BOUQUETS OF PRAISE FOR

Christmas Chocolat

"Magali, Colette, and Jacqueline are sisters living separate lives in separate parts of the world, but the ties that bind them tighten when their father demands their presence for Christmas at their childhood home in Pennsylvania. Filled with romance, adventure, and food, *Christmas Chocolat* is like a cup of *chocolat chaud* on a cold day. It is both funny and sad, hilarious and heart-warming. A terrific debut."

—T. Greenwood, author of *Bodies of Water,*
Two Rivers, and *Grace*

"Like sitting down to your favorite meal with a close friend, Kate Defrise's debut novel is many kinds of wonderful at once: warm, nourishing, irresistible. I thoroughly enjoyed this delicious story."

—Shilpi Somaya Gowda, author of *Secret Daughter*

"A confection of a novel, *Christmas Chocolat* is filled with the sugared scents of a holiday kitchen, forgiveness, and the endurance of family love. Fans of Mary Kay Andrews and Dana Bate will gobble this up!"

—Heather Webb, author of *Rodin's Lover*

Christmas Chocolat

KATE DEFRISE

KENSINGTON BOOKS
www.kensingtonbooks.com

KENSINGTON BOOKS are published by

Kensington Publishing Corp.
119 West 40th Street
New York, NY 10018

All Kensington titles, imprints, and distributed lines are available at special quantity discounts for bulk purchases for sales promotion, premiums, fund-raising, educational, or institutional use.

Special book excerpts or customized printings can also be created to fit specific needs. For details, write or phone the office of the Kensington Sales Manager: Kensington Publishing Corp., 119 West 40th Street, New York, NY 10018. Attn. Sales Department. Phone: 1-800-221-2647.

Kensington and the K logo Reg. U.S. Pat. & TM Off.

eISBN-13: 1-4967-0024-7
eISBN-10: 1-4967-0024-4
First Kensington Electronic Edition: October 2015

ISBN-13: 978-1-4967-0023-0
ISBN-10: 1-4967-0023-6
First Kensington Trade Paperback Printing: October 2015

10 9 8 7 6 5 4 3 2 1

Printed in the United States of America

à maman
encore et toujours

CHAPTER 1

Magali

Some families bred horses from one generation to the next. Others were rooted in the tradition of owning and managing land. In my Belgian family, survival skills consisted of going out into the world knowing how to make a perfect omelet and an infallible vinaigrette while sipping an *apéritif* and choosing the perfect wine. If you fed yourself well, with elegance, the rest would follow.

Let the plates be chipped, the platters mismatched, one would leave the table not just well, but *superbly,* fed. And this was never truer than at Christmas. It was all about the food. It always had been. Our mother taught my sisters and me all her secrets. We mixed and basted, roasted and sautéed. And later, we preserved and deglazed, creamed butter, beat eggs until they were white, whipped fresh cream and ourselves into a froth, in a frenzy to try to keep her alive.

When she died, our family deflated like a ruined soufflé.

Coming home after dropping my girls off at school, my morning resolve melted when faced with the pile of dirty breakfast dishes.

For this I needed a *Grand Diplôme* from the Institut Culinaire in Lyon? The dishwasher needed to be emptied and everything put away, piled dangerously in my inadequate cabinets. I drummed my fingers against my mug. My nails were too short to make any sound. If I didn't finish that chapter on main courses for the holidays this morning, I'd never make my deadline.

As usual, Charlotte, my four-year-old, had dumped two spoonfuls of milk-soaked Rice Krispies on the floor to share with the cat, who always obliged, but she would always leave a scrap or two. Her big sister, Elly, said it was to feed her pet mouse. A fairy-tale mouse, I hoped. Bippity boppity boo . . .

Oh, fairy godmother, I don't mind staying home from the ball. I just want someone to deal with the kitchen, laundry, cleaning. I promise, fairy godmother, that this magical cleaning person will be given meals—great ones, in fact. And he or she can turn back into a pumpkin to rest or go out on the town and get plastered on pumpkin schnapps or whatever tipple magical creatures favor these days.

So, work or dishes first? The phone rang, making the decision for me. I wedged the receiver between my ear and my shoulder—a great stretching exercise as long as I remembered to switch sides before the muscles and tendons stiffened like plaster. Then I'd have to stay that way all day, a good position for checking on the roast or appearing charmingly quizzical, a look I haven't been able to pull off since I was eight. "Hello?"

"It's me."

My father. I pictured him fully dressed as always, even before breakfast. Charcoal slacks, a pressed light gray shirt, a navy blue—no make that a *slate*-colored pullover, V-necked. His socks would be black and his shoes a soft gray. His hair, still full, but also gray as a November sky, would be perfectly combed. Even his eyes were gray. My father was in black-and-white.

When we were younger, on the way home from school, my older sister Jacqueline and I would play *What Would Daddy Be Wearing?* I always endowed him with a bit more color, a splash of whimsy. Jacqueline would win practically every time. Elegant to the tip of his buffed nails and polished leather shoes. Even his breath was classy: Courvoisier VSOP Cognac mixed with minty tooth-paste.

I stepped on a trail of Rice Krispies, now stuck to the green-and-yellow swirled linoleum, and pulled open the door of the new stain-less steel German dishwasher I'd bought when I got a royalty check from Australia, of all places.

"Hi, Daddy." My head felt thick with guilt.

"You are well?"

"Yeah, what about you?"

"The usual. The children?"

I laughed, "The usual too. Elly brought her baby shoes to school for show-and-tell. She swears she can remember learning to walk in them. With her memory, she just might. And Charlotte decided that her new favorite princess is Slow White, the sluggish sister of the celebrity. Hard being in somebody's shadow." I swallowed. *Tread lightly, Gali.*

"And yellow is no longer her favorite color. She only wears green. Today she went off to school looking like a Christmas elf in pigtails." Safer ground.

He chuckled. I offered up stories of my children on a platter, hoping for wholehearted approval, but knowing that in his eyes, we never quite made the cut. *Why can't you be more like your sister?* He never said this out loud, but I knew.

"Have you given thought to the holidays?"

October fifteenth, the day following Columbus Day, was his holiday kickoff date. He spent Thanksgiving in Belgium visiting Maman's family and my sister Jacqueline—forget that they don't have Thanksgiving over there—but Christmas was mine. So, guilt notwithstanding, I couldn't resist the urge to let him simmer.

"I don't know how I'm going to dress, but Elly is going as Wendy from *Peter Pan* and of course Charlotte will be Slow White."

Turn on the spit a bit, oh, ever-elegant father of mine. Who hated to ask.

"Maggie." Only my father called me Maggie. It was a time ma-chine: I was six years old and ever lacking. It was Gali to everyone except my godmother and the DMV, who used my given name,

Magali. I twirled a strand of hair around my forefinger, then dropped it.

"Okay, Daddy. Christmas. Go," I almost barked at him, feeling very military and take-charge. *Roberts, we must have that hill, cheerio and all that.* I slid a pile of plates back into the cupboard.

"Are you doing something else while talking to me? If you're busy, I can telephone later."

Busy? Who, me? "Uh, no, Daddy, the cat knocked over her dish."

"Humph."

Okay, great. Now he thought even my cat was clumsy.

"I think I'd like to celebrate it here at the house this year."

"Your house?" I stopped, a glass midway between the dishwasher rack and the shelf.

"Yes. Where I live. Don't be dense, Maggie."

I put down the glass and sat. "Are you sure? You know we can host it here. Or at Tante Solange's." My heart pounded.

"No, your godmother isn't well. We won't burden her."

Right. But we couldn't—not in our childhood home. Not since we lost Maman. "My house is open. And since we'd closed in the back porch—you haven't even seen it yet—and put in a great fireplace, we have lots of room." My words were coming out too fast. *Breathe.*

"No," he said. Wide open to discussion as usual. How could he ask us to have Christmas in our old home?

"Will it just be us?" I wondered if his latest companion, what was her name? Leigh . . . Lee . . . no *Lea* pronounced with the "a" at the end, would be there. It was hard to keep track. Since Maman died there had been two wives and a companion, as he called her, between the two. Then a couple of years of serial dating, and now, a new one. He hadn't married her. Yet.

"Just family. I expect *all* of my children to be home for Christmas this year."

What? All of us? But that was impossible. "But how—"

"This is important, Maggie. Is that clear? I will rely on you to invite your sisters and your brother. You are good at that sort of thing. And naturally, you girls will help with the cooking."

Oh crap! Here it was again. Maybe he wanted to present Lea to the family before sweeping into another round of 'til-death-do-us-part nuptial bliss. Or miss.

"Of course. Look, Daddy, I'm in the middle of something. Could I call you back?"

"In the middle of . . ."

"I have to work."

"Work?"

"You know what I do."

"Oh yes, the cookbooks."

So, Daddy wasn't proud of what I did. Nothing new. He thought they were frivolous, my chatty little cookbooks. But the *Hopeless in the Kitchen* series paid a lot of bills even if it didn't earn me star billing in my father's eyes. They were a collection of funny stories with recipes to get people away from their microwaves and play in the kitchen. Make memories, create traditions.

"I'll call you back," I said, hoping he couldn't hear my voice wobble. I forced a smile, knowing from my friend Syd that a smile could be heard through a microphone or telephone. "Keep in mind, before we decide on Christmas, that it will be a huge up-heaval, you know, with the kids, the mess."

"I know fully well what a Christmas feast entails. It's already been decided. Don't let me keep you from your work. Good-bye, Maggie."

Coffee, make more sparkled on the marquee of my mind. I picked up the pot.

I sat down at the desk I had built in to the corner of my kitchen, and flipped open my kitchen Mac.

How did he expect me to get my sisters—not to mention my lit-tle brother—home to Pennsylvania for Christmas? I drummed my fingers on the desk. Not that we never saw each other, but all of us, together in one place? In our old house? That hadn't happened since . . . well, since Maman's funeral. Never mind that Colette had been avoiding coming home altogether for years. Not enough money was her excuse. I was always the one who had to go to California. And Jacqueline? Leave Belgium for Christmas? She proba-bly had a performance or something. And she'd never leave our grandmother alone for the holidays. I looked at the clock. No way was I going to sit here with this on my own. Who first?

I picked up the phone, then realized Colette was probably still asleep. I'd have to time my call to get her after she woke up and before she went to the beach, or jogged to yoga, or whatever you did in San Diego.

Jacqueline would be getting ready for the theater. Not a propitious time to talk to her.

A gray cloud, the exact same shade as the bulk of Daddy's wardrobe, fell over me. I put the rest of the dishes away. There was nothing I could do right now about Daddy's request. It was more of a command, actually. A summons. Very royal. Maybe printing out formal invitations would do the trick. *Monsieur Philippe Arnaud requests your presence . . .*

I sighed, then turned to the screen, losing myself in a piece on how to make friends with your butcher, bypassing counters with meat packaged in plastic—not the easiest thing to make friends with, unless you were an alien and could communicate with shrink-wrap.

The phone broke into my thoughts. Maybe Colette's sixth sense had kicked in.

But it was Ana, my agent, calling to arrange a lunch date. I'd been wondering when she was going to get around to returning my call. I'd left several messages over the past few weeks and was feeling neglected, which I realized made me about as mature as a petulant first grader. We made plans to meet the next day.

She'd been acting strangely these past few months. I'd finally get to know what the big secret was.

Ana believed in my books. She felt people needed them because the world had become so alienating. Drive in, drive up, drive thru, pick up, and nuke.

So many grew up with moms whose idea of homemade was heating frozen lasagna in the conventional oven rather than the microwave.

Or others, whose mothers threw themselves into cooking and presenting food as if it were a life-or-death matter, tossing enough butter and cream in every dish to make even Julia Child cringe in her grave, while smiling graciously as their guests keeled over from massive coronaries, their whole identity wrapped up in what was on the plate and how it looked. No disrespect to Julia, of course. She was the queen.

Lately, a big crunchy trend had surfaced. Which was fine. I was all for farm-to-table, but it had to taste good. And be simple. Easy to make and delicious.

It was one of the reasons I'd not been unhappy to leave the restaurant. Too much effort went into presentation and finding new and interesting ways to incorporate the chic food du jour into everything from appetizers to dessert and every course in between.

I still had almost two hours before it was time to pick Charlotte up from the Jewish preschool she attended. I got down to work and finished the draft. It felt good.

So, I wasn't about to win the Nobel Prize. They didn't even have a Nobel Prize for cooking, though sometimes I think they should. After all, a good meal can keep, even create, the peace.

I made a mental note to write to the committee.

After a lunch of leftover ratatouille, reheated and eaten at my desk, I called my godmother to have her pick Charlotte up from school tomorrow. I hated to do it, much as I did love Tante Solange. She would unfailingly tote out the Virgin Mary medallion she'd gotten in Lourdes the year Maman got sick.

I rubbed cream into my hands. Someone could retrace the story of every meal I'd ever made just by reading the scars on my hands and forearms. I applied lipstick, then headed out. The day was too warm for a sweater.

What to say to my sisters to make sure they would both come out for the holidays? Maybe that I was having a baby? Or that I was ill? No, strike that. Bad idea.

And Art? None of us had a clue as to how to reach our baby brother. Jacqueline used to call him King Arthur, the adored, long-awaited male child. But he'd quickly morphed into the Artful Dodger. He'd disappear for months—sometimes even years—taking wildly successful photographs of wars and other disasters. Then he'd pop up as if nothing had happened. I'd gotten used to it over time.

Though right now, I wished I'd secretly implanted one of those microchips under his skin so I could track him down. Forget that I didn't have the slightest idea how to go about doing that. There had to be ways.

Why was it always up to me to deal with family matters?

Naturally, if they didn't come, it would be my fault. If I could make this happen, I bloody well deserved the Nobel Peace Prize.

I parked in the school parking lot while visions of siblings at Christmas danced in my head.

My spirits lifted. Tomorrow I'd finally find out what Ana had been cooking up these past months. A sharp northern breeze swept over me, giving me goose bumps. I should have brought my sweater. When would I learn not to trust unseasonable weather?

I parked my car in front of Ana's place so we could walk to the restaurant. Chestnut Hill looked like it had jumped right out of a storybook and settled itself in northwest Philadelphia.

Ana was waiting outside, her face tilted to catch the almost-warm rays of the October sun. Another one of those deceptive days that tempted you to leave the house without a coat, the sun almost too bright in a sky whose hue was normally associated with summer but belonged to autumn. The leaves dazzled, the maples red as blood, warring with the oranges, golds, and browns of the chestnuts and oaks. Touches of green from the fir trees that would soon proudly sport glistening Christmas lights, but were, for now, overshadowed by the last gasp of brilliance from the deciduous trees.

"It's so perfect for you to live here," I said.

"What happened to 'Hello, Ana, how are you, what a glorious day.' You know, what normal people say when they see each other?" She laughed.

"Of course, by all means, all you just said."

"Hello. Fine. It is a spectacular day indeed! So, why is it perfect for me to live here?" She kissed me once on each cheek.

There were two types of people in the world: the huggers and the kissers. Ana was the latter. Me, I could go either way. A switch hitter, a bisexual of physical greetings. Or would I be considered a hermaphrodite? So, I guess there are three kinds of people in the world.

"A storybook street in a storybook village. You're like a midwife for our books. Without you, they'd never see the light of day."

"Nonsense! You are all wonderful writers. If it weren't me, it would be someone else."

"No, it's all you. Let's go. I'm starving."

Ruth and John's was about a ten-minute walk from Ana's. I reveled in being outside on this glorious day, last year's boots crunching in the fallen leaves.

"You look beautiful," said Ana.

I smiled. I'd dressed a bit for the occasion, something I did only rarely. But today, my mother's Hermès scarf was knotted around my throat, and I wore a calf-length gray knit dress in wool so soft, I wanted to cuddle up and sleep next to it whenever Leo went away on business. A supple black leather belt and a long rust-colored sweater that everyone said brought out the reddish highlights in my tangle of hair completed the ensemble. I'd even applied a bit of eye makeup in addition to my usual lipstick. I felt good. I was doing my favorite thing with one of my favorite people, and it was even a tax write-off.

"So do you, Ana." In her black-and-white Chanel jacket and skirt, she looked a little like Grace Kelly. Only shorter.

Before this woman, agent, and friend, had taken me under her wing, I'd been adrift, starved for a mentor, my thirst unquenched by repeated stabs at becoming allies with Tante Solange, my godmother. Solange would run hot and cold like a faulty tap. Just when I would begin to bask in the glow of acceptance, she would turn around and slice me open with a remark she must have spent days sharpening.

Christmas. All of us together this year at the house. With Tante Solange. Trying to ignore the ghost of Christmas past at the table.

I pushed away the thought, couldn't sustain it right now, didn't want to. I zenned myself back to the postcard I was currently the star of. Well, costar. Ana was the star but in that Meryl Streep–deep way, not the Julia Roberts of-course-you-recognize-me-behind-these-glasses glam Hollywood way.

We turned onto Chestnut Hill's main shopping street, more charming than ever with its fall festival decorations.

"I am going to miss this," she said.

"Oh, me too. I can't believe this weather."

"No, I mean all of this." She swept her arm around her in a gesture that encompassed me.

My throat closed. I felt dizzy as I grabbed her hand and whirled to face her, my eyes and mouth open like a carp. Not my best look.

"Oh no, no, no. Don't worry. There's nothing wrong with me. As a matter of fact, there is something right with me." She gently pried my fingers from hers. "I'm retiring."

I must have misunderstood. My eyes focused and there it was, that look, the one she'd had periodically all during last spring and summer. I remembered it from my annual Fourth of July party. It wasn't just the cat-that-swallowed-the-cream look, it was more the cat who had gotten up during the night when everyone was asleep, sneaked down into the kitchen, opened the freezer, and downed a whole pint of Ben & Jerry's Sweet Cream & Cookies. I'd thought she'd met someone, had fallen in love. Since the death of Charles, her second husband, a little over six years ago, she'd been alone. Recently she'd dated this or that eligible divorced man or widower, usually an editor or someone involved in the arts. Last year, there had been a hand surgeon. Ana was far too attractive and full of life to grow old alone. Not for the first time, I wondered how old she was. She was that timeless age that only some women reach, between forty-seven and sixty-three, when they aren't a dewy-eyed twenty-five, but are more beautiful, the lines on their faces tell the stories of their lives, the laughter and tears, the quiet and loud.

My voice had returned. "But you can't retire. You're much too young!" For her to drop us like this, it had better be monumental.

She linked her arm through mine and steered me in the direction of the restaurant. The world suddenly took on a garish feel, like a carnival in an expressionist painting, or a play by Ödön von

Horváth. I rummaged through my bag for my sunglasses only to realize I was already wearing them.

"I wanted to tell you under the best possible circumstances."

"It's a man, right?"

"Nope. A woman."

I opened my mouth but nothing came out. Why was it that in situations that took me by surprise, I could never think of great and wonderful words. Why couldn't I be Anna Karenina? Lady Macbeth? Even Scarlett O'Hara? I needed to hire someone to write my lines. I wondered if Amy Sherman-Palladino was busy?

"She's a lucky woman," I said. "When can I meet her?"

"Gali, you are funny. No, the woman I am referring to is the muse . . . my muse."

This time I was sure I'd misunderstood. We started walking again, Ana's arm linked through mine. Ana was the nexus for a lot us, her *stable* of writers, which of course made us sound like a bunch of horses that are in the race, hoping not to be retired, or worse, sent off to the writer's equivalent of the glue factory: corporate America, with its demand for total commitment and the resulting death of the free spirit.

Ana was the cornerstone of my career, if you cared to call it that—which I did, only not in front of my father.

I'd met her through Syd—tall, blonde, stunning, brilliant Syd. I should have hated her, but she was my best friend, so that made it kind of hard. She worked in public radio as a researcher and knew everyone in the artsy crowd.

Syd was brilliant, but for one tiny detail: she couldn't cook.

Then she met Adam, and felt that, for once in her life, the relationship was serious enough for her to learn how to make a meal that didn't involve the excessive use of the microwave, with the preparation limited to carefully pricking plastic wrap with a fork.

"It's terrible. One of the most basic human skills and I have no clue as to how to even start. Even my mother could cook a little," she'd said.

I'd laughed, "Honey, I ate at your house a couple of times a month all through high school. For me it was exotic to have Dunkin' Donuts and Coke for dinner."

"Oh, but she cooked sometimes. Okay, so her idea of a home-cooked meal was Rice-A-Roni, at least she used an actual pot and a utensil or two."

We'd both started to giggle.

"Can you see me serving up Mom's specialty to Adam? The beautiful woven tablecloth I brought back from Greece, candles, soft music . . ."

"And mini-marshmallow-studded Hamburger Helper," I'd finished.

"Could I borrow your white Limoges? You know, to set off the marshmallows."

So, I'd e-mailed her some recipes.

I'd told her everything: where, when, and how to choose her meat, fruit, vegetables, and step by step, as if I were talking to her, "walked" her through the meal via e-mail. She'd prepared the easiest basic dinner I could think of that still said *you are special: boeuf bourguignon,* because it could be made the day before, and beef was an aphrodisiac of sorts, a mixed green salad with vinaigrette, spring beans, and new potatoes sprinkled with parsley and coarse sea salt. For dessert, fresh orange slices marinated in mint and Cointreau with a dollop of real *crème fraîche.* She nailed it and asked for more. We kept it up for about a year. Her love for cooking simple, elegant food never wavered, even if her love for Adam had, and he'd gone the way of the rest of her lovers.

"I can't believe I actually learned to cook for that jerk," she'd exclaimed, waving a glass of Bourgogne Aligoté in the air.

One snowy morning, a few weeks before Christmas, Syd arrived at my door, playing hooky from the station. She'd do this on a regular basis. Being a researcher she had to be out in the field quite often and would sometimes just research whatever was happening in my kitchen.

"This," she said, pulling off her wool cap, making her blonde hair stick out like an electric halo, "is a book."

"That is a stack of personal correspondence, much the worse for wear. This"—I held up the latest Barbara Kingsolver novel—"is a book."

"You don't get it. Do you think I'm the only one who never learned how to cook? You can call it, I don't know, something like *The I Wish I Knew How to Cook Cookbook*."

"Catchy." I turned back toward the kitchen, where I'd been washing leeks for soup.

By now she had removed her woolen muffler, mittens, and faux-fur-lined jacket and followed me into the kitchen. I served her coffee with sugar, no milk. Syd, even with her nose red and slightly chapped, her eyes watering and cheeks raw from the cold, looked like a model.

"I know what you're thinking." She was one of the few people privy to my secret ambition to become a novelist. To write fiction. Or rather Fiction. I pictured myself winning the National Book Award or the Pulitzer and casually dropping over to my father's house with a signed copy of my award-winning novel, rather than my usual offering of raspberry-filled genoise covered in Belgian chocolate icing or tarte tatin—never my famous spiked tiramisu, no sense in bringing coals to Newcastle. I could taste this image as strongly as the coffee I'd just brewed.

"This"—she waved the stack of papers at me—"is no impediment to that. Writing is writing."

"They're just silly. And kind of personal, you know?"

"Exactly. Just, you know, change the names to protect the guilty and all that."

I shook my head. "I don't have the time. In case you hadn't noticed, I'm with child." I placed my hands on my belly, smoothing Leo's old Princeton sweatshirt over my bump.

She stared at me.

"Okay, I do have the time. But . . . do you really think?"

"Would I be here in this weather if I didn't?"

"You'd come over during a hurricane." I returned to rinsing the grit out of the leeks.

"Point taken. Do it for me." She leaned against the counter and took a sip of coffee.

It took me about five months to pull the narrative together and turn it from a hodgepodge of messages to a friend into something fit for public consumption.

Then Syd introduced me to Ana and my life shifted subtly. Or not so subtly. A shift more along the lines of a small earthquake. By the time Elly was one, I had a contract.

Ana and I were just across the street from Ruth and John's. The light was red and we waited for the green WALK sign to flash on.

A car honked, capturing our attention.

"Hi, Maggie!" My father waved as he drove by in his black Mercedes. I lifted my fingers in reply, but he was gone before I could say anything. My father, honking and waving?

"Still a handsome man, your father. How is Philippe?" asked Ana.

"About the same. Probably on his way to lunch or something." Something like a bar. The storefront for his antique business was a few blocks from here. I should stop by one of these days, but there were always so many other things on my agenda. "Wants to have Christmas at his house this year." I sighed.

The light turned green and we crossed. I turned my attention back to Ana.

"It might be time," she said. "You look like you could use a drink."

I nodded, "Or three."

We were quickly seated, settled, and Chablis-ed. That was one of the best things about this restaurant; they were attentive like loving family, but not overbearing, obsequious, or at the other end of the spectrum, haughty. Ana twirled her full glass on the tablecloth. I willed her to meet my gaze but she was staring into her wine.

"Let me explain. I've always wanted to write—"

"But you never said—"

"Let me finish. I never said anything because I'm terrible at it. I'm much too good at recognizing quality writing when I see it."

Here her eyes rose and met mine and I saw such kindness there, I almost dissolved.

I busied myself draining my glass of Vaillons—a premier cru and quite nice—and refilling my empty one and Ana's almost full one.

"But even if I am bad at it, I still want to do it. So, I have bought a small house in Vermont and . . . you remember Charles had that condo in Dallas that he'd bought so we could visit my son, his wife, and the grandchildren? When I'm weary of the green or the cold, I will go to Dallas."

"But"—and here I wanted to cry *What about me?*—"What about us? I thought you loved your job."

"I love all of you, and your writing."

"But then how can you?" I bit my lip.

"Because it's time to move on, as they say." Her eyes sparkled and her cheeks were pink, as if she'd just drunk from the fountain of youth.

"What kind of books are you planning to write?" I tasted my sole and noticed in the back of my mind that it was truly excellent. It actually deserved my full attention, but I couldn't concentrate on food. I pushed my plate away.

Ana pushed it back. "If you eat, I'll tell you everything."

She had me there. Not one to resist any exhortation to eat, I picked up my knife and fork and cut another piece of fish. The flesh was firm without being rubbery and the lobster and cream-based sauce was delicately perfumed with truffle. It was so light, I could have used a spoon and fed it to a toothless six-month-old. I felt a pang of regret at no longer working at a restaurant, but it was dispelled at the thought of someone else raising the girls. This might make a good fish course for Christmas dinner.

I put my fork down. "See? I'm eating."

"Good. You already know I was an English major in college and, of course, I wrote. A lot. Notebooks filled with dreadful poetry and naïve-though-heartfelt short stories that I'd stay up half the night working on, but that would never bear the light of day." She waved her hand as if to dismiss these early efforts, then skewered a piece of fish.

The door opened, and the noise level in the restaurant went up a few notches. Ana put her fork and knife down, and we both turned.

Aidan Thomas, local news anchor and current darling of half of the greater Philadelphia area, walked in propelling a heart-stoppingly beautiful woman toward a corner table. It was Syd in that blue dress I liked so much, probably researching a show. I waved but she didn't see me. I'd go over later. I wouldn't mind a closer look at the hottie that had caused Channel Six's local news ratings to burst through the stratosphere.

"Syd and Aidan Thomas?" Ana raised an eyebrow.

"Oh, Syd knows everybody." I took a sip of my wine.

"Hmm. Well, I don't know."

"What?" I sat up a bit straighter. Ana's insight was sharp.

"A feeling. Did you notice how his hand was placed on her back as they walked through the room?"

"He's probably just a control freak." He wouldn't be the first overly handsome man to belong to that group.

"Look at her," Ana said.

I turned. She looked great, but she always looked great. However, there was a definite glow. "Not good. He's bad news. Hey, that's pretty good . . . the news anchor . . . bad news."

Ana smiled. "Syd can probably take care of herself."

This I wasn't so sure of. "Should we go over?"

"Let's wait until we're finished. Everyone is staring and trying not to show it."

"Playing *cooler than thou*. Okay, so what you are telling me? You're a terrible writer, yet you have decided to devote yourself to writing? What am I missing?"

She took a sip of wine and smiled. "Yes, I'm terrible. At least I was. But I've decided to use my time to do only the things I love. A privilege that comes with age and luck."

"You're probably better than you think," I said.

"I hope you're right. But Gali, much as I bask in your high opinion of me, I do not walk on water. If there is one thing I know, it's good writing."

"So, you are going to devote your life to writing crappy—sorry, I mean *bad* novels."

Our server, John-Paul, came over and asked if we'd like dessert.

"Let's split a crème brûlée. It's not as good as yours, but . . ." She raised her eyebrows.

I gulped the rest of my wine. "And coffee . . . espresso," I added.

"Make that two. And the check."

I played with my pink linen napkin, folding it again and again. I looked up and spotted a jagged crack in the molded ceiling. "But Ana, what's going to happen to us? To me?" I could hear my father now. *You lost your agent?* Great Christmas dinner conversation.

"You will be just fine. This might do you some good." She sighed. "I've made up my mind," she said so softly I could barely hear her over the din of the restaurant. I glanced over at Syd, absorbed in something the beautiful Aidan was saying. Odd that she hadn't noticed us sitting here. It's as if she were encased in a bubble—

Uh oh! The first heady throes of love, no one else existed except the love object. I'd seen her this way before. Anchors aweigh.

"I have also arranged"—now Ana's voice was more forceful—"for you to get in touch with two agents I think would be good for you." Before this lunch, I hadn't imagined a tempest would storm through my professional life.

I let her pay the bill.

Then, putting both hands flat on the table, I leaned forward. Time to pull out all the stops. "What about your godchild?"

"I'm not dropping off the face of the earth, Gali. I'll still be in her—and your—life."

We stood and, as we made our way across the crowded restaurant, I saw that Syd and Aidan had left.

We spilled out into the bright autumn sunlight. By the time I'd reached my car and we'd said our good-byes, my head was pounding. What was it about me that made everyone I loved leave me? My mother, my sisters, and now, Ana. Was it an aura I gave off, like a bad smell? Was there some sort of cosmic deodorant I could buy to protect myself against it?

The day I'd found so beautiful a few hours ago now seemed strident, overdone. "Shut up," I whispered to the colors.

That evening, once the girls were in bed, Leo and I cuddled up on the couch.

"Well"—he scratched his head—"could be worse." He took a sip of wine.

"Could be raining," we quoted. I smiled.

"Seriously. You don't have to do your Dad's bidding, you know. If he wants to have a big family Christmas at his house, why doesn't he take care of it?"

"Have you met my father?" I wiggled my toes in my favorite fuzzy striped socks that looked like they belonged on one of my daughters. "Remind me to introduce you."

"Just tell him you're too busy."

"Right." I pushed my hair back off my forehead. I'd never understand how some people got away with ignoring their parents. For me, the bond went beyond reason, beyond logic. I'd never stop trying to please him, to gain his approval. He was my father. End of story. I forced a smile. "It's fine. It's what I do. Besides, I think I might have a better shot at getting everyone to come than he does."

"Right. Well, coming to bed?" I felt him shift.

"In a bit. I still have a few more things I want to finish up." I got up off the couch and picked up our glasses. In the kitchen, I rinsed them out and loaded them in the top rack of the dishwasher. Leo came up behind me and encircled me with his arms. I leaned back into him and felt my muscles loosen a bit.

"Don't be too long," he said.

I turned and kissed him full on the mouth. A real boyfriend kiss is how Elly would put it. "I won't. I just need to get in touch with at least one of my sisters and figure out a battle plan to keep Ana here."

Plus the thorniest problem of all: how to pin down my mercurial brother?

I watched my husband of fifteen years leave the kitchen. I'd done my share of stupid things, made a gaggle of wrong decisions, but the day I said yes to the life I was sharing with this man, I'd gotten it right. I should forget about this whole family bash thing and go climb into bed with Leo.

But deep down, a secret part of me yearned to re-create the kind of Christmas we'd had when Maman was alive.

I grabbed a clean wineglass from the rack over the counter and uncorked the bottle of Crozes-Hermitage we'd started at dinner. With my glass half full, I sat at my desk. This was the only way left for me to have a drink "with" my sisters. One ritual we tried to keep in spite of the time differences. I dialed Colette's mobile. It was still relatively early in San Diego. *Pick up, pick up.* Voice mail. Damn. Leave a message or not? Leave one. Maybe I should send them e-mails, but it wasn't direct enough. I didn't want them to have any time to think up excuses. Ideally I would confront them in person, but the cost of two plane tickets just to get a face-to-face with my sisters seemed a bit much.

It was Alexander Graham Bell or nothing.

"Hi, baby, it's me. I need to talk to you. Call me. Love you. Bye." That ought to do it.

It was only eleven-thirty, which would make it . . . I used my fingers . . . five-thirty in Brussels. I didn't want to go to bed without breaking ground on Daddy's Christmas extravaganza, but Jacqueline would be no fun if I woke her up. It was always better if I were the one with the coffee and she the one with the wine. In the meantime, I had other problems to solve. My sisters, my brother, Ana.

I'd make a cake for Ana. A luscious chocolate cake full of life and love with a *crème pâtissière* lighter and creamier than a dream. A cake so good she wouldn't be able to bring herself to leave. The power of a truly outstanding dessert should not be underestimated.

I poured myself the last of the wine and placed the empty bottle in the recycling bin.

I put on my chef's apron and tied back my hair. Then, I pulled eggs and butter out of my stainless-steel fridge and the dry ingredients from the pantry. My hands knew what to do, my mind wasn't engaged. Some people meditated. Some did yoga. Some even ran. Me, I baked.

From a tin, I removed a slab of Côte-d'Or extra dark chocolate. It was impossible, even for the most inexperienced kitchen klutz, to ruin a dessert made with Côte-d'Or. I set the oven to 350 degrees, then melted the chocolate and butter in a double boiler, stirring constantly. The rich velvet filled my head with the smell of happiness and good times. Making a cake is the easiest thing in the world. Didn't we say "it's a piece of cake" to describe something easy and sweet and good? So, if a piece of cake is good, an entire cake could only be better.

If all I had to do was cook, Christmas would be a snap. I grabbed a spoon and tasted the batter. Wonderful. I washed the spoon, then tasted some more.

But Daddy expected perfection. If it didn't work out, the blame would be on the one he designated for the task. Leo was right. I should give it up. Refuse outright.

The heat from the oven warmed my face as I slid the filled cake tins inside. I tried to imagine what it would feel like to refuse to do Daddy's bidding. I could almost smell it, like mountain air. Freedom. I broke off a piece of chocolate and let it melt on my tongue.

Seated at my desk, I opened the bottom drawer. Concealed beneath a folder of random recipes and notes was my mother's diary. I didn't need to open it, I could probably recite it word for word. I'd filched the book from her nightstand right after she died, feeling guilty but never regretting the theft because, barely one week after the funeral, all of her personal belongings—clothes, jewelry, bags, letters—had disappeared. We each got a Hermès scarf and Daddy gave Art her worn volume of Rilke's *Lettres à un jeune poète*.

I'd planned on making copies for my siblings, but never got around to it. Maybe this year, as a Christmas present. I could have them bound.

The diary was thick. It related, in my mother's slanted European cursive, the years before she and Daddy were married. It stopped when she'd been pregnant with me. If there was a second book, I never found it, though not for lack of searching.

One last time. I would try one last time to make him proud of me, of what I could pull off. And maybe, just maybe, the man from the diary, the man my mother had fallen so in love with, would come back.

I whisked the pastry cream so hard it almost whimpered. Once done, I polished off what was left in the bowls before washing everything.

It was still too early to call Jacqueline in Brussels. She was the grumpiest morning person I knew. To her credit, she did go to bed late every night but Sunday and Monday. This being Friday, she'd had a performance last night. I toyed with my favorite fantasy, the one where I could slip into her skin at whim and live her life.

My gorgeous older sister with the sheaves of silky blonde hair and the lustrous voice, singing opera at night, going out to eat after the show because a large meal before singing, as she had repeatedly informed me, was bad for the voice and tended to make her sleepy. She lived off sweet lemony tea and then, after the show, with makeup stripped off, she'd hit a restaurant with the rest of the company. This in a city where it was almost impossible to get a bad meal. It was so glamorous, especially compared to my life. No wonder Daddy was proud of her. Even when we were kids, she'd been his favorite. Not that he would shower her with compliments. But when she'd master a challenging aria or dress with a certain flair, he'd give her a small smile and nod. "*Pas mal.*"

Why they weren't closer today was anybody's guess.

I tried Colette again, but no luck. I kept my voice light as I left another message. I imagined her out with Wayne-the-jerk. I wished she would just come home. And Art? I didn't have a clue about how to reach him.

My thoughts turned to frosting. Whipped or ganache? I could forgo the pastry cream mixed with raspberries altogether and cover the cake with ganache. I'd use an orange cream filling instead. I uncorked another bottle of wine and poured a glassful. Two cakes. A genoise with the pastry cream mixed with raspberries, frozen ones in this season, covered in ganache, and the chocolate with orange cream and whipped dark chocolate frosting. I broke off another piece of chocolate and popped it into my mouth. When it was almost gone, I took a sip of the wine and swirled it around my tongue. My heart smiled.

At two-thirty, I had a clean kitchen and two cakes. Now what? I needed another half hour at least before calling Jacqueline. Maybe a batch of brownies? With dark chocolate chips. I could freeze them then take them to school on Monday for the volunteers and office staff.

Once they were in the oven, I sat down with my wine and punched in the long string of numbers that belonged to my sister in Brussels. No answer. I got up, accidentally knocking my mother's diary to the floor. I placed it back in its drawer. I called again when the brownies were cooling. Still no luck. Fuming, I scanned my immaculate kitchen. What was the use of having sisters? Not only did they live on opposite ends of the earth, but it was also impossible to get them to answer their phones. Out of fashion though it was, the phone was my lifeline. I needed to hear their voices.

Chocolate mousse. Making *mousse au chocolat* would be a good use of my time.

When the last of the ramekins was in the fridge, I slumped down on a chair. Just fifteen more minutes and I'd give it another try.

The next thing I knew, Leo was shaking me. I opened my eyes and groaned. I'd fallen asleep. The mixture of batter, chocolate, and wine were churning in my belly and my head felt like it was going to explode. I rubbed my eyes.

He took in the two cakes, the brownies, then checked the fridge and whistled. "Cake or death?" My husband could get in touch with his inner Eddie Izzard at whim.

"Death, definitely death." I untied my apron and pulled it over my head.

"Go to bed. I'll take care of the kids."

"But what about school?"

He raised his eyebrows at me.

"Oh yeah, right, today's Saturday." I pulled my hair out of its ponytail and ran my fingers through it, in a pointless attempt to smooth out the tangles.

He helped me up and walked me to our bedroom, undressed me, then pulled the covers up around my shoulders.

"How did it go with Jacqueline?" he asked.

"It didn't. Love you," I murmured. "Monday I'm going on a diet."

"Whatever you want."

I don't remember him leaving the room.

Mousse au chocolat belge
BELGIAN CHOCOLATE MOUSSE

A truly superior *mousse au chocolat* is always welcome. It's perfect for any occasion, or even for no occasion at all. Use the best quality ingredients and take your time. The quantities seem a bit wacky due to the conversion from metric. If you have a metric scale, by all means use it.

7.5 ounces (200 g.) high quality dark bittersweet Belgian
 chocolate, like Côte d'Or (70% cocoa is perfect)
½ cup (125 g.) heavy whipping cream
5 fresh organic eggs (room temperature)
2 tablespoons, plus 1 teaspoon (20 g.) granulated sugar
¼ cup (30 g.) powdered sugar
¼ teaspoon salt
2 teaspoons coffee extract or 1 tablespoon very strong espresso
1 tablespoon coffee liqueur, like Kahlúa (*optional*)

For the chantilly cream topping . . .

1 cup heavy whipping cream
1–2 tablespoons sugar
1 teaspoon vanilla extract (or you can use vanilla sugar instead of
 these last two ingredients)
Dash of salt
Chocolate for grating

Break the chocolate into pieces and melt it over very low heat or in a double boiler over simmering water. You may also use a microwave. The safest method will always be the double boiler. Once melted, slowly stir in the cream and remove from heat. Let cool a bit.

In the meantime, beat the egg yolks and sugar until the mixture becomes pale yellow and creamy. This may take longer than you think. Don't skimp on this step.

Beat the egg whites with the confectioners' sugar and salt until stiff and glossy.

Add the slightly cooled espresso or the coffee extract (and coffee liqueur, if using—I generally don't) to the chocolate mixture.

Pour the chocolate into the egg-sugar mixture, scraping the bowl with a spatula. Mix well.

Very delicately, using a wooden spoon, fold in the egg whites, a spoonful at a time, being careful to not deflate them.

Pour into a large serving bowl, individual ramekins, or glasses, and cover. Chill for at least two hours, though your mousse will set better if you leave it overnight. This is a great dessert for a dinner party because you should make it the day before.

Just before serving, beat the remaining cream with the sugar, vanilla, and pinch of salt until it forms soft peaks.

Top each serving of mousse with a dollop of the chantilly cream and grate some dark chocolate on top.

There are many variations on this recipe and they are all delicious. But sometimes, simple is better.

CHAPTER 2

Jacqueline

Today was shaping up to be a glorious day. Didier De Meesmecker's interview of me and his rave review of our company's production of *La Bohème* just came out in this week's *Télémoustique*; it was Monday, so no performance, and I was planning to create a beautiful dinner for my family. It was warm enough so I could leave my Burberry raincoat open, a rare and welcome occurrence this time of year. A pale October sun was shining, making the wet cobblestones in my Brussels neighborhood sparkle, and best of all, I was three days late.

Through the thick wooden door, I could hear the phone ringing as I struggled to turn the oversized key in the ancient lock, juggling my bag, this morning's mail, and a straw shopping basket spilling over with what would become tonight's dinner, as well as two copies of *Télémoustique*—one for my father. It would have hurt the show if I'd sounded inane or didn't come off as the consummate professional who had it all: the golden voice, the golden home, the golden husband who adored her. Everything but the golden womb. But even that was about to change.

The key finally turned in the lock as the baguette slid to the floor. I picked up the bread and jammed it under my arm, hygiene be damned, and ran for the phone, which naturally stopped and went to voice mail the instant I reached it. *Merde!* I had forgotten to empty my mailbox, which was full. Again.

I hung up my raincoat, then turned back toward the door and closed it firmly, not bothering to lock it. We should really see about upgrading our security, but our leafy Brussels neighborhood was the picture of tranquility, right out of a gentler time. And I loved our home with the single-minded purity of first love.

The instant I'd stepped through the open doors and into the garden, I knew I'd found my home. Never mind that it was wild and overgrown. To make up for its gray skies and pouring rain, Mother Nature had given Belgium a green even emeralds would envy. The garden was walled with ancient bricks that went from gray to ochre, to a pink so pale it was almost too shy to be called a color. A huge chestnut tree dwarfed a weeping willow. Toward the back—the clincher—two cherry trees and a peach tree, both in need of serious pruning, sheltered a carved stone bench and a small pond, stagnant and choked with weeds and rotting leaves.

I'd made my way to the wall, glad I'd worn boots and had remembered to waterproof them. At the time, I wore a lot of jeans and boots and sweaters, topped with my one good Hermès scarf— a legacy from my mother—and outrageous earrings: *l'américaine,* they called me. I ran my fingers lightly over the rough surface of the bricks and soft moss that had taken hold of the wall here and there. A niche, onetime home of a saint or the Virgin Mary, was built into the wall. My baby sister, Colette, had made me a statue of Sainte Cécile, the patron saint of musicians. She would be at home in this garden.

So, we'd steamed off layer upon layer of faded wallpaper and painted the walls, we'd scraped the woodwork and sanded floors. A *vitrier* came to fix the windows, a *marbrier* came to restore the cracked marble fireplaces. We'd break to eat, either in the garden, when it wasn't raining, or in the *salle de séjour*—the family room— on a makeshift table. We'd had many picnics of bread, wine, and cheese, or sometimes we'd bring back *frites* and *cervelas* sausage, doused in golden Leffe or Trappiste beer. Then Laurent would tug off my paint-splattered jeans and we'd make love. All that food, work, and love had given me better muscle tone and skin than I'd ever had before.

I dropped the mail on the Louis Philippe bureau and walked through the formal living room, the baby grand piano gleaming in the light from the windows, through the dining room, and back to the *séjour,* where we spent most of our time. Two paned curved doors led into the room, and their twins out to the garden. An empty swing hung from one of the branches of the chestnut. The lawn was dew-covered and sparkled in the pale lemon sun.

I was living the life my mother should have had, had she not been carted off to the States by my father. Family lore had it that she'd wanted to leave as much as he did, but I didn't buy it.

All that was missing was a child. But not for long. Whoever said you couldn't have it all just lacked focus and determination.

Singing softly, I carried my bag to the kitchen, dropped the baguette, and started unloading fish, leeks, parsley, Bintje potatoes, a head of lettuce, eggs, crisp apples, the last of the good grapes, and five golden pears that had to be eaten today. I'd poach them in wine and sugar, then top them off with sweetened *crème fraîche* for dessert. There would be *potage de poireaux*—leek soup—followed by the *lotte en papillote* and *gratin dauphinois.* Then salad, cheese, and dessert. And wine, of course. It was my day off, after all. Laurent would pick up my grandmother, Mamy Elise, after work—long ago he'd fixed his schedule so he would finish early on Mondays. Being an interpreter at the EC Parliament not only paid well, but, ever since he took and passed the exam to become a *fonctionnaire,* it gave him a lot of freedom. Even if it was becoming a bit boring. Tante Charlotte and her husband, Gérard, would stroll over around six, in time for an *apéritif.*

La Bohème would run for three more weeks, then a few weeks off before rehearsals started for the holiday show. This year I would sing Gounod's "Ave Maria." Only one number, but clearly the choice piece for a Christmas concert. It was funny, working for the opera company. I was a bit like a *fonctionnaire* myself. I received a monthly salary with paid vacations, benefits, health care, the whole package. It wasn't really *la vie d'artiste* that everyone imagined. But it enabled me to live here where I belonged.

I sank down into the couch with my copy of the *Télémoustique* and was about to turn to the page with my interview when the phone rang again. Annoyed, I jumped up to get the cordless extension on the desk. And just in case it was another journalist calling for an interview, I made my voice as low and sultry as possible: think Brigitte Bardot meets Marlene Dietrich.

"*Allo.*"

"Jackie? Is that you? What's wrong with your voice?"

"Oh, Gali, it's you." I cleared my throat. "Nothing, Monet's frog, you know." It was an old joke between us when we were growing up. The idea of a frog in your throat was just altogether too gross and slimy so we decided it would be Monet's frog. Impressionistic.

"Ooh! I haven't had frog's legs in forever," said Gali.

"Come on out: frog's legs and mussels in white wine, *pommes frites,* and Côte d'Or chocolate . . . all these earthly delights waiting just for you. Not to mention a gorgeous, talented sister, a doting grandmother, aunts, uncles, cousins, you name it, we got it. And don't forget me!"

"You already mentioned you."

"Never too much of a good thing. More is more, haven't you heard?" I felt so good, I wanted to fling golden handfuls of joy everywhere.

"I'd love to, you know. Maybe after the holidays? For Epiphany? Or Chandeleur? We could make crêpes, like we used to."

I ran a finger over the top of the desk, checking for dust, but my fingers came away clean. "You know I can't wait to see you. Not to mention my nieces. *Comment vont les petites puces?*" My heartbeat slurred a little. I looked out in the garden at the swing Laurent had hung on a branch of the chestnut tree, now covered in green-gray mold. I headed for the kitchen.

"The fleas are fine. Jacqueline? I need to tell you something."

"Anything, my Gali. You know I am here to listen." I tucked the phone between my ear and my shoulder and started putting the groceries away.

"Yeah, well. It would be nice if you were *here* to listen," she said.

Guilt, guilt, guilt. Fuck, fuck, fuck. My family could give Woody Allen lessons in guilt. I took the phone to the sitting room and flung myself on the couch, its deep red fabric holding me, like a gigantic heart. This whole room was intended to coddle and please, to comfort. The south-facing windows let every scrap of light in, a huge ficus benjamina thrived in the corner. The sunlight grazed the fallen leaves. We should rake them but I love the loamy smell of rotting leaves in the fall. Reminded me of home. As did this. The guilt. *I couldn't go back with you, dammit! I'd lost my voice, remember? I was dying,* my mind screamed silently at my sister.

"Maybe someday." I fought the urge to sigh.

"Right, anyway, have you talked to Daddy recently?"

"No." I crossed my legs, tucking my skirt more neatly under me with my spare hand. Why was she asking me this? She knew I hardly ever talked to him. And when we did, our conversation was always stilted, like two polite people at a cocktail party who didn't know what to say to each other. It was exhausting. "I did send him a note a few weeks back with this season's program."

"Well, he called, about the holidays. He wants to have it at our old house."

"You're joking. You poor thing." I couldn't think of a worse way to spend Christmas. I shivered.

"He wants us all to be there."

I stood. "That's out of the question, I'm working."

"It was a summons, Jacqueline. I haven't heard that tone since before . . . since we were kids."

I paced around the room. "Impossible. Again, I'm singing." Not technically true since the final performance of the winter concert was on the twenty-third of December and after, there was a comedy starting on Christmas Day that would run till after the New Year.

"What, no comedy this year?"

Hell. Gali knew just how much Belgians enjoyed a good laugh during the holidays. I was the one who told her, extolling the sensibility of a population that preferred laughter in the face of almost any single thing. Besides I needed to see the tree in the Grand'Place during the holidays, and I always visited with friends, and Tante Charlotte . . . I had it! "But who will be with Mamy Elise? We can't leave her here alone for Christmas."

I'd sworn to myself that I would not go home again without a baby in my arms. And if, as I suspected, I was really pregnant this time, I would want a perfectly serene pregnancy. Which excluded Christmas with my father.

"He's invited her, too. And she accepted."

"How do you know?"

"He called me today and told me. Look, Jacqueline, don't make this harder on me than it already is, okay? He wants *everyone* there."

I heard a gulp at the other end. "Are you drinking?" I straightened up an already straight pile of magazines on the coffee table.

"Do you want to make something of it?"

I made a mental calculation, nine-fifteen here, that made it a quarter past three in the morning in Pennsylvania.

"Gali, it's—"

"Oh, don't freakin' tell me what time it is! All of a sudden you want to play big sister? I'll tell you what time it is! Time to book your fu—your flight home!"

"Are you alone?" Red flashing lights popped in my brain. Drinking, fine. Wine, even better. But alone?

"No. I mean yes. I mean the children, well, asleep. And so's Leo. Anyway, Daddy apparently has something to tell us. Some big secret." Her voice went quiet on the last word.

My heart shuddered. "Can't he tell us when he comes in November?"

"I don't know. Why don't you ask him."

"Right." I was glad no one else was around to read the lack of enthusiasm on my face at the prospect of Daddy's yearly visit. Gali's voice brought me back, her voice and a strange strangling noise at the other end of the line.

"Are you crying?" I asked.

"Ana's retiring, and I don't know what I'm going to do."

"Oh no. What happened?" Part of me listened to my sister while my brain searched for a plausible excuse to get out of this. Nothing. Yet.

"Gali, listen to me. Put the bottle away. Rinse out your glass. Drink water and go to bed next to that wonderful sexy husband of yours. We'll talk later but right now, you need to rest."

"Okay." Gali sighed and the sound made me tired. I stood and looked out the window. Try as I might, I couldn't recapture my earlier joy.

I got out the chamois cloth and a bucket of warm water with vinegar and cleaned the bay windows until they sparkled. When I was finished, I put on a sweater and went out to the garden to rake the leaves. Then I did something I hadn't done in years. I went into the kitchen and methodically, piece by piece, devoured the entire baguette slathered in butter. After throwing up in the bathroom, I washed my face, brushed my teeth, and redid my makeup. Then I went out to buy more bread.

CHAPTER 3

Colette

Everyone was saddled with a crazy family. Mine was no exception. In my family, we had an intense relationship with food. And we either were, or wanted to be, artists. Me, I was in the closet. Literally. My creations were draped on hangers, and when I was lucky, on willing bodies. Not that they weren't literary.

My family treated me like the baby. Not only was I the third daughter and youngest daughter, but I was also smaller than my siblings. I had fewer memories of my mother not being sick, of a time when my father was happy. I put some distance between my life and my family's, a distance that could be measured in miles, yards, inches, even. This was an accomplishment I held up to the world and to myself like a golden chalice. Not smug, exactly, but . . . okay, smug. And we all knew nature abhorred an uppity creature who thought she could climb out of her particular bog. Evolution took centuries for a reason.

I was driving home from work in my tan Honda Civic. This was California. Except for me, everyone had a tan, even my car. The sun was setting at the end of what had been a glorious October day.

From my crappy car, I had a million-dollar view of the shadowy blue mountains on one side, and the very rim of the earth where the sky fell into the sun-sprinkled ocean on the other. I loved taking the long, slow way home over Mount Soledad, avoiding the rodeo of harried drivers on cell phones that swarmed the freeway at rush hour. I couldn't remember the first time I'd heard that Southern California was laid back. This was the most stressed out place I'd ever lived. Not that I'd lived in that many.

My favorite time of day was when the light shifted. So, I felt good, approaching happy. I should have known better than to allow *eau de* joy to drizzle into my heart. I should have been *striving* for something more, something better. I taught French as an adjunct, one of the underpaid drones who did the bulk of under- grad teaching in universities coast to coast. It sounded fine in French, *professeur adjoint,* but without a contract, it was like living with one hand reaching for the HELP WANTED sign at the local Trader Joe's. Living atop a precipice was fine in your twenties, though I'd always been subject to vertigo. At thirty-two, it was time to move to lower, more solid ground. Or so I'd been told. Over and over.

Right now, the job was good enough. Better than good enough. It freed me up to spin my own dream. I fiddled with the dial, cut- ting off the latest KPBS sig alert. The Clash was wailing "Should I Stay or Should I Go?" on an eighties oldies station. My sisters had worshipped the group as teenagers, and, at the time, I'd wor- shipped my sisters, so I settled in for a bit of nostalgia, though why anyone with a past as whacked as mine should feel nostalgia baffled me. What I really loved was sixties pop. That it was before my time was beside the point.

My family was *artistic*. It was expected of us the way other fam- ilies expected their children to go into the family business or attend a certain college. I was supposed to have been the writer in the family. Even now, Daddy was disappointed that I hadn't pounded out the Great American Novel. But that was his dream. And Gali's secret one. But I did write. Words were key to my art. I used to dab- ble in painting and sculpture, anything three-dimensional with tex- ture and color, flailing around till I hit the right note. Until the day

I stumbled upon my one true joy. I made clothes. Not from patterns. I designed them, bringing together different fabrics and stones, glitter and buttons, combining natural and man-made materials.

And each piece contained a story or part of one. Literally. I stitched parts of stories, some my own, or some by authors I loved, or some I took from others, into the clothes. I'd just put the final touches on Gali's Christmas present: a swooping cocktail dress in midnight blue silk, with purple velvet pockets, with an off-the-shoulder neckline and asymmetrical hem shot through with the opening of Dinesen's "Babette's Feast" hand-sewn in gold thread.

This weekend would be devoted to Jacqueline's Christmas gift. It had to be superb and dramatic, yet a little wounded, like her. Maybe a cape with trailing feathers, dyed in brilliant colors contrasting with something modern, trashy and man-made like plastic or rubber. I'd use the lyrics to one of her favorite operas. Definitely something in Italian. I was leaning toward Puccini.

For my brother Art, I'd decided on a simple white shirt with snippets of *On the Road* stitched throughout. Or maybe something less obvious.

If Jacqueline was the voice of the family and Gali its heart, I was the brain. I had a double master's in French and English literature. Everyone thought I'd become a writer. Even me. But once I'd discovered I needed texture with my words, there was no turning back.

The ringing of my cell phone cut into my thoughts. It was my friend Sonya.

"How are you?" I asked.

"Terrible. Farley, he has the strep throat this week and I know I'm going to catch it."

"Is he better?" Farley, at six, was Sonya's middle child.

"Busy busy. I need to know if we still good for Saturday night." Her rolling Russian *r*'s trilled over the phone.

I'd forgotten we'd made plans to go out. Girls' night out. Wayne never minded. He'd go out with his surfer friends. Or they'd come over and play cards or watch a game or something.

"Sure." I made a right turn down Soledad Road.

"I made reservations at Mexican place Annick loves."

"Sounds good."

"Colette. We have decided that you must stop this crazy business about the food. What do the Americans call it? Intervention."

"Mmm." I could be very articulate when I chose.

"Is okay. We have all eaten there. Is good, I promise."

I did have this weird thing about food. I couldn't eat something if I didn't know where it came from or how it was prepared. Wayne said I should have been Jewish. But it went even beyond kosher. And it was getting worse. I couldn't eat in restaurants or at most parties. Nothing prepackaged or prepared too long in advance. It was getting so I could only eat what I prepared myself and only if it came from certain stores. Unless Gali was cooking but, unfortunately, she didn't swoop down from the sky with her magic pots and spoons to cook for me very often.

"I can always join you for a drink," I said. My aversion didn't carry over to alcohol. This saved my social life. Sort of.

"Seven-thirty, yes? And you will eat something."

My phone beeped. I'd forgotten to charge it, again. "My phone's about had it. I'll call you back from a land line, okay?"

"Not too late—" but my phone cut her off.

I had wanted to call Wayne to tell him I was on my way home, but no matter. I loved coming home to him. He was the only person who knew my secrets and faults, and bought me flowers anyway. I knew that whatever he did, I would always forgive him. I had already forgiven the unforgivable. Besides, I now got why he'd left me stranded at the altar, though at the time I felt like pulling a gun from my bouquet and putting a bullet through my head. Good thing florists didn't slip firearms among the blooms and ferns. Joining him out here in California—where the smell of jasmine made my body melt—was the right thing for us. Far from my family. My dead mother. And his living one.

I turned into my street and started the quest for a parking space. The search for the Holy Grail was nothing compared to finding a parking space in Pacific Beach, California, after six p.m. on a Friday. People came from all over San Diego to drink at the bars whose number was only rivaled by the grains of sand on the beach.

I was late for a good reason, though. I'd been chatting with Chantal, the head of the French department. My heart lurched as I remembered the spoils of our conversation.

This was going to make Wayne so happy.

I couldn't help grinning as I parallel-parked my car in a space just that second vacated by a shiny blue VW Beetle—the car I'd been longing for. After all, I lived in California and I, too, wanted to place fresh flowers in that little vase. It had to be an omen that I was taking the place of my dream car. Not to mention that nothing beat executing a perfect parallel parking on the first try. I felt competent, in control. Go-nowhere job or no, today I was Superwoman.

I grabbed my purse and NPR canvas book bag from the passenger seat, got out of the car, and went around the back to take a look. A measly five inches from the curb. I strode up the sidewalk, my four-inch heels echoing on the pavement. I couldn't wait to change out of my work clothes and into something that felt more like me.

I turned up the walkway leading to our place, a tiny yellow bungalow nestled in the backyard of a main house, which, here in PB, was known as a unit. My fingers scrambled to find the keys that inevitably played hide-and-seek with the objects in my bag until they finally hooked into the key ring. I pulled them out, together with a crinkled receipt from Whole Foods and an aging Altoid that had grown a winter coat of fuzz and grit. I threw the latter back inside with lofty intentions of cleaning out my purse sometime this weekend. I removed a cream-colored envelope from the bag and stuck the corner between my teeth, careful not to get it wet. It was the first thing Wayne needed to see. The content of this envelope had power. I felt like Santa.

For the past six—no, seven—weeks, ever since he was laid off from his high-tech job with the Sands Corporation, I'd find him laid out on the couch, wearing board shorts and old T-shirts, in front of a *Friends* rerun. Today was Friday, so he'd be holding a bottle of Pacifico beer. A ripped-open bag of those organic potato chips he loved would be balanced on his stomach. Mondays, Tuesdays, and Wednesdays, it was Diet Coke and carrot sticks with natural ranch dressing, Thursdays he switched to light beer, because he liked to watch his carb intake, and organic whole wheat crackers seasoned with sea salt.

Weekends, all bets were off, wine, tequila, vodka with Oreos, Ben & Jerry's, whatever. At least he was keeping to a schedule. And he still washed his hair, though shaving had become iffy. He didn't have much of a beard, so what grew on his face was sparse and sad. I was glad my father wasn't around to witness this.

But things were about to take a turn for the better. I liked to pride myself on my intuition, though seeing that I had none made it tough. The oblivious one, carrying on like a madwoman, that was me. Loath as I was to admit it, I confused intuition and wishful thinking.

But this was a sure thing. The CEO of OrangeCom, Wayne's dream company, was going to be honored at a huge university shindig. Buildings, the new library, even the coffee shop were named after him. They would probably end up renaming the whole university. But as long as the great Mark Jasper ended up being our personal benefactor, I didn't care. And what a coup, that I, a lowly adjunct toiling in the trenches, a nobody, had wrangled, by sheer will and charm, an invitation to the bash.

Wayne was always talking about the whiz-kid turned creative entrepreneur, hero of a high-tech California fairy tale, a legend in Wayne's world of beeps and wires and strings of numbers. Mark Jasper was rich, successful, attractive, married to a thin, dark-haired beauty, his former personal assistant, with the requisite two gorgeous kids and they were all living happily ever after in a mansion in the hills of La Jolla overlooking the Pacific Ocean. The stuff of turn-of-the-twenty-first-century fairy tales. And Wayne's dream was to meet his King Arthur and join the Round Table.

I hurried around the garage to the path leading to our bungalow, holding my keys in one hand and the envelope with the invitation in the other. Today, the cheery yellow paint with white trim, made even brighter with the Halloween lights we'd put up last weekend and that Wayne had hooked up to a timer so they'd flick on at sunset, suited my mood. I could smell the ocean and the breeze felt cool against my hot cheeks. I shoved the key in the lock.

Wayne always locked the door, even when he was home, a habit, one of the few, that I found irritating, just as irritating as he found my habit of never locking any door.

And if this party didn't work out, I thought, mentally placating a potential force in the universe that might want to shake up my plans just for fun, we'd make it anyway. We could go somewhere else, a fresh start in a fresh place, maybe a bit more affordable than San Diego. I wasn't married to California. I wasn't married at all. Not yet. I didn't even have a contract. We could go anywhere. Anywhere but back home.

Besides, I loved snow.

We were going to be fine.

The main thing is that I have a boyfriend waiting for me, I thought, as the door finally gave way and swung open. I looked from one side of the room to the other.

He was not on the couch watching TV. There wasn't even a TV to watch nor a couch to watch it on. The sound system was gone, all the electronics, the bulk of the CDs, his surfboard. The Persian rug, a gift from his mother, all gone. The gaps were everywhere.

God, was it a burglar? A murderer? A murglerer? Was he still here? Would I find Wayne bleeding in the bathtub? I froze and listened for some sound, some noise to indicate human life, ready to bolt.

Whoever it was left my favorite chair, an oversized faded-chintz affair. The Halloween decorations still dotted the room, a hideous ceramic pumpkin, a gift from our landlady, was now in the corner on the floor, no longer on the round bistro table that had held it up until this morning. The little witch doll I'd made years ago and pulled out every Halloween was gone.

What kind of nutcase would steal someone's doll?

The dining table was still there, surrounded by its army of four folding chairs, bought on sale at IKEA. Candles were clumped together on the table, a half-melted wax bouquet of gold, ochre, and burnt orange.

I couldn't move, couldn't talk. I barely took a breath. Then I spied it on the table, propped up against a fat orange candle, illuminated only by the light of the streetlamp streaming through the window. An envelope. White, not cream like the one I clutched in my sweaty hand. I didn't want to know, but I did. This was not the work of a burglar. Time hiccuped and my breath was stuck somewhere below my ribcage. *This must be what it feels like to drown,* I thought. I felt dizzy... knew I should move, sit down, close the door, at least.

After what felt like hours but couldn't have been more than a few minutes, I closed the door, dropped my bags, and went to the table. I was shaking. I threw the now-crumpled cream envelope with the invitation on its surface and read my name typed on the white rectangle. *Colette,* perfectly centered, something I strived for in life. It could have been the title of a short story: "Colette, Perfectly Centered." It was the kind of envelope we used to pay bills; security envelopes they were called. Just a dumb, cheap, functional, self-adhesive piece of paper folded and glued to hold words. Words that could pay debts, bring a smile, keep ordinary life going, or knife a dream.

I couldn't bring myself to open it. Instead, without switching on the lights, I went to the refrigerator and pulled open the door. The chilled air made my skin feel clammy as the light cast spooky shadows around the room. I kicked off my heels and stood on the cold tiles in my bare feet.

He'd taken the beer. Every last bottle. Even the high-carb stuff. Even that bottle of Chimay that Jean-Pierre, a Belgian friend of *mine,* had given us and we'd been hoarding. I grabbed a half-empty bottle of cheap Chardonnay, which I normally avoided because it invariably made my head pound thus nullifying any sweet oblivion the alcohol could bring. Tonight, it would have to do. My head was already throbbing.

I turned on the recessed light beneath the cabinet and, after finding a glass and three ibuprofen, drowned them in a gulp. I couldn't for the life of me remember which painkiller you were supposed to avoid when drinking. I refilled my glass and dragged a stool over to the refrigerator, climbed up, and opened the cupboard above it. I groped behind the vases and old phone books until I found what I was looking for. My stash. I stepped down from the stool with my pack of Lucky Strike lights and the beautiful gold lighter Gali had given me for my eighteenth birthday, when we both smoked like fiends.

Glass in hand, I went back outside, sat on the steps, and lit up. The smoke cleared my head at first, then made me dizzy. I was thankful, grateful for the deadly pull away from the horror I was going to have to live through. Again. As the smoke disappeared into the starry sky, I willed the whole situation to do the same. Just dissipate in a cloud of smoke. That's why there were still so many smokers around, I was sure. We wanted our problems to behave like the smoke, even if it killed us.

After my second cigarette and second full glass of wine, I went back inside, my head spinning. I wet the butts under the faucet to make sure they were completely out and threw them in the trash. A compulsive self-preservationist with a death wish, me in a nutshell.

I scouted around for something else to drink and came up with a full bottle of Porto. If I'd known, I wouldn't have bothered with the cheap Chard. I carried a wineglass full of the thick, sweet wine back to the living room then collapsed in my armchair. I stared out the window at the twinkly orange lights we had strung up last weekend, my mind numbing like an abscessed tooth at the dentist's after a shot of Novocain.

The envelope was leering at me.

"Shut up!" I said.

He owed me more than a typewritten Dear Jane letter. He could, should, would talk to me, dammit!

I reached for the phone we kept on the side table and realized they were both gone. Selfish bastard. How did he expect me to have a complete breakdown without a phone or a TV? The haze in my mind cleared and I remembered the glory of cellular communications. One more gulp of Porto . . . was the glass already empty? . . . this stuff was like lemonade. I needed—no wanted—more. Sugar was good for shock, my mother used to tell me. Of course, she was referring to chocolate. Should pick some up. Godiva liqueur.

After refilling my glass, I went back out and got my phone from the car. I plugged it in and pressed one on the speed dial.

Two rings and a charming voice: *Wayne Harper-Jones is not available to take your call and is not accepting messages at this time.*

I ripped the jack out of the phone.

By the time Sunday afternoon rolled around, I hadn't talked to a soul and I'd been out all of once, in a perfect breakdown uniform of pajama bottoms, a baggy T-shirt—I would have worn one of Wayne's but he hadn't left a scrap of clothing—and flip-flops, with dark glasses not quite big enough to cover the circles under my swollen eyes and my hair sticking out like a time-traveling punk rocker. I'd left the house briefly on Saturday morning to buy groceries. I loaded up on wine and food at Trader Joe's. And cigarettes at the 7-Eleven. Now, only the food was left.

Dumped, deserted, deleted. Most of the bad stuff that happened to you started with the letter *d.*

Divorced.

Diseased.

Dead.

I could go on, but why bother. I wondered if this was how my father felt when Maman died. Only worse.

I plugged the charger into my cell. I had eight missed calls.

Two from Sonya. Six from Gali. Zero from Wayne Harper-Jones . . .

Six calls from my sister?

I hung up. Christmas with my father? Impossible. Even more so than usual. For now, though, it was better to let Gali believe I was coming. I looked down at myself. My sweats were stretched out and looked tired. I needed a shower. I had to get cleaned up, do something, call someone. Someone other than my sister. On my way to the bathroom I spotted my bed and crawled in, rolled on my side, pulled my knees to my chest, and yanked the duvet over me. Only the tip of my nose was exposed. Just for a few minutes. Then, I'd get up.

I stared at an oil painting of a harbor done in shades of blue and gray hanging on the wall opposite my bed. A gift from my father. I remembered him restoring it in his little studio off the dining room. Originally a sunroom, it had the best light in the house. I would peek at him from the doorjamb and he seemed at peace when he was working on a canvas, the smell of solvents, special soaps, and varnish clinging to the air. The colors blurred and I closed my eyes.

When I woke up, the sun was high in the sky. Time to get it over with. I walked the eleven steps from the bedroom to the living room. The envelope was still there. Smug. Waiting for me to open it. Knowing I would.

I slid my thumb under the flap and felt a slice of pain. Blood filled a fine slit in the skin of my thumb. I sucked the blood out of the paper cut, then carefully removed the white sheet of recycled printer paper from its nest. I knew what it was going to say before I read the words, yet, I was curious. I forced my eyes to focus. Blood dotted the sheet.

Colette, baby—
Can't do this. It's not you, it's me. Sorry, babe.
Bye
W.

He hadn't even signed it with a pen. Just plain Arial on recycled paper.

I wondered which TV show he'd swiped the "It's not you, it's me" from. Not really his usual style. I held the bloodstained note and sat on one of the chairs, waiting for it. The pain. Last time it was excruciating. I waited. But nothing.

I jumped to my feet, crumpling the letter into a ball, then threw it as hard as I could against the wall.

"Shithead stupid fuck!"

It barely made a sound as it bounced off the wall and fell to the floor, weak, ineffectual.

For the rest of the day, I went through the motions of what could pass for life. I showered, put on leggings and a red-and-purple paisley dress—an outfit that usually made me feel better—and went to the laundry room off the garage. Evelyn, my landlady, had worked out a schedule. The main house got the washer-dryer during the week and tenants had it on weekends. I did laundry, sitting outside at the wrought-iron table, beneath a striped parasol. I went over my preps for tomorrow and finished marking student papers.

I needed a story. No one could know. I couldn't live through the shame another time. All the pity. Everyone knowing I'd failed. Again. I could still picture Daddy's face as my sisters ushered me away from the church.

When Wayne and I had started going out in high school, I couldn't believe my luck. Neither could anyone else. He was the hottest guy in our junior class. Athletic and smart; every guy wanted to be his friend, every girl had a crush on him. Me included. It was weird that both Jacqueline and Art didn't like him. Gali was just happy that I was happy. When he asked me out, it had felt like a miracle. To the rest of the class, too. I wasn't exactly A-list. The only A's in my life were my grades and my cup size. In the crook of his arm, I became visible for the first time. The others in the popular crowd had no choice but to accept me, some more grudgingly than others. Especially Tracy Harris, the head cheerleader, who'd earmarked him for herself. I knew she'd just as soon suffocate me with her pom-poms than be-friend me, but she did put up a good show. At least in front of the others. I didn't care. I had Wayne and the rest was just icing. Not even, just the decorations on the icing.

We both went to Shippensburg, though I'd won a scholarship to Bryn Mawr. Daddy still hadn't forgiven me for passing up a blue-chip education for a boyfriend, even if he was from an old Main Line family.

But Wayne was my life. My sun.

The first time it happened, we were supposed to go to the shore for a weekend. It was the summer between our freshman and sophomore years at college. We were both working to save money—me in a bou-tique owned by one of Tante Sola's friends and him as a lifeguard at the Shady Oaks Country Club. I was having a hard time putting money into my account because my thirty percent employee discount was a siren's call. I would snatch up different pieces of clothing, and on days when Wayne was working and I wasn't, I made them into something else.

We both had the weekend before July Fourth off. I'd packed my bag with a couple of bathing suits, sundresses I'd concocted, shorts, and about a gallon of sunblock. My mother had always said that she and I were children of the North, the sun was not a friend to our skin. "There are so many better things to do than lie like a crêpe getting brown on one side, then the next," she'd tell me. But as a teenager and even into college, forgoing the Jersey shore would have been like tossing an anvil through the fabric of my social life.

I was sitting on the porch swing rereading Colette's *Claudine* books, my packed weekender at my feet.

He never showed.

He'd quit his job. His mother, Eleanor, told me he had to get away. She was willing to bankroll his trip as well as the expenses for school in the coming year. "He has his entire life to work. He is young, time for fun, for foolishness. Poor thing, didn't he tell you he was leaving?"

"Must have slipped my mind," I'd mumbled before fleeing the look in her cool blue eyes. "Mine," said the look, "he's mine."

In the fall, back in school, it was as if it had never happened. He'd swept me up in his golden aura.

"I had to be on my own for a while. If I saw you, I wouldn't have had the strength to leave. Didn't my mother give you my note?"

I shook my head but no longer cared. He was back and he wanted me.

The second time was the day of our wedding—the happiest day in a young woman's life, I'd been assured by everyone and everything from bridal magazines to the manicurist, caterer, and every person I'd come across and who'd spotted the diamond on my ring finger.

Left at the altar, poor lamb.

Jacqueline and Gali saved me from the walk of shame and whisked me away to hide in Gali's house. Together they watched over me until Jacqueline had to go back to Belgium.

I sleepwalked through the next four years. I got a teaching job and a car. I lived with my sister and only came alive with Elly, who was just a baby at the time.

Then, one March day, I received a postcard from San Diego of two bikini-clad bottle blondes with weirdly large breasts. On the back, he'd written:

*Come to me, babe. I'm sorry. Will explain all. Love you.
W.*

And there was a phone number.

Against a wall of family shock, I packed and grabbed the money in what had been my honeymoon fund, took my sewing machine, quit my job, put my life into my Honda Civic, and crossed the country.

That had happened five years ago.

How did time slip by so fast? I'd thought that surely by now . . . I shook my head. The dryer was buzzing. I fluffed and folded, then went back inside.

"Yeah, his mother's sick. It is lucky that he isn't working right now. No really, Sonya, I'm fine. Don't come over, okay? The house is a disaster." *True enough,* I thought, looking at the depleted space. "Thanks. See you on campus tomorrow. Yes, coffee at eleven. Great."

I knew he'd come back to me. He always did. But in the meantime—and yes, time could certainly be mean—how was I going to survive? I took stock over a cup of tea.

My job gave me no benefits so I had to be careful not to get sick or hurt. On the plus side, I still had a good chunk of money stashed in savings, though it had shrunk a bit since Wayne lost his job. I checked my account online.

Empty.

I checked again.

Zero.

He'd taken my money. *My money.*

Nothing left.

I looked at my empty cup and fought an urge to fill it to the brim with vodka. I grabbed my phone and called Val.

"You up for a drink?" Val was my best friend and was famous for her disastrous romantic life. One loser after another.

"Always."

"The usual?"

"See you in twenty."

I could do this. I'd polish my story on Val. She was always so happy in spite of her string of lousy relationships. Something about being Irish, I guessed. I threw on a clean pair of jeans, my Camus T-shirt, and put on a bit of mascara and lip gloss. I should eat something. Later. I'd eat later. I'd figure this out. I could get a loan. A second job. But not tonight. Tonight was a night for soaking wounds in wine.

A soft click awakened me. I was still more than a bit drunk. What time was it? I looked for the alarm clock, but then I remembered that it, too, was gone. I listened, keeping still, my fingers clutching the covers.

Very light steps, barely perceptible, but my sense of hearing had always been highly developed. A gift I didn't know what to do with. It had never come in handy.

Wayne? But why would he pussyfoot around? Unless he'd left something and wanted to sneak in and grab it without my knowing he was here. Ha! He'd forgotten about my hearing.

I pushed the covers aside, ready for a fight, then froze. Maybe an angry, tearful confrontation wasn't the best tactic. But what? Just lie here and pretend I didn't hear him? Tempting. But what more could he want to take? I'd stay calm. Be charming. Throw him off guard.

And demand my money back, said a small voice in my head.

Funny. Be funny. He loved it when I made him laugh. Sadly, I was not in one of my more jocular moods. My head was thick with too much Pinot and the dull ache of dehydration was surfacing.

I heard a drawer slide open.

Maybe charming, funny, and naked?

I got out of bed and took a deep breath to dispel the fog in my head. Shouldn't have had that last glass of wine. I blinked several times till I felt steady. Well, steadier. I'd play it by ear. I could always whip off my pajamas in a grandstand gesture.

I padded to the main room and groped for the light switch.

Then, my heart shuddered to a stop.

In front of me, blinking like the proverbial deer caught in head-lights, was the most gorgeous man I'd probably ever seen. His glossy hair fell back in dark waves, framing a face of such classic beauty I wanted to paint him. Forget that I hadn't painted in so long I'd have to hit the art supply store in a big way and wearing pajamas to boot. His body, in black jeans and a tight black T-shirt, was lithe with those lean muscles that didn't come from a gym and his skin was the color of melted butterscotch. *And* his elegant fingers were riffling through one of my kitchen drawers. Actually, the light stopped him in mid-riffle, his hazel eyes wide. Brazilian?

I swiveled and bolted for the front door, my heart pounding in my ears. My ankle twisted, sending me sprawling. Cursing myself for drinking so much, I scrambled to my feet and swayed like a sapling in a strong wind.

"*Sc-scusi!*"

He placed a gentle hand on my arm, I pulled away, wrenched open the front door, stumbled out into the night. I felt strong hands on my shoulders holding me back. I opened my mouth to scream, but he pulled me to him with one arm and covered my mouth with his hand, muffling any noise I attempted. He turned me around to face him.

"*Scusi,*" he repeated.

Italian. And polite. I should have known. Only the Italians are intimate enough with beauty to grow humans as glorious as this. Instinctively, I curled my fingers into my palms, to hide my bitten fingernails. Was no one actually from San Diego? This place was like a colony.

"If I take my hand, you will not scream, yes?"

I widened my eyes at him and nodded.

"I will not hurt. I think no one is at the house." He lifted his hand just an inch from my mouth. I took a deep breath.

"At home." Now I was correcting his grammar? I quieted my inner language teacher and stared at his eyes. I believed him about not hurting me. Probably because he was just so beautiful I wanted to believe. Unexpected beauty can screw with your brain cells. Whichever ones were left after all those I'd murdered with wine tonight.

"*Si.*"

"What . . . Who . . . ?" I was so articulate. It was a gift.

"*Scusi.* I am Dante. Dante di Lucca." He inclined his lovely head.

"Nice to meet you, Dante. Could you tell me what you were doing in my kitchen?" That level of beauty was disarming. I couldn't believe he was dangerous. He looked as if he'd lost his way. On his way to where, via my kitchen, was an excellent question.

"Ah, *si, scusi.* Let us go back inside and I will explain." He waved his arm in a classic "after you" gesture. For some reason, in part due to my lingering inebriety, I went back in. If they found my bloody body on the floor of the living room, Wayne would be sorry. Dante followed me and held out one of the folding chairs. I sat.

I loved really nice manners. Especially in today's world. And in SoCal to boot.

"I come to"—he looked down, making a face—"to rob."

"To rub?" Was this some new nocturnal cleaning service?

"To *rob. Sono un ladro.* I am a thief." It rolled off his tongue like poetry.

Despite all the sleep I'd been getting this weekend, exhaustion fell over me. I snapped.

"Well, Dante. If you can find something worth taking, be my guest. Might I suggest my laptop and, uh, my cell phone. Please leave the sewing machine, you won't get much for it. I'm going to bed." I stalked back to the bedroom, concentrating on walking in a straight line, and crawled under my covers.

He followed me, looking horrified. "*Ma tu sei matta!* You are crazy. Someone could steal your *identità.*"

"If anyone wants it, they are welcome. I certainly haven't had much luck with it." Might be refreshing to become someone else.

I sat up, though. Seemed the proper thing to do when a gorgeous Italian burglar was in my bedroom in the middle of the night lecturing me on identity theft. Okay. I was dreaming. This wasn't happening. Maybe I should start cutting down on the wine for real.

His gaze alighted on Maman's Hermès scarf, draped over my dressmaker's dummy.

I shook my head at my apparition. "It's a gift. From my mother. She . . . died."

His gaze snapped back to mine. "*La tua mamma! Povera bambina.* Me too I am orphan from my mother."

I was now bonding with an imaginary gorgeous Italian burglar over the deaths of our mothers.

"You're the nicest, and one of the more creative, dreams I've ever had. But if you'll excuse me. I have to work tomorrow and need sleep."

"*Aspetta un'attimo.* You do not look good."

"Gee, thanks." Of course, next to him, who looked good? I couldn't believe I was being insulted by a figment of my imagination.

"No, you look not in good form."

"Healthy?"

"*Si,* not healthy. Too pale. You stay here. I have a wonderful idea. I go cook. Food always make life more beautiful. Not normal to want to give away *identità.*"

I heard him banging away in my kitchen dusting off my pots and pans. He was singing softly. He made a lot of noise for an apparition. Maybe he was real.

I got up, pulled on my silk Anna Karenina wrap, slipping my phone into the pocket just in case, and headed for the kitchen. The room hadn't seen this much excitement since I'd painted it two summers back.

"I know the stove works, but I can't vouch for the oven, it's a bit dicey at best."

"*Che bella,*" he said, admiring my robe, touching the fabric lightly. "So, what is wrong. Why so sad?"

"Well . . ." The whole situation was so weird, so otherworldly, that I found myself spilling the story. He listened without interrupting, all the while, cooking, setting the table, rummaging through the fridge, till at last he set a plate of the most luscious-looking eggs I'd ever seen in front of me.

"*Frittata con zucchini. Mangia.*"

I hadn't realized that I had the makings of *frittata con zucchini* in my fridge. I was impressed with myself. Gali would be proud.

"I'm not really hungry."

"Yes. You are hungry. I can see it. *Mangia!*"

I took a tentative bite. It was good. It was very good, in fact. Before I realized what I was doing, I finished off my plate of eggs. He served me seconds and I ate that, too. I felt as if I hadn't eaten anything this good, this necessary, in years.

"Do you have wine?"

I nodded toward the half-empty bottle on the counter.

"This"—he held up the bottle—"is not wine. It's *vinagre*. Not even to cook. It is not dignified enough to touch food." I was too embarrassed at my choice of wine, selected for thrift rather than quality, to utter a word of protest.

He poured the wine down the sink, then filled our glasses with ice cubes and bottled water. "And so?" he prompted.

"And so he pretty much took everything. Even all the money in my savings."

He shook his head with disgust. "No morality. This Wayne, he is a pig, *si?*"

I nodded. "*Si.*" I knew I'd change my mind at some point. I always did. But right now, that was exactly how I felt.

"What about you?" I asked. "What's your story? I know you lost your mother. And you're an amazing cook. How did you . . . break into the field of burglary?"

"*Domani.* Tomorrow I come back and we eat and talk and I tell you my story. *Va bene?*"

"*Si.*" My Italian was getting a workout tonight. Curiosity trumped any lingering anxiety about entertaining a burglar.

"You go back to sleep. I clean up."

Obediently I stood, feeling much more steady. There could be something to this whole feeding-yourself thing.

"*Aspetta!*"

I stopped.

"What is your name?"

"Colette. People call me Coco."

"*Bello!* Nicoletta. Yes? I call you Nico. *Ciao, Nico.*"

"*Ciao.*"

The next morning, I could have sworn that I'd dreamed the whole episode. I'd been drinking, after all. But when I got to the kitchen to make my coffee, a faint odor, not really an odor, more the memory of an odor, clung to the air. Last night's dishes were washed and neatly stacked on the drainboard with a bright orange dishtowel draped over them.

The rest of the day was a blur. I acted out the motions of my normal life, teaching and smiling, convincingly, I hoped, pretending to eat, probably less convincingly.

By the time I got home, I knew I would never see him again. Not a bad thing, considering he was a felon. Could you be a felon if you hadn't been convicted? I'd have to check.

On the off chance that he would be back, I'd stopped at Whole Foods and bought a bottle of Gavi di Gavi and a Santa Cristina. The wine buyer recommended both.

If he didn't come, at least I had two really nice bottles of wine for my dashed hopes. I showered and dressed in jeans and my *Breakfast at Tiffany's* sweater. I reclined on the bed propped up by pillows, since there was no more couch, feeling a bit decadent and rereading *Pride and Prejudice*. I set it aside, in the mood for something a bit more cynical, and picked up the latest Amélie Nothomb instead. Now this woman would never believe in love.

I got an urge to smoke. I rose and grabbed my pack and lighter from the jumble drawer in the kitchen. No need to hide them now that Wayne was gone. I stepped outside and sat on the steps. It was chilly but the cool air felt nice.

I smoked for a bit. I'd better not let myself get addicted again. Too hard to quit. I stubbed the cigarette out on the sole of my shoe and headed back in.

"*Ciao, Nico!*"

I turned, one hand on the doorknob. "Hi." He came. I stared at him. He was carrying a bag of groceries from Trader Joe's. He smiled and nodded toward the door.

"Oh yes. Sorry. Come in." Where were my manners? There was a certain etiquette to entertaining burglars.

"*Grazie.*"

Today, he wore a white shirt that brought out the honeyed hue of his skin, and jeans. I guess all black was his work wardrobe. He deposited the bag on the table as I went to the sink to run the cigarette butt under the tap and dispose of it.

"Many people in Europe smoke. Here you are rare," he said.

"I'm rare all right. But you . . ."

"No. I promise my *mamma* that I would smoke never."

"I guess you didn't promise not to steal, huh?"

The look that swept through his eyes made me wince. "I'm sorry," I said.

"No, you are right." He turned and, his back to me, unpacked the groceries. "Real food."

I saw pasta and vegetables, olive oil, garlic, and cheese. He pulled out a bottle of wine. I picked it up and read the label. "Barolo."

"*Si.* It is good. You will like."

"I bought some too." I showed him the two bottles.

His eyes widened with delight. I've never seen a grown-up whose features could be so transformed by simple joy, like a kid on Christmas morning.

"*Sei brava!*"

I felt as if he were painting me with warm chocolate. I should buy great wine more often.

He opened the bottle of white and breathed in the odor, held it in, then exhaled with satisfaction. My skin prickled. He poured two glasses, handed me one, then raised his glass. I matched his gesture.

"*Bella Nico.* To you."

I tried to think of something spiffy in return. "Cheers." Brilliant. I was brilliant. He was going to be bowled over by my sharp wit and unparalleled repartee.

The wine was cold and crisp, like a dip in a cool pool of water on a hot day.

I almost gasped. "This is wonderful."

"*Buono, si.*" He handed me a few carrots. "You cut."

"Sure." I began to chop while he washed tomatoes and flat-leaf parsley.

"So you want to know my story. Why I am here in San Diego, in such a strange . . . profession."

I nodded, though suddenly I wasn't sure I wanted reality to put a crack through this blissful moment.

"First, I am from Ravenna. Do you know it?"

"No." I picked up a carrot and began to peel it.

"It is a small city, on the Adriatico, beautiful."

"From what I've seen of Italy, it's all beautiful."

"You have been to Italia?" He was chopping an onion and blinked several times.

"A few times, a long time ago. Verona—" I threw the carrot peelings in the trash and start slicing them. I should invest in a better knife.

"*Per vedere la Casa di Giullietta.*"

"Yes, Juliet's house. But you are from Ravenna?" I prodded, curiosity getting the better of my reluctance to have this fairy-tale moment smashed.

He nodded. "Babbo, my father, was a good man. A sad man, but good. He never, how you say, recuperate?"

"Got over . . ."

"Got over the death of my mother."

I knew all too well what that was like. I had a sudden flash of my sad, gray father.

"*Allora,* my brother, he is very serious—study all the time. He is a doctor, very good, very brilliant." He finished with the onions and ran his hands under cold water. "To stop the stinging," he said. "My sister, Gabriella, is married and has three children. Always wanted to be a mother and is a fantastic *mamma.*"

"And you," I prompted.

"Ah, *si.* Me." He flashed a smile. "I play. I joke. My father gives me money. I spend it all on nothing. Last year, I win green card lottery. He gives me money again and tells me that this is the last time. No more. He says, 'Make a life. Promise me.' So I come to America and try to open a restaurant. I find a partner who has concept, *si?*"

"Yes." I finished the carrots and gave him my full attention.

"I know food, but I don't know business. I think it is enough, but no. We spend money on consiglieri—to give advice—for to start a business. They take and take, for permits and licenses and taxes. The money is gone and so is my partner. I have been, *come se dice,* conned."

"Oh Dante, I'm so sorry." I wanted to reach out and touch him, but I didn't dare.

"I cannot go home to Italy like this. No money, no job, no new life ... *niente*. So I become a burglar, like in American movies. I steal a little, small expensive things. I know quality."

I got that from the way he'd eyed my Hermès scarf last night.

"When I get enough, I go to Las Vegas. I make more." He picked up his glass and took a sip of wine.

"Wow." I lost myself in thought. "Can't you get back at these *consiglieri*? You could try to get your money back legally."

"They are professional. They disappear. I need lawyer. But with no money ..."

"No lawyer. I get it." The only lawyer I knew was Leo, my brother-in-law. Maybe he knew someone in California who did pro bono. But I couldn't begin to imagine explaining to my sister and her husband why I was trying to help a thief even if he was Italian and gorgeous and had been conned. Not to mention that I'd have to explain about Wayne.

"Can't you just get a ticket and go home? It's not your fault you were swindled."

"Impossible. It would kill Babbo. He would not believe. I must go home a success." He crushed a garlic clove with the flat of the knife.

I raised my glass. "Some people really suck!"

He burst out laughing and clinked his glass against mine. "But when the food is good and the wine exceptional, we eat and drink and get strong for life, yes?"

"Yes," I said to make him happy.

I didn't teach on Tuesdays so I spent a lot of time at my sewing machine working on Jacqueline's Christmas gift. The project took me to a different mental space. I no longer noticed the bareness of my surroundings. I allowed Dante to slip in and out of my mind like water rippling over pebbles.

Around noon I stopped to make coffee. I stretched, wondering if he'd be back tonight. I couldn't help hoping. Why? I had people to call. I could go out. I sighed and returned to my table, stitching and sewing. The machine whirred, its familiar rhythm a comfort. I stopped for dinner, a bit of leftover pasta and a glass of the Barolo.

I really should call Val or Sonya or any of the group. But the only person I wanted to talk to, outside of Wayne, was Dante.

Wednesday morning as I was driving to work, Chantal, the head of my department, called inviting me to lunch. I always looked forward to seeing her. She was one of those people who made others feel smarter and better than they actually were. Or maybe we were better around her. Her aura invited it.

After my two morning classes, I headed over to the café, my feet crunching through the brittle eucalyptus leaves that layered the path. The Santa Ana winds were blowing hot and dry and the sky had turned acrylic blue. Tempers flared in this weather, weird stuff always seemed to happen. Even in my sleeveless yellow cotton shift and lace-up espadrilles, I was too hot.

I nabbed a table near the window and sipped San Pellegrino, grading compositions until Chantal breezed in looking crisp and cool. She personified France. Her look was chic, but not in the clichéd fifties way most Americans picture French women. She was totally fashionable, hip, and pulled together. All her students worshipped her and she was personally responsible for many a student year abroad. I wondered what it would be like to be her just for a day. Live fully "*bien dans ma peau*," at home in my own skin.

Her body was slender, but not skinny, and she ate everything, even dessert. I didn't really know how she did it. It always seemed such an elegant way to live—not going off on dietary tangents where entire food groups were criminalized and banished on the altar of slim. I was far from fat, but I didn't eat like she did either.

Today, she wore a long, sleeveless cream sweater belted over wide-legged black pants, several long gold chains draped around her neck, and her dark hair brushed back from her face. There was even something quintessentially French about her eyes. Something I couldn't describe but that lived on the outer corners, between the eyelids and the laugh lines. She kissed me on both cheeks before taking a seat and pouring herself a glass of Pellegrino.

"What I'd really enjoy today is a glass of crisp dry wine, but all I need to do is show up in class with alcohol on my breath and the rumors . . ." She made a fluttering gesture with her hands.

"Not to mention that the campus is dry, so . . ." I raised my eyebrows.

"They would have visions of me sneaking whisky from a flask in my drawer." She leaned back in her chair.

"No one could picture you doing that," I said.

"You'd be surprised at what people will believe." Her smile was wide.

Our lunch arrived. Chantal was having a ham and brie baguette with a small green salad on the side. I chose the garden salad with dressing on the side.

She picked up her sandwich then set it down again with a sigh. "I have some bad news."

I looked at her and nodded.

"The university policy of giving teaching jobs to grad students rather than to experienced professionals is not a good one." She looked me straight in the eye. "This year I have three grad students who want to teach."

"Which means next trimester, I'm out of a job."

"I'm so sorry." She rubbed the bridge of her nose with her thumb and forefinger. "I have spoken to the dean, but the policy stands."

"So . . . Martin?" Martin was my colleague, also an adjunct in my department.

"Has more seniority and"—she looked down—"children."

"I get it." I crossed my arms and looked out the window at the branches of the eucalyptus trees swaying in the wind. I could smell Chantal's perfume, light and fresh like an ocean breeze.

"Oh, Colette. I hate to do this to you. Perhaps it is only temporary and next fall I will be able to have you back. *Je suis désolée.*" She took a bite of her baguette and made a face. "Too salty. I don't seem to have an appetite today anyway."

"It's hot." At least for once I had a good excuse for not touching my food. Usually I skewered a lettuce leaf and gestured with it before putting my fork down, discreetly removing it from the tines before spearing a tomato or cucumber, and starting the whole dance again. I didn't know where these vegetables were from, or who'd washed and prepared them.

Chantal's brow was furrowed. "And you do know that it is you and Martin who must train them."

"Yes." Which totally sucked. Until the end of the trimester, the grad student trainees, who were stealing my job, would be sitting in on my classes taking notes to familiarize themselves with the material.

She shook her head and pressed her lips together. I hated seeing her look so distraught so I forced myself to brighten.

"It's okay, I'll be fine." She looked up and I flashed her a smile. I had six weeks. My checks would stop just in time for Christmas. Oh goody. Christmas in Pennsylvania, sitting around the table with Daddy, having to explain that, not only had I been dumped again, but I was out of a job. The impending joy was almost too much to bear. My back was stiff. I rolled my shoulders to loosen the muscles, but it didn't help. And the Santa Anas had given me a headache.

So, how had this happened in less than a week? No boyfriend, no job, no savings, no furniture, even. Oh, and no Dante either. Even my gorgeous Italian burglar had abandoned me. Nevertheless, I waited for him, with a good bottle of wine I could no longer afford, for the next two nights. On the third, I gave up, drank the wine, and went to bed.

CHAPTER 4

Magali

The gorgeous Pennsylvania fall had surrendered to a rainstorm. I hurried into The Two Lions and scanned the crowd, surprised that there was one on a Tuesday. I removed my soaking wet trench coat and adjusted the neck of my black turtleneck. Since I'd been a mom and out of circulation, the world had become more sophisticated. Maman would have loved to pull her Jaguar up to a real Belgian tavern right here in Philly. Everything from the yeasty smell of beer to the strains of Brel in an art nouveau décor was skewed authentic. I was glad I was wearing heels.

I snagged two empty barstools when I felt a blast of rain-soaked wind wrap itself around me. A second later, Syd was there, damp blonde hair sticking to her cheek but gorgeous nonetheless. She was dressed in a sweater and jeans like me, but on her it looked fantastic.

"You look like shit!" She hugged me.

"Nice to see you, too. *You* don't, never have, never will." I'd stopped bugging Syd about her terrible vocabulary a while back, though I demanded she be careful around my kids.

"Let's ply you with alcohol and you can tell me what's up." She signaled the barman and he scampered over like a lovesick puppy. Not that Syd noticed.

I ordered a Leffe Blonde and she had a Lindemans Framboise.

"Do you know how much I love that you forgo the ubiquitous appletini and come have beer with me?" I said when our beers were served.

"Yeah, well"—she took a swig—"there's beer and *beer*, you know? Hip cocktails come and go—and appletinis are long gone"— she flashed me a sweet smile, the kind you give a child who believed long after an appropriate age that a bunny really did bring chocolate on Easter—"but beer is forever."

I shrugged and took a sip of my own brew; the Leffe tasted like sun topped with cream.

"Food?" she asked.

"When have I not wanted food?"

She scanned the menu. "I'm in the mood for *moules frites*."

Micheline came over. "My friends, I have your table." Micheline and her husband Piet owned The Two Lions and together they represented Belgium. Piet, a lanky blonde with pink cheeks, hailed from Flanders to the north, and petite Micheline, dark hair and hazel eyes, from Wallonia in the south. A mixed marriage. He was as mild and soft-spoken as she was boisterous and wild.

My eyes traveled to her belly.

"Micheline! You're—"

"Waiting for a baby, yes!" The way she got her words a bit wrong reminded me so much of my mother, I'd love her even if she secretly murdered people with her chef's knife in the kitchen.

"Congratulations!" Syd jumped up from the barstool and enfolded the smaller woman in her arms.

"We are happy," she said with a grin.

She kissed us each on the cheek and led us to a booth by the window beneath a black-and-white photo of the Brussels Hôtel de Ville. Between the sound of the rain, the heady smell of food, and Micheline's benevolence, I felt better than I had since my father's phone call. We placed our order.

"Now, back to the subject," she said.

"I didn't know there was a subject. Oh yeah, I remember, we were talking about how dreadful I look. You blame me for changing it?"

Syd looked at me with her cornflower blue eyes. It should be illegal for a grown-up to have eyes like that. They should be the exclusive province of babies.

Duncan, our server, came back with our beers. I took a gulp in an attempt to stem the tears that were beginning to fill my eyes. I choked and felt better because now I had an excuse for the tears running down my face.

"What's wrong? Gali . . . ?"

I wiped my eyes and made a stab at a grin. I could only imagine how grotesque I looked from the way Syd was staring at me.

"Okay, here goes." I ticked off on my fingers. "One, Daddy wants to have Christmas dinner at the old house with everyone there. Two, convincing my sisters, not to mention my brother—"

"How is Art?"

"Who knows? Last summer he popped up at Colette's. He was resting up before heading out to another overseas gig. According to Colette, he looked amazing. Get this: he's tanned, with biceps and a six-pack—and I'm not talking beer."

"Wow." She smiled.

"Eloquently put, but sums up my general reaction too."

"No one's heard from him since?" She leaned forward.

"Nope. *Rien*." I shrugged.

"Always at Colette's?"

I nodded. "They're closer, the two babies of the family."

The mussels came and they were perfect. Served in individual casseroles, they smelled like the North Sea. After depositing the platter of crisp *pommes frites* on the table between us, accompanied by a small bowl of mayonnaise, Duncan left us to our meal.

Syd knew the drill. You scouted one perfect mussel shell, used a fork to eat the first, then proceeded to extract the rest with the empty shell as a clamp.

"Do you know anything about where he is now?" she asked.

"No. It's always very cloak and dagger. We only really know where he is when his work pops up in the press and on the net. And by then he's usually on to the next assignment. He was talking about a change though."

"A change like settling down?"

I shrugged, picking at my food. I wasn't hungry anymore. I sipped my beer, but as always with beer, the first is always the best. Funny how that doesn't hold true for wine.

"And three." My voice came out so low, only dogs would be able to hear it. "Three, Ana is going to retire."

She stopped chewing.

"Don't swallow or you'll choke. Chew."

"Yes, Mom. But?"

"She wants to write novels." I took another sip of my beer.

"That sucks," she said.

"Yeah. Could we please not talk about it?"

She picked up a *frite* and bit it in half. "Cold."

As if she'd read our mind—it seemed, at times, that we shared just one, with Syd controlling the lion's share of the brainpower—Micheline removed the bowl filled with empty shells and replaced it.

"Let me bring you more *frites,* hot ones."

I shook my head. "I need to shed a few pounds before Christmas."

"You choose now, with Halloween, Thanksgiving, and Christmas all coming to make a diet?" asked Micheline.

"That's what I said," Syd interjected. "Great timing."

"Not a diet! You know how I feel about *diets!*" An exercise in futility and frustration. Sure to make you fatter and sadder. "I just want to cut down a bit and move around more."

"*Alors,* I will be back with fresh. *Regarde,* we have a celebrity." She cocked her head toward the bar.

I glanced through the mist of my misery and spotted a familiar profile. Syd looked over her shoulder, then snapped back like a mousetrap.

"Aidan Thomas." I narrowed my eyes at her. "Aren't you going to go over and say hi."

"Nope." She arranged and rearranged the salt and pepper shakers.

"Should I be writing you up a dinner menu?"

She shook her head and I felt . . . relieved, oddly enough. There was something about the guy that I didn't like. Nothing personal, just not for my best friend. He delivered the news as if he wanted everyone to like him.

But her face had gone pink. You didn't need to be CIA to figure out she was hiding something.

I whipped out my wallet. "Dinner's on me."

On top of everything else, my best friend didn't trust me.

Moules frites
MUSSELS AND REAL BELGIAN FRIES

This is one of those dishes that sounds scarier to tackle than it is. It's so delicious you won't be sorry you risked it, because here's the thing: it's really hard to mess up.

As a side note, true Belgian *frites* are twice-fried in *blanc de boeuf* (which is beef tallow or fat). The advantage to frying in fat rather than oil is that the fat does not penetrate the potato as the oil does, so your fries are always lighter, crisper, and less oily. Seems like a paradox. You can reuse it up to ten times. If you decide to take a whack at it, be sure to choose organic, pastured, grass-fed beef. However, nowadays in America and even in Europe, we tend to fry in oil. Choose one with a high smoking point (above 385 degrees F.) Safflower, canola, and grape seed are all good choices. Don't use olive oil, as wonderful as it is, because it is not intended to be used at high temperatures.

The potatoes: the true Belgian potato for *frites* is the Bintje, unavailable stateside. Use Yukon Gold instead. Make sure they are not new potatoes or you will never get a fry that is crisp and golden on the outside and meltingly fluffy on the inside. The older the potato, the better.

Serves 4.

Ready? Here's your shopping list.

For the mussels ...

⅔ tablespoons unsalted butter
3 ribs of celery, chopped
3 shallots or one onion, chopped
5 pounds mussels, debearded and cleaned (Count 1¼ to 1½ lbs
  per person—adjust the quantities.)
Fresh parsley, chopped
⅔ bottle (50 cl.) dry white wine
Freshly ground pepper

For the frites . . .

2 pounds Yukon Gold potatoes (or Russet or Idaho—as long as it
   is a starchy potato)
3 to 4 cups oil for frying
Salt
Electric deep fryer or a 4-to-6-quart Dutch oven or deep fryer
   with a basket attachment and a deep-fat thermometer.

First, the potatoes. Peel the potatoes and soak them in cool
water for an hour (this brings out the starch and ensures light,
fluffy fries). Dry them thoroughly. I mean it. Then cut them into
flat disks. Cut the disks lengthwise into even-sized fries. Don't mix
thick and thin, because the frying times will be different. In Belgium we prefer a thicker fry. Dry them again. The potatoes should
be as dry as possible.

Pour the oil into the fryer and heat to 325 degrees F. Working in
small batches, fry the potatoes for about 7 to 8 minutes. Do not
overcrowd them. Cooking too many potatoes at a go will lower the
temperature of the oil and your fries will not cook correctly. They
should be light yellow (not browned), but tender and cooked through.

Shake the basket to get rid of the excess oil and transfer them to
a large bowl or baking sheet lined with paper towels. Make sure
you maintain the temperature of your oil at 325 degrees. Then cook
the rest of the fries in small batches. Let them rest until they reach
room temperature. You can precook all of your fries several hours
in advance. It's important to let them rest and cool down before
cooking a second time.

When you are ready, heat your oil to between 375 and 380 degrees. Fry your potatoes in small batches until nicely browned. This
can take between 2 to 4 minutes. Keep an eye on them. Drain on
fresh paper towels and place in a paper towel–lined, pre-warmed
bowl. Season with salt and serve. You might want to cook half at
the beginning of the meal and the other half later on to ensure fresh
hot *frites*.

For the mussels . . .

Melt the butter in a pot large enough to hold all the mussels over medium heat. (If you are making mussels for more than four people, you may have to use two pots.)

Chop the celery and shallots or onion. Throw them in the pan and let them simmer slowly till they begin to soften, about 5 to 7 minutes. Add the mussels, some chopped parsley, the white wine, and freshly ground pepper.

Cover and bring to a boil over high heat, giving the pot a good shake now and then to redistribute the mussels. Cook until all the mussels are opened, about 5 to 6 minutes. Do not overcook, or the mussels will be tough. Remove from heat. Discard any mussels that have not opened.

Ladle mussels and broth into soup plates. Sprinkle with more parsley.

Serve with the fresh hot fries and a chilled white wine. Or a good beer.

Dip the fries in the broth or in homemade mayonnaise if desired.

This is paradise, Belgian-style. Great for a long, chatty meal with friends. It's also a wonderful romantic meal for two, since mussels are an aphrodisiac. Cut the recipe in half, light some tapers, and cue up your favorite music to play softly in the background.

CHAPTER 5

Jacqueline

I pushed open the heavy door of the Drug Opera—a café near the Grand'Place—and scanned the room. Nothing but the usual crowd of ladies feasting on tea, coffee, and pastries. When I first set eyes on the name, my reaction was "Wow! Mozart on mushrooms!" As it turned out, the café was as close to a stately British tearoom as you could get this side of the Channel. The name came from a truncated version of *drugstore*—the Belgians had been infatuated with American movies from the fifties with drugstores selling milkshakes and ice-cream sundaes abounded—and since it was located on a street adjacent to the Place de l'Opéra, thus the name Drug Opera.

I stepped aside for a couple leaving the café. She was wearing a loose white blouse over jeans, buttoning a hip-length blue sweater as she walked. He was in a turtleneck, with a baby strapped to his chest. The baby was still in the blob phase. I couldn't tell if it was a boy or a girl, and since Europeans had long ago abandoned the pink-for-girls blue-for-boys that, according to Gali, still prevailed in the States, I got no clue from the baby's clothing. As I stood and watched, the woman placed a bright blue woolen hat appliquéd with an orange elephant on her child's head. They both looked down on the little thing with pure adoration. My heart stuck in my throat. The father caught my eye and smiled. "Look what we made," his smile seemed to say. I smiled back. He put his arm around his wife and they left.

"I just hate overt public displays of affection," a voice behind me said. "Those three ought to get a room."

"David," I giggled. "Shh. They might speak English, you know. Most people do these days."

"It's becoming impossible to be snide in public. Saps the fun out of life." He always managed to look hip and urban despite his shoestring budget. Though he probably spent more than the average woman at the hair salon for the upkeep of his precision cut.

We grabbed the table just vacated by the young family, a choice spot by one of the mullioned windows, which at one time probably looked out on aristocrats in horse-drawn carriages clopping by on the cobblestones. I wondered if my parents had ever come here when they were dating.

He pulled out his cigarettes.

"David." I pointed to the NO SMOKING sign.

He sighed. "You know the old joke though, don't you? Why did the smoker cross the road? Because the nonsmoker told him not to."

"Tell it to the Belgian government. That is, if we have one right now. Do we?" I picked up a menu.

"Not sure. Pretty soon, it's going to be as bad here for smokers as it is in America. I might as well go back."

"You'd hate it there. Men don't dress." Shoshanna, my best friend and tenant, was standing beside our table, removing her coat.

"Why straight American males have an aversion to dressing well is beyond me," he said.

"There is that whole metrosexual trend that might work for you," I said.

"I hate that word. Makes it sound like you only have sex in subways."

Shoshanna slid in next to me. "Soon it'll be no more booths for me."

"How are you feeling?"

"Like I'm going to give birth to the Incredible Hulk." She was wearing a soft, midnight blue tunic over gray leggings, the fabric stretched across her belly. Her frizzy hair surrounded her round face like a halo. "I've been craving *croque-monsieur* for days. With a side of *frites*. And mayo."

"Sho, what would the rabbi say?" I nudged her.

"The rabbi would long ago have dropped dead from the shock. I'm about as Jewish as Grey Poupon mustard is French. Let's order, I'm starving." She scanned the room.

"I hope you've learned your lesson and this is the last one," said David. "Some women bloom when they're pregnant, you on the other hand, wilt."

"Nope, I'm just gonna keep poppin' them out as long as it keeps working." She caught the eye of a waiter and lifted her hand.

"You're kidding. You're not even Catholic," said David.

"Yeah, I am exaggerating a bit. We're thinking one more. Even numbers. If I survive this one."

"Makes sense," I said. I straightened the menus into a neat stack.

The waiter came over for our orders. Shoshanna's choice didn't even make him blink. I ordered the *tomates-crevettes*.

"*Filet américain,*" said David.

"You only order that because you enjoy saying it," I said.

"Filet of American, what's not to like? Same reason I come here, it's all about the name."

"You realize you have the emotional maturity of a preadolescent boy," said Shoshanna.

"At least I don't dress like one. Shoshanna, when you have four, isn't it going to get a bit crowded in that apartment?"

"Oh, yeah. About that." She put a hand on my forearm.

I looked at her pretty red nails. "Let's not have this conversation."

"Jacqueline, please?"

I'd known this day would come. Shoshanna and her husband, Josh, had been my tenants since we moved in. With two kids, it was already a bit tight. Though my head told me it wasn't viable for her to keep living there, my heart was stubborn.

"We won't go far."

"Has one of the houses next door gone up for sale?" I made a tidy pile out of the cardboard coasters and set them to the side.

"It's not as if we were back to the States."

Both David and I looked at her, horrified.

"Bite your tongue," he said.

"It sounds as if you already have a plan." Please, not outside the city.

"We found a small house with a garden in a great neighborhood." She waved her hands as if she could conjure up a vision to show us.

"In Brussels? Sounds like it could only be Boisfort." Clear across the city.

She shook her curls and mumbled something.

"I didn't quite catch that," I said.

She cleared her throat. "Rixensart."

Rixensart was a charming village complete with castle, about twenty minutes from the outskirts.

"We haven't seen the *notaire* yet. But it's a perfect house for us." Her cheeks were pink, whether with emotion, excitement, or hormones, I didn't know.

Our lunches arrived. I focused on the tomatoes stuffed with tiny shrimp. They didn't taste as fresh and briny as usual. But I ate every morsel. I reached for my glass of sparkling water. A warm hand stopped me.

"This is hard for me, too. I don't know how I'm going to survive without you." There were tears in her voice.

"I know." My voice was thick. Then the actress in me took over. "This is a colossal mistake you know."

She sighed. "Josh really wants this for the kids. Fresh air, great schools—"

"—snobby neighbors, no culture, nothing to do in the evening, no me," I finished.

Her face crumpled. What was I doing? Upsetting my pregnant best friend. Lovely. I should receive an award for outstanding strides in the field of empathy. I forced a smile. "I get it. But mark my words, you'll be back. Let's order dessert. I'm in the mood for a *dame blanche.*" I picked up the dessert menu.

"I don't think I've ever seen you this hungry," said David.

I smiled, feeling like a cat that found a leak in a vat of cream.

Shoshanna's eyes widened. "Unless . . ."

I giggled.

"Oh my God," she squealed.

"Don't squeal, darling. It's unbecoming," said David. He looked at Shoshanna, then at me. A slow grin spread across his features. "I want first dibs on godfather. Or at the very least, eccentric uncle."

"This would be the perfect time for David to move in." Shoshanna's eyes were dancing.

"I don't think David is the change-the-poopy-diaper type. It would cramp his style." I wasn't even sure I was the change-the-poopy-diaper type.

"You underestimate me. Story of my life." He raised his glass of Perrier.

After purchasing some early Christmas presents for my nieces, I went home and focused on preparing the weekly meal for my family.

I laid a freshly pressed light gold tablecloth over the surface protector on my dining-room table, set out the good dishes and russet-colored cloth napkins, followed by three glasses per person: one for water, sparkling and still; one for white wine; and one for red, though we wouldn't open the Bourgogne until the cheese.

Mamy Elise and my aunt and uncle were getting older. They deserved to be pampered.

By the time Laurent arrived with my grandmother, I was ready. I was wearing a simple wraparound knit dress and the gold earrings Laurent had given me for my birthday.

Mamy came in looking splendid as usual and smelling lightly of Chanel No. 5.

"*Bonjour petite,*" said my grandmother. I kissed her cheek, marveling as usual at the softness of her skin. She was elegant in a soft blue suit that brought out her eyes. She removed the hat from her head and readjusted her scarf. Her hair was freshly washed and set, her lipstick fresh. Just like my mother, Mamy Elise was the person-ification of coquette.

"*Tu es belle en robe,*" she said. My grandmother liked women to wear dresses, to look like women. Couldn't abide slopping around in shapeless pants and wasn't too crazy about jeans either. Here stood a woman who had survived a major world war and the occu-pation of her country, had lost her husband to the Nazis, raised her three girls on her own, and made sure they stayed in school.

And through it all, the poverty and the ease that came after when the government gave generous pensions to the widows of slain political prisoners as "*réparation,*" she had never let herself go, kept her house sparkling clean, and had always kept food—good food—on the table. If Maman had begun my education as a woman, Mamy taught me what it was to be a strong one. Grad school for life.

I was happy to spoil her once a week.

"It smells delicious." Her gaze swept over my immaculate living room.

Laurent came down in jeans and a gray shirt. "I'll get the *apéri-tif.* Porto?" he asked my grandmother. She beamed at him.

I followed him to the kitchen. "She's still absolutely in love with you."

"And right she is to be." He left the kitchen with the glass-and-bottle-laden tray I'd prepared.

The doorbell signaled the arrival of my aunt and uncle.

The dinner was a copy of our weekly Monday meal. My uncle, Gérard, kept us laughing with his usual batch of off-color jokes and we shared stories of the past week, eating the food I'd pre-pared, embraced in the soft candlelight.

My aunt, a sparrow of a woman, loved to talk about the past.

"Your mother and father," she said, "were fearless, full of life. Always looking for a new adventure. He owned a beautiful car, but here in the city, they spent their time dashing around on their little Vespa, even after the accident. Nothing could stop your mother. Everyone wanted to be them."

"That's how they ended up in America," said my uncle. He shook his silver head. "They tried to convince us to follow them, but ..."

"It wasn't for us. We belong here." She looked fondly at Mamy Elise.

"At least one of my daughters stayed with me," said my grandmother. Tante Solange and her husband, André, had emigrated about a year after my parents. He and my father started the antique business. They'd made a good team. He was the businessman and my father, the connoisseur. Uncle André, a bon vivant, had grown fatter and fatter as their business prospered and his wife devoted herself exclusively to their only son, neglecting her husband. He died of a massive coronary six years ago.

"I was always surprised that Tante Sola never returned," I said. I was so happy here, it felt so safe, I couldn't understand why my aunt stayed on in America.

"It became her home. And Vincent is there," said Tante Charlotte. "Children are the most important thing."

I drained my glass of water.

After dessert and coffee—the pears were fabulous, not too grainy and just the right degree of sweet—my grandmother rose.

I helped her into her coat and accompanied her to the door. My aunt and uncle were also leaving.

In a flurry of "*À la semaine prochaine!*"; "It was a wonderful meal"; "*Merci*"; and kisses all around, they slipped into the night, Laurent accompanying Mamy Elise.

I finished clearing the table, had the dishwasher running, scrubbed the baking dish, and hand-washed and dried the glasses. I was putting the tablecloth and dish towels into the washing machine when Laurent popped his head into the kitchen.

"Leave it," he said.

"I can't. Besides, it's done." I gave the counter a final wipe and wrung out the cloth, hanging it up to dry. "I want to show you something." I led him to the counter and unwrapped the plastic stick I'd hidden in a paper towel.

His face lit up. He lifted me and swung me around, kissing me hard.

"Careful. I'm bearing life here."

"So you shouldn't overexert yourself." He scooped me up and carried me into the bedroom, like a bride in a movie, and set me down on the bed as gently as if I'd been carved from eggshells.

I giggled. "I'm not an invalid."

"We're going to be careful this time." He sat next to me.

"You're one to talk, with the swinging me around." I bolted off the bed. "Why should I keep calm? This is exciting. It's more than exciting. It's stupendous."

"Of course. But . . ." He nodded three times, a habit he had that made him look like an earnest little boy. I usually found it endearing, but right now, I was annoyed. There were no *buts*.

"But?" I was veering close to dropping over the edge. "We said we wouldn't talk about it. Ever. We said we'd never think about it, even. And now you're bringing it up."

"I haven't said anything." He stood and began to undress.

"No, but you're thinking it."

"Okay. Sorry. I don't think I could stand to go through it a third time. If we stay calm . . ." He went to the bathroom. I could hear him brushing his teeth. I got up and undressed, hanging up my dress in the closet. I put my shoes on the shoe rack and my earrings back in the jewelry box on the vanity.

Laurent slid into bed. I put on a silk robe and sat down beside him.

"By *we* you mean me," I said, picking up the thread of our discussion.

He stroked my back, his hand going up and down my spine. It felt great.

"It's our turn, Laurent. It just feels different this time."

"Let's just not tell anyone yet, okay?" He kissed me.

"If it will make you happy. But we could. Because it will work, you'll see." I didn't tell him that Sho and David already knew. Technically, I hadn't *told* them.

In the bathroom, I stared hard at myself. "Maman, I know you are there. Please let this one be born." I turned away from the mirror, switched off the light, and headed for bed. I let my robe fall to the floor and pressed my naked body to my husband's.

* * *

The next morning, I was at the piano doing warm-ups. Joy, like a warm wave, lapped at my skin, until my father called.

And my wave of happiness sank into the sand, leaving it cold and wet.

Daddy rarely called. Or e-mailed for that matter. And when he did it was always curt. I looked at the clock. "What time is it for you? It's the middle of the night. What's wrong?"

"Nothing. Just been experiencing trouble sleeping."

That was new. A change from him passing out in his armchair at ten-thirty and staggering fully clothed to his bed sometime during the night.

"You're not sick?" I rearranged the candlesticks on the mantel, then put them back the way they'd been.

"Of course not." He said this as if sickness would take one look at him and slink away in terror. "I wanted to tell you I won't be coming for Thanksgiving this year."

I felt I should make some sort of protest or at least a heartfelt inquiry. I sat down on the piano bench, my back to the keys.

"There are things that I must take care of here at that moment." More bizarre by the second. I stood and plucked two flowers that looked as if they were on the verge of wilting out of the vase in the center of the table and dropped them in the garbage pail.

"Well, I . . . we'll miss you." It's what one said, wasn't it? Even if it didn't come from the heart? What kind of monster didn't want to see her own father? One that wanted a bit of serenity, perhaps?

"I'm sorry. I know this has come as a surprise to you."

"Yes." A welcome surprise. *Say something . . . think, think, think.* "I'm having a hard time believing it, that's all. It is tradition. It won't be the same without you." That, at least, was the truth.

"But I will see you at Christmas. Maggie told you."

"She did."

"It's settled." Now he was sounding more like his old self. Just when I was growing fond of his new self. "I shall leave you to your work. It was good to hear your voice."

After clicking off, I returned to the piano but suddenly felt too restless to sit there. A few seconds later, I was retching into the toilet. Just a coincidence.

* * *

I loved my job. I loved putting on supple black clothes, preparing my bag, getting on the metro, emerging from the underbelly of Brussels to the Place de la Monnaie and seeing the theater. And knowing that here was where I belonged. I felt keyed up, buoyant, like a cork in a bubbling brook, a little buzz in my brain. I was like this before every performance. Not something I took for granted.

I'd reached the stage door and sighed. I hated going to America. Another bout of nausea hit me and I ran to the WC without even saying hello to Thierry, the stage manager.

Stop it! I mentally told the baby inside. I brushed my teeth then ate some salty crackers I'd brought and washed them down with a slug of Perrier.

In my dressing room I grabbed a wilting bouquet of flowers from the vase by the makeup mirror and dropped them in the trash before heading out to the house for notes and warm-ups. Our director, François, felt that the company was a family and we all had to meet onstage before each performance. Not only the singers and musicians, but the stagehands, the costume crew, the stylists, and *accessoiristes*. In short, everyone who had a part to play in the success of the show.

Today there would be rejoicing at the great review we'd gotten and I couldn't help glowing from the rave I'd received.

Most of the cast and crew were already there. I joined the melee. The lights were up in the house, making the stage appear dim in comparison, like dawn preceding the bright daylight of the show.

"Are you okay?" asked François. "Thierry . . ." He trailed off, waving his arm in the direction of the stage manager.

"I'm fine." I was getting tired of saying this. "Just something I ate."

Just then, another bout of nausea swelled and, despite the smile that I wanted to be reassuring, I must have gone pale.

"Come sit." He sat down next to me.

"Jacqueline, since you've been with this company, have you ever missed a performance?"

"Never. And I don't intend to start." Except maybe when I have the baby, but that would be paid maternity leave.

He put his hand on my forehead. "No fever. When you are a parent, no need for a thermometer."

I smiled weakly, battling queasiness. A few more crackers and some Perrier and I'd be fine. Fine.

"You are a professional, but it is clear you are not well. Go home."

"But—" I rose.

He put a hand on my arm, guiding me back down to the seat.

"But the review." I was shaking.

"Ah yes! It was wonderful! And so much thanks to you. You must be careful. Take care of yourself. Not overextend."

"I can sing. I'm ready." I forced myself to take a deep, calming breath.

This was all Daddy's fault. His call and the ensuing stress triggered this avalanche of nausea. Babies hated stress. It was a known fact. "Really, François. I can do this."

"I know. But should you? Go home. Rest. Look, you are trembling. What if you are starting a bug? It could infect the entire cast."

"But I'm not sick. Your expert parental hand has verified that. I would never risk—"

"I know. But I want you to do as I say." His tone was gentle. "The body needs to rest sometimes. And the voice is part of the body. Go home. I will see you tomorrow."

There was really nothing left to say. I was banished. I felt everyone's eyes on me as I made my way backstage to collect my things. I glanced at my understudy, who was glowing. Young, beautiful, a native Italian . . . was he sleeping with her? I shook my head to dislodge the thought. This wasn't *All About Eve*.

The daylight was losing ground to the creeping darkness as I crossed the Place de la Monnaie. The cafés were overflowing with people savoring a beer after work before heading home. I was never at loose ends this time of day. I could head over to Cora Kemperman's boutique for some retail therapy. I could get on with Christmas shopping.

Instead, I crossed the street and stood staring at the window of a children's clothes shop. I shouldn't go in, really not. Maybe missing my show was the universe's way of telling me to concentrate on my impending motherhood.

I went in. Despite my good resolutions, I bought a tiny white cotton onesie, soft as a cloud, that sported a duckling delicately sewn in navy thread. I also bought two sweater-scarf woolen hat combos for my nieces. No pink to be found, though I knew Charlotte lived in and for that hue. I found a soft pearl gray for her that would set off any one of her pink ensembles. Perfect for Christmas.

My nausea had subsided, but too late to do me any good. I let myself get swallowed by the entrance to the metro.

It occurred to me that I still hadn't told Laurent about Christmas.

CHAPTER 6

Colette

Halloween

Every year at Halloween, Wayne and I would buy candy. Despite being single and almost broke, I couldn't disappoint the few hopeful trick-or-treaters who came to the door craving sweetness. It was just a handful of neighborhood kids who knew to come around the back, invited by my orange lights and jack-o-lantern—a Halloween-friendly house.

I finished carving two pumpkins. The pumpkins were organic, a fact I didn't broadcast for fear of being locked away in a loony bin. I justified the splurge by roasting the seeds and eating them with sea salt. The nutty smell of the seeds mixed with the spicy candle burning on the table made my little house smell like autumn—like back home. Here we liked to pretend to have seasons, but there really was only one.

This year I didn't have the heart to make a costume. Nevertheless, I dressed in head-to-toe black, with an aqua feather boa looped around my neck and a matching turban on my head.

Preparing for Halloween had kept me too busy to think. And tomorrow, I'd take everything down and pack the decorations away before cleaning. I didn't have a plan for Sunday...yet. I wished I had a couch and a TV to watch *It's the Great Pumpkin, Charlie Brown*. I slumped in my armchair, cradling the bowl of candy on my lap when the bell rang. I opened it to find a full-grown masked d'Artagnan, complete with boots.

"Nice costume," I murmured. I looked over his shoulder and didn't see any kids, let alone another musketeer. He was alone. What a creep.

"Trick or treat," he said. His rolling *r*'s gave him away.

"Dante!" I refrained from throwing my arms around him. Instead, I took a step back. Why was I so happy?

"*Ciao, bella Nico.*" He removed his mask. "*Venite qui,*" he called over his shoulder. Two men came up the walk carrying a sofa. I noticed a produce truck parked on the street.

"Where do you want it?" he asked.

"Oh, Dante, no. I couldn't." The last thing I needed was to get arrested for being in possession of stolen goods.

"No, no. Don't worry. The furniture is from the Goodwill. I clean and fix them."

"You bought me furniture?" I stepped back to let him in.

"*Si.* Very inexpensive but still nice quality."

The two men were still holding the couch.

"*Dai,* Dante," said the shorter of the two.

"*Si, si.* Come in. So where?"

I pointed to the center of the room in front of the fireplace. The couch was small and covered in green nubby fabric. It looked like something from the thirties. Dante pulled a large fringed shawl from the black mailbag he had slung across his body. He draped the shawl over the back of the couch. It looked...perfect.

I tried to swallow the lump that had taken up residency in my throat. I had a sudden flash of my father coming home with a Deco end table and my mother dancing around the room and clapping her hands.

"Th...thank you," I said, unsure of how to react. The two men left then returned, one with a floor lamp and the other with a small, round coffee table. They set one by the side of the couch and the other in front.

"It match the spirit of your chair," said Dante.

I nodded, feeling a big, stupid smile plastered on my face. I realized I was still wearing my turban and boa. I removed them both and set them on the table.

"*Grazie,* Paolo, Vincente."

In a chorus of *ciaos* they melted into the night, these angels bearing gifts, before I could properly thank them or offer them something. "I wanted to give them some wine or . . . candy," I said.

"They go to their families now. *Sono bravi.* I tell them you need furniture, they help." He grinned.

"Dante, I don't know what to say." The strange thing was that, had I been on my own all these years, it would have been pieces such as these that I would have chosen. Pieces with stories, a bit battered from life. Furniture with a soul. Wayne liked clean, modern lines.

"Come in, sit, make yourself comfortable—thanks to you I can actually say that again." I ran my hand over the nappy upholstery.

He sank easily into the couch, looking as if he owned the space he breathed in.

"I don't have any decent wine left. Or anything to eat for that matter, except for pumpkin seeds. And candy." I went into the kitchen and returned with the seeds in a ceramic dish.

He ate one. "*Buono.* Good for pesto."

From what I'd mistaken for his trick-or-treat bag, he pulled out a bottle of red wine—a Santa Cristina, I saw from the label. Then came two packages wrapped in waxed paper that turned out to be panini. I never ate panini.

I collected glasses and plates from the cupboard, suddenly hungry. We had a picnic bathed by the soft glow of my new lamp.

I ate almost half of my sandwich before I put it down.

"*Non ti piace?* You do not like?"

"I like. It's too big."

"Not so big. *Mangia!*" He nodded his head and resumed eating.

"It's delicious." To prove it I took another bite. It was one of the best sandwiches I'd ever had, with thinly sliced prosciutto and provolone topped with tomatoes, olive oil, and herbs. "But . . ." I shook my head and smiled.

"Something has happened, no? Something new?" His brow furrowed.

How could he guess? It would have given me the chills if it were someone else, but Dante was too gorgeous to give me the creeps. I wrapped the rest of my sandwich and put it on the coffee table.

"Your eyes. Very dark blue tonight, almost gray and also here." He touched a spot between my eyebrows and I realized I'd been frowning. "And here." He placed his hands on my shoulders and I felt how tight they were. His touch sent pinpricks of light through my body.

"Well." My voice would have given a congested toad a run for its money. I cleared my throat. "You win first prize. You're right. I seem to have lost my job."

His eyes widened.

I took a sip of wine and amended, "I will be officially unemployed come January."

After I'd explained, he gathered me in his arms. I curled up against him and lay my head against his chest, like a kitten. A tear rolled down my cheek. Then another.

"So, you will have no money?" he asked.

"Not a sou."

"And do you have a plan?"

"Nope. Haven't got one of those either." His shirt was darker where it had absorbed my tears.

He gently pushed me a few inches away from his body and looked into my eyes. "I have an idea."

CHAPTER 7

Magali

Halloween

I was removing my witch hat and untying my cape when the doorbell rang. The kids were finally in bed, so much corn syrup cours-
ing through their little bodies, I was sure they'd be up with
nightmares and a headache tomorrow.

Nine-thirty. A bit late for trick-or-treaters.

"Trick or treat!"

A six-foot-tall masked Mad Hatter stood on my porch. An
adult. Every year there was one or two. Talk about not ever wanting
to grow up.

His costume was nicely put together. I grabbed a few fun-size
candies and looked for his bag of goodies to drop them in.

"Actually," he said, "I could really go for a beer and maybe
some of that great pumpkin bread you always bake at Halloween."

"Art!" I flung myself at him, almost knocking him over.

"Nice to see I haven't been forgotten." He hugged me back.

"You dope."

"Dope? I see having kids has really transformed your vocabulary. How sophisticated."

I grabbed my brother's hand and pulled him inside. "You have no idea. I could have called you poopy pants, though we do discourage the use of scatological terms. Leo, look who's here!"

"Let me guess." Leo was using his plummy voice, the one he reserved for children. "Darth Vader? Ariel?" He came into the living room wearing a mask and cape, the Lancôme eyebrow-pencil moustache he'd drawn smudged on the left side.

"If it isn't the Mad Hatter," said Leo.

"See you're keeping up with tradition. Zorro again." Art grinned.

"What you don't get is that these are my actual street clothes. It's when I'm a lawyer that I'm in disguise." He lifted one end of his cape.

They went through that slap-on-the-back-bro-dude thing guys do to show how manly they are.

Art removed the tall purple hat.

"You look great." It was true. Beneath the kaleidoscopic suit, my brother looked healthy and strong.

Tomorrow I was going to start working out.

Art threw his arm around my shoulder. He towered over all of us, even Leo, who was a respectable six feet tall. Someone who didn't know us would be hard-pressed to guess we were siblings. Art, like Jacqueline, took after Daddy's side of the family, while Colette and I resembled our mother. The only thing that linked us physically was the blue of our eyes.

"The place looks beautiful," said Art. I realized we were still standing in the foyer.

"And those cobwebs? Real! Come in. Sit."

He sank into the deep red sofa. When I'd seen my sister's sofa in her Brussels apartment, I'd fallen in love and couldn't rest until I'd found one of my own. Though, the last time I saw hers, it was still in pristine condition.

"So you like my new décor? The island of broken toys mixed with stain du jour." I waved my hand and almost knocked over a burning candle. I caught it just before it toppled.

He laughed. "It all looks good to me."

True that with the candles lit, our ceramic jack-o-lanterns glowing on the mantel, two vases of pumpkin bouquets, one round, one square, and our not-so-wicked witch and cauldron, it looked cozy rather than spooky.

Big as he was, Art looked comfortable accepting a beer from Leo. I'd never seen him this at ease in his own skin.

"Have you eaten?" I got to my feet.

"Yeah, I had something earlier."

"How much earlier? Let me grab some cheese to go with the beer." I was already halfway to the kitchen.

"Gali, come back and sit down. I'm here to see you."

"I'll only be a sec."

"I forgot, I'm in the house of continuous feeding."

I needed a couple of minutes to figure out how to get Art to come back for Christmas. I needed a plan. Subterfuge. Scheming. *Come on brain,* I thought. *Jacqueline, where are you when I need you most?*

I grabbed a Petit Basque, a ubiquitous brie, and a lovely chunk of aged Chimay cheese—I'd been delighted to discover that the cheese, as well as the beer, was now being exported. I added grapes and walnuts and was back in the living room before I could figure something out. Maybe use the kids? Low, but it might work.

". . . finished up my latest assignment for the agency."

"And now?" asked Leo. He'd removed his mask and cape, but the mustache still graced his upper lip.

"Ah, my next incarnation." You never knew with Art. "The pay was great. I stuck a bunch of money into an account. That's kind of why I'm here. I want you to take care of it for me." He helped himself to some cheese.

"What's up?" My brother, Mr. Independence, I-don't-need-anyone-but-myself asking for help?

He swallowed. "This is great. Thanks." He drank some beer. "The thing is, I'm going away for a little while."

"Wow, that's huge. Really. Wait till I tell Colette and Jacqueline. The shock wave will be felt worldwide." I turned to my husband. "Leo, better call Al Gore."

He helped himself to some of the Chimay. "Only you would have Belgian cheese in the fridge."

Leo had poured me a nice glass of Crozes-Hermitage. I took a sip. "So, not exactly a news flash. Now hanging around, on the other hand."

"I've decided to write a book—"

"A book! You?" I spilled some wine on my shirt. Good thing it was black.

Even I heard my voice swerve into the panic lane. The guys looked at me oddly. Everyone, just everyone, was writing a book: Ana, now Art. A small voice that was Charlotte's age and level of maturity screamed inside my head, *Don't they know this is your dream they're stealing? What's wrong with these people?*

"Yeah, why should you be the only author in the family? Here." He handed me a napkin.

"I'm hardly an author." Yet. I dabbed the stain.

"And if you don't believe her, ask your father."

Art's eyes flickered. He sidled up next to me on the couch. "Don't you know how wonderful they are? Your books. Here, let me show you."

He disappeared into the foyer and came back with his old rucksack. Opening it, he pulled out one, two . . . four beat-up books, tattered, clearly read, reread, and loved. Every author's dream.

They were mine.

I drained my glass of wine and stuffed some cheese into my mouth, without tasting either.

He shrugged. "When I miss you . . ."

"You cook?" I managed to ask.

"Not that much. But, you'd be surprised."

"Don't steal my thunder," I mock-reprimanded. "I'm the chef in the family." And the writer.

"Anyway, you help people—don't argue. Reading them is like coming home and having a great conversation with you."

"So, you're going off to write a book?"

"Looking for my own Walden Pond, maybe. It makes sense. I have tons of photos. I want to pull it all together with a strong narrative." He looked so happy, I almost keeled over from the force.

An idea blossomed. "Art, stay here and write it. Please. We've got tons of room."

I looked at Leo, who nodded. "Yeah, dude."

"I thought you'd never ask." He cocked his head to the side. "You dope."

"Again with the dope? I'll chip in by doing yard work. And lots of photos of the kiddos in action."

I hadn't seen Leo look so happy since two years ago when I found a handyman to do all the little jobs around the house. He got up from the armchair and pulled me up, then kissed me. "I love your brother."

"Me too." This almost felt too easy. He'd be here for Christmas. Sometimes, I guess the universe could cut me a break.

My brother stood and put his hand on my shoulder. "Just one thing: don't tell anyone I'm here, okay?"

"Anyone?"

He looked me straight in the eyes. "*Anyone*. Meaning our father."

Figured.

CHAPTER 8

Jacqueline

Halloween

The passage of October thirty-first to November first was always rough, and this year was no exception. I liked it better before the Belgians began celebrating Halloween. In a country where most of the holidays were either about saints or Jesus and Mary, or national holidays like the king's birthday, Halloween came as an imposter. Nevertheless, I made an effort. I was usually at the theater so the effort consisted of some jack-o-lanterns and overbuying candy, which Laurent and I would end up eating until I forced him to take it to work. At least the candy here was really good.

Laurent would wear plastic vampire teeth and one of my old capes, assuring me he was "just doing it for the kids."

For me, it was too many memories. The nice ones were harder to bear. My parents had always gone all out: decorations, parties, and beautiful costumes. Even during the darkest times, after Maman died, a ghost of his old happiness seemed to visit Daddy on Halloween. I never understood why, but the spark was there. It was snuffed out at Christmas, which remained bleak. I shuddered.

The next day was a biggie for Belgians—All Saints' Day. School-children had the week off and Laurent almost never had to go in to work for lack of scheduled meetings. Everything except for the flower shops, restaurants, and cafés was pretty much closed so people would be free to bring large pots of chrysanthemums to the graves of their dead relatives.

Dressed in somber clothes, Laurent and I headed out to my grandmother's house, where the whole family was gathered. Not only Tonton Gérard and Tante Charlotte, but their sons, Pierre and Maxime, accompanied by their respective spouses, Isabelle and Marianne, and, of course, their brood of kids.

My grandmother offered us *une petite goutte*—literally a little drop—but meaning a tiny glass of liqueur or cognac to "guard against the chill."

It was an old tradition, no longer much followed by my generation, except in the villages that dotted the countryside where, on days like today, time seemed to have come to a standstill.

I usually accepted a small glass of Bénédictine, but this year I begged off.

Laurent sipped a calvados, a cordial from Normandy made from apples, but rich and smoky rather than sweet.

We left for the cemetery around nine-thirty, bringing umbrellas to protect us from the steady drizzle.

It was crowded when we arrived. Laurent dropped us off at the gate and went to park the car. While we waited, holding our pots of flowers, the kids ran around, playing an impromptu game of tag.

Laurent strode up the walk. He threaded his arms through ours and we went to my grandfather's grave. It was in the center of the cemetery in the beautifully groomed *pelouse d'honneur,* where the heroes were buried. We went to the section reserved for the political prisoners and placed our pots of russet and gold chrysanthemums. My grandfather had been captured by the Gestapo, tortured, and executed, shattering the lives of my grandmother and her three daughters. He'd been forty-two and a half.

The exact same age as Maman when she'd died.

We accompanied my grandmother to various graves, where she paid her respects. I kept my eyes trained on the gravel walk, unwilling to read the lives etched on the polished granite.

Then, the three of us went to Sainte Marie to light a candle for Maman.

Afterward, Laurent drove Mamy Elise and me to Chez Nous, her favorite restaurant. It was small but inviting, with snowy white linens and etched crystal salt and pepper shakers. A fire blazed in the open hearth and it was like being inside a cashmere cloak. Not to mention that they knew her well and always made a big fuss over her, treating her like a queen, which is exactly the way she deserved to be treated.

Laurent and the others had all gone off to the other sides of the families and another tour of the dead. Mamy, as the eldest and the matriarch, always came first.

She ordered a Porto and looked at me.

"*Un Perrier.*"

She looked tired. I covered her hand with mine. "*Ça va?*"

She sighed. "I just wish she was buried here, close to me. In her own country."

I nodded but was, in fact, relieved Maman wasn't here. A lot of the time, I could almost pretend it never happened. She was still alive, just living in Pennsylvania, so it was normal for her not to be around. So few of my memories of my life with her were here, just a handful of vacations, time out of time. In the States, her absence was too sharp. I didn't know how Gali could stand it.

I didn't know if I could get through a family Christmas without her. I pushed the bud vase to the side of the table and rearranged the salt and pepper shakers.

"So," my grandmother said, taking a sip of her drink, her blue eyes bright. "When are you going to tell me about the baby?"

"I . . . I . . ." How could she know? Laurent and I agreed not to breathe a word until another month had passed and we were in safer territory.

"I'm right!" She clapped her hands.

"We're not saying anything yet. It's too soon. Don't let Laurent know you know."

"Nonsense! It's wonderful news. I'm going to be a great-grandmother." She leaned forward and grasped my hands.

"For the . . . how many times would this be? Seven?" I asked.

"But every time is like the first." She signaled the waiter. "Antoine! *Deux coupes de champagne, s'il vous plaît!*" She rewarded him with a dazzling smile. The same smile Maman had inherited, then my sisters, and now, I hoped, the little one I was carrying.

"But Mamy, I can't drink."

"But you must! Champagne is good for the baby, lots of iron. And," she said, lifting one finger, "life must always be celebrated. Your mother would have been so happy."

I could never picture my mother as a grandmother. I couldn't picture her old. She remained in death as she'd been in life: young, beautiful, vibrant.

Still, when the champagne arrived, I hesitated. According to Shoshanna, most doctors here encouraged pregnant women to have a glass of wine, especially red. But the puritan American in me was frantically waving a flag, also red.

My grandmother lifted her glass. "In this day of celebration of the dead, let us drink to life."

I picked up my glass, the condensation cool on my fingers. We toasted.

"*A la vie!*"

"*La vie,*" I echoed. To placate the worried American in me, I only drank a little less than half. But Mamy had been right, as usual. The bubbles tasted like life.

That evening, after hanging up with my sister, I sank into the cushions of the couch and stared at the flame of the fat orange candle burning on the coffee table. I'd changed into soft jeans and a cream sweater, holding my cup of chamomile without drinking from it.

Laurent came back in, fresh from the shower, wearing a warm blue sweater and jeans. He joined me on the couch.

"How's your sister?" He put his arm around my shoulders.

"Fine. The same." I put my cup down and covered his hand with mine. "The usual harassment about getting plane tickets, you know. But it was the strangest thing."

"What?"

"You know how every year she brings flowers to Maman on the day of Toussaint?"

He nodded.

"This year, there were already fresh flowers on her grave."

"Probably your aunt."

I shook my head. "No. Tante Solange was with Gali." I shrugged. "Weird."

"A part of me still doesn't get it." Sho put down her tea. We were sitting in the kitchen. The rain pelted on the windowpane and it was still dark at nine in the morning.

"Me neither," I said, blowing on mine. "I'm the one whose only motivation for pulling myself out of bed each morning is getting to drink coffee. It's like a breakup."

"At least we have the same aversions."

"Practical. Though I can't seem to stand the smell of peanuts either. Even if Laurent has had so much as one and tries to kiss me . . ." I shuddered. "I make him brush his teeth."

"No." She giggled.

"Yes. And what about the cravings?" I rolled my eyes, but secretly I was so pleased to be able to share this conversation.

Shoshanna groaned. "Sardines on buttered bread."

"Apples. And eggs. I wonder if an apple omelet would taste good." It sounded really appealing.

Raising her cup and clinking it against mine, Sho said, "It's all for the good cause, right?"

"The best. I just wish I felt better." I hadn't even had the courage to dress this morning. I was wearing yoga pants and a wraparound sweater over a T-shirt. "If you move, we'd lose this." I waved my hands around, indicating the kitchen and everything in it. "Is that what you really want?" We shared coffee—or more recently—tea in the mornings several times a week. "We're like family. We're better than family because we don't have all that baggage. Can you just throw that away?" My voice was slipping out of my control. I cleared my throat.

Tears filled her eyes. "Don't. I'm trying not to focus on all I'm going to lose."

"Me, you're trying not to focus on me." I picked up a dishcloth and wiped the table.

"Would I really lose you?"

"Of course not! But it will never be the same." I wiped the counters and rinsed out the dishcloth. I wrung it out and hung it on its hook over the sink.

She heaved herself out of the chair. "We'll talk later. I'm going to be late. Thanks for watching the kids."

"Please."

"I'm going to ask the doctor how I can get that second trimester glow. This time it feels like I segued from first to third. I hope nothing's wrong." She had dark smudges beneath her eyes and a pained tightness around her mouth. Even her hair drooped.

"Nonsense! You're a pro. Aren't you the one who keeps spouting that no two pregnancies are alike and who confiscated my copy of *What to Expect When You're Expecting?*"

"Makes you crazy, that book. I'd love to have a Hollywood pregnancy for once, airbrushed into baby bump perfection."

"I think it's Photoshopped these days. I don't care what I look like, as long as I have a perfect baby."

"She of the flat tummy said. Just you wait." She ran her hands over her belly. "Even this dress is getting tight." She was wearing a stretchy, multicolored striped dress over tights and boots.

The kids were in the living room watching a *Sesame Street* DVD. She went in to kiss them good-bye, put on her raincoat, grabbed her umbrella, and was gone.

Back in the living room, I said, "Hey, guys. What do you say we turn off the TV. Are you hungry?"

"Yes!" They jumped to their feet and Myla switched off the TV.

"Come to the kitchen. You can help me make *chocolat chaud.*"

Once they'd eaten their buttered baguette dipped in the rich cocoa, they decided it was music lesson time.

At the piano, they clamored for one song after another. At eleven-thirty, they had mastered "Chopsticks" and were moving rapidly into "Twinkle, Twinkle, Little Star."

"Where's Mommy?" asked Myla, running her fingers up and down the keys.

Good question. "She'll be back soon." A routine checkup shouldn't take this long.

I set the kids up with a DVD and called Sho on her cell phone but it went to voice mail.

Once the DVD was over, I gave the kids lunch and settled them with drawing paper and colored pencils on the kitchen table. It was past one.

I called again, with the same result.

Then I called Josh. Voice mail.

I texted Laurent out of a meeting and he called back a few minutes later. He was reassuring but I wasn't reassured. I vacuumed the rug.

At two I put the kids down for a nap.

Where was Shoshanna?

At two twenty-five the phone rang. I almost jumped out of my skin in my hurry to answer it.

It was Josh.

"Shoshanna's in the hospital. She had the baby."

CHAPTER 9

Magali

Here I was off to New York for three days and having a panic attack. Ana had bugged me until I'd made the appointments with the two agents she'd referred me to. They'd both agreed to see me. I knew I should be grateful.

An open suitcase leered at me from the bed, a weekender mocked me by its side. There are two kinds of people in the world: those who know how to pack and those who are hopeless at it.

I pulled open my closet door and gazed into its depths of casual mommyhood. It was all jeans—not even the good designer kind—shirts, T-shirts, sweaters . . . boots, sandals, flats, a few nice pairs of heels. I liked to think of my clothes as throwaway chic but really, there was more throwaway than chic on the hangers. My one redeeming fashion rule: I refused to wear sneakers outside of a gym, which meant I had one pair bought two years ago and still in great shape. Which was more than I could say for myself.

At least my shoes were beautiful. They all fit perfectly, right down to the flip-flops. I'd wear my boots and build up from there.

I pulled out a pair of black heels and brown flats and put them on the bed. I'd get dressed first, then pack around what I was wearing. Though by the time I got to the city, the clothes I was wearing would be ready for the wash.

One lunch date tomorrow, and a late afternoon meeting. I was treating myself to an extra night at Leo's behest, with Art prodding me on.

I wasn't used to leaving the girls. But if they were ever in good hands, it was now.

What would Jacqueline wear? She'd know how to pack for a short jaunt to New York. I couldn't believe she'd traipsed off to Europe to selfishly further her career, leaving me not knowing what to wear or pack for this trip.

I had every intention of pitching, not my cookbooks or another cooking series, but a novel. It would all come together, but I had to look perfect.

I punched in my sister's number. Got her voice mail.

The thing was, technically, I really did know how to dress. Lunch with an agent, taking the train, shopping, so comfort was a factor. As long as I was methodical, it would work.

"I know, I'll phone Colette," I said to the cat, who had settled herself on the bed.

Voice mail.

What had I done to make my two sisters abandon me just when I needed them most? Syd was at work, and since that night at The Two Lions, there had been a rift.

I tried my sisters again.

Nothing. I wished I had one of those old phones I could slam down. Pushing a button doesn't vent frustration in quite the same way.

Deep breaths.

In my head, I heard a voice. All of a sudden I was Joan of Arc. It was Colette's. I closed my eyes and pictured the round blue eyes, cropped dark curls, waving her hands in the air, nails bitten down to the quick. Oh my baby sister, why did you leave me?

What would she say?

Okay, Gali. Your body is a canvas. Create.

I opened my eyes. I went to my closet and picked out a soft black, long-sleeved T-shirt and black pants. New York in November. I couldn't go wrong with black. I pulled out a cropped rust-colored jacket and low black ankle boots. My mother's Hermès scarf.

On automatic pilot I pulled things from my closet and put them on the bed. Pretty soon, I had a decent stash.

For the trip, I'd wear my best jeans and a soft gray sweater. It all looked great with my jacket. Jewelry. Big earrings and decent underwear. The Chanel lipstick I'd won at the preschool Renaissance faire/fundraiser went into my oversized black tote. Too much black? Never.

Done.

The phone rang.

"Gali? It's me. I got your message. What's the big emergency?" asked Colette.

"Nothing. It's over. How are you baby?" I closed my suitcase.

I kept finding little foil packets of peanuts in my bag. Leo had a habit of taking free stuff wherever he found it and stuffing it in my purse. I could be stranded for a weekend in the middle of a snowstorm and be able to survive on the contents of my bag alone.

The train rumbled its way to New York, it felt a bit like traveling in a washing machine. I sneaked a look at the man seated in front of me. Intent on the screen of his laptop, a Bluetooth thingy in his ear. He was wearing a coffee-colored sweater that matched his eyes, and jeans. A sports jacket was crumpled on the seat beside him. *Great shoes*.

"Thank you," he smiled. He spoke with a British accent.

"Excuse me?"

"The compliment on my shoes. Thank you."

I felt my face grow hot. "I hadn't realized I'd spoken out loud."

"It's fine. Women notice shoes. Fact of life."

I'm sure there are women out there who couldn't care less about shoes, I thought.

He laughed.

I clamped my hand over my mouth.

"It's fine. You're a writer," he said.

It wasn't a question. I nodded.

"I knew it. Writers spend a lot of time alone and end up talking to themselves. Trying out dialogue and such." He closed his laptop.

"You sound like you know a lot about it."

"Too much. My ex is a writer." His mouth turned up at the corners.

"I'm sorry," I said.

"I appreciate the apology. You were, after all, responsible for the breakup."

He was flirting. I tried to suppress a smile and averted my gaze. The Pennsylvania colors of autumn were tumbling out my window.

I thrust out my hand, knocking my purse to the floor. I went to pick it up but he beat me to it. I took my bag with one hand and stuck out the other. "I'm Nadia." I had no idea where the name came from but it sounded writerly and mysterious.

"Simon." His hand was warm and dry.

What a great name—solid.

"Thank you."

"Why do I keep doing this? My thoughts burst out of my mouth and I'm powerless to stop them."

"Maybe you need someone to talk to," he said.

I opened my purse. "Peanuts?"

He shook his head. I opened a pack to give myself something to do. "Where are you headed?"

"The city." His eyes crinkled at the edges. He must really think I'm an idiot. Normal, because I agree. Daddy's low opinion of me was justified after all.

"And you?" he asked, sparing me. "Are you headed to New York for business or pleasure?"

"Oh, both. I live there." Where this lie had come from, I had no idea. "You?"

"Business. I live in Philly."

He opened his laptop and went back to whatever he'd been doing, while I slipped away to my happy place: the inside of a Williams-Sonoma with unlimited cash. Simon's voice brought me back.

"... on Broadway."

"Sorry?"

"I thought you'd slipped away there for a second. I play the saxophone and have a gig in a reprise of *Seussical*." He tapped the instrument case beside him.

"I love *Seussical*! I've always wanted to play Gertrude McFuzz," I said.

"Then you should."

He really was too cute. "Yeah. It would be nice if I knew how to sing. My sister got all those genes." I shrugged.

"Your sister?"

I nodded. "Jacqueline. Jacqueline Arnaud. Opera. She sings with a small company in Brussels. Did you know that the inventor of the saxophone—"

"Was Belgian. Adolphe Saxe."

Our gazes met and held. How often was it that you met someone at large who could finish your sentences?

"I was born there." I tore my gaze away and stared out the window. We were slowing down, approaching a small station. My palms were sweaty. I took a peanut and offered one to him.

He shook his head. "Allergic."

"Oh I'm sorry!" I stuffed the open packet back in my bag. Great. Now I'd have peanuts all over everything.

"I'm not that allergic. I can still watch people across the aisle eating them."

I wiped my hands on my jeans. Sweat, salt, and oil. The picture of sophistication. Jacqueline would have tissues in her bag. Or even a real cloth handkerchief. I should have brought a pack of wipes. Next time, I'll suggest to Leo that he switch to dry roasted. Thinking of Leo made my stomach churn. I pictured him at home, packing lunches, making dinner, taking care of the girls. Making them laugh more than I ever did. And me, mother of the year, I hadn't even arrived at my destination and I was flirting with the first stranger I'd set my eyes on. At the drop of a hat. Or peanut, as the case may be.

"I don't know anyone in New York except a couple of musicians. Would you like to get together for a drink or coffee or something? It would be brilliant to have a true New Yorker show me the ropes." He smiled.

This was why I shouldn't lie. Most of my knowledge of the city came from shopping sprees when I was little, the only place Maman could find her favorite Côte-d'Or chocolate, a few trips with Leo and the girls, usually at Christmas to skate by the tree in Rockefeller Center and gawk at the windows in Bergdorf's. Plus my not-so-secret addiction to *Sex and the City*.

"You know I'm—"

"Married? Yeah, those rings on your left hand? Dead giveaway."

I twisted my wedding band and engagement ring around. I loved them. White gold. From Tiffany's.

"And while we're at it, I'm—"

"Not a New Yorker?" He laughed. He really had the most delightful laugh.

"That's amazing. If you went public, you could make a lot of money," I said.

"I could attribute it to my uncanny powers of perception, but true New Yorkers tend to choose a different sort of reading material."

We both looked at the book peeking out of my tote. The Michelin Guide to New York. I was nothing if not a traditionalist.

"Nadia," he said, leaning forward, his laptop forgotten. "Look, just a casual drink or dinner or something. No harm in that, right?" he said in his charming British accent. His deep brown eyes crinkled at the corners.

"Right," said Nadia.

With my feet pounding on the Manhattan pavement, I felt so jaunty I could have danced the jig. If I knew what a jig was, that is. Stopping somewhere to Google *jig* and take a lesson would most definitely detract from the spontaneity of the moment. I passed a homeless woman and gave her five dollars. She blessed me as I floated by. I should really have known better. The gods frown on too much unbridled joy. I suppose the gods prefer their joy more bridled, so as not to draw attention to itself.

I decided to shop for something to wear, something fabulous. I sailed down Eighth Avenue to drop off my bag at the midtown hotel I'd booked. My mother's diary had pages and pages devoted to her first trip to New York with Daddy. They'd hit all the tourist attractions, but she'd made them sound like an adventure. The Statue of Liberty, Central Park, the Empire State Building, which she absolutely wanted to visit and kiss Daddy at the top, like in *An Affair to Remember*.

I wished I'd planned my trip a bit later when the Christmas lights would have been up. I'd come back with Leo and the girls. I spotted a Starbucks and ducked in, ordering a *doppio macchiato*. I swear if Superman had been created today, he'd be ducking into Starbucks instead of phone booths.

"Sure," said the barista, her dreadlocks in sharp contrast to her trendy, designer glasses. "Name?"

"Nadia." Okay, onward and upward with the lying, but really, what was the harm? I looked over my shoulder. Everyone lied about their name at Starbucks.

We could try on and discard new dresses, new shoes, a new haircut, we could change everything. Why not try out a new name? What was wrong with being Miranda one year and Vikki with two *k*'s the next? How about Natasha?

I sidled over to the pickup line and waited.

"*Doppio macchiato* for Nadia."

What was set before me was a huge concoction topped with whipped cream and drizzled with caramel. Too late I realized my mistake. I picked up the drink and took a sip. It was so sweet, it made my teeth ache. I could just picture my dentist rubbing her hands in glee as she planned her next island jaunt to Tahiti or some such place that I wasn't positive even existed. It was just some plot to make the majority of us who had never been someplace removed and exotic feel left out.

Gali would have taken the drink and slumped in a chair, pretending to sip it for a while before discarding the whole sticky mess and leaving.

But Nadia? She'd stand up for herself. She'd been raised by

warm, doting parents who believed in her. I smiled and said, "I'm sorry. I wanted a double espresso topped with a spoonful of foam."

"No problem!" The lanky blonde barista dumped it. "Go see Amanda to get a refund and I'll have that for you in a sec."

"No, just tell her to ring up the refund and stick it in the tip jar. I should have been more specific." I smiled again and tilted my head. Here I was flirting with—I squinted at the name tag—Jason.

Was it a flirting epidemic? Was anything with a penis fair game now? Would I become compulsive? Have to join a 12-step program, Flirts Anonymous?

I shook my head to chase the thought and sat down with my coffee.

I had finally decided that head-to-toe black was my answer to how to dress for New York. Every year there was a new black—brown, gray, one year it was pink—none of which was as chic or slimming as the original. My butt in pink looked anything but. Did the fashion mafia think I was six?

What was I doing? I was on the verge of standing Simon up, hunting down the perfect pizza, heading back to my hotel, and watching a movie, when I saw the restaurant and immediately relaxed. Besides, the idea of spending one of my precious evenings in the city in front of the tube in Hotel Bland was too depressing.

I entered and my body relaxed. I smelled candles mixed with the aroma of something fabulous coming from the kitchen. It wasn't one of those stainless minimalist restaurants where more effort had been put in the décor than the food. Which was perfectly all right if you were out for the design. Not my case.

The walls were painted with warm golds, the lighting was recessed and just enough to set off both the food and the people enjoying it. Every table was a different size and shape. No two chairs matched. I breathed it all in.

Then I spotted Simon at the bar in head-to-toe black, smiling at me. I almost turned around to go back out. No one should look that good, even in this light. What was wrong with him that he was divorced? I made my way over and climbed onto a barstool.

"So how come you're divorced?" I asked.

"Never discuss unpleasantness before drinks and at least a smidge of food."

I looked down. "I'm hopeless, I'm a . . . social leper."

"No, it's charming." He signaled the barman.

"I'm glad you got the memo on tonight's color scheme."

"It makes everything easier. I do one load of laundry and three-quarters of my wardrobe is back in commission."

A man who did laundry. Now *that* was sexy.

"Do you think that's how real New Yorkers spot wannabes? A native would be secure enough to wear a little color?" I asked.

He laughed. "You look great."

"So do you." Very restrained. I turned my head and scanned the crowd.

"I took the liberty of signing us up for a table. Unless you prefer the bar? Or maybe you've eaten already?"

"No. Great. Sounds wonderful." Sounds wonderful? Could I sound more inane. Soon I was going to start using words like *yummy* and that would be the beginning of the end. Maybe I should switch to French. Not that I was wittier or more apropos or anything, it was just that fewer people would understand me, thus less embarrassment.

Before I could spout another inanity, the hostess came over and led us to our table. My heels clicked on the polished concrete floor. *Don't let me slip in front of all these people, please.*

We ordered drinks—a Pinot Gris for me and a Macallan Single Malt for him. Classy.

I grabbed the menu and started reading.

"So, when did you become interested in food?" he asked.

I was in a restaurant, what should I be interested in, the wait-staff's sense of style? I stared at him, annoyed. Did I look fat? My new black dress had a tapered waist and showed off my legs, which everyone said were good. Even my father once said I had inherited my mother's legs. *Only she was thinner than you,* I was sure he'd been thinking.

"It's just that you tore into that menu as if it were the latest un-putdownable page-turner."

"I ... cook." I didn't want to get into that whole Institut-Culinaire, worked-as-a-chef-in-restaurant, had-family, ended-up-writing-cookbooks saga. Plus, for tonight at least, I was a writer. A writer of fiction. I hoped he wouldn't ask me if he'd read anything I wrote.

He grinned. "Maybe you could give me some tips. I've just started. Found the most wonderful series of books: the *Hopeless in the Kitchen* cookbooks. Have you heard of them?"

"Rings a bell." Thank goodness I'd always refused to have an author picture on the covers. The food was the star. The books were my bread and butter, so to speak, but they weren't me.

"I love a woman who loves her food."

Did he just say *love?* I twisted my wedding ring on my finger, wondering where the heck my wine was. I moved the candle closer to my menu, keeping my head down.

Our server came with the drinks and asked if we were ready to order.

What I really wanted was a *steak-frites,* but I didn't want to look unsophisticated.

"I think I'll have the *frisée aux lardons* and the duck *confit.*" There. Simple but elegant. I set the menu on the table and reached for my glass of wine.

"I'll have the *steak-frites.* The house salad for an appetizer."

Figured.

"Why don't you tell me more about this cooking of yours?" said Simon.

"Nothing to tell. Besides, it's your turn."

He smiled, showing even, white teeth. Weren't Brits supposed to have questionable dental hygiene? Or maybe that went the way of the French-not-bathing cliché.

I pressed on. "You don't really live in Philly, do you?"

"Not anymore."

"Aha!" Aha? Who was I, Inspector Clouseau? I wished the food would arrive so I could do something with my mouth other than spout drivel.

"I used to live there. My ex and her new husband still do ... with my kids."

I winced. I couldn't imagine a life where I didn't see my children every day.

He took out his wallet and handed me a photo of a boy and a girl, about the same age as mine. They had his smile, but they could be from Sweden they were so blonde and blue-eyed.

He seemed to read my thoughts. "They have their mother's coloring. Tommy is ten and Shannon six." She was dressed in typical princess fashion and looked as if she were about to whack her brother over the head with her wand. The little boy looked sweet, with eyes so sad it was devastating.

"They're beautiful." The gold standard of parent-speak, but in this case the children were truly lovely.

"Thank you." He slid the photo back into his wallet.

"So, you actually live here now?"

"In a way, I'm rooming with one of the trumpets."

"The neighbors must be thrilled." You can take the girl out of the suburbs . . . But he just laughed.

"I came over from Bristol to attend the Berklee College of Music. One thing led to another and I never went back." He took a sip of his drink.

Nick Drake flowed from the loudspeakers.

"I love Nick Drake," I said.

"And good taste in music as well as charm."

I really liked this guy, I raveled a fantasy—can you ravel? Or is it like saying someone is gainly?—of living with him in a fabulous but artsy apartment in a not-yet-but-soon-to-be-trendy neighborhood. On the verge. A verge neighborhood. Our place would be a salon, I would make fabulous food, weigh ten pounds less, and be in the center of a vibrant literary and artistic world.

There was only one tiny hitch. Leo and the girls. I didn't mean any of it. Fantasies hurt no one, after all.

By the time the entrees arrived, we'd talked our way through the salads, my glass of wine, and a second Macallan for Simon. As the server put our food before us, I stopped in midsentence and devoted myself to what was on my plate. The duck looked crispy and succulent surrounded by juicy slices of orange, three tiny butter potatoes, and a bundle of five green beans wrapped in parchment and dusted with parsley. Simple, well presented without being overwhelming. *Just right,* I thought, feeling like Goldilocks.

"Would you like a different wine? May I recommend a Saint-Nicolas de Bourgueil?" asked our server, whose name was Raymond.

I looked at Simon, who shrugged his shoulders.

"Sure, why not? We'll take a bottle." I could, after all, write this off as a business expense. Or research. The beauty of working in food. It was times like this that I loved being a cookbook author.

I let my gaze fall on Simon's plate. His *pommes frites* and steak looked divine.

"Would you like a taste?"

"What?" I resurfaced.

"You're studying my *frites* as if you were cramming for A levels. Would you like one?"

I shook my head and felt my face grow hot.

"Go ahead, please. I value an expert's opinion. How often do you get to eat *pommes frites* with a Belgian?"

So I did. It was an act of intimacy to eat food off another's plate. I felt as if I were betraying Leo. Most women feel guilty for the fries themselves, all the starch and fat and salt, but that wouldn't be enough for me.

The fries were above average. Good, even. What if Leo could see me now? Or anyone I knew for that matter? I looked around the room and drank some water. No sooner had I set my glass down than a server came over to top it off.

"The verdict?" he asked.

I felt like saying *guilty*.

"On the fries?" he prodded.

"Oh. Not bad." I busied myself with my food, losing myself in the moment. Zen would be a lot easier if food were involved. I'd be a master for sure. Maybe I could create a religion? The church of divine morsels or something. That could be misconstrued. Our Lady of Chocolate?

I felt better. After all, what were a couple of innocent *frites* between friends? Then he grabbed my hand. I froze. I raised my eyes to meet his. His face was ashen, beads of sweat dotted his brow.

"What's wrong? Water! You need water." I handed him his glass.

Maybe he was choking. I'd never mastered the Heimlich maneuver. I suddenly flashed on Eddie Izzard's riff on Dr. Heimlich and his maneuver and, unable to stop myself, I burst out laughing. Everyone in the room was staring. I tried to think. The more I pictured how inappropriate my laughing was, the less I could stop. Finally, coughing and sputtering, I brought my fit under control.

Red, then blue, were the colors of someone who had food stuck in his throat. Simon was the color of a timid ghost.

"Simon?" Three servers had clustered around our table. "Simon? What's wrong?"

"Feeling poorly." His voice was a raw whisper. There was such a thing as taking the classic British understatement too far. He released my hand and slumped in his chair. I looked helplessly at the waitstaff.

"A doctor! We need a doctor." In movies, there was always a doctor in the house. A plump kindly man stood on the other side of the room. Dr. Welby. We were saved.

I rose, tipping my chair over, to the annoyance of the man seated behind me.

"Call nine-one-one," someone yelled.

"Done and done," replied a voice by the bar.

Dr. Welby came over. "Give him room. Stand back."

"You're a doctor?" I felt like kneeling and kissing his feet.

"Technically, no. I'm a vet."

"A vet? But you can't—"

"I'm not planning on operating on him with a steak knife. I just want everyone to move back. Does anyone have a blanket?"

I handed over my good black coat and Marcus Welby for canines draped it over Simon, who was now lying on the floor of the restaurant.

"Stay calm and breathe," said Marcus.

"Nadia? Where are you? Don't leave me," said Simon.

I got about seven dirty looks and a gorgeous woman in a short, slinky, low-cut dress that I couldn't pull off in a million years shouted, "Yeah, Nadia, don't leave him!"

"If she doesn't want him, I'll take him," said her companion.

"What a bitch."

"Never a good idea to impart bad news during a meal," Dr. Welby said, giving me a stern look.

"But, I'm not . . ."

Before I could explain, the medics burst into the room shooting sparks of testosterone.

Naturally, since everyone thought I was the bitch who caused the attack, I rode with him to the ER.

As the ambulance sped away, I thought of the duck I was leaving behind.

It was after two when I got back to my hotel, drained and with a headache from the wine I'd had earlier. Simon was going to be fine. It hadn't been a heart attack after all. Turned out Simon had had an anxiety attack. A severe anxiety attack can mimic the symptoms of a heart attack, I was informed by a twelve-year-old in an intern's white coat.

Hospitals always brought back memories of the last days with my mother. How Daddy looked sad and angry at the same time, all the time. We'd huddled together under the stark fluorescent-lit waiting room for our turn to see her. When she died, he'd hugged us, hard. For the last time.

Tonight, I'd gone through Simon's wallet, looking for information. Initially I'd called his wife—well, *ex*—who was still his emergency contact. She was the one who'd tipped me off. It had happened before.

"A trifle. Nothing to worry about." Had I ever worried about a trifle? No, it was a simple enough dessert to make.

"Are you coming?" I'd asked.

"I have a full schedule tomorrow. But do keep me informed, will you? What's your name?"

"Gali, but I'm not—"

"Gali, then. Cute name. Good night, Gali. You sound nicer than the last few."

Why was everyone persisting in treating me as if I were Simon's girlfriend? Was it impossible to have dinner with a guy in all innocence? The whole evening was a blur of trying to explain that no, I wasn't his girlfriend-wife-lover-sister, just some stranger he'd met on the train a few hours ago.

Going up the elevator, I felt leaden with exhaustion. Thank God my first meeting wasn't till twelve-thirty. The second was at four. Ana had arranged everything. I'd do a bit of shopping, go see a show tomorrow night, and return home the next day at noon.

I remembered that my phone was off. I checked it. Three missed calls. Home. Probably the girls wanting to tell me one last victory or adventure before bed. Suddenly I missed them. I hated not giving them their good-night kiss.

I swiped my key card, thinking only of bed, heavenly, wonderful, divine bed. Maybe just a bite of chocolate before.

"Hi."

I almost jumped out of my skin.

On my bed, looking rumpled but wearing a nice shirt and pants, sat Leo, with a huge smile on his face.

I stood there and stared. I opened my mouth but nothing came out.

"Surprise," he said weakly, rubbing his eyes. "Must have drifted off."

"Hi. But what—"

"I just wanted to surprise you. You know, have a night on our own, just the two of us in the city."

I noticed the chocolate on the table and an ice bucket with an unopened champagne bottle sticking out of it. I walked over, kicking off my shoes as I went, and sank onto the opposite side of the bed from him. My eyes felt gritty and all I wanted was a shower and sleep.

He looked at his watch. "Two . . . what? Where were you?"

"Just let me grab a shower and I'll tell you." I headed into the bathroom.

"Want some company?"

Normally I loved shower sex. Put all normal showers to shame. But tonight I needed to wash off Nadia and put Gali back on.

I shook my head. "I'll only be a few minutes, promise."

"Your loss." He leaned back against the pile of pillows and closed his eyes. "I'll be right here if you change your mind."

God, he was so familiar and gorgeous, yet weird and out of place.

I turned the water on full force, without much success. Probably one of those water savers that I saw on an episode of *Seinfeld*. But it was hot. I rubbed my skin almost raw, toweled off, and wrapped myself in the spa robe I'd brought from home. This wasn't the kind of hotel that supplied them. I padded back into the room and Leo's eyes snapped open.

"I was worried."

I didn't know what to say so I sat next to him on the bed and snuggled up. He was stiff next to me but slid his arm around my shoulder anyway.

"I was out to dinner."

"Till two-thirty?" His arm slid off my shoulder. "Come on, Gali, you can do better than that."

"Let me finish and then, if you want, climb right back up on that high horse."

He nodded, keeping his eyes trained on my face.

"I met someone on the train—a musician—who didn't know a soul in town. We hit it off and decided to hook up for dinner to finish the conversation we'd started on the trip up." So far so good, no lies.

"Long dinner. What did you do, go clubbing?" He tilted his chin up. He loved nightlife. I usually just went along to make him happy. It was one of the great untold advantages of having kids that so few opportunities for clubbing came along anymore. I always felt old and frumpy at those places, not a feeling I tended to seek out with any alacrity.

"God, no. You know me better than that."

He grinned and pulled me in closer, his body softening into mine.

"So she—"

"She, yes." He just assumed I'd met a woman. "She," I began.

"What was her name?"

"Si—*mona*. Yeah I know, weird pronunciation, huh, with the long *i*, anyway, she had some kind of seizure in the restaurant and I went along to the ER. Thought she was having a heart attack . . . so scary. But it turned out to be an anxiety attack and not life-threatening. I called her ex who told me it had happened tons of times before"—I needed to stop babbling—"but I still had a hard time leaving her. All alone and no one to come see her, isn't that sad?" I took a deep breath.

"Poor baby. Here, have some of this." He got up and retrieved the dripping bottle of champagne, popped the cork, and filled two glasses. "Of course you stayed. What choice did you have?" He clinked his glass against mine. "So much for surprises."

After we'd polished off most of the champagne and I'd had three truffles, we made love. As I drifted off, I could feel a knot of emotion in the pit of my stomach, something I couldn't quite identify.

I was almost asleep before I finally recognized it.

Anger.

The following morning, everything seemed perfect on the surface, like a cake that had risen unevenly but was camouflaged by a skillfully applied layer of luscious frosting.

We had room service, which I loved as a rule, and this one was no exception. Maybe this was a midrange hotel, but there was nothing midrange about breakfast. The coffee was strong but so smooth that even Leo refrained from adding sugar. Two fresh croissants, flaky and warm. There was nothing worse than a poor croissant. Either one that's so dry, it disintegrates at the first bite or one that has so much butter, it oozes grease between your teeth and leaves your hands gleaming with melted fat. Great for the skin, though. We had fresh orange juice and fruit that was juicy and ripened to a peak: sweet pears and crunchy apples layered with fat slices of emerald kiwi. The chef clearly loved food. I could picture him bundled up at the market at three a.m. picking only what would be perfect right now. No anemic strawberries or bland out-of-season cantaloupe.

And through it all, I smiled and ate and sipped coffee and seethed.

Once Leo had gone, I tried to settle down and figure out why I was so upset. Technically I should feel guilty because I'd sort of lied to him about Simon-Simona. I'd love a romantic getaway with him and he could even surprise me with it, but this was my getaway. I had wanted to be on my own, alone for once. Being Nadia was like a part in a play or a character in a book I might write. She was the opposite of me. Nadia was brave and confident and had loving, supportive parents. She would always rise to a challenge. It was . . . fun.

Too agitated—not to mention caffeinated—to settle down in bed, I got up and dressed. Black again today, but with a red silk tank top playing peekaboo at the V of my sweater. I belted my coat and headed out.

Once on the street, I felt better. I loved the purposefulness of a city waking up on a weekday. Weekend mornings, lovely as they were, just didn't have the same allure. I breathed in the energy that crackled through the air. I ended up at a big chain bookstore on Union Square.

If I lived here, I would be so skinny and toned.

I ducked into the superstore and bought a blank notebook with a picture of a 1930s-era Underwood and a cup of coffee on the cover. After grabbing a latte at the café, I sat down at a tiny round table near the window and dug a pen out of my purse. I opened the book. Here is where I would start to jot down notes for my Great American Novel. It would be hailed as a fresh voice. It would astound crowds. It would live on the *New York Times* bestseller list and Oprah would have me on her show. No one would have suspected that the little cookbook author had it in her. It would recount a journey from darkness to enlightenment in such a profound way that people would no longer look at the world with the same eyes.

And Daddy would sit up and look at me with pride. I would bask in it. I would bathe in it. Maybe I'd even get an offer by Christmas.

My latte was cold, my blank book still blank, my hand clutching the pen was still poised above the first page. If I didn't want to be late for lunch, I would have to take a cab to Café Ste. Claire, where I was to meet the agent who would surely be my angel of change.

As I fixed my lipstick, the taxi screeched to a halt, causing my hand to slip and draw a thick streak of Burnt Coffee across my cheek. A limp tissue rescued from the bottom of my bag among the loose peanuts did what it could to repair the damage. I scrambled for money to pay the driver and stepped out in front of the Upper East Side restaurant. The pale sun of morning had ceded to a steel sky.

I'd thought the Upper West Side was the trendy spot du jour but maybe I'd missed a chapter and the focus had shifted back to the other side of the park.

"*Bonjour,*" the hostess greeted me.

"*Ah, vous parlez français!*" Relief at being able to relax into French flooded my body.

She shook her sleek head. "Sorry."

"Oh! I just thought . . . you have a great accent, you know?" I could tell this from "*bonjour*"? So now I was Madame Irma with an advanced degree in comparative linguistics?

I'd trailed off, but this sleek, sophisticated creature with perfect skin and makeup came to my rescue. "Thanks. I mean *merci.* I'm an actress and also, apparently, a cliché." She glanced at a passing waiter, who grinned as if to say *Aren't we all?* "I've been taking an accent workshop. I'm auditioning for *The Maids* tomorrow."

"Jean Genet! I played Solange in college." It felt like another life, before culinary school had even crossed my mind. "Good luck to you. You sound great!" Could I stop gushing now please?

"*Merci.*"

We stood there a moment, staring at each other, her with an expectant gleam in her eye. Was I supposed to say something more?

The corners of her mouth tipped up. "Table for . . ."

"Oh. Oh yes. Of course. I'm meeting someone." And for the life of me I could not recall his name. Total blank. The last of my name-memory brain cells had gone to Charlotte. "Just a sec." I rummaged through my bag to grab my day planner, spilling a tube of lipstick and several crumpled receipts onto the floor. She bent down to help me as I flipped through the book. If this person was about to change my life, what did it mean that I couldn't even remember his name?

"Here it is. Terry d'Agostino."

"You are so charming, you remind me of my favorite aunt." I just hoped it was her mother's much younger sister.

"So you're a writer," she said over her shoulder as we threaded our way through the bistro. Each table held ceramic oil and vinegar bottles as well as the usual salt and pepper shakers. A bud vase with a single gerbera daisy sat in the center of each. The place was crowded and warm. The whitewashed walls sported vintage ad posters from France and Italy as well as some antique utensils and copper pots.

I relaxed. This Terry certainly had a flair for choosing an appropriate place for a lunch meeting.

"Here we are," my actress/hostess declared, waving her arm. We'd stopped at a rectangular table along the back wall of the restaurant. Sitting on the booth side was Terry. He slid out and extended his hand. It reminded me of Elly's, so smooth and still dimpled. He was dressed like a grown-up, in nice pants, a white shirt, but no tie, and a charcoal jacket.

"Magali?" He smiled, and adjusted his wire-rimmed glasses.

"Yes." I took his hand and shook it, then, horrified at the energy in my gesture, released it as if it had burned my fingers.

When exactly had these children taken over the earth? They were the doctors and businessmen, artists, and boutique owners. What had I been doing all this time?

I sat down, feeling old. Had I missed my opportunity while I'd been fussing around my kitchen jotting down my silly musings on food? I forced a smile. "It's very nice to meet you."

"And you. The day my mother learned to cook thanks to your books was better than Christmas."

I choked on the ice water I was sipping. His mother? Oh God! First an aunt, then a mom. When did I get so old?

"Really, it's an honor to meet you. You saved the latter part of my childhood and probably my parents' marriage to boot," he said.

I was feeling more and more like some ancient foreign dignitary who'd had a brilliant past and was wheeled out occasionally to be honored.

"Shall we order?" He opened his menu.

"Yeah, I mean yes, sure." I was pretty sure foreign dignitaries didn't say *yeah*. I scanned the menu while our waitress-server or whatever they like to be called these days filled our water glasses.

"Our soup is a pumpkin cream and our quiche today is mushroom spinach. Would you like a few more minutes?"

I shook my head, not being able to concentrate on the menu. "That sounds good. I'll have the quiche."

"It comes with salad," she said.

"Wonderful." Wonderful? What if it had come with steamed asparagus? Would I have swooned in ecstasy?

"Dressing?" She ticked off an impressive list of sauces while my companion scanned the menu.

"Champagne vinaigrette."

"Good choice," she said. Did they ever frown and say, *No, really, don't choose that, why just yesterday a patron got food poisoning from that salad?*

"I'll have the same. When dining with an expert . . ." He handed her the menu. "Do you know who this is?"

She shook her head, looking intrigued.

"Magali Arnaud!" he stage-whispered.

She looked blank, but expectant.

"She wrote the *Hopeless in the Kitchen* series."

"Sorry," she said. "I'm sure they're wonderful. But I don't cook."

"But that's the point, isn't it? They are for someone just like you." He turned back to me and removed his glasses. His huge, blue, near-sighted eyes made him look even younger, if that were possible.

"That's the problem." He wiped his glasses.

"What?" Smudged eyewear?

"Name recognition. I'm thinking just keep doing what you're doing but get you a blitz of media coverage, guest spots on morning shows and—" He put his glasses back on and leaned forward. So did I. I felt as if I were about to be given the map to the Holy Grail.

"Two words," he continued. "Food Network."

My mouth dropped open. "But—"

"And let's not forget an app. It's going to be fabulous. You'd keep helping people and be a star. We'll all make oodles of money."

Did he just say *oodles?* I could not confide my dream, my heart's desire, to this sweet-faced man-boy who said *oodles.* I must have looked crestfallen because he said, "Don't look so worried. You'll be amazing. Promise me one thing. Don't change. Just stay as you are and your *people* will build this around you," he said.

"I'm . . . I'll . . ." He was looking at me expectantly. I felt as if it were Charlotte sitting in front of me and she'd just had this great idea to tie-dye the cat bright pink so she would look nice against her purple pillow.

I twirled my water glass on the table, staring at it. Then I looked at him. "I'll think about it."

The food arrived and I realized that for once in my life, I wasn't the least bit hungry. I needed to call Syd and tell her. This was nuts.

He unfolded his napkin and picked up his knife and fork. "Are you seeing someone else?"

Baffled, I pointed to my ring finger.

"Another agent?" he prodded.

I nodded.

His confidence bubbled back up. "I know you'll make the right choice. We'll have so much fun."

"Oodles," I replied.

Becky Sternfeld didn't look like a Becky at all—more like a Rebecca. She was about fifty and gorgeous in that pulled-together-I-know-how-to-accessorize-and-maximize-my-good-points way that my mother had mastered. Or invented. I wondered if her suit was a real Chanel or not. Real, I decided.

After a quick smile and a signal for me to sit, she returned to her phone call.

"I don't know, Chris. The auction closes on Monday. I can talk to the author, but . . ." She shrugged. Her office didn't feel feminine: all black leather and chrome, hard surfaces, hard edges with nary a throw pillow in sight.

"Right, Monday then." She rolled her eyes at me and made a circular motion with her finger indicating that she was trying to wrap this up. "Sounds good." She cut the connection.

"Now, on to the present business." She scrutinized me and I couldn't help but sit up straighter. Then she smiled, seeming satisfied with what she saw. I repressed the urge to sigh with relief.

"It is wonderful to finally meet you. I've known Ana for ages and she raves about you." Really?

She held out her hand and I hesitated, almost wanting to hide my scarred fingers, but then took a breath and grasped her hand. It was surprisingly warm, as was the look in her hazel eyes. I suddenly felt as if I were the most important person on the planet.

"Coffee?"

"Please."

She pressed a button on the front edge of her desk. "Jenna? Could you bring two coffees, please? Thanks, darling." She turned her focus back on me. "I have such plans for you."

Please don't say cooking show.

"We," she continued, "are going to blast you out of the midlist to superstardom. Would you like to know how?"

I almost cringed. *Not cooking show,* I mentally shouted at her. In spite of myself, I leaned forward. The woman was magnetic.

"The first *Hopeless in the Kitchen* diet books. Gluten-free, vegan, paleo . . . As soon as it comes out, we release an adaptation. I'm sure I could even get a classic like Weight Watchers on board." She leaned back.

"But," I sputtered, "that's not—"

"—anything you've ever thought of before, I know. But Ana told me you were fast and dependable. A real pro."

"What my philosophy is all about." Had she ever read one of my books?

"And then," she went on, but we were interrupted by Jenna bearing coffee on a red-and-black lacquered tray.

I pounced on the interruption. "What I really wanted was a bit of a change." My voice was two notches too loud in my ears. She looked at me. "More than a bit. Maybe slightly drastic?"

"I'd love to hear your idea." She smiled.

"Fiction," I blurted. At the look of confusion on her face, I almost backed down. "You know, a novel?" My voice drizzled out to a whisper.

"Why not? Have you got something ready?"

"No, but—"

"It's a wonderful project but why don't we go with my idea first. Plus you haven't heard the rest of it."

I grasped my coffee cup, leaching warmth from it.

"We would expand: mixes, frozen entrees, desserts . . . prepackaged Magali. Everyone will go wild," she said.

"Again, it's not really what my books are about?" I felt hot and had a sudden urge to remove my jacket.

She went on as if she hadn't heard me, "—and not pots and pans, but our angle would be dishes, tablecloths, decorating items to make your kitchen into a Magali kitchen. Sponsoring a brand of appliance. You will be a first name."

Despite myself, I liked the idea of dishes. I could have my own shelf at Williams-Sonoma. Maybe I'd even get a discount.

She looked at her watch. "I will send you a contract. Leave all your info with Jenna before you go. Try to get an outline on the first diet book to me by next week. And a few sample recipes. I think we should start with gluten-free and go from there, don't you think? Because, frankly, it might have a more limited shelf life than the others." She drained her coffee. I hadn't touched mine.

Without waiting for a reply, she was leading me through the door. "I'm excited."

Once out in the street, I felt hot with shame. Right now I wanted a bath, wine, and chocolate. Lots and lots of the latter two.

I turned my phone back on. Three missed calls again—one from Colette, one from home, and a number I didn't recognize.

I put in a quick call to Colette and my family—I put off telling anyone about what had happened in the meetings. The third message was from Simon. I pressed redial.

As I fended off his apologies for the night before—after all, having a medical condition wasn't his fault—I realized that there was one thing that would make this day go away.

I stepped to the right to avoid a group of gorgeous Amazons coming in the other direction. Models, probably.

I wanted—no, *needed*—to cook food. To buy raw ingredients, put them together into something edible. I stopped at a red light and stepped back as a taxi careened around a corner.

After establishing that he did have something resembling a kitchen in his apartment, I told him to text me his address. I'd be there at seven. He could take care of the wine.

The light turned green but I was lost in mental menu preparation and made no move to cross. A woman pushing a stroller jostled me from behind.

I called Terry d'Agostino and asked him where I could find a good quality grocery store. He gave me directions to Fairway, and there I purchased veal, three different types of forest mushrooms, onion, Belgian endives, garlic, mustard, cream, potatoes, nutmeg, butter, cheese, then after a bit of thought, salt, pepper, and sugar. Who knew what state the cupboards were in. I added pears and chocolate for dessert, as well as a baguette, a St.-Marcelin, and an aged Comté.

Thus laden, I hailed a cab and told him to take me to the nearest Williams-Sonoma. There I purchased a Wüsthof chef's knife and, what the hell, a new whisk. I'd have to sneak this one into the house and squirrel it away while Leo wasn't watching.

I remembered the best part of the pastry-making kit from the Easy-Bake Oven Syd had bought the girls was a doll-sized whisk for beating a tablespoon of egg. I'd been about to tuck it into my whisk drawer, just for safekeeping, when Elly had caught me.

"We can keep it safe," she'd said.

"Yeth," had added Charlotte. "Safe from what?"

So I'd left it with their things. But not without a pang.

Feeling reckless about the amount of money I was spending, I grabbed another cab and gave the driver Simon's address.

"How ARE you?" I asked, when he opened the door.

"I'm fine, really. I do want to apologize for last night. What a horrible way for you to spend an evening in New York. Bit of an embarrassment for me as well."

"Really, it was no problem. I'm just glad you're okay."

"You spoke to her, then." His voice was flat.

"I did."

"Yes, she was on the phone first thing this morning informing me in no uncertain terms of how she no longer wishes to be woken in the middle of the night and would I please remove her name from my emergency contact list."

My heart almost broke, right there in the foyer.

He shrugged then caught sight of my load. He burst out laughing, then put down an open bottle of wine—white, I noted with satisfaction, the perfect *aperitif*—before unburdening me of two of my bags.

"Shall I pop around the corner and invite a few of the homeless to come join us?"

"Too much?"

"Maybe a tad." He was dressed more casually tonight, in jeans and a crew-neck navy blue sweater. "But who am I to complain? A beautiful woman invites herself over to cook me dinner."

I followed him to the kitchen. "You'll have leftovers." I put the other packages down on the counter. I'd never met a kitchen I didn't like. But Simon's put that to the test. Cramped and not about to win an award for cleanliness, though I detected the odor of scouring powder. He must have given it a once-over.

"Do you have any more of that scouring powder? And maybe some rubber gloves?" I removed my jacket. I hadn't gone back to the hotel to change.

"Under the sink. No gloves though, I'm afraid. You know, I just did that."

"Sorry, I'm compulsive about sinks." I set about making the sink sparkle, the most necessary prep step to cooking after washing your hands. "I have something I have to confess," I said.

"Of course, anything." He was pouring wine into two glasses.

"It's bad," I said.

He handed me my wine. "How bad can it be?"

I took a sip of wine. Not great, but not horrible. A little too fruity for me. "My name . . . it isn't really Nadia."

"Oh, well. No harm in that, is there?" He tasted his own wine and made a face.

I shook my head. "My real name is Magali."

"Just like . . . the cookbook? You're one and the same?"

"Guilty as charged. Sorry." I unpacked the groceries and washed the new knife.

"What's to be sorry about? I was already looking forward to the meal before, but now I feel like royalty. A famous chef in my kitchen." He raised his glass to me.

I winced, but let it go.

As I set about chopping onion and celery and sautéing them in a pan over low heat, I relaxed for the first time all day. All told, it took me an hour and a half to prepare the veal, *gratin dauphinois,* and braised Belgian endive. An hour and a half during which we'd polished off a bottle of wine and opened another. A better one.

We went into the living room while the meal finished cooking. I'd bought some tapenade and broke off a few chunks of baguette to have with our wine.

Moving easily together, we set the table—Simon even managed to dig up a half-melted candle.

"Ambiance is everything," he said.

Since there was no dining table per se, we ate at the coffee table, sitting on cushions piled on the floor.

The veal and gratin were fragrant and tender. Paired with a tart salad, the meal was a joy.

I raised my glass. "Simon, thank you. I haven't felt this good all day. How about you?"

"Fine." He cleared his throat. "My . . . *condition* is brought on by stress, and at the moment I'm quite mellow."

He clinked his glass against mine, a nice Nuits-Saint-Georges.

After the poached pears dipped in melted chocolate and topped off with a generous spoonful of *crème fraîche,* I was slightly woozy and it was almost one in the morning. I didn't remember where I put my shoes. Simon and I were side by side, on the floor leaning against the couch.

"Where did the time go?"

"Lost in music, food, and wine. Can't think of a better use for it." He leaned into me and I allowed myself to relax into him, feeling his body warm against mine.

A red light flashed in my brain. What was I doing?

It would be so easy to sink into this man further and further and allow him to completely sink into me, so to speak. I sprang up, almost toppling him.

"I've really got to go. Let me clean up a bit first." I grabbed two plates. He took them from me. I found my shoes near the kitchen.

"Leave it. I'll do them in the morning. Stay a bit longer." He put his hand on my arm. My skin tingled.

I wondered what his penis looked like. I hadn't been with another man in so many years I had no idea what it would be like to have an unfamiliar penis inside me.

I turned away and grabbed my coat and scarf, winding the latter around my neck. I was buttoning my coat when Simon put a hand on my shoulder.

"Let me take you to your hotel, at least. It's the gentlemanly thing to do."

He was behind me and so slowly his hand drifted from my shoulder, caressing my side and landing on my hip.

It started to inch its way toward my lower belly inside my not-quite-buttoned coat.

"Please," I whispered.

His hand stopped. I was throbbing. "Please what? Please go on?" His hand pressed a bit harder on my skin.

"Stop," I croaked. "Please stop."

He released me and spun me around to face him.

"I know you're married. But no one will know. Who could it hurt? It would be just a lark. Two people coming together for an instant of happiness."

My eyes inadvertently slid down his body to the bulge in his jeans. He grinned.

I turned and fled. I stepped out into the chilled night. Luck was with me. An empty cab was cruising down the street. I hailed it and, once inside, I shook all the way to my hotel.

I was still shaky twenty minutes later when I slammed—or tried to slam—my hotel room door behind me. It was one of those doors that had a brake on the hinges.

It was fine. Nothing happened. I didn't do anything.

But I'd wanted to.

I was almost asleep before I remembered I'd left my whisk at Simon's.

Chicons braisées
BRAISED BELGIAN ENDIVE

This side dish is as easy as it is spectacular. Braising reduces the bitterness of the endive, rendering them almost sweet.

7 or 8 Belgian endives
2 (or more) cloves of garlic
2 tablespoons butter
Water
Juice of ½ lemon
Sea salt
Freshly ground pepper
1 or 2 teaspoons sugar—any kind: raw, white, or brown (*optional*)

Rinse the endives, pat dry, and slice off the bottom (not too much so they don't fall apart). Remove any browned or wilted outer leaves.

Peel the garlic, slice the cloves in half, and remove the green sprout (or germ). Mince and reserve.

Melt the butter in a large stainless-steel or enamel pot with a tight-fitting lid. Throw in the garlic and let it cook for about a minute.

Place the endives in a single layer in the pot. Add a bit of water (start with ½ cup and be prepared to add more if needed), the lemon juice, the sea salt, and pepper.

Cover tightly and cook over medium-low heat for 25 to 30 minutes.

Remove the lid and check the liquid. Add more water if necessary. Increase the heat to high and cook uncovered until brown. If you are using sugar, add it at this stage to further caramelize the endives.

This is one of my biggest hits with guests. Just don't tell anyone how easy it is. *Bon appétit!*

CHAPTER 10

Colette

I glanced at Dante behind the wheel of the Toyota. If Art could have seen me now. Our family's danger junkie probably never tried this. Though with him, you never knew.

I wondered if anyone would come visit me in prison if it came to that. Gali. With files hidden in chocolate éclairs so I could break out. Wouldn't it serve Wayne right, though. Driven to a life of crime by a louse. The stuff of great novels.

I steeled myself against thoughts of paternal disapproval. Where had being a good girl gotten me? And Daddy thought so highly of Wayne. Well, maybe not of Wayne himself, but certainly of his family.

I was dressed in the same clothes as on Halloween, black jeans and black sweater, minus the boa and turban. I figured stealth would not have benefited from extravagant headgear, even in Southern California. My feet were clad in soft-soled flat ankle boots in a deep black suede. Interestingly enough, I didn't feel short and I could walk so easily. Maybe it was time to rethink my devotion to heels.

"Ready?"

I nodded but my insides trembled. He squeezed my hand. "You will see. It will be the breeze."

"A breeze," I whispered back.

It was two-thirty in the morning and the streets were empty. I could see my breath in the chilled November air. Before living here, I'd imagined that Southern California was balmy, like Florida. But the climate was mild—never too hot, nor too cold, as if it were afraid of undue extremes. Of course, on occasion, it would shudder at being so constrained and buildings would tumble, roads would crack. Nothing came for free, nothing could be easy all the time.

We crept through a backyard, careful not to bump into the patio furniture. Dante passed me a black balaclava. I thought he was kidding. But when he slipped his on, I did the same, feeling silly. Then, his magician fingers worked the lock on the door. He had beautiful hands. I curled my fingers in, hiding my nails, though from whom, I didn't know. He'd made sure there was no alarm and he'd seen the owners leave with packed bags earlier in the evening. I felt a pang at the thought of them returning home from a carefree weekend jaunt to discover they'd been burglarized.

The lock sprang open with a soft click and we stepped in. It was eerie to be in someone's house in the middle of the night.

He nodded and I headed down a hallway off the living room, looking for the master bedroom, while he went over the living room, office, and kitchen. I passed by a smallish room with a bed and paused, then continued on my way. The furniture looked staged. A guest room offering hospitality for the owners' friends and family. I felt myself chickening out as my heart pounded in my ears. *Too late now,* whispered a voice in my head. These people would be fine. Dante's instructions were specific. No personal computers or cell phones. No digital cameras unless we could easily pop out the memory card. Nothing with information that couldn't be replaced. On the other hand, any jewelry, cash, expensive accessories like designer bags, scarves, or even high-end shoes, if they weren't too bulky. One of his friends, a master whiz-geek, hacked into insurance companies to glean information on policies. Dante only hit houses with plenty of coverage. I took a breath. He also checked out the targets and ruled out anyone who came from a lower-income background. That's how he hit us. Wayne's family was Main Line aristocracy.

The couple who lived here were Texas oil money.

In the bedroom, I hit pay dirt. A jewelry box sat open on an antique vanity table. I emptied it into my black canvas mailbag—a twin to the one Dante carried. A few great scarves were draped over the mirror and I stuffed them in the bag, too, pushing them around the jewelry so it wouldn't jingle. It was hard to catch my breath. My heart pounded against my ribs. On the shelf of the closet, I spied four designer bags, a Chanel clutch, a Chloé, a Hermès—though not a Kelly or Birkin—and a ubiquitous Vuitton. I saw a gorgeous shirt in a plastic bag. Saint-Laurent. In it went. My bag was just about full. I spotted an iPod on the nightstand, hesitated, then, tossed it into the bag. It was all insured, I kept repeating to myself. Replaceable.

When I got to the back door, Dante was waiting for me. His teeth gleamed in the dark. Together we crept through the yard and down the alley to his car, parked a few blocks away.

I clambered in and he turned the ignition. Suddenly, I was flooded with a surge of adrenaline or endorphins or whatever it was that made you feel fantastic. I pulled off my damp balaclava and took a deep breath. Then, before I could stop myself, I squealed, like a three-year-old let loose in Barbie's palace.

"That was . . . beyond description!" I said.

He grinned. "So you see, it is easy. And no one is hurt." He drove easily through the dark streets, keeping well within the speed limit. By the time he dropped me off in front of my house, my heartbeat had slowed down to almost its normal rate.

"Go inside," he said. "Go to sleep. I will be back in a few hours."

But I was so keyed up, I couldn't sleep. I felt like telling someone. My mind relived every moment of the heist, over and over. I sat at my sewing machine but my mind was too full to leave room for anything else. I stepped outside to smoke.

It was after seven when Dante came back, still wearing the same clothes, carrying two takeout cups of coffee. I'd changed into a short denim skirt and UGG boots, topped with my deep purple Dostoevsky top. In a mixture of black silk thread and black-and-white appliquéd letters shot through with fine gold thread, was the quote: *Why am I going there now? Am I capable of that? Is that serious? It is not serious at all. It's simply a fantasy to amuse myself; a plaything! Yes, maybe it is a plaything.*

He set the coffee down on the table and pulled a roll of cash out of his inside coat pocket. He handed it to me with one of the lattes. I took a sip before counting the money. There was almost five thousand dollars.

I started to split it in half but he stopped me. *"La tua parte,"* he said, removing a similar wad from the other pocket of his coat. "I look like I have breasts, yes?"

"Not really." But I was still staring at my share of the money.

"My 'connection' he is very happy. Soon, we will be rich."

"If we don't all burn in hell. What's the penalty for stealing in Dante's *Inferno*?" I tore my eyes away from the money and looked at him.

"Ah, yes. Very bad." He shook his beautiful head. "The eighth circle, thieves go to the ditch of serpents."

"A snake pit?" I shuddered. "That's cheerful." I put my hand to my mouth, about to start biting my nails, when he stopped me.

"But that's a different Dante."

"Thank God. What are you going to do with the money? Go home?"

"No. It will be redemption, redemption by sinning, but still, redemption. A friend from Italy, his family makes wine. They buy a small vineyard near to Sonoma. The son, my friend Domenico, comes to America to take charge of it. He offer me to be a partner. Better for business and more *conviviale* for life, no?" He held up two fingers and pressed them together.

"Yes." My coffee was smooth, almost nutty.

"Mio padre tells him I have money. So I need to get the same amount back," he said. He rose and went to the window. The morning glory vine clinging to the fence was blooming with fat violet flowers. *"Bello,"* he said.

"How much?" I asked.

"Three hundred thousand dollars."

I almost dropped my cup. "That's how much you lost? Were conned out of?" I gulped.

"*Si*. But I have a little bit more than half, now. I invest in winery, become a real partner, not just a worker with salary. We will make beautiful wine. And I will go home a hero." He turned back to me. Backlit by the morning light coming through the window, he looked as if he were surrounded by a golden aura.

"Your father . . ."

"Will be proud, *si*." He came back to the table, sat down, and drank his latte. "To make wine is noble."

"But Dante, what if you . . . we . . . get caught?"

"It will not happen. We are too careful, *si?*"

"I hope so."

"And you, what will you do?" he asked.

For a moment I wondered what it would feel like to return home, married and wealthy. I would show Daddy what a success I'd made of myself. But then what? "If I don't end up in jail or in a pit of snakes, I'll . . . I don't know. Buy a small house somewhere affordable, make a new life. I won't be dependent on Wayne when he comes back."

"You think he will come back."

"Absolutely. He always does. We're soul mates. It's destined. But I won't take him back unless he marries me." I stood and paced around the small room. "And I won't let myself be financially insecure ever again."

"Do you not have another dream? You look like someone who dreams."

"Well . . ." I'd already bared my inner secrets to him, why not go all the way?

"So there is something more."

I nodded. "There is. I love to make, design, clothes. I'd like to have my own line one day. My own business."

"And this makes you happy?"

"Yeah, it makes me happy."

"Are the clothes you wear of your own?"

"A lot of them are. Not the skirt. But the top."

"All the ones you wear with the words and the designs and layers?"

I grinned. "Yeah, those are mine."

"*Ma, è squisito. Straordinario. Superiore. Tu sei bravissima.*" He punctuated each word with his hands.

My Italian, far from adequate, was still good enough for his words to register. "Not all that."

"Yes, Nico, you will bring joy and beauty into this world."

"And you will bring a marvelous wine."

We clinked cardboard cups.

"To the future," I said.

"May she smile."

I willed myself to sleep, to be still. I kept twisting and turning in my bed. It was too hot. Then a few minutes later, too cold. Finally I got up and opened my closet. I grabbed a plastic bag full of brand new men's T-shirts that I got for a song at Costco last summer. They were simple, soft, and, most of all, unadorned. I selected a black one. Next I pulled out a box full of fabric scraps and trim from under the bed. I found what I was looking for: a shiny black silk, the kind you usually see on tuxedo lapels. I cut and sewed a crescent moon and stars and appliquéd them onto the stretchy cotton. Next I picked over my plastic box of multicolored spools of thread and chose a silvery one, with just a touch of the palest yellow in it.

I studied the shirt and thread.

I plugged in my laptop. It only took Google a few minutes to pinpoint exactly what I was looking for.

In the shape of a triangle on the lower left-hand corner of the front of the T-shirt I embroidered in flowing script:

Remember tonight . . . for it is the beginning of always.

Tomorrow I'd look up the original quote in Italian and put it on the back.

After all, Dante wasn't only about poor souls drowning in mud, or with their heads screwed on backward, or being trapped in a pit of writhing snakes. It was also about Beatrice, his feminine ideal, and love that defied all boundaries.

I finally fell asleep.

When I awoke, it was late afternoon and I felt displaced. Maybe I should get a cat to have a focal point outside of my own head. At loose ends, I went outside to check the mailbox. A few flyers, the water bill, and a letter. My heart skipped a beat, but although the handwriting on the envelope was familiar, it wasn't Wayne's. Not that he was the letter-writing type. Inside, I dumped the rest of the mail on the table and opened the envelope.

I drew out a letter and a photograph. It was a snapshot of my parents and a baby. My mother was looking directly into the camera, a smile on her lips. My father was gazing at the bundle in my mother's arms, one finger on the baby's cheek. His eyes crinkled at the corners and his mouth curved with some private joy. The baby's big blue eyes were wide open and it was staring up at my mother's face. The picture was taken on the porch swing of my parents' house.

The letter was short.

Dear Colette,

I came across this photograph the other day and I thought you might like to have it. It's you the summer you were three months old.

I'm looking forward to seeing you this Christmas. It's been too long.

I hope you are well.

Love,

Dad

Love, Dad?

I'd never seen this picture before. I stared at it while minutes ticked by. Then I went to the bedroom. From the closet, I pulled out a fat album. It was where I pasted anything I came across that reminded me of my mother. There were pictures of my sisters and a few of Art when we were children.

I took the album and a tube of glue over to the bed. I sat down cross-legged and pasted the photograph on the first empty page. On the opposite page, I glued Daddy's letter.

I stared at them until the light dimmed. Then I put the album back in the closet.

Since that first time, my life had taken on an otherworldliness. Nothing felt familiar yet I spent my days as usual. I taught, joked with my students, saw friends, sewed Christmas presents, went to movies, listened to problems, and offered solace. But it was as if I were packed in cotton. If anyone noticed, they didn't say. Nobody asked about Wayne anymore either, not since the "he went home because his mother is ill" explanation. Only witchy Sonya ticked. She kept telling me how good I looked and asking me for my secret.

My senses sharpened only when I was on a job with Dante. The adrenaline rush, the joy of finding treasures that brought us closer to our goals, was intoxicating. I barely drank at all but oddly enough, I was eating. I must have needed the strength or stamina. Even my nails looked better.

On the Friday before Thanksgiving, I invited Dante over to dinner. Over the phone, Gali talked me through a pot-au-feu. She was thrilled, the desire to cook always a beacon of mental health in her book. I pretexted a dinner party with some of Wayne's colleagues.

After triple washing and peeling turnips, carrots, and potatoes, and slicing onions, I browned the meat and covered it in cold water to seal in the juices. I really didn't have a proper pot to cook the dish in but I made do. It took me hours to prepare and even longer to cook but it made the house smell just like my sister's. A pang of what could only be homesickness coursed through me.

When Dante arrived, he was astonished but in a delighted sort of way. I'd even broken into the fund, as I'd come to call my ever-increasing pile of cash, to buy a really good bottle of Gigondas recommended by my sister.

We ate and laughed and drank. It was all easy and comfortable.

After the pear gelato, I pulled out the package containing the finished T-shirt. He unwrapped it with gentle fingers, then stared at the shirt without saying a word.

"You don't like it," I said flatly. "That's okay."

He looked up and met my gaze. "No," he said, "I don't like. I love." He stripped right there in the living room. I could have charged admission. His chest and back were as perfectly chiseled as his face. My mouth went a bit dry and I took a sip of wine to give myself something to do rather than gawk. He pulled the T-shirt over his rippling muscles and spread out his arms.

"How do I look?"

"Good," I said, nodding several times in quick succession. It wouldn't do to start gushing and drooling, very gauche.

"It is the most lovely present from the most lovely lady."

I'd never been called a lovely lady before. He stepped close to me, our bodies almost, not quite, touching. My eyes locked on his. He leaned in and placed his lips on mine. At first, his kiss was soft, tentative. He cupped my face in his hands and kissed me more firmly, with intention. I opened my mouth and welcomed his tongue, tasting him. I put my arms up around his neck. Without breaking our kiss, he led me to the couch. My legs buckled and we both sank into the cushions. He began to stroke my body with his magician's fingers. Every pore, every cell sang at his touch. He slipped his hand under my shirt and I gasped at his fingers on my bare skin. I arched into him, wanting his mouth all over me, wanting all of him.

Suddenly he stopped and pulled gently away. His eyes were unfocused and his breathing heavy.

"Don't stop," I whispered.

"I am sorry," he said. "I should not have."

"Yes! You should!" I panicked like a raft cut adrift from the boat it had been tethered to.

"No, you are a woman in love with another man." He moved away from me on the couch.

"Who isn't here."

"But you still love him?"

I looked down. I couldn't deny it. Wayne was a part of me. And had been for so long, I couldn't fathom not loving him. Even now, as furious as I was.

"I do not want to be how you call it, the rebounce?"

"Rebound. But you wouldn't be. You're not."

"Too soon for you to say." He sighed. He planted a light kiss on my forehead. "*Grazie mille* for this most beautiful present." And just like that, he slipped away.

I stared at the door, biting my nails. Then I did the dishes and cleaned the kitchen. Afterward I sat some more.

But he never came back.

The next morning I awoke, steeped in humiliation. There was a job tonight and for once, I dreaded it. *See masterpiece of a man, a man who comes from a country that arguably has the most beautiful women in the world. See Colette throw herself at said man. See Dante run. Run Dante run. See Colette make a spectacular fool of herself. Silly, silly Colette.*

No wonder Wayne kept dumping me. Around two, I hauled myself out of bed, threw on an old pair of jeans and my faded blue-and-red hooded Shippensburg sweatshirt. Not my style, but at the time Wayne had pressed me to buy it. I headed out to the beach, hoping the air would clear my head. I had to cut ties with Dante. But the money was a promise. He'd planned a long weekend in Vegas in December, a time where I'd be singing carols and sipping hot chocolate or eggnog before heading to the skating rink with my nieces if I were still living in Pennsylvania. Maybe I should move back home, live the seasons I loved, be part of my family again. It could even be temporary. I could stay just long enough to figure out my next step.

Tonight I'd play it cool. Pretend I'd been drunk. After all, I wasn't in love with him, it was pure lust. I loved Wayne, always would. Dante was right. I'd been using him. Shabby.

Later, as I was dressing in what I'd come to consider my cat burglar costume, I realized that being in costume and going on heists when I would have normally been asleep was what made it so easy for me to slip into this criminal persona. None of it felt real. It was like being in a movie.

The money was real, though.

At one, Dante slipped quietly inside. I told him not to bother knocking anymore, but now I wondered if that had been such a bright idea.

He smiled at me and I looked away.

"Look," I said. I was about to apologize but seeing him brought such a lump to my throat that I could hardly breathe. I felt like an annoying gnat that he'd had to swat away.

"I . . ." I didn't know what to say.

He came over to me. "I am so sorry. It was my fault. Your beautiful gift."

"No need to apologize," I said, surprised at how cool I sounded. "It was a mistake, could happen to anyone."

"But I need to say something—"

I stepped back. "Dante, please. Please let's not talk about it. It's past, okay?" I knew I sounded desperate but I couldn't believe how easily I was off the hook.

We had two houses tonight, nice ones, in La Jolla. According to Dante, it was rare to find places in the community with no serious security.

The first one, halfway down Mount Soledad on a street perpendicular to Via Capri, went off without a hitch. We got an astounding haul.

We drove south to Ocean Beach and I stayed in the car while Dante grabbed the grocery bags from the trunk and disappeared into a bungalow. It never looked suspicious to carry groceries.

I never knew what happened to the merchandise after the drop. Mexico? eBay?

While he was inside, I tried to figure out why all this taking from the rich was so satisfying, so easy. He was Robin Hood with a corrupt Maid Marian. Except that Robin Hood loved Maid Marian, of course.

There were only a half a dozen or so more jobs before stopping and going to Vegas.

Dante got back in the car and started the engine.

"Dante?"

"*Si*." He was still a bit cold but at least he gave me a hint of his old smile.

"Why stop now? Why not keep going until you have all the money rather than run the risk of losing it all in Vegas?"

"Because, Nico," he said, "the lady of the luck, she may leave like that." He kissed his fingertips. "You must walk away before she does. Same in Las Vegas, know when to walk."

It made a wacky kind of sense. But what if I became completely addicted to this double life?

"So after Vegas?" I was blinded for a moment by the headlights of an oncoming car.

"I go to Sonoma. In January, I will start my new life. And you?"

"I'll start one too." Gali had guilted me into going home for Christmas and I was almost looking forward to it. My main problem was explaining Wayne's absence. What if he spent Christmas in Pennsylvania with his mother? It seemed likely. I could corner him. But the prospect didn't fill me with seasonal cheer. Holidays were such a problem when living a sham.

I'd been invited to spend Thanksgiving with Sonya and her family, but my friends were going to start to find it odd that Wayne was still gone. I didn't know how much longer I was going to be able to keep up the charade.

And as much as I loved Sonya, her family, and the other waylaid expats that were always a part of her bashes, it was always hard to be in the middle of other people's families when you were on your own. Val, whom I depended on to be single and present, was going home to Ireland to spend a week with her family. Her brother was getting engaged. Which left Sonya and Annick, and all their children and husbands. And yet, the thought of spending Thanksgiving alone in my little house made me too sad.

"Dante, what are you doing for Thanksgiving?"

CHAPTER 11

Jacqueline

Shoshanna was sleeping when I arrived at the hospital. Or rather, she was drugged into unconsciousness.

"Are you family?" A nurse with exhaustion etched around her eyes barely looked up.

"Yes, I'm her sister." Which was the truth. Being sisters didn't always have to do with blood and sharing a parent or two.

She waved me in. "Your brother is already here."

I turned to look at her. She smiled. "The one with the Canadian accent."

David. He pretended to be Canadian to make life easier. No one hated Canada.

I hurried down the hallway, the heels of my boots clicking on the gleaming tiles. Edith Cavell was a small, top-rate private hospital. But private or no, all hospitals the world over smelled the same. A mix of disinfectant and something sweet, almost cloying—the smell of illness and suffering. I hated it. Hospitals robbed you of your power. I remember Daddy's words to me when Maman was dying. *No matter what I do, what I want, how much I strive, I can't change this.* We'd all withered in that room, Daddy most of all.

I pushed in the door and saw Josh and David standing by the bed hovering like bodyguards minus the dark glasses. Josh crossed over and hugged me.

"The kids?" he whispered.

"Tante Charlotte has them. Laurent is on his way to pick them up." I hung up my coat and put my bag on a chair.

"Thank you. At least they will be well fed." A feeble smile toyed with his lips before giving up.

My aunt was a force of culinary excellence. She'd been one of Gali's great role models and her books were sprinkled with things she'd learned from Tante Charlotte. I still didn't get why my sister had turned her back on a career as a chef. She would have been a star.

David kissed me on the cheek and only then did I allow my gaze to fall on my friend.

Pale, much too pale. I looked at Josh. "How is she?"

"Knocked out. She'll probably sleep through the night," he said. Josh was wiry, energetic, always looking as if he were about to take flight. I never figured out how he could be happy doing marketing in a big company.

"Emotionally?" I asked.

"Strong. Unbelievable." He smiled.

Instinctively I put my hands on my belly. "And ..." I couldn't finish the sentence.

"She's here." Josh led me to a glassed-in section of the room. "We named her Rachel."

In the corner of this human-sized aquarium stood an incubator with the tiniest baby I'd ever seen. She was only as long as my hand.

"So beautiful. What happened? Sho was fine. Just a few hours ago. Fine."

"She fell. Forward. Slipped on something. Her pouch ruptured and she was losing amniotic fluid. She had the presence of mind to call Dr. Cellier, who sent an ambulance."

"And ..."

"Emergency C-section. The baby . . . Rachel . . ."—he cleared his throat—"wasn't strong enough to take the stress of labor."

"She's fine, though, isn't she? They both are." My fingernails were digging into my palms. I forced myself to relax my hands.

"Yes, right now, thank God, they're fine. The baby's lungs aren't developed yet but they've managed to simulate as closely as possible the condition of the womb."

"Six and a half months," said David. He rubbed his scrappy goatee. "She's a knockout," he added. "Just like her mother."

My heart doubled in size as I looked at my sleeping friend. Her hair seemed too dark against her pale skin. Her lips were dry. She hated those scratchy hospital gowns. I'd bring her some soft ones from home.

I went back to the incubator. How could something so tiny be strong? I hoped human strength was inversely proportional to size. I sent a thought to Maman—*protect her.*

"Aren't you singing tonight?" David had put his hand on my shoulder and was looking at Rachel as well.

"I'm supposed to."

"Go. Everything is fine," said Josh. I went to the mirror, where I wiped the smudged mascara from beneath my eyes and applied lipstick. If there was one lesson I'd learned both from my grandmother and my own life, it was *don't let it show.*

I spent the better part of the week cleaning out my closets, finishing up my Christmas shopping, and buying baby clothes for my secret stash. Each day I went to the hospital. Shoshanna had been released and Rachel had been moved to NICU. It was a small city of miniature human beings in glass cases attached to life by wires and needles and machines that breathed for them. Sometimes it didn't even feel like part of the world. It was like a baby museum with the most precious of all treasures protected and preserved for the future. The nurses knew me and let me in to sit with Rachel every day. And every day I would go and sing softly to her.

Thursday we were going to David's for Thanksgiving, just the five of us and Shoshanna's kids. Sunday was the annual banquet in honor of fallen political prisoners from World War II. This year, they were honoring my grandfather. The whole family would be there, right down to his great-grandchildren. I knew my grandmother was angry at Tante Solange for not making an effort to come when her own father was being honored.

At least Tante Charlotte would get a break from cooking a turkey this year. I still wondered what had gotten into Daddy. He was such a stickler for tradition. It made no sense. Or maybe it did. Maybe he was tired of imposing an American holiday on his Belgian family.

Not a chance.

It was something else.

I sighed. I wasn't sure I wanted to know.

CHAPTER 12

Colette

Thanksgiving

"The pumpkin is tender. And the apples look pretty good." I poked them with a fork.

"Okay, throw in the cranberries and let it cook, uncovered, for about a minute."

After hanging up, I took the apple-cranberry mixture off the stove to cool before using it to fill the pie. Gali, not bothering to hide her shock at my spontaneous desire to make pastry, gamely talked me through two pies. One of her *Hopeless in the Kitchen* books lay open on my counter, but I'd wanted to hear her explain it to me. Jacqueline's voice from my iPod speakers provided the soundtrack to my culinary experiment. Caught in a bout of missing both my sisters, I made them a part of my day the only way I could.

I was wearing a short russet skirt over tights and boots with a tight long-sleeved black top with a segment of *The House of the Spirits* stitched in orange and yellow. Wayne always said it was one of his favorite outfits. I put my thumbnail up to my mouth, then stopped myself just in time. My nails had grown out a bit. I looked at them. In a week or so, I could maybe even polish them. Or get a manicure, something I'd never dared to do.

By the time Dante came in, wearing a nice pair of khakis topped with the shirt I'd made him, the pies were cooling on the table and I'd just finished an e-mail to Jacqueline. Her voice filled the room with glorious notes, coming from the iPod dock that I broke down and bought with some of my "earnings." He sniffed the air, and when he spotted the pies, his eyes lit up with delight. How did he do that? His hair was damp from the light rain.

"You make these? And you listen to such beautiful music?"

I smiled. He always made me feel so good about myself. "Dante, have I ever told you about my sisters?"

Jacqueline provided the soundtrack to our drive to Sonya's.

I was apprehensive about introducing Dante to Sonya. We'd fabricated a story about his being a friend of my Belgian cousin Max, in America for an extended visit. Max had urged Dante to look me up and I, not wanting to leave him on his own for his first American Thanksgiving, was bringing him to Sonya's annual Thanksgiving of stray lambs, a motley collection of expats and far-from-homes.

Plausible, but Sonya was one of those people who could spot a nontruth from two towns away. Through thick fog. I was counting on her to be too busy with the party to question my story. Besides, she would probably be so bedazzled by Dante that there would be no room for anything else. She was, after all, in full possession of two X chromosomes.

The rain pelted down more seriously when we arrived at Sonya's Carmel Valley house. Protecting the pies with the um-brella, which, as a true Belgian, I always had in my car, we hurried to the door.

We were engulfed in hugs and hellos, adults, kids, and two cats scampering around us in a fanfare of welcome.

I went into the kitchen holding one pie, with Dante on my heels holding the other, as well as the bottle of wine we brought. There was such a blur of people, I wondered if two pies would be enough.

"Colette!" Sonya hugged me as I set my pie safely on the counter. "You look beautiful!"

"So do you." Sonya was all smooth skin, sleek hair, and green cat eyes. All offset by chunky jewelry and a wild silk print tunic belted over a fabulous pair of black satin pants.

"Such a shame Wayne—" At that moment, she spotted Dante setting down the second pie next to the wine and her mouth dropped open.

She recovered more quickly than I'd expected, and gave him a charming smile, raising her arm in welcome, her chunky bangles sliding down her arm. If I looked like her, I'd reproduce too, as often and quickly as possible. She held out her cheek for Dante to kiss, which, ever the gentleman, he obliged.

"Please, have a drink. We are all having champagne."

I grabbed two flutes and Dante filled them from a dripping bottle of Mumm Cordon Rouge plucked from a tub of ice.

We clinked glasses and we made the rounds.

A hand grasped my arm and pulled me away from the group and into the kitchen. "So, this is the famous Italian friend of your cousin?" Sonya let go of my arm.

I nodded and gulped the dregs of my glass.

"He is magnificent! You didn't say!" said Sonya, a hint of accusation in her voice.

"The place looks great, Sonya," I said.

"If Val were here," said Annick, who had materialized at my side, "she would be in instant love."

"Again," added Sonya.

I laughed good-naturedly but was suddenly glad Val wasn't here.

"Do you need any help in here?" I again tried to steer the conversation to a safer course.

"And you made *tarte aux pommes,*" said Annick. "So uncommon for you to bake. And your cheeks are round. With good color." Nothing physical escaped her eye. She built her whole fashion consultant business on her powers of observation.

"Thank you. I just felt like making dessert. Contributing something other than alcohol for once. Not that big a deal."

"Oh no. Not big at all." They exchanged a look.

"I'm standing right here and I can see you." I picked up a bottle of chilled champagne and raised it. "Refills?" They both held out their glasses.

Sonya handed me a tray of blinis topped with thick cream and caviar and sent me into the living room. Annick trailed me with another tray, this one laden with crackers spread with her famous salmon *rillettes.* The fire crackled, people were talking, and there were candles everywhere. The rain made the house feel cozy and warm. Annick's and Sonya's kids looked spiffed up shiny in their good clothes. I loved that they had their children dress for special occasions.

Svetlana, Sonya's daughter, came over to me brandishing a sketch pad.

"Oh, have you got new ones?" I asked.

She nodded. "Would you like to see them?"

"Wouldn't miss it. Let's sit." I set my tray down on the coffee table and settled on the couch, pulling the eight-year-old close. I opened up the pad full of drawings of different garments and exclaimed over her sense of style and color. She turned rosy with pleasure.

"Do you see how one sleeve is longer than the other, and they are different colors?" she asked.

"It's very original, I love it," I said.

"I have to go make some more. I need to work on a winter collection." She dashed off.

Annick sank down in the spot vacated by Svetlana. I watched Dante, who was now chatting with the Spaniards, displaying the kind of ease you were either born with or had to do without. Wayne had excellent breeding but always remained just a tad aloof. If you didn't know him like I did, it wasn't even noticeable. But it was often as if he felt he was talking to someone below his social stature. Dante, on the other hand, flowed around people like a warm bubbling brook, easy and loose.

"So," said Annick. "I notice he is wearing one of your creations."

Drat. "Yes. It's a welcome-to-America present."

"Is he just here on vacation? You never said. What does he do exactly?" she asked.

There were a lot of things I never said. "Oh, this and that. He was working in a restaurant. Now he's . . . exploring his options."

"Is he legal?"

In our world, legal didn't mean old enough to drink but rather in possession of a valid visa.

"Gee, I don't know. We're not really that close." I shrugged.

"Yet you made him a gift?" she pressed.

"It was the polite thing to do. Why do you want to know about his visa?"

She sighed. "It would be a shame to lose such a man over a technicality. How is Wayne, by the way? Does he say when he will be back?" She helped herself to a blini.

I did the same. "He will probably stay through the holidays."

"So many things you don't know. I had no idea he was such a devoted son." She bit into the blini.

I glanced at my friend; the ironic smile on her lips didn't escape my notice. She wasn't buying a single word of my story.

And if Annick wasn't swallowing the story, neither was Sonya.

The rest of the day passed quickly. I ate a lot, talked with maybe a dab too much animation. Dante was adorably attentive to my slightest desire. And throughout the entire meal, my two friends exchanged knowing looks and cocked eyebrows. Very smooth.

By the time pie and coffee had been devoured, and vodka offered and refused by all but a few diehards, it was almost nine. I couldn't help feeling a degree of satisfaction at the empty pie plates. Wait till I told Gali.

At the door, Sonya whispered in my ear, "And tomorrow, you will tell me the truth. Yes? All of it?"

"Okay." I pretended to concede defeat, wondering what story I would conjure up. One that she wouldn't see through.

Because the truth?

Out of the question.

Friday passed in a blur of snoozing, reading, dreaming up new designs in my sketchbook—Svetlana, like most children, served as both inspiration and motor to get on with my own "winter collection"—and dodging calls from my friends. I pushed thoughts of my impending trip home for Christmas to the back corner of my mind.

Around eleven on Saturday morning, there was a knock on the door. *Please not Annick or Sonya. Or worse, Annick and Sonya.* I hadn't yet come up with a credible story. Plus the change in decor would surely elicit a barrage of questions.

I opened the door to find Dante standing in the sun, wearing a big grin, and holding up a blue spruce.

I laughed. "What?"

"I know that in America, *Natale* comes directly after the Thanksgiving. So . . ."—he gestured toward the tree with a flourish—"Christmas!"

"How do you know that?" I was glad I'd felt good enough this morning to dress in something decent. With my blue-and-black retro sixties tunic over black leggings and white boots, I felt like a go-go girl. I even had on a bit of mascara and lip gloss.

"Because, *bella,* you tell me."

"Oh, right. It must have slipped my mind. Don't just stand there, come in."

"You have the balls and garlands?" He was standing in the middle of the room still holding the tree.

"You bet."

We set the tree up in the corner by the window and hauled four cartons of Christmas stuff in from the garage. Around one, we took a break.

"We are working well," he said. "Let me take you to a *ristorante.*"

"You know how I feel about eating out." I was placing red votives in small glass jars.

"But this place is very different. I promise. Very clean, all fresh. Italians directly from Italy."

"I don't know." I turned to him.

"*Dai! Per piacere.*" When he started speaking Italian with the look of a hurt puppy in his eye, every particle of will I could conjure just zipped out the window.

"Okay." I felt so happy right now. I wanted to make him happy too. Wayne hated holiday decorating. It was so much fun to have a partner to do this stuff with.

He took me to Caffè Bella Luna, a restaurant I'd passed by hundreds of times, but being me, had never entered, much less eaten there.

The modest exterior was deceiving. Inside it was modern and quirky, with gauzy fabrics draped artfully from the ceiling and partially covering the windows. Two richly textured tapestries adorned the walls, saving the decor from the clinical chill of many trendy restaurants.

Dante ordered for me.

Our server brought the wine almost immediately and I was grateful for the warmth and courage it gave me.

Soon, she returned with two steaming bowls of soup.

"*Minestrone della casa!*" she announced, as if she were heralding the arrival of royalty in our midst. "Is organic."

I took a spoonful of the vegetable-laden broth and blew on it a bit. Both the waitress and Dante leaned in toward me. The pressure was crucifying. I swallowed. "Wow," I said, "this is . . . delicious!" I took another spoonful. The broth was rich but light, not greasy, and somehow the vegetables retained both their texture and flavor. They both relaxed, the waitress smiled and left.

"You see, Nico. You should always trust me." He broke off a piece of bread.

Because I didn't? How much more proof did he need? Before I realized it, I'd drained the bowl.

"*Brava!*" said our waitress. "It will be a while for *le pizze, va be'*?"

"*Si, si, va bene. Non si preoccupi.*" He turned to me. "I tell her not to worry, to take time."

Our long lazy lunch was like vacation. Two services came and went, and still we lingered.

"*Americani,*" said Dante. "Eat too fast. Do not savor."

"I'm going to get fat if I keep hanging around you." But I knew there was no danger there because our relationship was on a timer.

"No. *Sei bella!* You should not be so skinny. And the body and the soul need great food and wine to be happy." He punctuated his words with a dessert spoon.

"I suppose." I scooped up the last of the *tartuffo nero* we shared for dessert and took a sip of smoky espresso.

We returned to my place. Dante strung the outdoor lights while I fiddled with the details inside, placing branches of holly and tree clippings on the windowsills, the mantel, and above the kitchen counters. It was dark by the time we finished and turned on the lights. They obediently twinkled against the inky sky.

"*Magico!*"

"It is."

"*Ma* . . . ?" He tapped his index finger against his chin.

"What?" I looked around. It looked perfect.

He was frowning. "*Dov'è* . . . where is the crèche?"

I shrugged. "Haven't got one."

He looked horrified. "But it cannot be Christmas without a crèche! Come."

"Where?"

"To buy crèche."

We were in the car when he asked, "So, where do they sell crèches?"

"I don't know. But when in doubt . . ."

"*Si?*"

"Target."

Just like everything else, shopping with Dante was easy. Fun. It felt as if I'd known him all my life. We found a decent wooden manger and figurines. I loaded up on candles and we headed home.

"Dante, don't we have a job tonight?" I asked, when we'd finished setting up the crèche. I had a sudden flash of my father handing me the figurine of the baby Jesus and telling me to place it in the manger. Growing up, it was a magical moment.

He sighed and his shoulders drooped a bit. "*Si*. It is almost the last. Soon we can stop. Do not worry."

After a walk on the beach, he went home for a nap and a change of clothes. I tried to rest but couldn't help pacing.

At a little past two he pulled up in a car. Each time it was a different vehicle, with different plates, remarkable only for their blandness.

"Are you all right?"

He seemed jittery, unlike himself. "*Si*. Do not worry."

We headed north to Del Mar.

CHAPTER 13

Magali

Thanksgiving

"So, he called back?" Syd was peeling and coring apples for the apple-cranberry lattice pie.

"A lot. Last time was this morning. Mostly he's apologetic then asking me stuff like which restaurant I'd recommend for a solitary Thanksgiving dinner."

"Gunning for an invite. But he's a Brit, what does he care about Thanksgiving?"

"He was married and has two American kids." I wiped my hands on my apron and got the dough out of the refrigerator.

"His ex should have him over." Syd was concentrating so hard on the apples, she looked as if she were about to give a speech to the president of the United States.

"I doubt that family is about to be blended, whirled, or in any way mixed together. Anyway, I feel awful for him. Holidays on your own . . ." I shuddered. "So, speaking of tomorrow, is Perfect Hair coming?"

"Stop."

"Seriously, do newscasters have a special stylist just for insiders? There must be a secret code or handshake to get The Cut."

"I don't know if Aidan will be here."

"Do you want him to be?"

"Good question. But if he does come and you start talking about any type of mousse other than chocolate, I'll smite you with a drumstick."

"Got it. Though I don't see why. A lively conversation on hair products could carry us through an entire course." I was layering sweet and regular potatoes for a gratin. Between each layer, I sprinkled a mixture of fresh herbs. "But Syd—"

She stopped chopping and held up her hands, the right one still brandishing the knife. "Please. Not the lecture again. I know I have a thing for divorced men. Like I could fix them or something. They always go back to their wives." She rolled her eyes and went back to work on the apples. "I bet I could turn it into a business or something. Forget about couples therapy, just date me for a few months and any broken marriage will mend." She downed half a glass of the hot Pimm's we were drinking.

"Maybe you should try Simon. I doubt he's going back to his wife, seeing as she's newly married and pregnant and all." I'd finished layering and started on the garlic, which would be added to the cream. I would heat it up then pour it over the potatoes.

"Two problems: One, I don't do out of town. And two"—she lowered her voice—"he's crazy about you."

"Who's crazy about you?" Leo walked into the kitchen.

Syd bit her lip and handed me the bowl of Jonagolds.

"Uh . . . Terry, the baby agent." I dumped the apples into a pot of hot clarified butter and added the seasonings.

"Just coming in to get a beer. Need any help?" He stood behind me and his arms encircled my waist. I leaned back for a few seconds.

"No, we're fine," I said.

Leo left to watch the game and Syd widened her eyes at me. "Anyway," she said loudly enough to be heard two doors down, "there are still days I can't believe I'm helping to prepare a meal that other people are actually going to eat."

"As opposed to?"

"I don't know, scrape into the disposal like we did with Mom's meals."

"How is your mom?"

"Still on a diet. Will do anything to get out of having to eat." Syd started rinsing dishes.

"Could you grab the rolling pin out of the middle drawer? Today, you roll pie crust."

"But—"

"Syd, not brain surgery, remember?"

When the apples had boiled and reduced, I threw in the cranberries to precook for about a minute, then set the filling aside to cool a bit.

"To get back to the subject"—I lowered my voice, throwing what I hoped was a meaningful glance in the direction of the family room—"I'm afraid he's just going to show up. He'll be in town, he'll want to see his kids."

"Gali, he's a Brit, remember? Now Boxing Day, that's a whole other pair of shoes. Or gloves. Or whatever. Besides, doesn't he work on Thanksgiving? The show must go on, and all that."

"Not on Thanksgiving Day. All weekend though," I said.

"That hardly seems right. What about the people who don't have a family, hate parades, are averse to football? Don't they get to do something fun on Thanksgiving?"

"Somehow, I doubt that *Seussical* would be their musical of choice. Besides, that's what restaurants, DVDs, and movies are for. Not to mention NPR. I'd like to play hooky from the whole thing, just once, and sit around, watch movies, and relax."

"Sure. And that's the day monkeys in christening gowns will rain down from the sky. Gali, you did Thanksgiving even when you were still living in Belgium, for Christ's sake."

"You're doing great with the crust. You know, I regret ever having translated that expression for you."

"Too late," she said.

Art sauntered into the kitchen wearing a white shirt over black jeans. He hadn't lost any of his muscle tone since he'd been living here and the yard had never looked better. "Hey Gal—oh, sorry. I didn't know you had company."

The temperature in the room could have frozen the dough Syd was suddenly so intent on rolling out.

"You goose. It's not company, it's Syd. My best friend? Used to almost live here?" I rapped my knuckles against his skull.

"Hi," he said without looking at her. He opened the fridge and got a beer, then vanished as if my baby brother had just developed supernatural powers.

I looked at Syd with one eyebrow cocked, an expression it had taken me years to perfect. Wasted years apparently, since she didn't even notice. "You can stop torturing that pie crust now. What has it ever done to you?"

She looked up. "What's wrong with your eye?"

I relaxed my facial muscles, musing that Joan Crawford had nothing to fear from me. "What the hell is going on between you two?" I put the dough in the pie plate and handed Syd a fork so she could prick it.

"What do you mean?"

"Oh, come on, Syd. We don't have enough oil to heat this house for an entire meal with you two in the same room!"

"We had . . . an argument."

"About what?"

She shook her head. "Too silly to talk about. I'll call him later and fix it." She slung an arm around my shoulder, making me feel tiny, a feeling I didn't dislike. "Promise."

"I'll hold you to that. You know how I get if there's even the slightest tension at my table."

"Drunk?"

"That's the least of it." I stirred the cream. The first pie was ready to be popped into the oven. "Here, brush some egg wash across the top."

"I can't believe I actually know what you're talking about when you say egg wash, that, you know, it's not—"

"Something to wash eggs. Though why anyone would want or need to do that is beyond me. Anyway, I do admire how you veered off the subject."

"You're the one who changed it in the first place. As I recall, we were talking about Simon."

"Simon? Who's Simon?" Leo had just padded into the kitchen. I really needed to lay down some rules about wearing just socks around the house. Tap shoes maybe.

"Smells fantastic in here. Maybe I'll switch drinks." He indicated the pitcher of Pimm's on the counter. "Refills?"

"You really need to ask?" said Syd, smiling.

"So, who's Simon?"

"Oh, just this divorced guy I met . . ." Syd finished spreading the egg wash over the top of the pie.

"I thought you were already hooked up with your divorcé du jour."

"Hardy har har," she said.

"Children. Behave." The cream was hot. I poured it over the potatoes. Tomorrow I would sprinkle grated cheese over the top and pop it in the oven.

"We are, Mommy." Elly and Charlotte had just entered. "We're hungry."

"And thirsty."

"Okay, time to eat." Saved once again, by food.

That night, after we made love, I curled up against my husband and felt very, very thankful.

Thanksgiving Day

I awoke, feeling a bubble of happiness for a day that would be filled with good food and great people. By the time the day had dawned properly, the orange-cranberry and pumpkin muffins were already cooling on the sideboard, ready for breakfast. I'd serve them with yogurt and juicy Comice pears.

During breakfast, I surveyed my brood: my husband, daughters, and my baby brother, gathered around the kitchen table, eating and joking.

"This is my favorite time of any holiday," I said.

"Why?" asked Elly.

"Because every morning is a promise but a holiday morning is an extra special promise."

"If this is the high point of the day, why bother going through that whole feast thing?" asked Art before helping himself to another muffin.

I punched him.

Once breakfast was over, Leo went out back to chop some firewood, the only chore he liked to do. He must have been a lumberjack in a previous life. I shooed the girls into the den, where they were watching the Macy's Thanksgiving Day Parade on TV, and Art had disappeared on some mysterious errand. Hopefully, to patch things up with Syd.

This year, Thanksgiving would be intimate, not many strays. It would just be us, Tante Sola, Syd, and a young couple from Leo's firm, newlyweds far from home who knew no one. Syd had called this morning saying Aidan wouldn't be here. Ana said she'd stop by for an *apéritif* before grabbing a plane to have dinner with her son and family in Texas. And Daddy was in Belgium, as always, which, as much as I hated to admit it even to myself, was another reason to be thankful.

My kitchen was fragrant with the smell of cornbread baking. The turkey was stuffed and ready to go. Thanksgiving was my one absolute wholehearted concession to American cuisine. Every other holiday remained stubbornly Old World. Probably because that's how Maman and her sisters had done it.

I'd even prepared a Thanksgiving dinner on my own in Belgium one year, not without trepidation, feeling a bit protective of this holiday. It had been a huge hit, until we'd come to the pumpkin pie, which cleaved the table in two: half thought it was incredibly disgusting, and the other that it was surprisingly delicious. I was certain it had to do with an attitude toward cinnamon, a spice admittedly overused in American cuisine. I loved it though, and couldn't imagine pumpkin without it. Apples could go either way: I'd made both that year, a traditional deep-dish apple and a *nor-*

mande. Thinking of *tarte aux pommes à la normande* made me crave it. Oh, what the hell. I began peeling apples.

Leo, smelling like a forest, stepped in and stomped his feet on the mat. After removing his work boots he came over and put his arms around my waist, making me instinctively suck in my stomach. He looked over my shoulder.

"What are you doing?"

"Making a *tarte aux pommes à la normande.*"

"Good idea. I was worried that with only two pies, we would be faced with a pie shortage." He shuddered. "Terrible fate."

"Don't you know"—I swiveled to face him, taking in the woodsy smell of his plaid shirt—"that it's inadvisable to tease a woman holding a knife?"

"I'll risk it. I'm going to grab a shower before everyone gets here."

Everything here was under control. I made an *espresso lungo* and went to watch the parade with the girls.

They were already wearing their party dresses and looked like they'd stepped out of a painting.

"Mommy, watch with us. Please?"

Life was good. They say love is blind. But, actually, happiness is the one that needs its eyes surgically enhanced.

The fire was roaring, the maple tree outside the living room window was crimson, everyone was talking, laughing, eating, drinking champagne. We were all beautifully dressed. I was wearing the dress I'd bought in New York. The day was shaping up to be everything I'd hoped. I was pulling off the perfect Thanksgiving. Mentally I saluted Maman. I was sure I'd culled the cooking gene from her side of the family. Though I'd never inherited her love for fast cars.

We were finishing our drinks when Art walked in. Not alone. I almost dropped the tray of appetizers I was passing to go grab my sunglasses. Dazzling didn't do his companion justice.

"Hi, guys, this is Brandy," he said.

Of course it was.

Syd shot them a look that could have sliced steel. A second later it was gone, as was her champagne.

Leo refilled her glass and she glowered at him.

"I'm going to run up and get my camera. All this"—I swept my arm around the room, sloshing a bit of champagne on my wrist—"deserves posterity."

It would be fine. I had no idea what was going on between my best friend and my brother but I'd deal with that later. Not on Thanksgiving.

The girls followed me. I pointed the camera at them. "Strike a pose." They were both such hams. They twirled in their party dresses, dark curls bouncing, eyes bright, almost out-shirley-templing Shirley Temple.

"Ready?" They were always ready. When did it stop, the wanting to bask in the spotlight, the basic love affair with any mirror? I took a few shots, then Elly scuttled to her room to dig out her own camera.

Memories of my own first camera washed over me. I'd been ten. We'd all been ten. It had been like a rite of passage. At least I'd gotten a few good years of pictures before Maman left us. I sent a silent promise to my girls: *I will not abandon you so young. I'll be here for you and your kids. You won't ever have to know.*

I chased the thought away. It wouldn't do to start crying today.

"Gali! Come down. Ana's leaving," called Leo.

By the time we were all seated around the table, it was almost three-thirty. The afternoon light was already fading, making the lit candles, if not strictly necessary, at least inviting.

We were still on our first servings. It was my intention that everyone have, at the very least, seconds, if not thirds. Well, everyone but Brandy, who was making a great show of rearranging homeopathic portions of her food around her plate. I guessed her to be about seventeen. Her jeans hugged hips the size of my upper arm, and her sweater, which ended just above her amber belly-button ring, was shorter than her sheaves of black hair.

"Arthur? Could you give me a refill?" she beamed, holding out her empty water glass.

"Yes, Arthur, do take care of your guest," I said.

He made a face at me and filled Brandy's glass. She rewarded him with a brilliant smile.

"Thank you so much for having me at your table," she said to Leo.

"Oh, no problem . . . uh . . . anytime." He was actually stammering. To her breasts.

At that moment, the phone rang and Leo sprang up to answer.

"Just leave it, we're eating," I said.

"Which everyone knows. It might be important."

Not as important as hiding that flush spreading up across his face. Syd and I looked at each other.

"This is delicious, Magali. The turkey is not at all dry this year," said my godmother.

"Thanks, Tante Sola."

"And I must say, you look *très belle.* The extra kilos make your face look younger." She took a forkful of gratin and smiled.

I would not let her spoil my meal.

"You know what Coco Chanel said. After a certain age, a woman must choose between her face and her derrière." I knocked over my glass of wine. Luckily it had been almost empty. I sprinkled salt on the stain.

"Only after forty, *chérie*. But there is no harm in getting a head start."

"Mama is perfect." Hotly blurted by my precocious seven-year-old.

"*Naturellement.*" Tante Sola raised her glass. "A toast, to the most fantastic cook in the family."

I refilled my glass. Had I gained weight? I shifted uncomfortably in my chair, sucking in my stomach. If I'd gotten fatter I'd have to starve myself between now and Christmas to pass Daddy's scrutiny. Didn't want to spend that holiday in his line of fire.

Tante Sola was past sixty now, her eyes must be going. I was sure I hadn't gotten any heavier. The dress I was wearing, the one I'd bought in New York, fit perfectly. I picked up my knife and fork. The young couple from Leo's firm, Paola and Mark, was chatting with Brandy and *Arthur*. Syd looked miserable and was eating at an alarming rate. The girls had polished off most of their meal and were starting to fidget.

"Charlotte. Elly. You may both be excused," I said.

"But what about dessert?" asked Elly.

"I'll call you in when it's time." They went to the family room to watch a movie. Art left the table with them to set it up just as Leo returned holding out the phone.

"Your sister," he said.

"Which one?"

He grinned. "Which one do you think?"

The ever-dutiful Jacqueline. "I'll call her back."

"She insists. Do you want me to hang up on her?" It wasn't a question.

Annoyed, I stood and left the table, taking the phone into the kitchen.

After handing the phone to my reluctant brother, I went to find my godmother. She was just leaving the guest bathroom when I cornered her. "Where's Daddy?"

She gave me one of her *don't be daft* looks. "Where he always is this week every year. In Belgium."

I shook my head.

"*Non?*" Her eyes widened.

She scurried to the dining room, and Art said a quick good-bye before handing the phone to Tante Sola. She went to the kitchen. Art was still standing. I hated when people left the table during a meal. I felt like shouting to please sit down and eat. "Sit," I said to my brother.

"We have to get going." He grabbed Brandy's hand and she rose.

"What?"

"I promised Brandy I'd take her out." He slung his arm across her shoulders.

"Today? What about dessert?"

"Later. Look, I'm not hungry right now," said Art.

"Oh," said Brandy, with a giggle, "I never eat dessert. Do you know what all that fat and sugar do to your body?"

"Pure poison, yes, I know." I tapped my fork on the table.

The young couple looked uncomfortable. "Maybe we . . ."

"Stay." They didn't move. I turned to Art and Brandy. "Sit down. Both of you."

"Yes, Mom." But Art sat, tugging Brandy's arm till she perched on a chair beside him.

Tante Sola came back, looking worried.

"We will sit and finish. No more phones," I said.

Obediently, they all passed around platters and resumed eating.

"So, has anyone been to the movies lately?" asked Syd.

I threw her a grateful look. "Oh, I just saw—" I began, searching my brain for the last movie I did see.

The doorbell rang. I threw my napkin on the table and blew all the air out of my body as if I were about to do a deep-breathing yoga pose or something. Tomorrow I was going to get the phone and the doorbell disconnected.

"I'll get it," I said.

"Too late, I'm there," Leo said.

"So the movie?" prompted Syd.

"Yeah, it was that new Meryl Streep thing. What was the title? She had a British accent in it?"

Leo was back with Ana in tow. My spirits lifted.

"They closed DFW. An ice storm just hit."

"Thank God," I said.

"What?" said Ana.

"You know what I mean. You could have taken off and—" So intent was I on Ana that I only then noticed a second person trailing behind her. My mouth hung open.

"Everyone, this is—" Ana started.

"Simon. What are you doing in my house?" asked Leo.

"I hope you don't mind my crashing the party. Hi, Gali."

"How do you two know each other?" I asked Ana.

"We don't. We just met outside."

Leo looked confused but stuck out his hand. "So, Simon, apparently you know my wife?" His tone was cold.

"Technically, that would be correct, though we haven't known each other long." With an easy smile, he grasped Leo's hand, then turned his gaze to me.

Cold fear spread through my veins. Leo knew him? And didn't seem overly fond of him either. "Food." I sprang up. "Have you eaten? Never mind. You'll eat more."

Leo shot me a bewildered look and went to get two more chairs while I hurried to the kitchen, glad to hide. I would have happily stayed there for the rest of the evening. Syd appeared at my side, as if by magic.

"Oh my God," she whispered.

"I know. Leo *knows* him?"

"It's a nightmare. But honey, you didn't mention he was so hot."

"Yes I did." My hands shook as I got two fresh plates out of the cupboard. "What am I going to do?" How did Leo know him?

"I know. Seat him next to me," she said. "You can say you met Simon and intended him for me. Which, if you were a true friend, would be the case."

"Yeah, except we already told Leo that you'd met a Simon." I bit my lip and my sore finger throbbed.

"We'll wing it. It will work. Come on. Let's get back out there before Leo comes in asking questions." She tugged on my arm. I took a few deep breaths and tried to quiet the pounding in my chest.

The rest of the meal took on a surreal aspect—I kept expecting a train to drive through the living room wall, or something. Syd flirted brazenly with Simon, who clearly enjoyed the attention, though his gaze kept sliding back to me. Leo ignored me and spent his time with Art and Brandy and her breasts. Ana chatted and charmed Paola and Mark. Which left me with Tante Solange and several glasses of wine. By this time she was quite tipsy and teary-eyed about her son, whom she hadn't seen in the past I-can't-recall-how-many years. Time was always a bit fuzzy with my aunt.

And through it all, concern for my father needled me.

I wished Syd would stop laughing so loudly. What was wrong with her?

If only that train would make its entrance. It would have been a welcome distraction. Where was Magritte when you really needed him? Surrealism wasn't to be trusted.

By the time dessert had been demolished, the girls had fallen asleep on the couch, and everyone, including Syd, had left, it was after nine o'clock.

We carried the girls to bed before starting on the kitchen.

"So where did you meet Simon?" asked Leo, carrying dishes in from the dining room.

"In New York—I thought he'd be perfect for Syd."

"Apparently she thought so too. Is he any relation to Simona?" He put his hand on my arm. "Quite a coincidence, wouldn't you say?"

Busted. "Okay. There is no Simona."

"Gee, I'm astonished." His voice flatlined. He turned his back to me. "I can't believe you lied."

"It's not a big deal. It just seemed . . . simpler." I scraped food into the disposal, my heart racing.

"Why? Why did you need to lie?"

"Look, it was nothing. I didn't want you to get the wrong idea." I put down the plate I was holding and it broke cleanly into two pieces. It was too hot in the kitchen. I couldn't breathe.

He swiveled and faced me. "And you thought lying about it was going to achieve that?"

I remained silent.

His eyes went so dark, they looked gray. "You're my wife. I trust you. Or should I say trusted you."

The tense sliced through my legs.

"Look. It just seemed . . . complicated to explain that I'd been out half the night with a guy. It was late, I was tired, and I didn't want to get into it."

"Why? Unless you felt guilty."

"No. I just thought you might misunderstand, okay?" I took a step toward him. He stepped back.

"There was no misunderstanding those looks he kept giving

you. Pretty eloquent." He picked up the dishrag and started wiping the counter.

"He spent the whole time talking to Syd."

"Who was putting on a great show."

"How do you know him?" My voice croaked.

"Handled his divorce. I represented his ex." He folded the dishrag and put it on the drainboard.

"Oh." *Shit*.

"He has quite the reputation. Likes them married."

"Leo." I reached for his arm, but he backed away.

"I'll be in the living room straightening up."

And so we cleaned in silence.

"I'm going up. Good night." No look, no kiss.

"I'll be just a few more minutes." I didn't dare look at him. To tell the truth, I wasn't thinking, or seeing straight, for that matter. I felt too full. I wondered how many calories I had consumed. With all the wine and cognac, probably about five thousand. Or maybe ten. I sighed. Tomorrow it would be nothing but fruits and vegetables. And lean protein. Had lots of white meat left on the turkey.

I was finishing up the dishes when the phone rang. I pounced on it, heart beating. I checked caller ID, hoping it wasn't Simon. Not that there was anyone I wanted to talk to at this point.

Anyone except my baby sister.

I tried to keep my usual light banter, but my heart wasn't in it. She must have heard it in my voice. At her insistence, I spilled. It tumbled out of my mouth as I slumped at the desk, head in hand.

"My career is a disaster, I haven't convinced Ana not to leave me. Our brother has turned into a cradle-snatcher, unless he's planning to adopt his current date—"

"Again?"

"Yeah, and I'm pretty sure this one isn't even legal. What is it with him?"

"Nothing new. Not a hell of a lot we can do about Artie."

"I think you mean Arthur."

"Oh no! You're kidding?" She began to giggle. "Gali, sweetie, your career is fixable. Ana leaving isn't the end of the world."

Then why did it sometimes feel that way, as if someone had just thrown a shroud over the sun? Hey, that was good. I should write it down to use in my novel, the one I would probably never write because who gave a shit about what I had to say anyway? Shut up and cook.

"Not finished with the list, yet. So"—I ticked off my fingers—"Ana, Artie, my marriage is probably over—"

"What?"

"It's bad, Colette." Tears stung my eyes. I blinked.

"It can't be that bad. How much have you had to drink?"

"Too much."

"Besides, if it was really serious, you would've led with that, instead of Ana."

"Maybe I just don't want to talk about it." Which was the truth. "By the way, is Daddy with you?"

"What? Is he on his way here?" Her voice swerved.

"Not that I know."

"Gali,"—back to her normal voice—"you know Daddy doesn't recognize California as part of the United States. It wasn't one of the thirteen original. Besides, he spends Thanksgiving in Belgium."

"Not this year."

"Huh." Colette paused. "He's probably fine. I'm sure he's fine. So, what's up with you and my yummy brother-in-law?"

I got up and poured myself a fresh glass of wine and told her. Everything. The train ride, the restaurant, the hospital, Leo's visit, my lie, that night in his apartment, and his showing up here.

"Thank God Syd was here to deflect the horror," I finished.

"Well, it's weird, I'll give you that. But nothing happened, right? And you were feeling alone and vulnerable," she said.

"But I wanted to be alone."

"So you say."

"When exactly did you get your PhD in psych? Anyway, it was the lie that did it. I told him Simon was a girl: Simon-a."

Colette started to laugh.

"Not funny."

"Sorry. So, he made the connection."

"Worse than that, he knows the guy. His firm handled his divorce, represented Simon's ex."

"Oh, *merde!*"

"My sentiments exactly. So, Daddy, Ana, Art, Simon, Leo . . . what did I miss? Syd. She's acting like a lunatic."

"Again, nothing new."

I let it pass. "And . . . oh yeah, I'm fat. But it suits me." I took a sip of wine without tasting it.

"Let me guess. Tante Sola?"

"Bingo."

"The girls?"

"The girls are amazing and oblivious and happy."

"I miss them."

"They miss you, too. The light at the end of the tunnel is seeing you at Christmas."

"Uh, about that?"

"If you bail, I will come out there myself and drag you here by the scruff of your neck."

"Impossible, neck has no scruff to speak of." She paused. "Of course I'll be there," she said very—too?—brightly.

"You'd better."

"Okay, now, listen to me. Empty that glass in the sink, rinse it out. Go to bed, go directly to bed. Do not pass go, do not collect two hundred dollars. Got it?"

Guiltily, I poured the wine I was drinking into the sink. California was doing wonders for her powers of perception. "Done."

"Call me tomorrow."

She clicked off and I realized I had no idea how she was. How long had it been since I'd had hard news from her? I mounted the steps, the cat trailing behind me. Something else to worry about. I felt like having a cigarette. Maybe I should take up smoking again. Lung cancer, after all, is a great solution. I stopped in to check on the girls and pulled up Charlotte's duvet, smoothed Elly's hair back. I planted a light kiss on each perfect forehead.

"Don't worry, I'll never let anything bad happen to you, I promise." But even as I said it, I knew it was a lie.

Black Friday

As per tradition, still wearing pajamas, the girls and I made pancakes the next morning. I couldn't understand how, after eating such a huge amount the day before, I was starving in the morning. I remembered the diet I was going to start today.

No one started dieting on a Friday. There was probably a law against it. I'd start Monday. Besides, I didn't believe in diets.

Charlotte cracked the eggs and beat them with the milk. Elly measured the flour and salt, though I did rectify her pinch, which in her tiny hands ended up being all of four grains.

They'd even set the breakfast table themselves.

By the time Leo came down, the setting was picture perfect. "Hi, Daddy, look what we made!"

He picked up a girl in each arm and spun them. "You two are the most fantastic chefs. I can't believe how lucky I am."

They giggled and basked in his love and approval. My stomach clenched. I had to make sure nothing would ever take that away from them. I set a cup of fresh, hot coffee in front of him.

"Morning. Thanks."

I tried to gauge his mood. I knew from Maman's diary that my parents had argued hard and often. They both had strong personalities, but just like milk that was boiling over, tempers died down as soon as the heat was removed.

He took a sip of coffee. "No kiss?"

Was it really over? That easily? I leaned over and kissed him, but his lips remained tight. Or was it my imagination? Guilt was a mirage-maker, after all.

"Should we start on putting up the lights once the Thanksgiving stuff is all packed up?" I forced a note of insouciance, of brightness, into my voice.

"Sure. Maybe Simon can come over and give us a hand."

"He's nice. And he talks like Harry Potter," said Elly.

I kept my eyes on my plate and began to eat.

"Are they good, Momma?" asked Charlotte.

"Perfect," I said. I swallowed and took a sip of coffee. My appetite was gone. Probably not a bad thing. "Could you come and help me with something in the attic? Once you're done?"

"I'll be right there."

I went up and started getting the empty Thanksgiving boxes down from the shelf. The last one had just toppled on my head when Leo came in.

I swiveled. "Look. If you have something to say to me, just say it. Don't spend all day innocently throwing poison darts at me in front of the girls."

"Look, I'm trying, okay? It's not that guy—not just, anyway. It's that you found you needed to lie to me."

I looked down at the dust balls at my feet. "I'm sorry. I just thought it would be easier. A white lie. Don't you ever tell white lies?"

"Not to you."

"Oh come on. When you tell me I look great when I'm clearly fat."

"Not a lie. You look great. I mean it every time. Okay," he said, "how would you have reacted if I'd been the one to tell the lie?"

I opened my mouth but before I could formulate a thought, he put his hand up like a cop stopping traffic.

"Yes, I know—we would have had to dig ourselves out of a blizzard of pastry." He smiled at me and I felt my own mouth begin to twitch. "But how would you have felt?"

"I . . . I wouldn't know if I could still trust you," I said, my voice small.

"Exactly. And that's what I'm going through right now because I still don't truly understand the need." He put his hands on my shoulders. "This is us."

I felt tears welling up in my eyes. "I know. That's why it shouldn't matter. It's us."

"Not to mention that the guy's a bastard."

"Huh?" I could be very eloquent when the need arose.

"Things aren't always what they seem. It's that accent. Makes him sound like that actor you like."

"Hugh Grant? Colin Firth?"

"Yeah, him."

"If he's so awful, should we say something to Syd? She seemed . . . smitten."

Leo rapped his knuckles against my temple. "For such a smart woman, you're not always very perceptive."

"What?"

"Look, I'm freezing up here. Let's grab some of those cartons and head back down where it's warm."

"So what am I not being perceptive about?" I picked up a carton and followed him.

"Because . . . think about it. I shouldn't be the one to tell you. I'm going to get dressed before digging out the ladder."

I suddenly felt suffocated, I needed air. I headed to the kitchen. "C'mon, girls, let's clean this up, get dressed, and go shopping."

"For us?" asked Charlotte.

"Sure, for all of us and the house, too."

Once on the road, my claustrophobia had abated a bit. I drove over to Plymouth Meeting Mall and almost lost control of the car when I spotted the line of cars and orange-clad parking attendants. Of course. Today was Black Friday.

"Mommy, where are we going?" asked Elly.

I was maneuvering out of the line of cars, signaling and peering over my shoulder.

"Aren't we going in?" she persisted.

"I want to go in," said her sister.

"Change of plan, sweeties. We're going to the drugstore. Pick up some more lights and stuff."

We were almost there. I was fiddling with the dial on the radio scanning for some Christmas music.

"You're not listening," said Elly.

"Of course I am. What?" I found a station that was playing "Winter Wonderland."

"Then *are* they?" she asked, her voice rising above the music.

"Are they what? Who?"

Elly gave an exasperated sigh worthy of a seven-year-old drama queen. "Told ya you weren't listening. Are Uncle Art and Aunt Syd getting *married?* And are we getting new dresses?"

"I wanna be a flower girl," said Charlotte.

"Why would you think they're getting married? Silly goose." I turned into the parking lot and cruised up and down the lanes, looking for a space.

"Cause they were loooove kissing—" said Elly.

"—in the backyard," said Charlotte.

"Yeah. Then Aunt Syd hit him on the face." She giggled.

"That's bad, right, Momma? Aunt Syd needs a time-out."

If I hadn't been in a moving vehicle, I would have banged my head against the steering wheel. On purpose. Repeatedly.

Dumbkoff! Imbecile! Idiot!

I couldn't decide which of them suited me better. I'd have to have all three engraved on my tombstone. Expense be damned.

CHAPTER 14

Jacqueline

Thanksgiving

"I don't know, I'm a bit nervous," I said. We were getting dressed for Thanksgiving at David's. Laurent had taken the day off.

"I don't understand you. These are your friends." He was trying to decide between a black shirt with light gray stripes and a midnight blue one. He looked at me. I nodded toward the blue.

"Yeah, I know. Probably hormones." I discarded a pair of black Gaultier jeans that were suddenly a bit snug around the waist while Laurent gave me a puzzled look. "My good jeans are too small," I told him with a smile.

"Ah, you are going to grow fat and lazy like a cat in the sun."

"Don't even think it," I said with a shudder. "I intend to be one of those women who don't look pregnant from the back." I put the jeans back on the hanger.

"I don't think you have much of a choice. It's genetic. Look at tiny Shoshanna." He buttoned his shirt.

"She says swelling up like a balloon is the worst part." I stood in front of my open closet.

"*Ma Jackie,*" he said, putting his arms around me, "you are the most beautiful pregnant woman there ever was or ever will be."

"So I'm ugly when I'm not pregnant?"

"You are impossible always."

"You say whatever you like, but I bet you don't come near me if I get huge. You'll just look at me with revulsion like the monster from the planet of the blimps."

"Is that really all you think of me?"

I found a pair of tan pants that had a bit of stretch in them. "No. It's what I think of me." I pulled them on. My father had always criticized women who let themselves go. For him, the F-word was *fat.*

"Not me. I love you. All of you. For better for worse, remember?" He sat on the bed to tie his shoes.

"They should add 'for thinner for fatter' to wedding vows. I've known more than one marriage that split up because of body issues."

"Not a good marriage to begin with," he said. He turned to the mirror and splashed on some Eau de Vetiver.

I pulled my boots on over my pants, added a chocolate brown sweater and Maman's Hermès scarf.

"You look beautiful. How are you feeling?"

"Good. No more nausea. Do you think it's a bad sign?"

"Stop worrying. We'll have all the details tomorrow. You know, it's relaxing to celebrate Thanksgiving at David's rather than the big dinner at your Aunt Charlotte's house."

We smiled at each other. What we left unsaid was that it was nice not to have to deal with Daddy for once. Not that he wasn't always gracious. But I always felt as if I were auditioning for a part when he was there. But the gift of a Daddy-free Thanksgiving came with a price. Sacrificing Christmas. "I really need to get those tickets."

"It's done," he said.

"What do you mean?"

"I was worried that we wouldn't be able to get on the same flight as Elise and then she'd have to travel alone."

Anger flared briefly, then died. "You are a wonderful man." I kissed him.

We headed downstairs.

"Oh yes, before I forget, this came for you." He picked up a letter from the Louis Philippe bureau and handed it to me. It had a US stamp.

"It's from my father," I said, and slit open the envelope. "I wonder . . . Oh! It's a photograph. Look at this." I showed it to Laurent. It was a picture of me as a baby. I was smiling and looking at the photographer. Beside me were my parents, gazing at me as if I were a queen. I read the note.

Dear Jacqueline,

I thought you might like to have this. It was taken the summer you were five months old.

I miss you and am looking forward to seeing you at Christmas.

Love,

Dad

"I remember this picture. It was hanging on the wall of the staircase, along with similar poses of my sisters and brother. After Maman died, they all vanished," I said, running a finger over my mother's hair. "I wonder why he's sending this now?" I pressed the photograph to my heart.

"Maybe he's mellowing with age, like a fine cognac." Laurent grinned.

"He's a fine cognac, all right." I stared at the photograph again. "They were such a gorgeous couple." I sighed. If only I could conjure up that time, just for a day, and observe them. See that light in my father's eyes.

Laurent nodded. "And you were a beautiful baby. And clearly very loved."

"Do we have a frame?" I looked up. He shook his head. "I'll

buy one tomorrow." I went to the piano and propped up the photograph on the music stand.

When we got to David's place it smelled like a Virginia farmhouse in autumn. I lived in a vibrant, culturally dynamic city that was my home while maintaining a link to the place where I grew up. I really had the best of both worlds.

CHAPTER 15

Colette

The streets were tree-lined and gorgeous. Old Del Mar was old-money Republican and one of the most beautiful communities in the area.

"Something in the air ... it doesn't feel right to me tonight." Buying and setting up a crèche just prior to committing a mortal sin might have had something to do with it.

Dante kept passing his hand through his hair. "It will be fine. Is almost over."

"Can I ask you a question?"

"*Naturalmente.*"

"Are you going to be able to just ... quit? What about your partners?"

"It's not what you think, *bella*. It is very, how you say, relaxed?" he said.

"Casual."

"*Si.* I am independent agent."

I relaxed. Besides, the moon was shining so beautifully in the night sky, it had to be a good sign.

We parked the car on an adjacent street and cut through the backyards to our mark. The door off the deck slid open. Dante threw me a smile. Piece of cake. All I wanted was for it to be over and to be back home with my bedecked halls of Christmas cheer.

I headed off to the side of the house to where I thought the master bedroom would be while Dante made a sweep of the living areas. I padded down the dark hall past floor-to-ceiling built-in bookcases.

A California King flanked by two tables. I was opening a drawer in the nightstand when the atmosphere of the house shifted.

"Oh my God! Oh my God!" A woman's voice pierced the stillness. Suddenly Dante was beside me, a dog barking at his heels. He grabbed my hand and thrust open the bedroom door leading to the back patio.

"I'm calling nine-one-one. Angie, stop screaming. They won't get away. Sic 'em. Toby!" But Toby, a golden lab, just rubbed up against me. I patted his head and was rewarded by a warm, wet lick and a wagging tail.

Dante pulled me toward the fence surrounding the pool and pushed me up and over, then scampered up after me. We ran through the alley, our soft-soled shoes hitting the asphalt in a way that sounded too loud in my own ears. I tripped and scraped my knee, tears stung my eyes. Dante helped me up and we kept running. Once on the street we slowed to a fast walk. We reached the car but Dante shook his head. We continued down toward the ocean until we hit Highway 101. Sirens wailed in the distance. We crossed the deserted highway. With no one around, if we were spotted, we were cooked.

Once at the beach, we crouched behind an outcropping of rocks to catch our breath. A wave lapped up, soaking my canvas shoes with liquid ice.

"Now what?" I whispered through my now-chattering teeth. The noise seemed too loud in the night.

"Now, we walk."

So we did. We walked along the sand's edge from Torrey Pines Beach all the way to La Jolla Shores. I shivered the whole way. We cut through a few neighborhoods before hitting the Cove, staying off the roads as much as possible. Sometimes we had to climb over rocks. I slipped a few times, the pain in my knee throbbed, but Dante's strong grasp on my hand kept me from falling. At others, we were hand in hand along the smooth, damp sand, looking like a couple in love out for a moonlit walk on the beach. In November.

By the time we got home, I was shaking more than ever. Dante drew me a hot bath and set about making tea with honey. I was immersed in bubbles and he brought it in, hiding his eyes.

"You can look, I'm decent."

He set the cup carefully on the edge of the tub and brought in a warm, clean pair of soft cotton sweats in midnight blue.

Once I was out of the bathroom, he bandaged my knee.

We sat in the darkened living room, lit only by the fire in the fireplace and candles.

"The car?"

"Tomorrow I will send friends." He placed one of his beautiful hands on my shoulder. "Time to stop. Our luck . . . *finito*."

Dante stayed with me. Every time I dozed off, I was jerked awake by images of red lights flashing in the night, silvery handcuffs, and steel bars. Finally exhausted, I fell into a black sleep.

I woke up to Dante making more tea. I grabbed the cream pashmina shawl that Jacqueline sent me last year and headed to the kitchen.

"Did they see your face? Can they recognize you?" I asked.

He shook his head. "I wear the ski mask and pull up the collar of my sweater like this." He demonstrated, unrolling the turtleneck up over the lower half of his face. "Maybe they see my nose. Eh."

I couldn't help it. I giggled.

"I leave the bag. They will be less angry, nothing taken. The police will not pursue."

It made sense. I sat at the table and bit my nails.

"We are not in danger. Do not worry, okay?" Gently he moved my hand down to the table.

"Okay. But we could have been." His hand was as cold as mine.

"What could have is not. It is air." He gestured upward with the palm of his free hand. Now I go home to change the clothes."

"Oh, my God. You must be freezing."

"No, *tutto bene*. The fire is warm."

I knew he was lying.

"I make arrangements to go to Las Vegas. It is time," he said from the door.

I blew on my tea and took a sip. It was sweet without being cloying.

"We leave on Thursday. Come back Monday."

I was about to open my mouth to say that I taught on Fridays but stopped. I didn't feel as if I owed any loyalty to an institution that was about to discard me like a bunch of wilted flowers. It also occurred to me that Friday was the big university bash. The one I'd hung so many hopes on all those weeks ago. It felt more like a couple of centuries. I closed my eyes and couldn't quite picture Wayne's face. His general demeanor, yes. But his actual features were fuzzy.

But my students. They were not responsible. But how much more could I give them in one fifty-minute class? The carrots were cooked, as they said in French.

"Nico? Where are you?" He was still in the doorway.

"Sorry. Right here. Thursday sounds good. I'll be ready and waiting, Captain."

"It will give you an opportunity to wear your most beautiful dresses."

I hadn't thought of that. This was going to be fun.

Although Dante could wear burlap bags and still steal every other man's thunder, some ideas popped into my head. I hadn't had much practice designing for men other than my brother—Wayne thought my designs were too chichi—but I'd never had a Dante in my life either.

I spent the better part of the next three days designing and making a suit for him. I was absorbed, wanting to do his beauty justice.

After I lied to Chantal with a poise I never knew I possessed, she arranged for one of the grad students to cover my class and she wished me good luck on my job interview in Dallas.

I was just an ever-replenishing pool of vice.

CHAPTER 16

Magali

"Daddy! Where have you been?"

"Where I always am. Working here or at the shop."

"Not Thursday you weren't."

I was standing on my father's doorstep the Saturday after Thanksgiving bearing Tupperware. I'd dressed with care, wearing high-waisted gray pleated pants with a white shirt and charcoal jacket. Very Annie Hall, but it was a look I'd always liked. Besides, it was slimming.

"Jacqueline was frantic."

"I have a difficult time believing that. Jacqueline isn't one to give in to emotion." As opposed to me. "I'd informed her that I wouldn't be traveling for Thanksgiving this year. I thought I'd told you as well. Come in, put that in the kitchen."

"She assumed you'd spend it with me. I was worried," I said to my father's back. After all these years I still had a hard time passing this threshold. The house defined everything I thought of as home: roomy, ramshackle, solid, bursting with light, and surrounded by green growing things. Still, with every visit, I'd feel sad at how shabby it had become.

Even in the early years when money was tight, the rooms were always filled with flowers—I remembered the wildflowers in jars all over the house. She'd plant vines and flowers from seeds, and everything would spring magically to life through her fingers. I still saw her, pregnant and stunning, an old white shirt of Daddy's over loose slacks, a scarf wound through her hair. This was before anyone looked gorgeous when pregnant. How much more beautiful would she have looked today, when it was hip to have a bump.

Me, I'd gained too much weight, as my father—and my aunt—had repeatedly pointed out. I'd schlepped around my life in baggy sweatpants and Leo's old Princeton sweatshirts and tees. My only indulgence had been a vintage baby-doll nightie I'd found at a resale shop and bought because it reminded me of my mother.

"Why are you still standing there? Come in," he said. "I have something to show you."

"Sorry," I said, my thoughts still on the nightie. Maybe I should pass it on to Jacqueline as a talisman. It might bring her luck. Then a thought, swift as a very small, very mean hummingbird, zipped through my mind: *why should she have everything?*

I made my way through the foyer to the dining room on my left. He put a hand on my back and gently pushed me in the direction of the kitchen. He hadn't taken the container of soup from my hands.

In the kitchen, I froze.

He smiled. "What do you think?"

"You had the kitchen painted."

"Almost."

"*You* painted the kitchen?" Never in my life did I recall my father ever doing any physical labor.

"I thought the house could use a little freshening." He rocked back and forth on the balls of his feet, his eyes bright.

The walls glowed with warm gold, the newly white wooden cabinets were crisp and clean in contrast. He was smiling. He looked . . . I couldn't put my finger on it.

"Do you like it?" he asked.

"I do." But I was torn. Where were the traces of our dirty fingers? The nick in the pantry door where Jacqueline had thrown a mug of milk at me when she was thirteen and I was eleven and I'd borrowed her charm bracelet without asking and promptly lost it.

I felt erased. My childhood was hidden, covered up. Pretty.

I felt like opening up the cupboards and cooking something.

"Would you like some tea?" asked my father.

"Tea?" Now he drank tea? "I didn't know you liked tea."

"I have recently come to enjoy it."

I narrowed my eyes at this stranger inhabiting my father's body. "Tea would be . . . lovely." All very *Remains of the Day*.

He busied himself getting the water boiling in the kettle. When he opened the pantry door, I saw four sets of horizontal marks with our names. Our height charts year by year. He noticed me looking.

"Come here, Maggie."

I did.

"Stand right there."

As I had so many times before, I stood with my back against the pantry door and he drew a line level with the crown of my head.

"Look how tall you've gotten. You're all grown up."

When we were settled with our tea, he looked at me across the table. "I have something for you," he said.

"And then, he *thanked* me for the soup. We had our tea—really good tea, by the way—and he brought out a plate of lemon cream scones from All Things British."

Leo, Art, and I were sitting around the kitchen table. I'd already sent an e-mail to both my sisters and was waiting for their reaction. We'd just finished our supper of leftovers and were lingering over the last of the wine. I still hadn't mentioned to my brother what the girls had told me about seeing him with Syd. I wasn't sure I was going to. Respecting Art's privacy was the norm, if I wanted to hang on to him. It was like having a secret agent in the family.

Syd, however, was a different matter. It felt as if the world had tilted in an unexpected direction, as if I no longer knew my best friend. I'd called her several times and stopped by her house, but so far, no luck. Being kept in the dark was making me crazy.

"Alien abduction. That's my only guess," said Art, bringing me back to the present.

"Or a new British Invasion—some kind of drug in the tea that makes the mind go Brit? A nice bloodless way to get back those pesky colonies," said Leo.

"Those bloodstains are murder. And we know they have a flag," said Leo, grinning.

Then Leo and Art in unison: "No flag, no country!"

"Does everything have to turn into a reference to Eddie Izzard?" I asked. But I was laughing.

"Excuse me for a minute." John Lennon was singing about peace and Christmas over the speakers.

"Where ARE you going?" Leo asked, still channeling his favorite British comedian.

"Oh, thought I'd run up and grab my go-go boots, to keep in the spirit—if we go Brit, might as well go all the way," I said.

If Colette knew I still had the vintage boots, she'd jump out of her skin with longing. I decided to give them to her for Christmas.

"Gali can't get rid of anything," said Leo.

"Lucky for you, huh." Oops, maybe not the right time for that kind of teasing. "We have a big house, might as well fill it up." My motto tended to be empty space, wasted space. "But to get back to Daddy, I haven't told you the strangest part. He gave me a baby picture of me with him and Maman. It was weird." I turned to my brother. "Do you remember them? There was a series of them. One of you, too. They used to hang on the wall of the staircase."

"Nope," said Art. "Doesn't ring a bell."

I wasn't surprised. He and Colette had both been so young when our mother died. "I'll bet the only reason he didn't give you yours is that he has no idea that you're here." I put my hand over my brother's. "And he has no idea how to get in touch with you."

"If you say so," said Art.

The oven dinged.

"Ah, the first batch of Christmas cookies!" sighed Art. "And none too soon, either. It's been, what, *hours* since Thanksgiving?" Art stood. "Save me some. I'll be right back." He went out the back door. Through the window, I saw him take a cigarette out of a crumpled pack and light up, bathed in the glow of the Christmas lights. He hadn't even bothered to put on a jacket. Something about his stance stopped me from taking one out to him.

I'd started baking earlier this month. I figured I could freeze the dough, so that both my new spartan regimen and my novel would have a free schedule starting Monday. I'd finished my last cookbook on Tuesday, so apart from edits, I was in the clear. My new life as a thin writer of fiction awaited. I hadn't told anyone, especially about the diet, since technically, I didn't believe in them. Maybe I was wrong. In any case, it wasn't something I would ever want to write about.

So, no more writing about food.

Leo and I were alone at the table.

"You did a nice job on the lights," I said. I was waving my olive branch as hard as I could.

"Thanks, just a couple finishing touches and we'll be set," he said. "Except for the tree."

"I'll call Syd and see if she's free next Friday to help us trim it." *If she ever answers her phone, that is.* I was looking at the photograph. "I look just like Charlotte."

He stood behind me and looked at the picture over my shoulder. "It's the other way around, she's the one who looks like you," he said.

"Leo?" I grabbed his hand. "Are we okay?"

"Yeah, we are. I know nothing happened. I can't stay mad at you. You're too good a cook."

I hoped I'd never lose the ability to cook, because I don't know if I'd have anyone left in my life.

"Just don't ever lie to me again."

I stood and faced him. "I promise."

He stared into my eyes. "I believe you." We kissed and I felt some of the tension melt away from my body.

"Do you think he means to sell it?" I said against the soft fabric of Leo's sweatshirt. "The house, I mean. And that's why he's painting."

"I don't know."

"I'll bet that's it. And that's what he's going to announce on Christmas." Tears came to my eyes.

"We don't know that's going to happen so don't get yourself so worked up," he said, releasing me.

The cookies were now cool enough to be transferred to a plate. Art came back in smelling like cigarettes.

"Want a cookie?" I asked him.

"Ah, Sis. You've got a big heart. The biggest in the family."

"Aren't you having one?" he asked, with his mouth full.

"Don't speak with your mouth full." I shook my head. "Not hungry."

"Since when do you have to be hungry for a cookie?"

I shrugged. "Okay. Just to taste. To make sure they are good."

"They are sublime," he said, helping himself to another.

They turned out perfect: slightly crisp on the outside with a moist, warm center.

Perfect.

CHAPTER 17

Jacqueline

It was raining in Brussels the day of my first ultrasound. In the US, it was Black Friday, the biggest shopping day of the year. Despite the dreary weather, I sang as I got ready. Laurent had taken the day off to accompany me.

We were in the waiting room but I was too excited to read any of the magazines I usually indulged in. Laurent was flipping through *Première,* a film magazine. Her office was in a beautiful *maison de maître* in Ixelles, decorated in soft browns with butterscotch accents and dark orange curtains. How many times had we sat here like this? But we'd never come this far. Our first ultrasound.

Dr. Cellier, wearing a white coat and sporting a new short haircut, opened the door to her office and waved us in. When I first came to Belgium, I was surprised at the simplicity of doctors' offices. No nurses or office managers, receptionists or secretaries. Some doctors and dentists did use an outside billing service, but most did it all themselves. Here, when you called your doctor, you talked to your doctor.

It was all very easy, very humane.

I removed my skirt and panties and boots in the curtained-off area in the far corner of her office. I shivered as I hopped up onto the table. These old houses were wonderful, but despite central heating, they always let in a bit of the cold.

"So, how have you been feeling?" she asked.

"Better. No more nausea, which is a relief," I said. "I like your hair."

She smiled and patted the short bob. "I read the review in *Télémoustique*. Congratulations."

"*Merci*."

She adjusted her glasses. "But the nausea. It can come and go. It's all very normal and different from one woman to the next."

I lay down on the table and she squirted gel on my tummy. I flinched.

"I'm sorry. I know it's cold."

"No. It's fine." We were going to see our baby for the first time. Laurent grasped my hand, both of us intent on the magic screen.

"So, we will be looking for the heartbeat. We will see it and hear it. It will be very fast, which is normal," she said.

Normal was good.

She smiled as she rolled the probe over my abdomen. A whooshing oceanic sound filled the air. Every cell in my body yearned toward the image that was soon to appear. So far, it was like bad black-and-white reception from a sixties television, grainy and indistinct.

"Hard to believe we are going to get to see a picture on that," said Laurent. He remained laconic but I know he was as jumpy as I was.

"Here is your uterus. Looks good." She kept rolling the probe back and forth. It seemed to take a long time. I tore my eyes from the screen, gave Laurent a smile, then looked at my doctor. A slight frown had appeared on her forehead.

Then, she stopped. I couldn't hear anything but the whooshing. "I can't really make out anything," I said. I saw a small circle, lighter than the background, but that was all. No rapid *boom boom boom,* either.

She shook her head. "*Un oeuf clair.*"

"I don't know what that means," I said. *This can't be good.*

"In English," she said, "an empty amnion or sac. The gestational sac is there but there is no embryo." She shook her head gently.

"Look again. There has to be a baby. All the tests were positive. Even you told us everything was fine at her last visit." Laurent turned pale.

I was dizzy. "I had all the symptoms. Even the nausea. Did I do something wrong? Did I kill it? Look again, please?" The champagne. I should never have had the champagne. I should have stopped working. Rested.

"I'm sorry." She switched off the ultrasound machine, then gently wiped the gel off my abdomen with a soft white towel. I couldn't move. She tossed the towel in the hamper. "Why don't you get dressed and we'll discuss it in my office." Her voice was gentle. "Take your time."

"Thank you," said Laurent. I had no voice.

He gathered me in his arms and held me. Wordlessly, he helped me down from the table and took me to the dressing area. Then he dressed me, like a doll. Panties, tights, my skirt. The zipper stuck at my waist, then slid up. Last came my boots.

He pulled a handful of tissues from the box on the small Deco table in the corner and wiped my face. I took them from him and blew my nose.

"Ready?"

I nodded. Dry-eyed and hollow, I let him lead me through the tall double doors. We sat in the two chairs facing Dr. Cellier's desk. My file was open in front of her and she was writing something in her neat cursive. She looked up.

"What happened is"—she put down her pen—"that the egg was fertilized, but some condition made it stop developing. There can be many causes. Even a virus."

"But that's so cruel." I was shaking. "I really was pregnant, right? I didn't imagine it."

"No, you didn't," she said. "It is cruel, but mostly, it's Mother Nature's way of elim . . . stopping a defective embryo. One of them, at any rate. But under no circumstances did you do anything wrong. Do you understand? There was nothing that could be done to change this."

I nodded, not really believing her. Her words were a happy face sticker on a gunshot wound.

"We need to schedule a D&C as soon as possible. Monday?"

I stared at my nails. "When can I get pregnant again?"

"You have to wait for at least two months. You really should take the pill for two cycles." She tapped her pen on the prescription pad on her desk.

"*Quoi?* The pill? But . . ." I was horrified.

"It's best. It will help your body get back in order." She slid a card across her desk. "Here is the name of a good therapist. You should see her, talk about what happened."

About being a total failure? About my body betraying me? About having a womb so hostile it consistently refused to grow a baby? Talking would do no good. I'd deal with this the way I'd always dealt with everything. On my own. Therapy was for the weak.

She leaned forward over her desk. "There is a *deuil,* a grieving that must follow."

"But what I really want is to start as soon as possible," I said. I looked at Laurent. He was staring into space.

"I know. But you must follow the steps. It is important." Her eyes were soft. "It is better to deal with the emotions." She fluttered her fingers up and down her torso in the vicinity of her heart, as if emotions were butterflies.

"*Docteur.*" It was my turn to lean forward. "I really just need to get pregnant again. As soon as possible. It's the only way for me. Unless . . ."

"Unless?"

"Unless there is something really wrong with me?"

"We've run many tests. So far, nothing has indicated that you could not have the baby you want. But . . ." she said.

"Yes?" Laurent found his voice.

"Maybe it is the stress." She raised her eyebrows.

"But everyone has stress," I said.

"Yes, and it affects different bodies in different ways," she said.

"So what I need to do is stay calm?" I asked.

"Not as easy as that. What you two should do is forget about all this for a while." She looked out the window, where, true to form, the Belgian sky continued to unleash its usual torrent of water. "Take a holiday. Go somewhere warm and sunny. With palm trees and a spa. Christmas vacation is coming up."

"I'm going to Pennsylvania for Christmas." But as I said it, I realized how impossible it was to make the trip.

Her face brightened. "Perfect. Being with family can be very therapeutic. Especially around the holidays."

Right. She probably came from one of those perfect families where discord was something only the piano had. If it dared.

"I'll see you on Monday." She made a note on my chart. We all rose and she walked us to the door. "And please," she said, "call Anne de Meyer. She is a friend and a very competent therapist."

We left the warm cocoon of the house and stood looking at each other in the downpour. Laurent struggled with the umbrella, pulled me close, and led me to the subway station.

Black Friday. Whoever came up with that one?

CHAPTER 18

Colette

Upgraded to first class. It was a short flight, but fun to fly in the lap of luxury, sipping chilled champagne. We were both dressed up a bit, him in black pants, a white shirt, and a soft leather jacket, and me in a multi-patterned off-the-shoulder Save the Queen dress I'd picked up for a song at a resale shop. It was the perfect dress for traveling because, not only did it fit great, it was comfortable and the fabric didn't wrinkle.

We landed just as the sun was setting, making the pyramid of the Luxor glow in the dying light. We breezed out of the airport, each holding a carry-on, and got into a cab for the Bellagio. Before checking in, we watched the dancing fountain right across from the Eiffel Tower. Daddy would say it was tacky but I was entranced by the whole splendiferous show. "I'm a bit surprised that you chose the Bellagio rather than the Venetian," I said as the fountains died down and we headed for the lobby. I bet Maman would have loved it here.

"Ah, well, the Venetian is very beautiful, but is Italian for tourists."

"Whereas the Bellagio?" I went through the door he held open for me.

"Is for true lovers of beauty." The multicolored sculpted glass everywhere in the lobby backed up his view. I drew a sharp breath and let the colors and soft light wash over me. The Christmas decorations enhanced rather than detracted from the décor.

We were treated like royalty as we checked in. Either the personnel had been magnificently trained or it was the Dante effect again. Probably a bit of both. We had two adjoining rooms. Dante slid over his credit card, but stopped me from pulling mine out.

"Later," he said. "We will arrange ourselves."

We passed through a garden with hanging birds, plants, and flags. The effect was one of being in a past era as designed by someone from the future.

"Here we will come and have our first drink in Las Vegas," he said, pointing to a glass-fronted room that housed a bar that was a wall of shimmering water.

"Wow. I mean, sure."

We were at the elevators. Two elevator doors sporting the telltale intricate *B*'s glided open. "How much did you bring? To gamble?"

"*Tutto.* All."

I gasped.

"But I will only risk one half. The other half I give to you. We put in the hotel safe, *si?*"

"Yeah, we wouldn't want to get burglarized or anything." Still, it was a lot.

"And you?" he asked.

"Ten thousand," I whispered. He whistled. I put the other twenty in the bank but I decided, win or lose, I'd play with my ill-gotten gains. It would almost be justice to lose it all. It seemed like a lot but it still didn't cover the thirty-two thousand that Wayne took. The bulk of which my mother had left me.

"The luck will smile on us. You will see."

I couldn't help but believe him.

Our rooms were gorgeous. I jumped on the bed and touched everything, even the miniature bottles of shampoo and conditioner in the bathroom. I unpacked and headed for the shower. I put on a bit more eye makeup than usual and dressed in one of my clingy black off-the-shoulder asymmetrical pieces, leaving one arm bare and the other covered. A passage from *The Great Gatsby* covered the entire sleeve and shoulder down to the top of my breast. I added red lipstick and earrings and mile-high heels.

I knocked softly on the door between our rooms, feeling a bit shy.

He opened the door wrapped in a robe, his hair damp. I couldn't help imagining his naked body underneath.

In my right hand I held up a hanger with the suit I'd made for him this week. I'd worked hard on it, staying up till past two every night. The suit was black with text around the cuffs and hidden under the lapels, tone on tone. To complete the ensemble, I chose a shirt the color of bluebonnets with tiny dollar signs in white silk embroidered down the front.

"It is *meraviglioso!* Almost as beautiful as you."

I would never get used to his big reactions. Delight radiated from his entire being. More payoff than I was used to.

He kissed my cheek and I felt my body react. *Down, boy!* I chided it. No replays of my night of shame. "But, what are these words?" He fingered the text. "*Francese?*"

"Yes, it's French. Serge Gainsbourg's lyrics to his version of the legend of Bonnie and Clyde."

"*Naturalmente.*" His grin was wicked. "He sing it with Jane Birkin."

"Also with Brigitte Bardot. I left out the tragic end, though." I grinned.

"Good, because we will have a happy one." He disappeared into the bathroom to change. I drifted to the window, the view a carbon copy of the one from my own room, feeling as if I were floating. I gazed down the Strip and, again, felt touched by enchantment, an undercurrent of excitement beginning to thrum through my body.

Dante came out of the bathroom. He spread his arms and turned with feline grace. "*Allora?*"

"Perfect. Almost." I retrieved my sewing kit from my room then kneeled down to cuff the pants. When I finished, I rose and pinned the sleeves to the right length. Every time my fingers grazed his skin, my body tingled with a thousand hot pinpricks. I moved away.

"It fits like you measure it on me. How?"

"I have a good sense of ... proportion, I guess. Space. Some people call it an eye."

"More than an eye. To make this, you have a soul. You are a genius, so much talent. This is your life, your devotion." He punctuated his words with his hands.

"It's not what I devote myself to. It's a hobby. Not real work."

One day, I must have been about fourteen, I was working at my sewing machine when my father peered over my shoulder and said, "You have a great mind. Don't waste it on being a seamstress. *Une midinette.*" I knew he wanted the best for us. And you didn't turn your back on family. Ever. Even if you created distance, the ties were eternal. For better or worse, he would always be my father.

"Nico, teaching is a profession *molto nobile, si?* But you, you create such beauty, give so much happiness. It is a gift from God." Dante stroked the fabric of the sleeve.

No one had ever put it that way before.

"This is a life's work. You are born to do this. Do you see?" He placed his hands on my shoulders and his eyes locked on to mine.

"I see that you look wonderful." But the raw material was of the highest quality.

"*Grazie a te.*" He went to the full-length mirror and looked at himself from the front and side.

Seeing him there wearing what I'd made, what I'd thought up and put together, how happy it made him hit me like a slap. "Now, go take it off, it will only take me a minute to hem and press."

"Then we go have drink?"

I smiled. As I threaded the needle, I looked proudly at my fingernails. Short, but not ragged, covered with a layer of pale pink polish.

A half an hour later, we floated down to our first night in Vegas. Being dressed up with Dante on my arm felt better than the prom or even how I felt on the day of my wedding. Before I realized there wasn't going to be one. We all grew up wanting to be princesses, at least for a few hours. This surge of pure joy was what the fairy tales were about.

We stopped for our first drink. Wine, of course. Cocktails, according to Dante, ruined the palate and made the mind fuzzy. After admiring the chocolate fountain and putting a leather satchel with half of Dante's money in the safe, we headed for the floor.

We got some chips, then, he led me to a blackjack table. We stood watching for a bit, then he took me to another.

"Do you know this game?" he asked.

"A bit. I know the principle. You?"

"I grow up in Italy playing with my family. Also with friends." He shrugged.

"And you always won?"

"Always. Until I begin to lose," he said.

He selected a table and we took our places. I bet the table minimum but Dante rolled higher. And we won. Several hands. Nothing excessive, but up just the same. My glass of champagne forgotten at my elbow, I played like a child. This was better than Christmas. I was about to place another bet when Dante took a chip off his pile and handed it to the dealer with a smile.

"*Grazie*," he said, "you bring much luck." And this tough-as-nails pit dealer's face turned scarlet as we left the table. We hit another. Not so lucky this time, but we were still up. Then another. I felt so vibrant, I wanted to keep playing. All night long, to keep this rush going. Dante touched my elbow.

"We must go." Another chip, another smile. "We have reservations for dinner."

"I don't want dinner. I want to play."

"Play or win?"

"Both." I looked over my shoulder at the gambling area we were leaving.

"Then you must trust me."

I really hadn't thought that much about food and that I'd be eating in strange restaurants. I could pretend. But my stomach rumbled.

He steered me to a restaurant. "The food here is very fresh, organic. And you see, the kitchen is impeccable." He swept his arm, as if he were showcasing the place. "Come. The kitchen is here." It was open to the dining area and I could see everything. It sparkled.

One of the chefs grinned at me. I took a deep breath. "Okay. Let's do it."

He had steak. While I couldn't quite bring myself to order red meat, I did get the wild Alaskan salmon that had still been swimming in the frigid coastal waters that very morning, the waiter assured me.

It was superb. All of it. It was so good that I even hazarded a bite of Dante's steak. It was wonderful. After sharing a crème brûlée and the ubiquitous but exquisite espresso, we left the muted elegance of the restaurant. I felt like a normal person.

"Thank you."

"No. You have given me so much. *Grazie.*" Our eyes locked. Slowly he pulled me toward him and kissed me. My entire reason for existing was wrapped up in that one kiss.

It's just lust, whispered my brain. I pushed him away.

"Dante, we don't want ... I don't want ..."

But he didn't release me. "I am crazy in love with you, don't you see?"

"But what about the other night?" I broke away, embarrassed by the memory. He took my chin in his hand and lifted my head so I was looking at him again. At his mouth. Then his eyes.

"You were not ready, still too broken. Now, you are changed." And he kissed me again. My whole body sang. I could no more have pushed him away than voluntarily stopped my heart from beating.

"Come, we play some more." He took my hand.

"I have a better idea."

"We play. We wait. Trust me." And I did. It was becoming a habit. Could I help it if he was the most trustworthy criminal I'd ever met?

That night, after winning, quite often, and quite a lot, he took me to bed for the first time. When his body united with mine, I felt whole. This was the way it should be. When a person paid so much attention to the other, with both body and heart, the result was ecstasy. I wanted to be one with him forever. We lay locked together for a long time. I felt him stiffen and slowly, so slowly he began to move again within me. I willed this to go on and on, to never stop.

When he finally pulled away, I didn't feel lost, the way I thought I would. I was complete. Making love with Dante was like performing a very slow, very intricate dance of joy.

I fell asleep in his arms. When I woke up, he was still sleeping. As if my gaze weighed heavy upon him, he opened his eyes and smiled.

"*Ciao, Nico.*" And that was when I knew. This was a man I could ride off into the sunset with. On a Vespa.

"I call room service for breakfast. What would please you?" He was propped up on his elbow.

I burrowed deeper into the snowy sheets and pulled him to me. "Let me show you."

We eventually had breakfast and returned to the outside world.

The entire weekend was a string of food, shopping, gambling, sex, more gambling, more sex. We went swimming. For once I barely drank. I wanted all my senses sharp. And despite the fact that everyone around me was smoking, even inside the casinos, never had I so little desired a cigarette.

On Sunday afternoon, we were playing blackjack at the Mandalay Bay when Dante's whole body stiffened. He put a warm hand on my arm and said, "It is time."

"Time?" I was focused on the game and the pile of money I'd just won. "Just a few more. Look at how much I'm winning." And I was. Beginner's luck, they called it. I'd more than doubled my original stake, which covered the money Wayne had taken and then some.

He shook his head. "No. Nico, look at me." I did. "It is time, now we walk away."

We both tipped the dealer. I felt bereft but as soon as we left the pit, I was okay. More than okay. Fantastic.

"Now what?"

"Now, we shop, we swim, we eat. Tonight I have a surprise." We left the casino. The desert wind chilled me. It was much colder in Vegas than I'd expected it to be.

"So what would you like to do now?"

"I'll give you one guess."

We did manage to make it out of bed eventually. We wound our way through the Bellagio until we reached a theater lobby.

"*O*," I said. "I've always wanted to see this. Did you know the creator of Cirque is Belgian?"

"*Cara,* his name is Franco Dragone. He is pure Italian."

"He was born and grew up in Belgium. In La Louvière. He still lives there." Jacqueline knew him.

"But still Italian. And a success in America. The best of all the worlds. *Come noi.*"

We had fifth-row orchestra seats. I lived and breathed the performance, quivered with every scene, every dive, every note of music and swirl of fabric. My heart spun up into my throat and stayed there.

The voice.

Like Jacqueline's.

The tears slid down my cheeks. It was for this gloriousness, to be able to produce such soaring heights of beauty, that she'd turned her back on us all those years ago. She'd stayed in Belgium when we returned to the States. Art is both selfish and selfless.

At intermission I almost texted her to tell her I loved her. Not wanting to deal with her astonishment stopped me. I'd tell her at Christmas. For the first time there was a glimmer of excitement at the prospect of our holiday reunion.

Dante and I headed back into the theater.

The costumes were a visual feast. I was almost, but not quite, on overload by the time it drew to a close. And suddenly, I knew what I had to do. I had to play my part in the world of pure passion, intense joy.

I was trembling as we walked out of the theater. "They should have called it *D* instead of *O*."

"Why?" asked Dante.

"Because it's the closest man can come to the divine here on earth."

Then, we walked in silence through the flashing lights, which suddenly seemed obscene, gaudy. Gambling no longer held the slightest attraction.

We stopped and bought rich dark chocolate and then went to the bar from the first night, the one with the wall of streaming water. We ordered champagne and clinked glasses.

"To Vegas," I said.

"No. To life."

"Yes."

Later that night, lying naked in bed, Dante was feeding me morsels of the best chocolate I'd ever had in my life outside of Belgium. I savored it.

"I finally get it," I said.

"What?" He handed me a glass of champagne.

"Why some people, lots of people actually, like my sister Gali, equate chocolate with perfect love, perfect sex." I felt as if I'd never really tasted it before. "It's . . ."—I searched for a word—". . . sublime." But for the whole experience and the man at my side, *sublime* didn't even come close.

I took a sip of champagne. "I'm developing expensive tastes," I teased. "You never should have brought me here. I wish we could stay this way forever."

"No. It would lose the magic. Always know when to walk away and when to stay. It is the secret to life."

But I didn't want to walk away. I wanted to stay like this for as long as I breathed. San Diego, the university, packing up my things, all seemed removed from the force of this single moment.

He shifted so he was lying on his side facing me, his head propped up on his hand. "You will come to Sonoma with me?"

I looked at him, at everything he was. Not what he had been, not what he would become, but just what was.

"Yes."

* * *

On the plane on the way home, coach this time but I didn't care, we made plans. I'd already asked my landlady if I could stow my stuff in her garage till after New Year's. I wasn't sure at the time where I would be taking it. Home to Pennsylvania had been the best I'd come up with. But here I was, the girl with a plan. I'd get in touch with Annick today, start talking to people. Sonoma was perfect because it was so close to a major city. A major city I loved, at that. If I needed a storefront boutique, I could set up there. Eventually. But I would start small. The Internet.

We were about twenty minutes from landing when I squeezed Dante's hand.

"*Si, cara?*"

"What are you doing for Christmas?"

He shrugged. "My friend, he is coming to California in January. I have no plans."

"Would you like to come and meet my family?"

"I thought you never ask." He grinned.

When the taxi dropped us off in front of my little house, I couldn't wait to start our new life. I put my key in the lock. Dante was right behind me on the stoop holding our bags. I pushed the door open.

And saw Wayne, sitting at the table eating a sandwich.

"Hey, babe." A lazy smile spread across his face.

I was stunned, as in, shot by a stun gun.

"Come here," he said, "otherwise I'm going to think that you aren't glad to see me." He put down his sandwich and got up. I took two wooden steps in his direction then stopped. He came over to me, pulling me close. I hardened like plaster.

"Hey, Colette, what's up with the surfboard act? Oh." He saw Dante standing in the doorway. "Who's your friend? Where are your manners? Come on in." He dropped his arms and I took a step back.

I found my voice. "Dante, this is"—I almost choked on the word—"Wayne."

"Nice to meet you, Dante." Wayne held out his hand. Dante

dropped the bags on the floor and looked at the proffered hand-shake as if it contained the herpes virus before taking it. I could tell Wayne was sizing up Dante. His chin lifted ever so slightly, a tiny smile played on his lips.

"Wayne, what are you doing here?" My voice was hoarse.

"Later, babe. Don't you see we have company?"

His hair was a bit shorter in the back and he'd lost his Southern California tan, but otherwise he looked the same: brown hair that flopped over his forehead above dark puppy eyes, same boyish good looks. He was wearing jeans and an old navy-blue college sweatshirt. He was so familiar, so much a part of who I was. My knees buckled.

I stole a glance at Dante. His eyes were narrowed and his lips were pressed in one straight line. He was also in jeans and a simple wine-colored crew-neck sweater. Such similar clothes, but they didn't look like they'd come from the same planet.

"You a friend of Colette's from the university?" asked Wayne.

"No, I—"

"—Something like that." I covered his words. "Dante, could I speak to you for a minute. Outside?"

He nodded. "Of course." He picked up his bag and turned to go.

"Bye, dude. Nice meeting you. Any friend of Colette's, you know?"

For an instant he hesitated then kept going. I followed him out to the sidewalk by the main house, out of earshot.

"Nico, you—"

"Listen. I have to do this my own way. I can't just kick him out," I said. I gnawed at my thumbnail. He took my hand away from my mouth and held it gently.

"I will have no problem with the kicking. Allow me." I'd never seen Dante's eyes so black. His body tensed.

"No." I realized I was being abrupt. "Please."

"But he is a monster." He shook his head.

"Don't you think you're exaggerating just a little?" I shivered. The sky was overcast, threatening rain.

"He cause you so much pain." Dante put his other hand on my shoulder.

"I know. I haven't forgotten. But I have to do this on my own. Make a clean break. He's a part of my life."

His eyes flashed.

"Was, I mean. He *was* a part of my life. A big part. I owe him this."

"You owe him nothing." He looked as if he were about to throw something. Like a car.

"Maybe not." I took a breath. "But I owe it to myself. I need closure."

"I do not like to leave you with him."

"It will be fine. I promise. Trust me."

"So now it is my turn to trust you?" he said.

"Yes. Do you?"

"*Bene.*"

"Tomorrow I'll meet you at—"

"Caffè Bella Luna," he said.

"That was just what I was about to say." It was our place. I smiled.

His hand moved to my cheek. "You see, Nico. We are of one mind, one heart."

"One o'clock?" I said.

He grinned. "*Si.*"

I watched him disappear down the street before I went back inside.

"Miss me? Still biting your nails, same old Colette," said Wayne. I dropped my hand. He tried to pull me to him once again, but I stepped away. It would be so easy to fall into his arms. It was where I'd lived for so long. The one constant in a world of variables. Colette loved Wayne, scratched on my heart like graffiti.

But things had changed. I'd changed.

"What did you do with the place? What's all this?" He indicated the furniture and suddenly my anger burst out.

"What did you expect me to do, Wayne? Would you have preferred I sit on the floor for the past two months? And with what money? How *could* you?" All of the old anger, old hurt resurfaced and I banged my hand on the table. Hard.

"Yeah, about that." He began to pace. "I did it for us."

"Us?" I laughed.

"As in me and you." He swiveled and looked at me.

"Could you explain how taking the furniture and all of my money, leaving an 'I'm sorry' note was for *us*?" I grabbed a chair and sat down, glaring at him. "Enlighten me." If he got out of this one, he could take his act to Vegas and make a fortune as king of the escape artists.

"Aww, babe, don't be like that. I was hoping we could skip all this and just take up where we left off."

"Not a chance." My body felt like cold steel. "And stop calling me babe."

"Okay, okay. If that's the way you want it. But just hear me out, all the way through. Don't interrupt me. I'll tell you my side." He started pacing again.

"Sure. Because frankly, from my side, it really stinks." I stopped myself from biting my nail.

"See, you're already doing it," he said.

"What?"

"Being all hard and cynical and shit."

"I'll make an effort."

"Good. You look great by the way." He gave me a big smile.

I looked down at my glittery Vegas T-shirt and black leggings. The shirt was tacky but I loved it anyway. "Don't change the subject. You were about to tell me how taking the furniture, my money, and abandoning me was for my benefit." I ticked his crimes off on my fingers.

"I'm getting there." He ran his hands through his hair and sat opposite me. The smell of his half-eaten sandwich was nauseating. "Back in September, I felt like a failure, you know?"

I nodded once, unwilling to give in to the pity he was trying to inspire in me.

"No job, no prospects, just hanging around the house all day."

"I remember that part."

"Geez, Colette. Give me a break, wouldya?"

"All right." I relented.

"So I decide to go back East and see if I couldn't drum up some, uh, family contacts, you know? And it worked. It took a while, but I just landed a great job with Multitech in Boston—"

"But—"

He held up his hands. "You promised to hear me out."

"Okay."

"It was really hard at first, lots of dead ends. But I finally got picked up by Multitech. I used the money to put a down payment on a great apartment. One of those brownstone tree-lined streets you always go on about. And the furniture, well, I used it to start furnishing the place. I've been sleeping on the couch, figuring we could pick out a bed together."

"But why didn't you tell me all this?" I started on my nail again.

"Because what if I failed? I couldn't face you until I succeeded. And Colette, there are so many colleges out there, it'll be a cinch for you to line up a new teaching job. You just have to give your notice—"

"That won't be a problem." My voice sounded gray to my ears.

"Great! Fantastic! See? It's all falling into place."

"But Wayne, an e-mail, would that have been so hard? I would have understood."

"You don't get it." He covered my hand with his and started playing with my fingers. "I love you. I felt I needed to be worthy. You stood by me all those months when I was a mess. You always stand by me. You know I love you, right?"

I didn't trust my voice.

"And you love me." It was not a question.

I looked at him. His brown eyes pleaded. How did you stop loving someone who'd been a part of your life for so long?

You didn't.

"Yeah. I do." It was true.

"Colette, baby." Suddenly he was kneeling on the floor at my feet, both of my hands clasped in his. I realized how cold my hands were when they made contact with his warm ones. "Will you marry me?" He let go to reach into the pocket of his jeans. He pulled out a pale blue box and flipped it open to reveal a round solitaire in the classic Tiffany setting. It glittered in a sudden shaft of sunlight from the window.

Here it was. Everything I'd always wanted. Right here, at my feet.

I took a deep breath. And held it.

"Say something. In case you hadn't noticed, I just proposed." His eyes were wide.

I let my breath out.

"Yes." This was stronger than I was. Destined. He grinned and slipped the ring on my finger. It was too big.

"Great! Terrific!" He got up and gave me a quick kiss on the lips. "You hungry?" he asked, sitting down again.

"No." I looked at the ring hanging lopsided on my finger. I could get it resized. I waited for the rush of joy I was supposed to feel, the giddy excitement, but so far, nothing. Maybe it took a few minutes to kick in.

"Same old Colette." He wolfed down the rest of his sandwich. "What did you do, get religion?" He pointed at the crèche.

I shook my head.

"Besides," he said, after swallowing the last bite, "you need me. You have terrible taste in furniture when I'm not around."

I put the ring back in the box. I was afraid I might lose it.

I arrived at the Bella Luna a few minutes before one. Dante was already there chatting easily with the waitress. He was wearing the T-shirt I made for him after our first job. Wayne's ring was in the inside pocket of my bag. I was just back from Tiffany's in Fashion Valley with the news that the ring couldn't be resized in time for my trip home.

Dante smiled when he saw me and it felt like the sun had just come out. He waved me over. When I reached the table, he was standing and holding out my chair. He leaned in to kiss me but I turned my head and the kiss landed on the corner of my mouth.

He sat opposite me, his grin gone. "So, he is kicked out? *Sì?*"

"Dante—"

"You tell me after. First we order."

I realized I was starving. I hadn't eaten anything since breakfast yesterday morning in Vegas. I set my bag on the floor beside my chair. My heart was beating too fast, too hard. *Whoa boy!*

"Shall I . . . ?" He indicated the menu.

"Go ahead."

He ordered two *risotto ai funghi* and a bottle of white wine.

"*Come stai?*" asked our waitress.

"*Bene. Grazie,*" I said. I realized I wasn't going to have much of a chance to learn Italian after all.

"So, now," he said, and watched the young woman leave before turning to me. "You have thrown him away?"

"Out"—automatic grammar correction still on strong—"No."

"I understand it is difficult. *Quando, allora?* I can help you."

"Dante, I'm sorry," I said to the saltshaker.

"For what? You not look at me. *Perché?*"

I could feel his gaze. I looked up. "What we have, it's great, but—" I said this to his left ear.

"It is better than great. Great is a meal, the one we will share now. We have, together . . . the true life."

I turned my fork over and over on the tablecloth. "No. It *was*"—I paused and insisted on the past tense—"amazing but it wasn't real. It was a fairy tale."

"You are *molto intelligente,* Nico. But right now, you say stupid things."

I finally raised my eyes to meet his. He didn't look angry. Or confused. Our waitress came and filled our water glasses. I gave her a smile, grateful for the interruption.

I took a sip of water. "Let me explain."

"No. I will explain. Seeing him again was a shock, no?"

I nodded.

"And you have been together for *tanti anni?*"

"Since I was fifteen," I admitted.

"Too long. It is normal that it is difficult. But such a man. He is not a man. He is a little boy who takes money from a woman, who abandons her, not once, but twice. How can you believe he will not start again?" He finished, sounding like an attorney who had just delivered the irrefutable closing argument in an open-and-shut case.

"He's changed. He's . . . grown." I needed to make him understand.

Our waitress came back, this time with our wine. Dante tasted it and nodded. She filled our glasses and placed the bottle in a sweating bucket. Another Gavi, I noticed. Suddenly I was very thirsty.

"*Grazie,*" I said. Might as well get as much practice in while I still could. I drank half of my glass of wine. I knew it must have been good, but I could barely taste it.

"Nico, I know this type of person. He is a taker—one who steals."

I shot him a glance.

He made a face. "Not of things. Things can be replaced. But of the heart. He will break you again."

"You can't know that. You don't know him." I drained the rest of my wine. His glass was still full.

"But I do. He is the kind who will love you only when you are broken. To feel strong." He took my hand. I curled my fingers in to hide my nails, bitten down to the quick.

I kept shaking my head, probably looking like some stupid windup doll. "It's not like that."

Our food came but neither of us touched it.

"So what we have, for you it is . . . *niente?* Nothing?" A slight frown appeared between his eyebrows.

"Of course not! It's something. It's a big something. But Dante, it's not real life. It was a lovely dream. Wayne is real."

"Life does not have to be hard to be real." He picked up his knife and fork, then set them down again. "Can you say that you do not love me?"

I bit my lip. "No, I can't." I loved them both. I had a sudden flash of myself as the Jeanne Moreau character in *Jules et Jim,* loving two men, the absolute ménage à trois. But the thought of Dante and Wayne being friends was so absurd, it made me smile. Life was not a French film.

He caught my smile and latched onto it. "*Allora,* I do not accept." He put his napkin on the table, abandoning all pretense of eating. "I will give you one week. One week from today to think about what life you want."

"But—"

"Listen to me. In one week, it is the day before you go home for Christmas. If you want our life, you come to me. Here. I will wait for you. Tuesday. Eight o'clock. If I don't see you, I go."

"No, Dante, this has to be good-bye," I whispered.

"What are you frightened of?" He threw some bills on the table and we both got up, leaving our untouched risotto to congeal.

CHAPTER 19

Magali

As the middle sister, being neither the star, the son, nor the adored baby, I'd chosen to play the role of keeper of traditions. I made the holidays happen. I created space in my home and my life. My gaze swept across the house. It was perfect—well, as perfect as my Pennsylvania two-story colonial would get. The Christmas decorations were up. I had enough cookies in the freezer for the annual ice-skating fundraiser for school and all the bake sales, caroling parties, unexpected drop-ins. There was still the half-finished art project and occasional Barbie, along with Elly's and Charlotte's books lying around, but they were more or less contained. For the moment.

Nevertheless, today marked my "it" day. Waiting till after the New Year was a cliché.

I'd had half a grapefruit for breakfast and was feeling virtuous. I'd forgotten just how filling grapefruit and black coffee could be.

I was dressed all in black, my hair pulled back, a long silk scarf wound around my hair with the ends trailing over my shoulder, my glasses perched on my head. With better makeup, this would be my look for my jacket photo.

I flipped open my Mac, then stopped. I was at my kitchen desk, where I'd written all seven of my previous books. I needed to find another space. Great American Novels weren't written in kitchens.

With mounting dismay, I realized I didn't have a workspace of my own outside the kitchen. Leo had converted one of the four bedrooms into an office. He often holed up in there catching up on work. The other spare room would have been ideal but Art was still staying with us.

The dining room table?

Too formal and public.

Maybe building a fire and curling up in the soft leather armchair in the living room? That would be cozy and inspiring. I could be the Great American Armchair Novelist.

I set about building a fire, crisscrossing logs from the pile, adding dried twigs and newspaper. I lit last Friday's *New York Times* front page, feeling a bit guilty for burning words—*Fahrenheit 451* had had a huge impact in junior high.

Smoke promptly poured into the room, setting off the smoke detector. Gasping, I reached over, yanked the flue, then grabbed a pillow and fanned the device until it stopped shrieking.

Once everything seemed to be under control, I grabbed the accordion thingy—what was it called? A writer should know the names of things. Note to self: Google accordion thingy before starting novel. Soot flew into the room, covering me as well as a good portion of the hearth and floor. *Merde!*

At least the fire seemed to be catching. And I was wearing black, albeit with a nice smoky scent.

The alarm went off again.

"Shut up!"

I tried to open a window, then remembered we'd put in the storm windows three weeks ago—so I opened the front door instead, tracking soot all over the floor and my freshly-shampooed-for-Thanksgiving rug.

Leaving the door ajar, I fanned the fire detector until it quieted.

The fire itself was now roaring, but my perfect room and serious author clothes were covered with a fine layer of ash. I lugged the vacuum cleaner out of the hall closet and vacuumed the floor, then went up to take a shower and change clothes.

Back in the living room, in jeans and a baggy sweatshirt—note to self: buy more black—it was freezing. I'd forgotten to shut the door and the fire was dead.

Maybe the living room in front of a roaring fire hadn't been such a hot idea after all. The metaphor made me wince. I should be better than that if I wanted to be a great novelist. More original. More something.

Anger fizzed as if someone had shaken a bottle of soda inside me. I slammed the door. There was no space for me. How was I supposed to dedicate myself to great literature without, to paraphrase Virginia Woolf, a room of my own?

In the kitchen I put on a fresh pot of coffee. I should run to the discount kitchen-supply store and buy one of those single-cup espresso machines. I think better with caffeine.

My stomach rumbled but I ignored it.

When the coffee was ready, I poured myself a cup and sat down. My stomach growled again. Giving up, I cut myself a large slice of the pumpkin cranberry walnut loaf to have with it. After all, pumpkin is a squash so technically a vegetable and everyone knew how good cranberries were. Besides, I'd burned tons of calories vacuuming.

I mentally scanned every room in the house: master bedroom, girls' bedrooms, two spare rooms all occupied. Dining and living room, for everyone, which left me . . .

Out in the cold.

Or in the kitchen.

No.

But since I was here, I might as well check my e-mail and Google the accordion thingy.

A message from Terry d'Agostino, the boy-wonder agent, which

I didn't open. I knew I should. Ana kept pressing me to make a decision. One from Jacqueline telling me not to worry about Daddy, it was probably a midlife crisis.

I've heard of sports cars and hot blondes, but tea and scones to make yourself feel young? I answered.

A *bellow*. That was what that accordion-thingy was called. I sipped my coffee, feeling writerly.

Then it hit me. I snapped shut my laptop. A stroke of genius. The attic. I'd clear out a space in the attic, I could put all the boxes to one side, and take over the other as a writing space.

I went up, looked around, and sneezed.

It was dusty.

And cold.

And messier than I'd remembered.

I'd do it anyway. If I could tackle this, I could tackle anything.

I carried all the cartons and stacked them against the right wall, then pushed a trunk that had belonged to Leo's grandfather in front of them. I used the trunk to store fabric and old clothes suitable for costumes. I opened it and pulled out a large oblong tablecloth with a paisley pattern and draped it over the cartons.

I shoved Tante Sola's old table and a chair across the floor and by the dormer window, facing out.

I swept and vacuumed, cleaned the windows, polished the table and chair. I climbed on a chair and covered the naked bulb hanging in the center of the room with a faux-Tiffany lampshade.

In the kitchen, I grabbed a cobalt bud vase and plucked a gerbera daisy from the Thanksgiving bouquet Ana had brought and set both on my table. In the garage, I found an old space heater we'd used when the oil heater had gone on the blink six winters ago.

When I was done, I surveyed the result of my labors. My laptop sat in the center of the table flanked by freshly sharpened pencils, a spanking new notebook, and my Montblanc fountain pen—the one Leo had gotten me for my first cookbook signing. Something was missing. I ran back downstairs and grabbed three picture frames from the kitchen: one of Leo and the girls on a sailboat last summer; one of me and my sisters; and lastly, one of Maman, a candid, snapped as she was striding down the city street, a scarf around her head, oversized sunglasses and holding a clutch à la Jackie. Then I got out my mother's diary and the photograph Daddy had given me.

I had created my very own writer's garret. Sitting down, I drew a breath, feeling more than a bit like Colette. Author Colette, not kid sister Colette.

I flipped open my Mac and created a new blank document in Word. I typed *Chapter One* and centered it.

Then I began:

All her life, she'd known that she was destined for greatness.

Or was "for great things" better? No, "greatness," definitely, "greatness." Now what?

She would change the world.

A good start. A great one, in fact. This would be an Important Book. Daddy would sit up and take notice. Jacqueline would be envious of me for a change.

I pictured myself at my publication party, drinking champagne and wearing couture. Or even better, one of my sister's original designs. I'd compare notes with Barbara Kingsolver, who would become a dear, close friend. I'd say something witty and Michiko Kakutani—whom I would call *Michi*—would laugh in delight.

Ana would wonder if retirement had been such a good idea after all. Daddy would be telling everyone that I was his daughter.

Colin Firth would star in the movie version.

Life would be perfect.

I looked at the clock and realized with annoyance that it was time to pick the girls up from school.

I saved my document and named the file "Novel One."

On my way out, I realized I was starving so I cut myself another chunk of pumpkin loaf and, for once, didn't set the table.

I ate it in the car.

Serious novelists don't have time to eat properly. Besides, I hadn't had that many calories today.

I found the note propped on the counter when I got home.

Bye, Sis,
Had to leave. Thanks for everything.
Merry Christmas. I love you,
Art.

Wringing my brother's neck now topped my to-do list.

The food for our annual Christmas caroling party needed preparing. I couldn't help but feel that it was my fault for not being able to hang on to my brother. At least Daddy never knew he'd been here.

And Colette, sounding oddly flat, had told me that she had exciting news. Also that she would be bringing Wayne. My heart sank at the thought. Not that I disliked him, I just basically couldn't stand the guy. Especially for my baby sister. Of course I told her it was okay. I picked up my offset frosting knife and dipped it into the chocolate mousse.

Colette and I had decided to set aside the twenty-third for just the two of us. Which would go over big with Jacqueline, missing out on the sisterly reunion. I dusted the *bûche* with confectioner's sugar, then added a few sugar mushrooms.

Although since she was flying in on the twenty-fourth and was staying with Tante Sola, it probably wouldn't register.

I turned my attention to the appetizers. With a spatula, I slid the tiny cheese pastries onto a green tray.

Done. I just had to clean up the kitchen and change. I looked around and spotted my new boots waiting for me at the bottom of the stairs. I'd bought them at Saks during a whirlwind Christmas shopping spree with Tante Sola. I couldn't wait to show them to Colette. They were Collection Privée, black, low-heeled, supple as if elves had hand-stitched them for my feet. I also paid way too much for them, a fact that Leo waved off with a "You deserve them."

These were boots made for walking . . . into my new life. Serious writer boots. Boots that made a person worthy of notice, of respect. Boots that said, "Now look here. I expect to be taken seriously."

Tante Sola had offered to pay for half but I'd refused. She was always generous. I wondered if she would ever be content. My god-mother was the person you could count on to phone on June twenty-third to lament the fact that the days were now officially growing shorter and winter was on its way.

As I finished wiping the counters, my thoughts turned back to my brother. I'd bet Syd knew something. Maybe tonight when everyone had gone home, I'd corner her.

I'd wear my new boots with new jeans, also from Saks. I'd never believed the rumors about how well-cut designer jeans could trans-form your derrière, but seeing my ass in these made them worth every cent. I was spritzing on perfume when I heard the back door open. Leo. Right on time.

I needed him to build a fire. Following Monday's fiasco, I'd de-cided to delegate this duty for the rest of my days.

He came into the bedroom. "Everything looks great. And you look amazing." He grabbed me and put his hands on my ass. "Do we have time? Where are the girls?" he murmured into my hair.

"With Tante Sola. At Saks. She took them to buy Christmas dresses."

"Sweet." He kissed my neck.

"But they should be here in about ten."

"Enough time. Let's get you out of these jeans."

"But I just got dressed."

"Then you know how. Won't be hard to do an encore."

The phone rang.

"Let it ring."

"I can't. We're having a party, need I remind you? It might be important." But suddenly my body wasn't cooperating with my head. After all, voice mail had been invented for a reason.

Afterward, I really did look good, for me. My hair was just a little bit tousled and my face glowed. All the creams and facials in the world couldn't replicate that.

I checked my messages.

It's Syd. I'm sorry Gali, but I have to cancel for tonight. I'm sick. She coughed. *Don't want to contaminate everyone at the party. Sorry. Love you.*

Merde! I'd have to corner her some other time. We had plans to go out on Tuesday. If she cancelled, I'd march over to her house with a gallon of chicken soup (or maybe a nice beef bouillon) and have it out.

Tuesday. Syd, plied with alcohol, and grilled.

There was a missed call from my father. I'd call him back tomorrow.

Downstairs I saw that Leo had already gotten the fire blazing. The door burst open and in bounced the girls followed by Tante Sola, laden with bags from—where else?—Saks.

"Momma, we got the prettiest dresses!"

"Really? Let me see."

They pulled red velvet and lace from the bags, held them up in front of themselves, and twirled. Dresses from a storybook. Plus shoes, ribbons, and tights.

Leo whistled.

"It's too much," I told my aunt, kissing her cool cheek.

She waved away my protest. "They are angels. Absolute angels." There were a lot of iffy things that could be said about my godmother. But I loved that, as far as she was concerned, my girls could do no wrong.

"You should have more children, Magali, you do it so well. The world needs more beautiful children."

I was in shock. A compliment. I waited for the backlash, the sting, but nothing. Her eyes were shining at my girls who preened before their captive audience of one.

"Come now. We will choose the perfect clothes for tonight." Charlotte put her hand in her great-aunt's. Elly gave me a kiss and galloped up the stairs behind them.

I turned to Leo. "That was Syd. She cancelled."

"Interesting."

"What's interesting about it?" I was more than a little annoyed.

"Art is gone and now Syd is sick? Two plus two . . ."

"Doesn't always equal four." I felt hot and pushed up my sleeves.

"Hey, take it easy."

Tagged onto my nagging worry-worm about my brother and Syd was an ever-underlying fear that Simon would show up again—though he should be working at the theater on a Friday night in December. I still couldn't accept that he was a shady character. It was one of the topics I'd been wanting to rehash with Syd.

It would have to keep until Tuesday. Sick or not.

My aunt and the girls came down. They looked beautiful. Their hair was freshly brushed and held back by new barrettes. Each one had on a pair of jeans and a Christmas sweater. Elly's was red with a Christmas tree appliquéd on it, Charlotte's green with Rudolph.

Tante Sola sidled up to me and whispered, "It's Saint Nicolas, I assume you are ready? Where are the carrots for his ass?" I put down the tray of glasses and mugs. There would be eggnog, both spiked and unspiked, hot wine, and a nice Crémant de Bourgogne for those who didn't like sweet drinks. And for the children, sparkling apple cider and hot chocolate.

"His donkey."

"It is the same."

"So it is. We don't celebrate," I whispered back. In Belgium, children put out their shoes at night after the parents had set out a glass of cognac or schnapps, and a few carrots for the donkey who carried the children's gifts. Not as PC as Santa with his milk and cookies, but if given the choice on a cold December night, I'd probably choose a nice warming brandy too. Good children would wake up to toys and candy while those who weren't so good would find coal in their shoes, left by the Père Fouettard—a character used by parents to scare children into good behavior. Saint Nicolas was also the patron saint of teachers and students, so it was a big deal in Belgium.

"Why not?"

The girls had disappeared safely into the kitchen. "It's just complicated. I told the girls that since Santa is always so very generous with them, we'd instructed Saint Nicolas to give their share to poor children who aren't as lucky."

"It is a nice story. But the tradition." She raised an eyebrow.

The party was a success. Once all the savory appetizers were devoured and everyone had had a drink, we went around the neighborhood singing carols. Syd's house remained stubbornly dark through a rendition of "We Wish You a Merry Christmas" that probably registered on the Richter scale.

Once back home, I put out the desserts: *tarte au Maton,* a meltingly delicious pastry from Grammont whose recipe has been classified as part of our national heritage and is protected by the EU; as well as traditional galettes from my grandmother's recipe; and some homemade *speculoos,* a spicy biscuit eaten in Belgium during the holidays. And the *bûche,* of course. The desserts disappeared gratifyingly quickly. I loved friends who ate.

When everyone had gone home and the house was cleaned up, I sat on the sofa with a glass of hot wine. Leo was in his study. I was always a bit wired after a party and it was only ten-thirty, normal when a party included children. The warm wine would help me sleep.

Leo walked into the room cradling a two-inch stack of paper.

"What's that?"

"Something I've been working on."

"A big something."

He seated himself next to me. "I've been working on it for a long time."

I looked at the sheaf of paper in his arms. He put it down on the coffee table, wiping the already clean surface with the sleeve of his sweater before laying it down.

"It's something I'd like you to read," he said.

"Because I know so much about the law. Good choice. Commendable."

He stood and squatted before the fire, poking the embers. "It's a novel," he said to the grate.

"A what?"

He turned to face me, a bashful grin on his face. "A thriller."

"You wrote a novel? *You* wrote a novel?" I felt a stab of emotion I couldn't put my finger on.

"I know it's a cliché. Lawyers writing novels." He laughed.

"Why didn't you say something?" Betrayed. That's what I was feeling. I was the writer, the aspiring novelist. That was my dream.

"Aw, Gali." Suddenly he was beside me on the couch, pulling me close. My limbs were novocained. "I didn't know if I could. If I could finish it, you know?"

I did know. I stared at the stack of paper as if it were about to jump up and attack me.

I pulled away. "How long has this been going on?" I couldn't help it, I felt as if he'd cheated on me.

"A year give or take. Look, it's probably lousy. I need you to tell me if it's any good." He looked at the manuscript, then at me.

I swallowed. "Sure." I forced a smile. "When? Now?"

He looked hopeful.

I laughed in spite of myself. "I'm exhausted. I need sleep."

"Of course. Of course. But this weekend?"

"Sure," I repeated.

My thoughts drifted over the week I'd just had. Though I'd visited my garret several times, I hadn't written a word. How could I already have writer's block after just two sentences? There were so many things going on in my life, my head was brimming. Maybe I should take up yoga? But how would that stop all the demands that kept calling me away—calling me away from my calling. If I could just sort it all out, I could clear enough mental space to get the book done. The cookbooks had been so easy and . . . fun. I sighed. I grabbed my laptop and tiptoed up the stairs to the attic. I switched on my lamp, noticing the fine layer of dust that had resettled on my table. I ignored it and opened my computer, then stared at the screen.

"Write! Just write it! Write something profound!" I willed myself. But nothing came.

I went down to the kitchen. I opened a cupboard and stared at the pans and tins. But for once, I didn't feel like baking.

CHAPTER 20

Jacqueline

Monday dawned bright and cold. Figured. For once there was sun in Belgium and all I could see was how it spotlighted every defect, every speck of dust. The procedure was swift. I sleepwalked through most of it. The drugs helped.

Upon returning home, I went back to bed. This time, my legs could barely hold me up. Someone had put on fresh sheets. Not smoothed out the way I liked them but I was too groggy to care. They were soft and smelled like summer.

By the time I woke up, it was dark. I wrapped myself in a cream pashmina and went downstairs.

Laurent was sitting at his keyboard, looking a bit rumpled in jeans and an unironed shirt. He had earphones on and hadn't heard me come in. I went over to him and smoothed back his hair. He looked up and pulled me down on the bench next to him, removing the earphones. He hung on to my hand.

"I'm happy you're up. How do you feel?" he asked.

"Okay. I feel okay." I was spotting a bit, but really couldn't feel anything.

"Are you hungry?"

I wasn't. "Maybe a little," I said. To have this talk, I needed him not to be worried, to trust that I was back to normal. "Working on something?"

"Yeah. I was about to go to Alain's house. We're going to play around with it a bit. And to rehearse for our gig at Soleil Bleu."

"That's right. I'd completely forgotten."

"We both had other things on our mind."

"I'm fine. Come on, let's have some wine and cheese." I closed the fallboard and stood, pulling him up.

"I didn't buy any bread."

"We'll figure it out." We went to the kitchen and I yanked open the refrigerator door. It felt like months rather than days since I'd been here. "Oh, I know. What about this?"

"David's care package from Thanksgiving. I'd forgotten about it," he said.

Tears pricked my eyes. On Thanksgiving, I'd still been blissfully pregnant. I swallowed. "Let's heat it up. It would be a crime to let it go to waste."

"I'll get the wine," said Laurent.

Once we were seated with David's feast in front of us, I found that I did have an appetite.

Laurent filled our glasses. "Did you give any thought to calling that therapist?"

"No. I don't need it. What I do need is something no therapist can give me." I drank. "This is nice. What is it?" I turned the bottle to look at the label. A Chateauneuf-du-Pape.

He cut a piece of duck. "Jacqueline, it's too soon."

"I'm not entirely sure I believe that. I think it's just standard procedure. She's worried about my psychological state. But again"—I took a bite of *gratin dauphinois*—"I'm fine. Or I will be once we get another baby on the way."

Laurent sighed and put down his knife and fork. He took a big gulp of wine before speaking. "I don't think I can do it again."

"What?" I stopped eating.

"It's too hard, Jacqueline. On you, on me, on us."

"But that doesn't mean we should give up. Is that what you

want? To give up?" I realized I was becoming shrill. I took a deep breath and drained my glass of wine.

"You see? What it's doing to you?" His tone was gentle.

"But we *want* children." I didn't understand.

"Of course. But I also want to live. Now. Not throw all my heart into a future that I have no control over."

"So, you don't want a baby anymore?" I banged my knife against the edge of my plate. "Sorry."

"I don't want another three-ring circus of hormones and doctors' appointments. More hormones, Jackie?" He shook his head.

"If that's what it takes. It's not that bad," I lied.

"No? I've had a lot of time these past few days to do research on IVF. It's not a panacea."

"You Google a subject and all of a sudden you're an expert?" I drummed my fingers on the table.

"It's nuts. Did you know that some people go broke putting themselves through several IVF attempts? Sometimes, it never takes. I've been giving this a lot of thought. I want you back. I want us back." He tried to take my hand but I snatched it away. Then I reconsidered, and placed my hand in his.

I took a deep breath. "We can have it all. Us and a baby. You're not really giving up on our baby, are you?"

"Stay here." He got up and left the room. When he returned he was carrying a manila file. "This," he said, handing me the file, "could be our answer."

I looked at the folder on the table. In his neat European script, he'd written *Adoption* across the top.

I stood, nearly toppling my chair. I grabbed it just in time.

"*Pas question!* Out of the question." I couldn't even look at it.

"But why?" He picked up the folder and held it toward me.

"Because! Because . . . I want my own baby." I was blinking back tears. "I mean *our* own."

"I think you were right the first time."

"Just . . . take that thing away." I wrapped the pashmina tight around my body and went upstairs. There were things I could not talk about. Not even to Laurent.

Back in my bedroom, I heard the clink of plates and silverware, water running. Then silence. I sat on the bed and waited for him to come up.

Then came the sound of the front door opening and closing.

I stood and remade the bed, exactly the way I liked it. Then I got in, curled into a ball, and pulled the covers over my head.

The next morning we managed to avoid saying a single word to each other.

The advantage of not having announced my pregnancy was that I didn't have to tell anyone in the company what had happened. Laurent had been right about that.

It felt good to be back at the theater. The people surrounding me were like a motley second family. I embraced Thierry, having forgiven him his betrayal from a few weeks back. François was almost dancing in his excitement.

"*Allez*. Let us begin," he said.

Odd. The concert was a tradition. We knew the drill, though the selection changed every year. But this was our time to relax and enjoy. I felt light and happy. Here, I wasn't the one who couldn't. I was good enough. Better than good enough. And with a light rehearsal schedule, no stress about learning lines, great clothes and makeup but no elaborate costumes and accessories, I was excited. It would be just us and the musicians. It would be me as me on the stage, not me playing a part.

I opened my mouth, prepared to sing, but nothing came out.

I didn't want to talk. To go home. To see anyone I knew. I ducked into a café and ordered coffee, but didn't drink it. The garçon came over to ask me if anything was wrong with the coffee. What was he, American? I shook my head. Put some coins on the table and fled.

I ended up at Edith Cavell and sat by Rachel for a while. One of the nurses came over and placed a hand on my shoulder. "No singing today?" she asked.

"No," I whispered. "My voice is tired."

"That happens. You should drink some hot tea with lemon and honey."

She left and I whispered to Rachel, "Beautiful little baby. It's all in front of you. Be deliriously happy. And strong."

Back outside, I wandered. It was dark, though it couldn't be later than five-thirty or so. Without realizing where I was heading I ended up at the one place I needed to be, the one place I could be. I used my key to let myself in.

My grandmother's face lit up at the sight of me.

I burst into tears.

And told her everything. Almost. How unbearable it was to lose yet another baby, how I knew I should get some therapy but was afraid, Laurent and his adoption file, Rachel, Shoshanna moving away. And how I'd lost my voice. Maybe this time for good.

"Nonsense," she said. "What you need, is some food. Unless you're sick? You are not sick, are you?"

"No." *Just my heart.*

"Then you need food. *Ça va s'arranger.*"

I sighed. "I'm not hungry."

"*L'appétit vient en mangeant.*" Your appetite will come as you eat.

She poured me a glass of Martini blanc—sweet white vermouth in a small glass with one ice cube. I sipped it. It tasted both sweet and bitter at the same time. The cool syrupy drink slid easily down my throat.

"What are you making?" I asked.

"Just a *biftek-frites-salade.*" Steak, french fries, and salad, one of Belgium's national dishes, the other being mussels and *frites.* Mamy used a lot of garlic when cooking her steaks. It was wonderful.

"Let me help," I said.

"You should rest." She took her yellow bowl and went to the cellar. When she came back, it was filled with potatoes.

"I've been resting. I need to do something," I said.

She eyed me and probably decided I could be trusted around a knife.

"*Alors,* peel these." She handed me the bowl. "I'm going to telephone Laurent and tell him you're having dinner with me."

"Okay." I set to work. I unfolded a section of yesterday's newspaper over the table and started peeling. I listened to her speaking with my husband with half an ear.

It felt good to be doing something, anything I could actually complete. Once peeled, the potatoes were set to soak in water, so some of the starch would seep out. While they were soaking I peeled and crushed garlic while my grandmother washed and spun some lettuce for our green salad. Once the potatoes were dried and sliced into thick sticks, she began the actual cooking. I cringed a bit at the amount of butter she used for the steak but the aroma of garlic butter was intoxicating. While she was busy, I set the table in the other room. In traditional Belgian homes, the kitchen was for cooking, not for eating. A kitchen in which you ate was called, unsurprisingly, a *cuisine américaine*.

The bell rang.

"Answer the door, *ma belle*." I hoped it wasn't Laurent. I just wanted to be alone with my grandmother. Have dinner. Watch some TV with her after the dishes were done. I opened the door and there stood David, holding a pie.

"David?"

"Right the first time."

"What are you doing here?"

"You have just perfected the art of the gracious welcome," he said. "Well? May I come in or shall I just stand out here freezing my tush off and letting a perfectly wonderful apple pie go to waste. Besides, shouldn't you be at rehearsal? You're dressed for it."

I was still in my black rehearsal clothes. "Of course. I'm sorry. Come in." I stepped aside, still perplexed.

Mamy Elise came into the hallway drying her hands on a dishtowel. "David. How nice. Right on time. *Ah! La belle tarte. Merci.*" He kissed her on the cheek. She took the pie from him before disappearing back into the kitchen.

"*Fais comme d'habitude,*" she said.

"*Merci.*"

Comme d'habitude? As usual? He noticed my confusion and reddened a bit.

"Do you make a habit of this?" We walked to the dining room.

"Well, I adore your grandmother, that's no secret." He sat.

"No, you're not alone in that," I said. I got him a glass from the cabinet. I held up the bottle of vermouth.

He nodded. "Exactly. So, once or twice a week, I come over and have dinner with her. She always makes too much for just one. Then I clean up and we play cards."

The vermouth I was pouring sloshed over the side of the glass.

He got up and got a dishrag to wipe up the spill. "Gin, actually. She's a master card shark."

I thought back to the endless games we used to play when I was living here and going to school. She was fierce. I felt myself melt a bit. "That is so incredibly sweet. But why didn't you tell me?"

"I have a reputation to preserve. I'm supposed to be the single gay man living the high life." He took a sip of his drink. "Needs ice. I'll get it." He went back to the kitchen.

"And instead," I said, when he returned, "you spend your evenings playing cards with my grandmother."

"Not all of them. Are you mad at me for not telling you?"

"No. Just . . . surprised."

"I'll get the wine." He went to the cellar to fetch a bottle.

When he got back, I said, "Still. You could have told me."

"I didn't want you to think that I was stomping on your turf." He got the corkscrew out of the drawer and opened the wine.

"Is that what you think I'm like?"

"I know what you're like. You, darling Jacqueline, are a cat. Very territorial." He set the open bottle in the center of the table.

I'd been compared to much worse so I let it go. Besides, he was right.

"I like coming here. She tells the best stories." He grinned.

"And gives the best advice."

"And makes the best *frites* in a country known for the quality of its fried potatoes."

"*A table!*" My grandmother came in bearing the meat and salad. "Sit down and help yourselves while I get the potatoes."

The wine was still a bit cool from having resided in the cellar but it would warm up quickly in the cozy room. It was like being in a museum dedicated to my family. Photographs from the beginning of the last century up to the most recent school pictures of her great-grandchildren adorned every wall and flat surface.

She may live alone, but if photographs did in fact contain parts of their subjects' spirits, she lived in a crowded house, surrounded by generation upon generation of love.

As usual my grandmother was right. Once I started eating, my appetite came. It was wonderful—the steak was seared to perfection, the *frites* were crisp and golden on the outside and fluffy on the inside, light, not greasy. The vinegar in the salad cut the richness and cleansed the palate.

When we were finished, we cleared the table and attacked David's pie—and it was a pie, not *une tarte*. A real deep-dish American apple pie with just the right combination of tart and sweet, not too much cinnamon and a crust so flaky it was like eating the wings of angels.

"What's your secret? For the crust?" I asked him.

"I'll never tell."

"Maybe if I threw the rest of the pie at you?" I looked at the pie, then at him.

"Ice water. And frozen butter," he said.

"I'll try it." I helped myself to a second piece.

Then we played cards. I couldn't remember the last time I'd felt so relaxed.

Around ten, David stood and stretched. "I'd better get home and try to restore a bit of my self-respect. Good thing we never play for money or you two would have cleaned me out. I would have had to look for a new place to live."

"Like grandmother, like granddaughter," I said, grinning.

"Already I regret giving you the secret to my crust."

Mamy Elise patted David's hand. "But you are improving. Maybe one day you will win."

"Unless I begin to play your great-grandchildren, I'm not counting the seconds. And I would never put money on it."

"You are a wise man," said my grandmother. He kissed her cheek and I walked him to the door.

"You bring her so much joy," I whispered.

"It's reciprocal. There's no one else like her. Especially not in my family. Are you okay? Are you sure you don't want me to get you home?" He glanced at my middle. "I didn't ask you about . . ." His eyes came back to mine.

"Yeah. I'm okay. It's . . . hard. Thanks for not talking about it tonight."

"Kind of what I figured." He opened the door and a blast of freezing wind hit us.

"Jacqueline! Close the door. You are letting the cold in."

He took a finger and rubbed it under one eye, then the other. "Smudged mascara. Very unlike you." Then he was gone, holding his empty pie plate under his arm.

I returned to the living room where Mamy was sitting in the soft glow of the floor lamps. She looked twenty-five years younger. Knowing the benefits of good lighting was a talent.

"I should go too." But I sat down next to her.

"Jacqueline?" She was playing a game of solitaire.

"*Oui?*" Maybe I should just stay here tonight.

"You must try to understand why you want a baby, a family," said my grandmother. "What is it that would make you want to risk your marriage, your profession—"

"But—"

"Let me finish. A baby isn't just about blood." She turned over a nine of spades and placed it on the ten of hearts.

"But it's not really a part of the family. It won't resemble any of us. Inherit any of our traits." I indicated all the photographs around the room.

"And so it wouldn't be worthy of love?" My grandmother put down her cards and looked at me.

"That's not the point. But I've read that the bond comes when you are carrying the baby. I've felt it." I wanted the picture of my baby on the mantel. Or the wall. Or the buffet. Or all three. He or she would look like a mixture of my mother and Laurent. With someone else's baby, you missed out on all that.

She sighed. Took a sip of water from her glass. "Would you like some? Help yourself." She pointed to the bottle of Spa Reine in front of us.

I poured myself a glassful. "You had your own children. You can't know what it's like."

"True." She stood and straightened an already-straight photograph on the wall. "I am going to tell you a secret."

My heart was beating hard.

"Your aunt Charlotte. She couldn't have her own children." She turned back toward me.

It didn't register. "But Pierre and Maxime—"

"Are adopted."

I was stunned. "Do they know?"

"*Oui.* But no one else does. I don't know why she wants to keep it a secret. It seems silly, after all these years. It's her choice. But listen to my words." My grandmother sat back down and took my hand.

Still reeling, I tried to focus on what she was telling me.

"Carrying the baby is but a small part of having children," she went on. "The loving them and taking care of them, that is what makes the family."

"But if I hadn't been my mother's real daughter, would you have taken me in?"

"Do you think it would have made a difference?"

"I don't know," I said in a small voice.

"You are my grandchild, regardless. As are Pierre and Maxime." With that, she released my fingers and gathered up the cards that were still scattered on the table.

"I don't want to stop trying."

"Why? Did you ever consider that there is a reason you cannot conceive? That there is a baby out there who needs you to be his mother?" she asked.

I shook my head.

"Consider this. If Rachel were an orphan, what would you do?"

"But I love Rachel! As if . . ." As if she were my own.

"*Exactement,*" she replied. "I am not telling you what you should do. I'm asking you not to reject Laurent's idea without giving it serious thought." She shuffled the cards and began a new round.

When I got home, I wasn't sleepy. I put the piece of pie for Laurent in the kitchen. He wasn't back from his rehearsal yet.

In the bedroom I opened the bottom drawer of my bureau and carefully removed a tissue-wrapped bundle from under a stack of

T-shirts. I then unfolded and looked at every bootie, every sweater, every Petit Bateau onesie, every hat, every minute sock I'd bought over the past two months. Impossibly tiny. I stared at my clandestine purchases for what seemed like a long time.

I was inalterably flawed. Never would I live up to my father's image of what he thought I should be. My stabs at perfection were wounding not only me, but everyone I loved.

When Laurent came in, pink-cheeked and bright-eyed from the night chill, he found me cross-legged on the bed surrounded by baby clothes.

"What's all this?" He looked panicked.

"It's clothes. For a baby. What does it look like, the makings of *coq au vin?*" I got off the bed and walked into his arms.

And I cried.

Again.

"Does this mean you've changed your mind?" He still had his worn leather jacket on, his musician's jacket I called it. It was soft against my skin.

"I don't know. I don't know what it means." I looked at the baby picture my father had sent. It was now framed and sitting on my nightstand.

He stiffened a bit.

"Can you give me some time? Can we maybe not talk about it right now?"

He nodded and kissed my hair. I turned my face and found his lips. We undressed each other and made love among the tiny clothes on the bed. For once, I didn't stop to turn down the sheets. Afterward, I clung to him, hard. I had to hang on, because if he knew the truth, he wouldn't love me anymore.

CHAPTER 21

Colette

Leaving San Diego was proving to be easier than expected. It was a sign. I spent the week tying up loose ends. Laura, our landlady, already had a new tenant lined up for the fifteenth of January so we could leave the furniture until after the first of the year. My grades were in and I sleepwalked through my good-byes.

I spent Tuesday evening, the night of Dante's ultimatum, wrapping the gifts I'd made in tissue paper and packing them. I couldn't get in the spirit, despite the lights and the Christmas carols. For my father, I'd bought a beautiful gray silk robe. The inspiration wouldn't come so I'd settled for a simple *Merry Christmas, Love, Colette* in darker gray thread. I needed a suitcase just for the presents. I felt like Santa.

Wayne had borrowed a surfboard and got in some last days of surfing before leaving San Diego. Boston and our new life dominated our conversations. I figured my feeling of being outside my body observing my actions, listening to—rather than living—my words stemmed from how suddenly all this came about. And also how crazy I went when he'd left. What had I been thinking? Stealing, going to Vegas, gambling. Lucky thing Wayne returned some sanity to my world.

My thoughts skirted around the image of Dante waiting for me at the Bella Luna. He was probably gone by now. It was late. How late, I didn't know because I didn't dare look at the clock. Saying good-bye would have been too messy.

I'd also confessed everything to Gali during a long phone call. I didn't leave out a single detail. She went from outrage at Wayne's abandonment, to shock at my life of crime, to a touch of envy at my enchanted Vegas weekend, to relief that it was over and I was safe. She even promised to be on her best behavior with Wayne.

I'd never had a wild teenage phase so I guess it had been time to get it out of my system.

"Babe, can you come give me a hand with this?"

I went into the other room. Wayne was holding up one end of the couch. "I figure we can get a head start on moving and get rid of some of this junk. We can set it out on the sidewalk, some Mexicans are bound to pick it up."

"Just leave it. We'll deal with it later. Besides, it's started to rain."

"Rain might actually improve it." He made a face.

I winced. "Look. I'll take care of it when we get back from Pennsylvania. We have time. I don't want to tear up the house just yet." My hand lingered on the back of the sofa.

"When we get back from where?"

"Pennsylvania, you remember? Christmas? All that good cheer. Tons of good food? Courtesy of my sister?" I rapped my knuckles lightly against his skull.

"I never said I'd go."

"But—"

"I booked a condo in Aspen for Christmas. Get in some good West Coast skiing before slogging back East." He grinned.

"But I promised. I assumed you'd want to spend Christmas with me," I said, tugging at the neck of my sweater. It was too hot in the room.

"I do. In Aspen. Aww, Colette, don't make me waste Christmas with your family. You can't ask me to do that."

"I can't?"

"You know how I feel."

"No. Enlighten me."

"You're asking me to choose between skiing in Aspen and Christmas with your sisters and father, and oh, that aunt. Come on, it's a no-brainer. You gotta see." He lifted his hands, palms out.

And all of a sudden I did see. The no-brainer was me. I looked at the clock. Eleven-thirty. Maybe there was still time. I grabbed my bag from the counter and pulled on a jacket and headed for the door.

"Where are you going?"

I didn't answer.

He grabbed me. I twisted away.

"Let me go, Wayne. It isn't going to work."

"What isn't?'

"Us."

"What the fuck are you talking about? We belong together. You need me."

I yanked my arm away from his grasp. It was going to leave a bruise. I looked at him straight in the eye. "Wayne, baby—Can't do this. It's not you, it's me. Sorry if I hurt you, babe. Bye. C."

I dug the light blue box out of my bag and put it on the table. Then, I rushed off into the night. I didn't even stop to look for my car keys. The restaurant was only seven or eight blocks away. I jogged through the drizzle, passing all the twinkling Christmas lights, candy canes, and Santas. *Please let him still be there.* I broke into a run. It was not midnight yet.

I was panting as I turned the corner and headed across the street to the Bella Luna.

My heart sank.

No. It was still Tuesday!

But the café was shrouded in darkness. I pressed up against the plate glass door and peered in, with my palms pressed on either side of my face. Nothing but empty tables dressed for tomorrow's customers. I looked over to "our" table by the window where I could see nothing but the ghosts of what could have been.

I turned and slid down the glass door to the pavement. I put my head between my knees and let go.

"Hey, kid. Are you okay?"

I looked up and saw a cop leaning over me. He was short and stocky.

"Sorry," he said. "You're not exactly a kid, are you? It's just that you look so small sitting there. Here, get up."

I took the hand he offered and he pulled me to my feet.

"Nothing can be that bad." He handed me a tissue. I wiped my eyes and blew my nose. "You look like you just lost your best friend or something."

"Something like that."

"You can fix it in the morning."

"No," I said, my voice a shaky whisper. "I blew it."

"You can't know that. Things have a way of working themselves out. Unless you're doing something illegal, that is." He chuckled. "Like you would be the type. Go home, get a good night's sleep. It'll look better in the morning." He looked at his watch. "It's midnight."

"Midnight," I echoed. And I would forever be a pumpkin.

"It's really starting to come down. Let me give you a ride." He pointed to his car.

I shook my head. "No. I live really close to here."

"If you're sure. You know, there really aren't that many mistakes you can make that can't be undone."

At least there was one mistake I would sidestep. Going off to Boston with Wayne.

We turned onto the street and I almost expected to see Dante standing there at the corner, his hair plastered to his head by the rain.

But this wasn't a movie. In real life, very few of us got an Audrey Hepburn moment.

CHAPTER 22

Magali

Syd was late. I was seated at our usual booth at The Two Lions, trying to block the thought of her standing me up. I knew she'd been avoiding me. I was hungry and exhausted, having spent the better part of the day walking around Valley Forge Park, trying to make sense of what was happening in my life. I'd been doing a lot of walking lately. The movement soothed me and tired me out so I could sleep.

Micheline and Piet were sitting across from me with expectant looks on their faces. Micheline was rounder in the belly but otherwise didn't look pregnant.

"Oh, Magali, *s'il-te-plaît,* at least say you will think about it?" Her eyes were shining, definitely in the second-trimester-glow part of pregnancy.

"She must make her mind, yeah?" said Piet.

"You would be perfect."

Would I? Micheline and Piet had just offered me a job as head chef for the first shift, lunch. With the baby on the way, they wanted to cut back, but were determined to maintain the authenticity of their kitchen.

"Of course! You are *belge,* expertly trained, and a wonderful chef. You would be in charge. You could change the menu."

"Carte blanche," Piet added.

Micheline shot him a look. I didn't think she was completely on board with the "carte blanche" idea. I sipped my beer, a St. Feuillien Cuvée de Noël.

"I haven't worked in a restaurant in years." I shook my head.

"It's like a bicycle," Micheline said.

I wanted to say no. This was not my dream. *But it had been once,* said a stubborn little voice in my head. *And your current dream is two sentences long and gathering dust in the attic.* Maybe this was the universe telling me to forget about being a Great Author and pushing me in the direction of the kitchen. Again.

Syd walked in.

"I'll let you know."

"Before New Year? Because if it's no, we must interview chefs."

"Hi," Syd croaked.

To her credit, she did look as if she'd been sick. Her skin was pale and her nose was red and chapped around the edges.

"I don't think I'm contagious anymore but no hugging, just to stay on the safe side." She sat.

Micheline and Piet rose, he cradling her elbow. She shook him off.

"Soup for you," she told Syd.

Then she looked at me.

"I'll have the same."

When they were gone, I said, "I wasn't sure you were coming."

"What part of 'C U 2nite' left any room for doubt? God, I'm beginning to feel almost human again."

"I tried to call. I even stopped by your house." I tried for lightness, but missed. I knew I sounded accusing.

"I went to a friend's house. He nursed me back to health," she said. She hadn't removed her coat.

"I thought *I* was your friend." I couldn't help it.

"And I'm yours. Which is why I refrained from spreading my germy self all over your house and your girls."

"Which friend?" I asked.

She took a deep breath and coughed. I softened. "Oh, you poor baby. You should take off your coat. It's warm in here and you'll just get colder when you leave."

" 'Bout time I got some sympathy out of you." She opened her bag and pulled out a crumpled tissue.

"Oh, for the love of Mary. Here." I opened my bag and pulled a pocket-sized pack of tissues and handed it to her. She took one and pushed the pack toward me. "Keep it. I could open up a shop I have so many." The legacy of motherhood.

"So what's your news?" she asked.

I debated about telling her about Leo's book but didn't want to get into that with anyone at this point. I had read it over the weekend, with Leo hovering like a mother hen concerned about her favorite chick. Finally I sent him out to the park with the girls so I could read in peace.

The book was good. A page-turner with a strong plot, offbeat humor, and a solid dose of understanding of human behavior. It needed work but nevertheless, envy pierced my heart with every well-turned phrase. I don't know why I was surprised. The very qualities I married him for were the same qualities that made his novel wonderful. One part brilliance, one part humanity, and two parts quirky sense of humor.

My jealousy made me feel small.

"Nothing much," I finally answered. "Missed you at the party, though. We also missed Art." I looked at her, hard. "Did you know he'd left?" I asked, all wide-eyed innocence, but Syd knew me too well.

Her face crumpled. "You know?"

"I don't know what I know. I know Elly and Charlotte saw you two kissing and then you slapped him?"

She nodded, but didn't speak. My pocket tissue packet was getting a workout.

Duncan came with our soup. "Soup du jour. White asparagus with chervil."

"Chervil? How did Micheline get her hands on chervil?" Chervil—*cerfeuil*—was Belgium's national herb. Soup made with it tasted like a tender spring garden.

"Secrets of the trade. But seeing as if you might join the family—" He leaned in and peered around the room, as if he were about to impart top-secret information. What a clown. Syd shot him a questioning glance, but he didn't notice. "Micheline has a garden—a greenhouse."

"So that's how she does it." Brilliant woman brimming with energy. I'd always toyed with the idea of having one myself but it had seemed too overwhelming. Not to mention my decided lack of a green thumb. If unleashed in the Amazon jungle, I could probably kill it in a matter of weeks.

"What was that about?" demanded Syd.

I stared her down. "First, you."

"Maybe we should eat our soup while it's still hot."

"Maybe we should stop looking for delaying tactics. But fine, yes, let's."

"We don't want to incur Micheline's wrath."

"True." So, we ate in silence for a few minutes. The soup was a masterpiece, not too thick or creamy, light and flavorful, exactly what this evening needed. Soup was the original comfort food.

"Besides," added Syd, "you need to eat. You're looking thin."

I put my spoon down. "Thin?"

"Gali, you must have lost at least ten pounds since you got back from New York."

"But it can't be. I'm not dieting."

"Clearly, because if you were, you'd be miserable and a few pounds heavier than before. You can't not have noticed."

I shook my head, comprehension spreading through my body. "It's the jeans. They're magic."

"Nope. Not just the jeans, though they are nice."

Come to think of it, the waistband was feeling loose. Since I spent most of my time these days in yoga pants and sweats, I didn't have much of a reference point. And Leo had thrown out my scale years ago after seeing me obsess about gaining and losing the same three pounds over and over.

Maybe it was all that walking. After sitting in front of my screen and fidgeting, my heart would start pounding and I felt as if I were suffocating. Walks were the only thing that seemed to help.

"Thanks." Would Daddy also find me thin? Or at least thinner? I shook my head. "Much as I love you for telling me I'm thin, you're not off the hook."

"Okay. I won't cry. I won't cry." She tapped her spoon against the rim of the soup dish. "Art and I have . . . I don't know how to say this."

"You like my brother?"

"What are we, in seventh grade?" She grinned. "Actually"—she took a deep breath—"it started in high school."

"But he's . . ."

"Four years younger than I am, exactly. Not to mention he's my best friend's brother."

"And he . . . ?"

"Feels the same way, yeah. But nothing's happened, Gali, I swear. I promise."

It was strange, I had to admit, the thought of Syd and Art together, as a couple.

"It never will." She put down her spoon and started tearing little pieces off a slice of baguette. "I wouldn't ever want anything to jeopardize our friendship. Guys come and go, but friends are forever."

"Let me get this straight. And stop persecuting that piece of bread, it hasn't done anything to you. You have been holding each other off because of me?"

"Of course because of you. What if it didn't work out? What would it do to us? You are my family." She looked miserable.

Suddenly it made sense, why neither of them, luscious as they were, could sustain a relationship. Years under my nose and I saw none of it. How observant of me.

"So you're the reason he keeps disappearing?"

"You see? It's starting already. No, it's in his nature. But"—she ate another spoonful of soup—"he did ask me to give him a reason to stay."

"And?"

She shook her head. "Too risky."

"Are you crazy?" I slammed my palm on the table. "You know where he is?"

She nodded, her eyes shiny.

"Go after him."

"How can—"

"How can you not? Don't you know how short life is?" I waved to Duncan and mimed signing my name on my palm. "So where am I driving you?"

She shook her head. "What if we break up? You would have to take sides and it would drive a wedge . . . I can't lose you."

"Not even in a relationship and already planning the post-breakup? How did you become so optimistic?"

"Sheer talent."

I jingled my car keys. "Where to?"

"The Poconos."

I felt my eyes widen. "Our cabin?"

She nodded.

Duncan came over with our check and a chocolate mousse with two spoons. "Compliments of *la patronne*."

"We should leave."

"Yes." Our gazes locked on the mousse.

"It would be a shame," I conceded.

"A crime, really."

"And Micheline might get upset."

"And we wouldn't want that. Not in her condition. What if something happened? It would be our fault." Syd picked up one of the spoons.

I picked up the other. "Plus, we need energy for the drive."

So, we fell in.

"Amazing." Nothing could create happiness like a truly wonderful chocolate mousse.

"Almost as good as yours." Syd scraped the dish.

"Better."

"No."

"Yes." And it was okay. There could coexist many different yet divine chocolate mousses in the universe, each special in its own way. And each necessary.

"I can't believe he's been so close all this time." I squinted my eyes at the glare from the headlights of an oncoming car.

"He knows no one uses it," said Syd.

Too many happy memories. "I may have to strangle him."

"You see? Problem." She blew her nose.

"Kidding."

"Oh."

We got on the turnpike, having already stopped for gas and Starbucks.

"Gali. I'm going to say this once, then we can drop it if you like. You have no idea how much I missed you those years you were in Belgium. When you came home, I swore I'd never let you get away again. I can't lose you."

"You think I can? You are my sister. We chose each other. Let's stop talking about this or I'll start bawling and won't be able to see and end up running us both off the turnpike."

"Okay." She handed me a tissue.

"Funny thing, though. I really thought you'd go for Simon. I also knew Brandy was not a contender the minute you asked her what kind of eyeliner she used."

"And she answered 'On my eyes?' I thought I was going to explode."

"And Art's face!"

"I told him that if he was going to bring someone to make me jealous, he should rustle up a more plausible girl."

"*Girl* being the operative word," I said.

We drove for a long while in easy silence listening to Roxy Music. We were off the turnpike and almost at the cabin when Syd, keeping her eyes straight in front of her, said, "Since this is the night of hard conversations, I need to tell you something. About Simon."

"I still think you two would have made a good match." I felt in control, bringing Syd to Art with my blessing. If it didn't work out, so be it but at least they'd have taken their shot.

"He told me you tried to seduce him."

"What?" I yanked the car over, in a shower of gravel. Probably nicked the paint on the Volvo. Damn.

"He said you insisted on coming to his apartment. You cooked for him and got him drunk. Then you left. 'Chickened out' was how he put it. But he's sure you have feelings for him." She turned and looked at me.

"That bastard. I told you what happened. It wasn't like that at all!"

"I wanted you to know how he saw it. Because I don't think he intends to leave you alone."

"But I didn't lead him on." Or had I? Was that the way I'd come across—like some unhappy married woman on the prowl? Was he lying for Syd's benefit? Out of a sense of revenge? Had he planned the whole thing to get back at Leo?

Either way, I'd have to confront him. I sighed. Unless Syd was wrong and it would go away on its own.

I pulled back onto the road and headed toward the cabin. I drove carefully, refusing to let my fury rise.

"You okay?" she asked.

"Yeah. You know it was nothing like that. I'd had a lousy day. I needed to cook. I felt sorry for him all alone. He was fun and had a kitchen."

"I know."

I couldn't let this pass. Was this him trying to manipulate me into getting in touch with him? I turned into the driveway. "Here you are."

"You're not coming in?"

"No. I'm going home. Art can drive you back." I kissed my friend on the cheek and watched her go into the cabin. Then I drove home.

My kitchen was now laden with an assortment of cakes, pies, and pastries that would put the most bountiful pâtisserie to shame. I barely had any counter space left to make dinner.

I knew I had to have it out with Simon.

Had the whole thing been my fault? I'd flirted on the train, even lied a bit, but that had been a harmless game. People did it all the time without it turning around and biting them in the *derrière*.

I picked up the phone and booked tickets to *How the Grinch Stole Christmas*. The girls wanted to see *Seussical* again, but I thought it best to avoid physical proximity of my family with Simon.

I eyed the stack of Christmas cards waiting to be signed, addressed, and mailed. If I didn't get them done soon, they'd never arrive before Christmas.

Feeling a bit Grinch-like myself, I decided to take measures. Music. Strains of "Carol of the Bells" filled the air. That was more like it. I made coffee, grabbed a cookie, and sat at my desk. My mug was festooned with grinning, rosy-cheeked snowmen. Very cheery. Then why did I just want to lie down and take a nap? I felt as if my veins were shot through with sludge.

I dug my mobile from out of my bag and dropped my keys in the process. Simon's number was still programmed. Phoning was the coward's way out, but I couldn't bring myself to take a day trip to the city and face him. And I certainly didn't want to see him around here. The phone was a great invention, after all. Especially when dealing with dangerous people, those who could, with one flick of a pinkie, topple my beautiful house of cards.

I cut the music.

"Hello?"

That accent. It got to me every time. It's just an accent. A way of pronouncing words. I hardened myself. "It's Magali."

"Oh. Hello there. Wondering when I'd be hearing from you."

I shut my eyes. Might as well plunge right in. "You told Syd that I tried to seduce you."

"And as I recall, you would have succeeded had you not chickened out at the last moment."

I couldn't believe I was hearing this. "But you know the day I'd had. I needed to cook, and you were alone, I was alone, you had a kitchen, end of story."

"You were giving out mixed signals." He chuckled.

"I'd had too much to drink." Why was I feeling guilty? "It was all in your mind. My signals were very separated." As I said the words, a new thought hit me. "Did you know who I was? On the train?"

Silence.

"You did!"

"I recognized you from a photograph on your husband's desk."

"So you planned this? It was deliberate?"

"I didn't plan on us being on the same train, if that's what you mean."

"But once you recognized me? You . . . decided to get back at Leo?"

He sighed. "The thought had crossed my mind. Not often you get a chance at hurting someone who hurt you. He was ruthless."

"So you used me?" I couldn't breathe. Of course. Why would he want me? An old married woman.

"It did amuse me that you were playing at being someone else. That doesn't really scream 'happy marriage,' you know. I saw a chance and took it."

"Leo is right. You *are* a bastard." I was seething.

"Wait. It started out that way. But as the game went on . . ." He stopped and I could hear him taking a deep breath. "I became smitten. You're quite wonderful."

"And you expect me to believe that? Just leave me alone. I have a home. A family." As soon as I hung up, I would go somewhere and die of embarrassment. "Hanging up now."

"No, wait."

For some reason, I did.

"Are you listening? That's exactly what I want. What you have. What you make. It was gorgeous. You're gorgeous."

I swallowed. "But you had it and threw it all away."

"What makes you think it was my doing?"

"My husband was your wife's lawyer."

"It wasn't what it seemed."

"It never is." I went to the kitchen and stood by the window. A squirrel scampered up the maple tree.

"Do you have any idea what it's like to live with someone who wants you to be perfect? Always?"

My breath was stuck in my throat.

"I never measured up to her standards. She was always finding fault. So I ended up having an affair."

"And that didn't work out either?" I asked, my gaze still on the squirrel. He was on a very small limb but seemed completely at ease.

He sighed. "She was married too."

"You make a habit of this."

"No. She ended up patching things up with her husband. But Elizabeth—"

"Found out."

"Yeah. In some crazy way, I thought it would make her see me in a new light. If someone else wanted me, maybe I wasn't so flawed."

"That didn't really work out for you."

"Couldn't get rid of me fast enough." He chuckled, but it was a grim sound.

I was trying not to feel sorry for him. He'd played me. I went to the counter and broke off a piece of brownie. "So you decided to show up here at Thanksgiving . . ."

"I hadn't really thought it through. But yeah, I wanted to try my luck."

Fury overtook me again. "Your luck? At breaking up my marriage?"

"Sounds awful, I know. But how was I to know your marriage was any good? You certainly didn't spend the evening with me extolling the joys of marital bliss."

"It would have seemed insensitive, seeing how your ex reacted to your accident."

"I thought I'd take a shot. I'm sorry. But I miss being a family, having kids running around, the whole thing."

"Should have thought of that before." I crushed the brownie, then swept the crumbs into the trash.

"She would have found a reason to unload me regardless."

"But what you tried to do to me? Good-bye, Simon."

"Wait."

"Don't call me. Don't come here." I hung up, feeling queasy. Air. I needed air. I laced up my shoes and left the house. I don't know how long I walked, my mind numb. I couldn't shake an underlying feeling of guilt. I kept hearing him ask, "Do you know what it's like to live with someone who wants you to be perfect?"

When I got home, there was a carton waiting for me on the porch. I brought it in, recognizing Ana's scrawl. Advance copies of my book already? Impossible. I left the carton by the door and went up to take a nap. Just before drifting off, it hit me. I'd said no to Simon. That was why I felt so guilty. I was the one who always said yes.

That evening after supper, Leo asked, "What's in the box?"

"Oh, just some stuff Ana sent. I'll get to it in the morning." I was finally addressing Christmas cards. Rote work was just what I needed to keep my mind numb.

The next morning, I opened the carton. Inside was a gift-wrapped package and a note. *Open before Christmas.* She'd probably been mistaken and rushed, forgetting the *Do Not.* I hid them on the top shelf of my closet till Christmas Eve when all the presents would go under the tree.

Soupe aux asperges blancs et cerfeuil
WHITE ASPARAGUS AND CHERVIL SOUP

We love white asparagus in Belgium. Every time I taste this soup, it feels like an explosion of spring. So whatever you are planning on making for dinner, if you come across fresh white asparagus and chervil, change your menu and make this instead.

You're welcome.

For 4 to 6 people.

1½ pounds white asparagus
6 tablespoons unsalted butter
6 cups chicken broth (homemade or high-quality organic)
Generous handful of freshly chopped chervil, plus leaves for
    garnish
3 tablespoons flour
Sea salt
Freshly ground pepper
1 large egg yolk (*optional*)
½ cup heavy cream (*optional*)

Peel the asparagus. Remove the tips and reserve them. Meanwhile, melt 4 tablespoons of butter over medium-low heat in a soup pot. Snap the stems into smaller pieces.

When the butter is hot but not brown, throw in the stalks and let them cook for about 5 minutes, stirring regularly. Add 2 cups of broth, cover, and simmer until tender, about 20 minutes.

Serve yourself a nice glass of chilled white wine. You deserve it after all that peeling and chopping and stirring.

Chop a generous handful of chervil and set aside.

When the stalks are tender, remove from heat and let cool.

Meanwhile, cook the asparagus tips in boiling salted water for a few minutes, but no more than 2 or 3. Drain in a colander and rinse under cool water.

Once the stalks have cooled down a bit, purée them, in batches, using a blender or food processor. Set them aside to be used later.

Melt the remaining 2 tablespoons of butter. Add the flour and mix with a wooden spoon. Once the flour is bubbling, grab your whisk and, whisking steadily, add the remaining broth. Bring to a boil then remove from heat.

Now, take a sip of wine.

Add the puréed asparagus to the broth, mixing well. Season with salt and pepper. (*The soup can be made ahead up to this point and chilled.*)

Here you get to make a decision:

1. Throw in the chervil and the asparagus tips and serve the soup with a garnish of chervil leaves. The sun comes out from behind a cloud and birds are chirping.

2. Or, for a richer, creamier, altogether superior soup, mix the egg yolk with the cream. Add it to the base along with the chervil. Then in go the asparagus tips. Serve and garnish.

If you chilled the soup, then reheat it slowly but do not bring to a boil or it will curdle.

Voilà! It's springtime in a bowl.

CHAPTER 23

The Reunion Begins

Christmas Eve

"Remind me again why I agreed to do this?" I opened the oven and pulled out a genoise. Leo was brushing mushrooms. He hadn't shaved yet and looked comfortably rumpled in a soft, plaid flannel shirt and jeans.

"You didn't have a choice? That's the last of them." He set the bowl of shitake mushrooms on the counter. "Do you want these sliced?"

"That would be great."

"Besides, you know you love it," he said.

"You know me too well. Make sure the slices are very thin."

Elly came into the kitchen, holding *How the Grinch Stole Christmas.* "Could someone read to me, please?"

"You know how to read, baby. Would you mind getting Mommy a fresh apron from the middle drawer in the pantry? And throwing this one in the hamper?" I was whisking pastry cream.

"It's more fun when you or Daddy do the voices."

I removed my soiled apron and replaced it with the fresh one Elly was handing me. I glanced at Leo.

"In exactly four minutes I'll be in to read, okay? You have to count out loud though," he said. She left, counting in a voice that could be heard two streets down.

"How does this sound? Next year, Christmas: you, me, and the kids. Agreed?"

"Absolutely. And we can send photos, or maybe even a video, to Tante Sola. She can fend for herself. She'll understand. And your father, any stray sister, or a brother, well, why else do they do a turkey dinner special at Denny's, right? I hear it's lovely. Absolutely heartwarming."

"I don't know if we'd go as far as Denny's. Maybe we could spring for Applebee's."

"Right. Good idea. Applebee's. And we'll send Syd off to join them. There . . . done." He scraped the sliced mushrooms back into the bowl.

"We might not have to *send* Syd anywhere."

"Send Syd where?" My best friend had just let herself in the back door. "Where shall I put this? I love your kitchen like this." She removed her fur-lined parka and hung it up.

"Yes, it does have a certain air, doesn't it? Dorothy Gale's, post-tornado."

"So where are you sending me and do I have to pack any bags? If so, how many?" She pushed a bowlful of peeled potatoes aside and set a foil-covered baking dish down on the counter.

"Next year," said Leo, "Gali has decided that she's not doing Christmas."

Syd snorted. "Oh God, did I just snort? See what you made me do?"

"A lovelier sound has never been known to man . . . or woman for that matter," said Leo.

"I love it when you snort." Art had come into the kitchen bearing a case of wine. "It humanizes you." He looked around for a place to put it and finally settled on the desk.

"Shut up or I'll bonk you with this dish of cranberry-stuffed pears."

I was impressed. "Honey, I'm so proud of you. You strayed."

"We'll see the result. I don't know where to put the dish, though."

"Got it," said Leo, relieving Syd of her dish. "I'll put it in the spare fridge."

"Good thinking. I'm so glad I married you. You are a wonderful, brilliant man."

"At last. My worth is recognized at last." He brandished a fist in the air. "Had I known, I would have mentioned the spare fridge years ago."

"Just go, you goon!" I said, flicking him with my dish towel. "And when you're done, could you both go to Stefano's and pick up the seafood? Guys?"

"It's early yet. And I promised Elly I'd read to her."

"Right. But right after? Remember three years ago when they messed it up?" I shuddered.

"What I remember was almost having to take you to the emergency room for an intravenous Valium drip," said Leo.

"Sounds lovely. We'll go as soon as you come back with the seafood," I said.

"That works."

"Besides," I added, "I want to get the bisque done before my sisters get here."

"While you guys are doing that, I'll get started on the cranberry relish," said Syd.

"You are the cranberry queen," said my brother. He kissed her before heading out behind Leo.

Syd put some oranges on the cutting board and opened a drawer, looking for the grater.

"Here." I handed it to her. "I never knew Art to be so . . ."

"Mushy, I know. It's weird."

"I was going to say romantic." It would take some getting used to.

"So, who's here and who isn't?" Syd started zesting an orange.

"Laurent and Mamy Elise arrived yesterday and spent the night at Tante Sola's. But so far, no sisters. They'll both be here around two. Weird that their planes get in around the same time. Colette was supposed to come in yesterday, but she changed her ticket. Said she would explain when she got here."

"And Jacqueline?"

"Her concert was taped during last night's performance and will be aired tonight." I breathed deeply, inhaling the sharp smell of fresh oranges.

"I hope we get to see it. I love the "Ave Maria" at Christmas."

"Knowing Jacqueline, she'll make sure we do. She probably snagged a copy." I felt a bit disloyal to my sister. "I'm sure she's amazing."

"Laurent is such a prince to have flown out a day early with your grandmother. Why is it that the women in your family nab all the good ones?"

I eyed my friend.

"Moving right along," she said.

Elly came rushing into the room, her sister trailing behind her. "Mama, there's a package that says 'Open before Christmas.' It says '*before*' and it's for you. Open it!"

"I wish I had a present for before," said Charlotte.

"How did I miss that?"

"It was under the tree with the people presents. The not-from-Santa ones. You better open it right now. Because it says '*before*.' And it's almost Christmas."

"Okay, okay." I dried my hands on my apron. "Do you want to take over?" I offered my knife to Syd, who'd zested enough orange to last us until Easter.

She leaned heavily on the counter and put the back of her hand on her forehead, miming a fainting spell. "You're trusting me with the *celery?*" she gasped.

"Oh be quiet. I'm not that bad."

"No, baby, of course not. Why don't you have a glass of wine?"

"Too early. I'd just as soon keep a clear head until everyone gets here." I grabbed the carafe. "Coffee?"

She nodded. I took two cups adorned with snowmen from the cupboard and poured, placing one near her on the counter.

"*Ma-man! Viens!*"

"*Je viens.*" I trailed behind my daughters carrying my coffee. How could I get anything done with all the interruptions? But I watched how their beauty intensified with their excitement. Their cheeks were pink and eyes bright, hair every which way. If I never did another thing in my life, at least I made these two amazing little humans. I'd had help, but still. Is that how Maman had felt when she died?

I saw that the box they were referring to was the one from Ana. Whether she'd intended to add the "do not" and forgotten, now that the girls had seen the package, there was no going back.

I knelt down in front of the Christmas tree, an act that made me feel about as old as my girls. The house smelled piney and fresh. The decorations, old and new, made the place feel as if it could be plopped down in merry olde England. At least from the inside. Outside, it was nothing spectacular. Typical two-story suburban colonial.

But it was ours.

We'd worked hard at getting the house to look beautiful. I balked at the idea of having to haul a bunch of foil-covered dishes over to Daddy's tomorrow morning. After presents and before breakfast. At first, he'd wanted to have Christmas Eve at his house but for once, I'd put my foot down.

"Daddy, the girls expect Santa to come here. It's a ritual. So, you are more than welcome to join us. The supper will be simple. Seafood, oysters, lobster bisque, and some scampi for the girls. Jacqueline is smuggling in some foie gras for appetizers. We'll leave some for Christmas Day, and have the main meal and the *bûche* at your house."

"Fine," he'd said. But he'd sounded a bit . . . what was it? Hurt? No, that couldn't be it, Daddy never let anything slip out. Still, I'd felt guilty. Even more so when he declined to join us for Christmas Eve, under the pretext of having a lot of things to prepare for the following day. That my guilt was tinged with relief was my own slimy secret.

I couldn't imagine what his "a lot of things" consisted of, since I was doing all the cooking.

"Too long," said Charlotte.

"You can't open it just by looking," said Elly.

I laughed and brought my attention back to the brightly wrapped box on the floor, happy at this moment of peace, my body flanked by my daughters. They were still in their pj's. The house glowed with lights and candles. Around the base of the tree, we'd set up a Christmas village surrounded by train tracks. The train had derailed and was lying on its side by the post office. In the bay window, the crèche was waiting for the tiny figure of baby Jesus to be placed in the cradle at midnight by the youngest member of the family still awake. Technically Charlotte, but she usually conked out long before the strike of twelve.

In the center of the mantel throned a lovely silver menorah that had belonged to Leo's grandmother. It was almost more because of the Jewish preschool Charlotte still attended and the girls' expectations, than out of any true desire on Leo's part that we followed the tradition of lighting the candles on each of the eight nights of Hanukkah. On the final night, the menorah blazed in its celebration of light. I loved this time of year.

I wished I was looking forward to tomorrow more.

Charlotte had already removed a piece of tape from one corner of the package.

"I'm scattered today. You girls need to help me."

That was all the permission they needed. With glee, they tore through the wrapping paper like a pair of jackals.

Elly put a restraining arm on her sister. "Let Mommy open the box."

Charlotte scowled at her sister from under her bangs. "You're not my mommy!"

"Mommy, she said—"

I held my hands up, palms facing out, and arranged my features in an expression of dismay. "What would Santa say to hear you two arguing on Christmas Eve?" They fell silent.

What would I do when I could no longer use Santa to exact good behavior? Although as far as I was concerned, there was absolutely no reason to stop believing—I don't think I ever really did.

I opened the box. Inside was a stack of books and a note.

*   *   *

To help you along on your journey. If it's the right one for you.
Ana

I sifted through them. Books on the craft of writing. And one about birds.

"It's books," said Charlotte.

"Mama loves books, right?" said Elly.

Looking at them all made me feel tired.

"Right," I said. I closed the box and put it in the closet.

The airport was jammed. My sisters were arriving within forty minutes of each other, really quite thoughtful, if you looked at it a certain way. Completely overwhelming if you looked at it another. To be honest, it really wasn't a problem getting used to having Colette around. It was like slipping into a favorite sweater that had fallen off the back of the pile, gotten squished up against the wall and that you rediscovered with joy. You didn't know how much you'd missed it till you found it again.

Jacqueline was a different story.

I took off my parka. It was Christmas, maybe all that peace on earth goodwill toward men would spill over to include sisters. And a brother. At least they would be split up. Jacqueline would be staying at Tante Sola's with Laurent and our grandmother, while Colette would bunk in with us. Art had graciously vacated the guest room. Probably loving the excuse to stay with Syd without having to come out and admit it.

Laurent was already at the gate. He was just wearing pants and a sweater, with a striped wool scarf around his neck, and a leather jacket, yet he managed to appear more stylish than any other guy around. Was it the cut of European clothes or the way Europeans wore them? I'd have to ask Colette, she'd know. I strode over to my brother-in-law. He towered over me.

"Magali. It is wonderful to see you. You look beautiful." Compared to what, I wondered, a three-week-dead lizard? I'd only had time for a quick shower and my hair was unwashed. I felt dowdy. I shouldn't have worn old jeans. He bent down and kissed me on both cheeks, then turned to shake Leo's hand. Europeans never felt as if they'd properly greeted another human unless there was physical touch.

"It's great to see you, too, Laurent." And it was. "Where's Mamy Elise?"

"Taking a nap for the jet lag to pass."

"Smart woman."

"The smartest. And you? How are you holding up?" He looked worn out. Jacqueline would be here soon. That would perk him up.

"Fine. It's easier this way, on the way home we lose a night."

"I know. Pure torture."

"Ah, here they come." He scanned the crowd pouring out of the arrival gate.

"We made it just in time," said Leo. He slung his arm around me.

"I keep forgetting how long it takes to get to the airport on holidays. Though I would have thought the rush would be over, that people would be home. Cooking."

"*La voilà,*" said Laurent.

I took a deep breath and wished really hard that I'd worn a dress and my beautiful boots. Or at least my good jeans. Because here was my sister and she still looked like Catherine Deneuve. Only younger.

And we were off.

"*Mamy! Que fais-tu?*"

"*Je donne un coup de main.*" My grandmother bustled around the kitchen, Syd in her wake. She had peeled what looked like a wheelbarrow full of potatoes and had cleaned and mopped the kitchen till it sparkled. Syd had finished chopping vegetables and browning meat for the stuffing and it stood fragrant in a bowl, waiting to cool before being put in the fridge until it was ready to go into the bird tomorrow.

"*Mais . . .*"

"*Chut.*" My grandmother held a finger to her lips.

I turned to Syd. "She was supposed to be taking a nap."

Syd shrugged. "Your aunt dropped her off. Did you expect me

to tie her to the bed? She wanted to help." She looked at me. "Are you all right?" I nodded and she poured me a glass of Pinot Noir from a bottle that had been opened to let the wine breathe.

"I'm going up to change." With Jacqueline around, I at least needed to feel I looked good. My good jeans and cream cashmere would shore me up.

But before I could make my getaway, Colette came into the kitchen wearing the sweats and UGG boots she'd traveled in, looking nothing like her usual self. She saw our grandmother and rushed to her side. They kissed and immediately started talking in rapid French, as if they'd been in the middle of a conversation that had been interrupted.

Syd cleared her throat.

Colette squealed, "Syd!" and jumped into her arms.

"Hey, baby. I've missed you. I love your hair like this. Very French."

Colette passed a hand over her close-cropped hair. "Why don't you ever come out to see me? Oh, forget it. I know, allergic to California. It's not really that bad, you know."

"You living there certainly improves it greatly. And you still have your own breasts. I'm so proud. So, what juicy tidbits of news have you brought me?" asked Syd.

Colette's light visibly dimmed.

Before she could answer, Jacqueline came in. "I don't know about all of you but I'm ready for a bit of Christmas cheer. Of the red variety." Laurent was right behind her, hand on her shoulder. More hellos were said, wine was poured.

Colette looked relieved at the interruption.

Jacqueline took a sip of the Pinot. "Lovely!" she said. "I still can't believe I had to fork over actual money for the swill the airline attempts to pass off as wine."

"Bloody Marys," said Colette.

"Gin and tonics," I added.

"Good advice and I will make great use of it on the flight home." She smiled. "The house looks beautiful." She came over and gave me a peck on the cheek, then whispered, "What's up with Colette?"

I shrugged and shook my head.

"So," Syd said, "Colette, tell us all."

"Maybe not quite a story for now?" I tried to let her off the hook.

"Why not? No time like the present." Syd's happiness was like a thick fog, blinding her to signals she would normally pick up.

"Fine. First, Wayne is a thing of the past."

I probably wasn't alone in having a hard time resisting the urge to whoop and applaud. "I'm so sorry, baby," I said, to cover up for it.

"I know he wasn't exactly popular around here. And second"— she took a small sip of wine—"I seem to have lost my job. I'm quite the conquering hero come marching home, aren't I?"

That part I'd known about. Syd put her arm around Colette.

"But what about—" I started.

She shot me a look that shut me up. I was about to ask about Dante. The last time we'd talked, the loss of her job had been a distant second next to him.

"Time to make Santa's cookies. Santa's cookie time." The girls ran into the room.

Colette grinned. Jacqueline, who'd barely said a word since she landed, stooped down and scooped up the girls, one in each arm.

"You two would make wonderful cookies. And I'm just the one to do it. Bet you didn't know I was the gingerbread witch, did you?" she cackled.

"No! Don't!" But they were giggling and squirming.

"So, who would like to be first? And exactly what kind of cookie would you like to be?"

I pulled out bowls from the cupboard and cookie sheets from the wide bottom drawer beneath the counter. No point in changing now. I grabbed my apron and tied it, then pulled my hair back into its usual ponytail. "Grab the eggs and butter, would you?"

"So, who will be here tonight?" asked Jacqueline, putting the girls down.

"Everyone. Well, everyone except Daddy."

"Oh?"

Was I mistaken or did a look of relief flit across her face. I must have imagined it. Jacqueline was my father's favorite. She was the one who got to bask in warm pools of approval while the rest of us shivered naked on the banks, watching. So why did it feel as if the relief in the room was so thick you could plate it and serve it up as a main course?

"Will he be okay?" ventured Colette. "All alone on Christmas Eve." She shuddered.

"It's the way he wants it," I said. "He said he wants to get things ready for us. And who's to say he's alone?"

"I wonder which things he means, since you are doing all the cooking right here," said Jacqueline.

Mamy Elise was at the stove making hot chocolate for the girls, explaining to them that the only way to make really good hot chocolate is to melt real Belgian chocolate, add a little milk and *un ingrédient secret*. Naturally the girls were enchanted by the idea of a secret ingredient.

"That's what he says, anyway. Maybe we should go over there and get him," said Jacqueline. The Good Sister. The one who always knew the right thing to do in any given situation and made sure everyone knew it. "Then again"—she shrugged and smiled at me—"I haven't been around, have I? I'm sure you did everything you could. Once Daddy makes up his mind, it would take a world war to change it."

My sister giving me a break? That was different. First Daddy, now her. Was the whole family going to be abducted by aliens? Would I be next?

Art came in through the back door. "If he wants to be alone, let him be alone."

"Hey, Scarecrow! I think I missed you most of all." Colette charged at him.

"Dorothy! So, still happy at the other end of the yellow brick road? How does it feel to be back in Kansas?"

Art and Colette used to be obsessed with *The Wizard of Oz*. They'd spent countless hours reading the books and watching the movie over and over, until they knew every line and every note by heart. As Dorothy and the Scarecrow, they'd venture out to the woods behind our house and fight the forces of evil.

"Feels . . . pretty good, actually." She punched him on the arm.

"Hi, Art," said Jacqueline.

"Hey," said my brother. "Long time."

She nodded. "You look great."

"So do you. As always."

There they went again, behaving like they were acquaintances who had run into each other unexpectedly. Something had happened between those two way back. It was when Maman was still alive. One day, everything was fine. The next, they would barely speak to each other. It poisoned every dinner, every family moment. It carried over to this day.

Then Jacqueline did a strange thing. She went over to Art and gave him a hug. They made a pretty picture, the only two tall, blonde siblings. After a moment, he hugged her back. She pulled away and her eyes were damp.

"I'm sorry," she whispered.

My ears pricked. Sorry? Sorry for what? Looks were exchanged like Valentine's Day cards in a schoolroom on February fourteenth.

I clapped my hands together, breaking the spell. "All right! Now, who wants to make cookies for Santa?"

"I thought you'd never ask," said Elly.

"When did you turn forty?" asked her dad.

She shrugged.

Seven dozen cookies later, we'd gone our separate ways to rest and clean up for dinner. The girls, too excited to nap, were watching *Mr. Magoo's Christmas Carol.* They'd be out by nine-thirty or ten at the latest, the better to get up while it was still dark and pull us out of bed, breathless to see what Santa had brought.

The kitchen had gotten itself put back together without any effort on my part. I carried a cup of coffee up to the bathroom where I ran a bath with some essential oil bubble bath Colette had brought back from San Diego.

It was called Peace.

As I soaked, the smell of jasmine and vanilla filled my head and I tried to relax my shoulders. Something was off with my sisters.

I lathered up to shave my legs. I couldn't put my finger on what was wrong. It was as if there were a great big bowl of the lightest, creamiest *crème pâtissière* into which had fallen tiny pieces of eggshell. It looked perfect but beneath the surface, it was all wrong.

Maybe it was just apprehension about Christmas dinner tomorrow. I turned on the handheld shower and washed my hair.

I breathed in.

Peace on earth.

Goodwill toward men.

All of them.

Even my father.

And siblings.

I was drying my hair when Leo came in carrying the phone. "For you," he said. "Your father."

Speak of the devil. "Daddy? Hi, did you change your mind about tonight?"

"Hello, Maggie. No. This is not about tonight." He coughed. "I wanted to invite you, your sisters, and your brother to breakfast tomorrow morning."

"Oh." I put down the towel. "Just the four of us?" I twisted a strand of hair around my finger.

"Yes. Let's say at nine?"

I took a deep breath. "Daddy, tomorrow is *Christmas* morning. The girls will be opening their presents from Santa. It's tradition. I don't want to miss it." I closed my eyes, waiting for the storm.

To my surprise, he chuckled. "I'm sure they'll be up before the first light of dawn."

He had a point.

"Say nine-thirty?" he asked.

I felt like whining *Do we have to?* I stared at myself in the mirror. "I'll check with the others, but how about between nine-thirty and ten."

"Good. I'll be expecting you. Merry Christmas."

"Merry Christmas, Daddy. See you tomorrow."

"I wonder what your breakfast will be like? More scones maybe?" said Leo that night as we lay wrapped together in bed.

"I've never eaten my father's cooking. Ever. Maybe I should bring something." I ran my finger up and down his forearm.

"How bad can it be?"

"I don't know. That's the kind of question I like to avoid when it comes to my father. It's always linked closely to 'how much has he had to drink?' "

"He sounded different."

"I know. He's been different these past few months."

"That was quite a Christmas Eve." We'd switched off the lights and just left a strand of tiny white Christmas lights lit around the mirror. "It was . . ."—Leo scratched his head—"uh . . . *fun*."

"It was. What's up with that? Normally, fun and my family are mortal enemies. Heartbreaking, critical, excruciating, those are the adjectives normally associated with family reunions." I looked at my husband. "In mine, at least. Your family is out of a book. I didn't even know what normal was until I met you."

"If we all lived in the same town, trust me, you wouldn't find them so normal."

"Yeah, well, I guess all that open love and respect, the laughing, even. Not normal. You're right. I mean, seriously"—I turned to him, propping myself up on my elbow—"when we go visit them, I actually look forward to it. It's a vacation. Sheesh."

He grinned and kissed me.

"To get back to Jacqueline, I wonder what's up? She isn't herself."

"You might want to have it out with her at some point, but maybe not on Christmas?"

I gasped. "You mean you want us to spend all of Christmas Day together without a huge, emotional, wrenching scene? Sounds kind of dull, no?"

"No," he said, grinning.

"I'll be on my best behavior if she will."

"C'mere," said Leo, and pulled me close. "I have an early Christmas present for you."

CHAPTER 24

The Reunion

Christmas Day

"We look like something out of a movie." Jacqueline and I were wearing the dresses Colette made us for Christmas and Art was wearing the Artful Dodger shirt. "You've really outdone yourself this year."

"Thanks. I wonder what Daddy's going to say," Colette said, smiling.

I could hear him now. *Do you really think you're dressed appropriately? Aren't you confusing Christmas with Mardi Gras?* But it was so much fun to wear these clothes, and the season was supposed to be about joy.

We turned into the lane that led to my father's house. Frost-crusted fields hemmed in by wood rail fences flanked the car. The horses were out today under the overcast sky. It had turned bitterly cold during the night. The girls had been disappointed at the absence of snow this morning. What was it about a white Christmas that was so ingrained into our collective memories? It couldn't just be about a song.

We pulled up in front of the house and I went into shock. Daddy had strung Christmas lights around the windows and trees. Snowmen and candy canes dotted the lawn. A nutcracker the size of Elly stood sentinel on the porch. Red ribbons were tied around every post. There was a wreath on the front door and a small sign just below that said BELIEVE.

"Wow," said Colette.

The house hadn't been done up for the holidays since our mother died. I swallowed and latched onto Jacqueline's hand and squeezed. She squeezed back. She remembered too.

"The girls are going to love this," I whispered. The house, well over two hundred fifty years old, was gorgeous in itself. Dressed for the holidays, it looked like something out of a postcard, lacking only a blanket of snow. I wouldn't have been surprised to see Santa himself open the door.

We sat in silence looking at the house.

"I guess we should get started carting all the food in," said Art, slinging his camera bag across his body.

I sighed. "Do we have to?"

"You sound like Charlotte." He smiled for the first time since we'd gotten in the car. "You know, I'm doing this just for you."

"I figured." I leaned over and hugged my brother. "Thanks, Art."

Still, I sat gazing at the house.

"Shouldn't we get out of the car?" asked Jacqueline. We all looked great in Colette's creations, but she looked spectacular. She'd left her hair long and loose, unadorned. Her only jewelry was a pair of dangly gem-encrusted earrings.

"I don't know. The house looks so warm and inviting. Maybe it's a trap," I said, only half-joking. Whatever was going to happen today must be pretty dire if Daddy had gone to all this trouble. Could he have lost his mind? Was there a mental illness that caused excessive holiday decorating?

"When I see how nutty you are, it makes me feel better about myself," said Colette, putting a gloved hand on my shoulder.

"*Joyeux Noël* to you, too." I took a deep breath. "Let's get started." Whatever it was, I could get through it. At least I wasn't going in alone.

We got out. I shivered and pulled my coat tighter. Art popped the trunk. We were carrying part of the food for dinner. Later, Leo would bring the rest.

"I've never been less hungry in my life," said Jacqueline.

"I know," answered Colette.

"Christmas breakfast is a tradition." I hated when people said they weren't hungry when it was time to eat.

"And no one messes with tradition, especially if it's about food, right? At least not in our family." Jacqueline put her hand on my arm. "Don't look so alarmed. We'll eat. We always do. But aren't you worried you're going to put back some of the weight you lost?"

"Me?" I looked down at myself.

"Yes, you. Who else am I talking to? You look great by the way. You have to have been dieting."

"Nope," I said, grinning. "But I have been walking. Miles and miles."

"It suits you. Want to go for a walk?" She cocked her head toward the woods behind the stables.

"Don't tempt me. But we could," I said. "After breakfast, I mean."

"Or maybe we could go for a ride. Remember?" We hadn't ridden here for years. Daddy still kept horses, but I was never comfortable asking if I could take one out.

She nodded. "It was the best part of growing up here."

She took the *bûche* and I grabbed a foil-covered dish of *gratin dauphinois* and my straw bag full of the ingredients for a salad. I liked to make my salads fresh, at the last minute. Art picked up the turkey, which was dressed and ready to go into the oven.

The front door opened. I'd only been joking about Santa opening the door, but there stood my father, wearing a stiff smile and a . . . was that a *red* sweater?

"*Bienvenus! Joyeux Noël!*" he said. He wasn't wearing a false beard, so I still recognized him. I caught Jacqueline's eye.

Red? she mouthed.

I shook my head. There was no way he'd bought that sweater himself unless he was a victim of sudden onset color-blindness.

"He's getting married again," I whispered to Colette, who had appeared at my other side carrying a shopping bag full of brightly wrapped packages. "I'm sure of it."

"I hope not. I hate it when he gets married."

"What else would get him out of the land of charcoal gray and tasteful beige?"

"She must have superpowers if she got him to wear bright colors. Maybe she's from a cult." Colette giggled.

"What? Worshippers of all things bright?" I said.

I would have crossed my fingers but my hands were full. We walked up to the front porch and, each in turn, walked up the steps, kissed him, wished him a merry Christmas, and went through the door, as if we were going through an amusement park turnstile. And everyone was tall enough for the ride.

If there had been a part of my brain that clung to the idea that the outside decorations were a fluke, it dissolved as soon as we entered. A lump the size of a cantaloupe lodged itself in my throat. Christmas carols drifted from the speakers. Pine boughs and candles were everywhere. On the mantel, above a crackling fire, was a Russian doll set depicting Santa that we had when we were little. Each doll was lined up from tall to tiny.

I sniffed. "Did you roast chestnuts in here?" It was too weird.

"Yes, for the *purée de marrons*. It's better than the canned chestnut mash they sell. Don't look at me like that. I do know how to cook." He took our coats and went to hang them up in the hall closet.

It was as if he'd been possessed by the ghost of Nat King Cole.

Then there was the tree. By the fireplace in the multipaned bay window surrounded by a window seat towered a magnificent fir. I blinked back tears. All the decorations from when we were kids hung from the branches. My angel. Colette's kitten in a pearl basket with a red ribbon. Jacqueline's nutcracker. And my mother's favorite, a cut crystal globe with an intricate snow-scene village inside. A perfect world within a world.

Art went up and fingered a small wooden train he'd made and painstakingly painted when he was nine.

"I didn't know you still had this," he said.

My father cleared his throat. "I never threw anything away, actually." He spread his hands. "You all look very . . . festive."

"So do you. New sweater?" I asked.

"As a matter of fact, yes." He looked down and pinched the fabric between two fingers. "Does it suit me?"

"It looks great, Daddy. Red is a good color for you," said Colette.

We followed him into the dining room.

"It's not just the chestnuts. Something else smells wonderful," I said.

"Cougnole de Noël."

"How on earth did you find a *cougnole?*" I asked. My father turned on the threshold.

"I made it. I, how do you say it again? Ah . . . *Googled* the recipe."

My father not only cooks, he uses *Google* as a verb. I hadn't even known he'd gotten Internet access. *Cougnole* was a special type of bread eaten on Christmas morning in Belgium. It was sweet with a texture somewhere between brioche and challah.

"Wow."

"Yes, well, we shall see about the result. It might not deserve so much excitement. Please, come into the dining room."

We did as we were told. I hoped the *cougnole* was edible because I couldn't see any of us telling Daddy otherwise. He disappeared into the kitchen.

"Do you think he's on some sort of medication?" whispered Colette.

I shrugged. "If he is, it seems to be working."

"Maybe we should invest in a lifetime supply," said Art.

"How long has he been like this?" asked Jacqueline.

"I don't know for sure. A few months?" I answered.

"You are the one who's here. You should know," said Jacqueline.

Now I recognized my family. The guilt came whooshing through the door and settled around me. Looking in on my father was something I did out of a sense of duty rather than desire. I shot Jacqueline a look and, to her credit, she looked away.

"Sorry. It's just that I wasn't expecting this."

"And I was?" The dining room matched the rest of the house. Gone were the piles of newspapers, the dust, the empty glasses and half-drunk cups of coffee, the cluttered air of cold indifference. The table itself was out of a photo spread from *Gourmet* magazine. It was like being jerked out of an Ingmar Bergman film and plopped down into a Bing Crosby Christmas special. I wouldn't have been surprised to see my mother emerging from the kitchen bearing a pot of coffee and a huge smile.

"Maybe he's marrying Martha Stewart," said Colette.

"Whoever she is could give Martha an inferiority complex," I whispered back. "It would certainly be a change from his usual fare." A coterie of skinny, neurotic, self-absorbed beauties made up my father's circle of exes. Blonde, brunette, or redhead, it didn't matter. They were all the same. They looked great, dressed great, and were well-spoken. And about as deep as my daughters' kiddie pool.

But today, nothing fit the picture I'd formed in my head. The table was set for breakfast with the hand-painted china my parents had received for their wedding. Colette fingered a plate.

"This is stunning," she said.

"Don't you remember it?" I asked.

She shook her head. I kept forgetting how young she'd been when Maman died.

My father returned holding a tray with coffee, hot chocolate, and a pot of steeping tea. I was still holding the food I'd brought in.

"Why don't you put that in the kitchen and then we can eat," said my father, setting the tray down on the table.

We trooped into the kitchen and placed dishes and bags of food on every sparkling surface.

"Talk about unexpected," I said, going to preheat the already-hot oven.

"Something's up. I'm not sure I like it," said Jacqueline.

"I'm not sure I trust it," I added.

Colette looked out the window. "Do you think he's . . . ?" Colette broke off, unable to say what we were all thinking.

"Sick," finished Art, with the lack of affect that had fallen over him as soon as he'd stepped inside the house. "If he is, he's hiding it pretty well. He's never looked better. And have you smelled the air in here?"

"It's hard to avoid, isn't it? It smells like fresh-baked bread, coffee, and chestnuts, with undertones of pine and candle." I breathed in.

"You should be a writer, you know that?" said Art. I punched him on the arm.

"Yes," said Jacqueline, "it smells like the inside of a good *boulangerie.*"

"Exactly. Notice anything else?" Art leaned up against the counter and crossed his arms.

We all sniffed the air like a bunch of bloodhounds.

Colette gasped. "Cigarettes. It doesn't smell like cigarette smoke." How could I have missed that?

"Maybe he's been smoking outside?" she ventured.

"Our father? Please! He thinks it's vulgar," I said.

"If he stopped smoking, then something is probably really wrong," said Jacqueline.

She had a point. We looked at each other.

"Oh, God," I groaned. Wouldn't it be just like my father to set a beautiful heartwarming scene, become the perfect father and grandfather, the one we've all been yearning for, just to announce that he has some sort of late-stage incurable cancer. This *would* be the worst Christmas ever.

"We'd best get on with it," said Jacqueline.

I opened the oven door and Art hoisted the turkey in.

"After you," he said. Then he wrenched the door from my hand, closed it quickly, and cackled, "Ha! Now I've got you!"

"You goon."

"I guess it's time we all went back in, huh?" He turned back toward us.

"Maybe one of us should say something?" I ventured.

"Like you?" asked Jacqueline.

"No, I was thinking of you, actually," I replied to my older sister. She was, after all, the favorite child.

"Are you out of your mind?" She rolled her eyes.

"So we are all just going to sit there and eat and wait for the ax to fall." I looked from one face to another, meeting sheepish looks and blank stares.

"Why change such long-standing habits? Hasn't that been the way this family has functioned forever?" asked Art.

"Maybe it won't fall," said Colette.

"Maybe it's something else," said Jacqueline.

"Another marriage? Even that sounds good if it's an alternative to..." I sighed.

"If it were another marriage, wouldn't she be here? The intended? Besides, isn't he getting a bit old to sail off into the sunset with his bride?" asked Art.

"What are you, a romance writer all of a sudden?" I asked.

"Oh Art, how can you ever be too old for love?" asked Colette. She lowered her eyes, looking for a moment as if she'd just lost everything in a raging fire. Then it passed.

"I'm not talking about love. I'm talking about our father getting married," said Art.

Jacqueline broke in. "Let's just go and get this over with." She left the kitchen, shoulders back, head high. We trailed behind her. I braced myself.

Jacqueline went over to our father. "Daddy, this is beautiful. You've had the house repainted, right?"

"Actually, I did. I have been preparing this for a few months. The last one especially." He was sitting at the head of the table, clearly waiting for us. He kept unfolding and refolding his napkin.

"But..."

"Most of these things"—he indicated the china, the decorations, even the paintings—"have been in the attic since...since your mother...since Camille...passed."

No one said a word. I'm not entirely sure anyone was even breathing anymore.

We don't talk about Maman in Daddy's presence.

We don't speak French.

We don't ever allude to the past.

I'd been furious with him because, though he never used any of it, he didn't want us to have even one of Maman's things. Other than one scarf each. He'd just hidden it all away, as if she'd never existed. He didn't know I'd swiped her diary.

And here he was, saying her name.

"Why don't you all sit down and we can talk while we eat," he said.

We did as we were told. I sat facing him, with Jacqueline on one side, and Colette and Art on the other. I picked up a knife and cut five slices of the *cougnole*. I was methodical, as if I were to be graded on the results.

"Coffee?" Jacqueline lifted the pot. I nodded gratefully and held out my cup, as did the others. All except our father.

"It's tradition to have hot chocolate with buttered *cougnole* on Christmas morning," he said, pouring the cocoa into his cup. It was probably spiked. He made no bones about pouring brandy into his coffee in the morning.

"I don't think I've ever seen you drink hot chocolate," I said, sipping my coffee. It was fragrant and strong, and cleared my head.

"I felt like a change."

"I'll say," said my brother.

"What he means is, we've noticed," I said. It almost felt as if we should set another place for Maman.

I buttered my slice of *cougnole* and took a bite. It was perfect. "Daddy, how on earth did you manage to bake perfect *cougnole* on the first try?" It was neither too light nor too dense, not chewy but not crumbly either. This was no simple feat.

"To be honest, it's not my first attempt. I've been practicing." He looked down at the slice on his plate. "Trial and error. There were many errors." He met my eyes.

"Would you mind showing me?" I blurted before thinking it through.

"So that you could write about it in one of your cookbooks?" He leaned forward.

"No! No, of course not." I felt hot. A piece of *cougnole* lodged itself in my throat. I forced myself to swallow, washing it down with coffee.

"Oh. Too bad. I would have been honored."

My head snapped up so fast you could almost hear my neck crack.

"Okay. That. Is. Enough." Jacqueline's voice rang clear and sharp, her head high on her graceful neck. At that instant, standing up to my father, I had never loved my sister more. Nor had I ever been prouder. Something was different about her, but she hadn't lost one bit of her edge. "Daddy, what exactly is going on?"

Though she was sitting at the table, in apparent calm holding her half-empty cup of coffee, in my mind's eye she had crossed arms, narrowed eyes, and was tapping her foot.

My father cleared his throat. "Yes, I have every intention of explaining certain things to you. I know you have questions."

"Like where were you at Thanksgiving?" asked Jacqueline.

"Why was it so important to have all of us here this Christmas?" said Colette, in a small voice.

"And all you've done in here," I added. "It's incredible. But, what . . . why . . ." I was beginning to sputter so I shut up. Jacqueline and I exchanged a look. She raised her eyebrow, I didn't bother trying. But we still understood each other perfectly. And what's up with the red sweater?

"One question at a time. I was here at Thanksgiving. Working on the house."

"By yourself?" I thought nothing my father could do or say could still have the power to shock me, but I was wrong. This was just too sad, even for him.

"Yes. I wanted to see all of you together." He poured himself another cup of hot chocolate. Dutch courage, I guessed. He cleared his throat. "The reason I asked you all to be here this Christmas was to tell you something that should have been said a long time ago." His gaze swept around the table and lingered on each of us for a few seconds. He cleared his throat again.

"Daddy, just say it, whatever it is," said Jacqueline.

Unless you'd like a throat lozenge, I thought. My father cracked a smile.

"No, but that's very kind of you, Maggie."

Oops. I'd said it out loud.

Everyone grinned at me and you could feel the tension in the room loosen, just a bit.

Art stood up. "Look, let me put all of you out of your misery." He looked at our father. "I know why you wanted us all to be together today. I know what you want to announce." He shot a look at Jacqueline, who was shaking her head, mouthing a silent *no.* She stood too.

"Look, Art, I—"

"Just let me say it. It's time everyone knew anyway. I'm tired of living this lie. It sucks."

"Please!" Jacqueline's fist down on the table startled everyone.

"Look, Jacqueline, put a lid on it, okay?"

She plopped down on her chair, her mouth open. Who was this guy who looked like my sweet, crazy baby brother but had the super power to shut my sister up? This was turning into one of those down-the-rabbit-hole experiences that usually only happen when you're dreaming.

"I know," said Art. "I've known for a long time."

"Known what?" asked Daddy.

"I'm not your son. I'm not really a part of this family."

Colette put her cup down so hard, coffee sloshed over the edge, staining the good tablecloth.

"What are you talking about?" I asked. Shocked beyond words doesn't apply to me. I was never beyond words.

"That is the most ridiculous thing I have ever heard," my father's voice roared from the head of the table, his composure gone. Ah, back to normal. "Of course you are my son. Where did you get such a preposterous idea?"

"Artie, look at me," I said. Now it was my time to stand. We were like a bunch of contestants on a game show. "I remember Maman being pregnant with you."

"Yes, she was pregnant, but not with me. She went into labor, went to the hospital, had a baby boy. But he didn't make it. So you brought me home in his place. My real mother was a strung-out seventeen-year-old who could no more look after a baby than get a job at NASA."

"What?" I went over and put my arms around him. If I could have picked him up and cradled him, I would have. "That's nuts. You just don't walk away from a hospital with someone else's baby, even if it is to be put up for adoption. Do you even realize how hard it is to adopt?"

Art looked lost for a moment. "But she said . . ." He looked at Jacqueline.

"I don't understand," I said.

Art kept his eyes on my sister.

"What? Jacqueline?" I still didn't get it.

Jacqueline kept her gaze locked on her hands clutching the coffee cup. I wished someone would switch off the Christmas carols.

"I'm sorry," she said to her cup.

"Sorry?" I was confused.

"I was the one who told him that story. It's my fault." She still hadn't met anyone's eye.

"But why?" asked Art. "I was just a little kid. I believed whatever you said."

"Because I was jealous. I wanted you to disappear. It never felt like there was enough love to go around even before you got here. I was afraid that, with a son, a boy, not another girl, there wouldn't be enough left for me." She finally looked up, shaking. "I never meant for it to go on so long."

"That makes no sense. You were always the favorite," I said, then realized that Daddy was right here listening. "Sorry," I whispered. He looked pained but to my surprise, didn't say a word.

She began to cry. I'd never seen her cry except onstage. "I know," she continued, "I'm a monster. Go ahead. Gang up on me. I deserve it."

"So, it's not true?" Art looked dazed. He'd raked his fingers through his hair so much that it stood up in untidy tufts.

She gave a slight shake of her head.

"So you never believed you were a part of the family? All those years?" Colette asked.

He looked down.

We all went back to staring at Jacqueline in shock. My father broke the spell.

"Leave her alone. It's Christmas. Everyone, just sit down. If this situation is anyone's fault, it's mine." He turned to Art. "Of course you are my son. You look exactly like my brother."

"The one who—" Would I ever keep my mouth shut?

"Died, yes." Another taboo. We never discussed Daddy's family. I just knew the bare facts. When he was twelve, his brother had fallen out of a tree while building a fort and was killed instantly. His mother killed herself two years later. And his father became a drunk. I didn't remember him. He'd died from a bleeding ulcer about the time I was born. Daddy got all the money. He'd packed up and moved to America with his wife, three-year-old Jacqueline, and me. He bought this beautiful house and started his import-export antique business.

But Art just stared at my father. He looked as if he were about to cry. "You never told me that."

"There are many things I haven't told you. All of you."

Jacqueline still had her head bowed.

"It's not her fault," my father went on. "Jacqueline. Look at me." She did. "Don't blame yourself. Blame me," he said, softly, looking at her, then at Art. "I was at fault. I just wanted you to be strong. To withstand."

"Withstand?" Me again.

"Withstand losing your mother."

"But you were like this before she died," I said. I had no memory of him being warm and giving. I don't recall him laughing. That was the paradox I couldn't wrap my mind around. The man in Maman's diary was the flip side of the man I knew as my father. Then, a piece clicked into place. "Wait. You knew?"

"What?" Jacqueline snapped to attention.

He picked up his cup and drank from it. "Cold." He grimaced and set it down. "It was a long time coming. And she was in remission for so long. We knew that with each pregnancy, the sickness . . . the lupus could reactivate."

"So you blamed us?" I asked.

"Not intentionally. She wanted a big family." He sighed.

"And you let her?" My hand clenched. "She knew that she was condemning us to grow up without a mother? Without her?" My vision turned dark and I saw spots in front of my eyes. I felt queasy.

"Let me explain."

"Be my guest." My anger turned cold. "I'm listening. We all are."

"I was against it. I knew this desire to have a big family could kill her. But she wanted it. I couldn't refuse her anything. But I hated my weakness. If I'd been stronger, I would have stopped her. I could have had an . . . operation." His shoulders slumped. "If I'd been a better man, I would have. Because when she wanted something, she wouldn't let anyone or anything stand in her way."

He had a point. For all her easy elegance, her will was formidable, almost electric. But he could have saved her. And he had to live with that.

"So," said Colette. "You never wanted us. Art and me?"

"The truth is, I wanted her more." He picked up his empty plate and seemed to ponder the motif. He set it down and looked at his two youngest children. "But not quite enough. I'm sorry."

It all made perfect sense. Why Jacqueline was favored. She was the only child who had been desired by both parents.

"So, when exactly did she get lupus? You never said when it started." My breath was coming out in short spurts.

My father gazed at me, wordless, then averted his eyes.

"Oh," I said in a small voice. I killed my mother. Merry Christmas. I pushed back my chair. The air was having a hard time getting to my lungs.

I stood. "I need to get some air. Outside."

"Maggie. Hear me out. Please?"

But I couldn't. I had to get away.

"She went into remission," he shouted after me. I stopped but didn't turn around. "She was fine, but as the years passed, and her condition remained good, it receded in her mind. She thought she had it beat. So she decided to get pregnant. Without telling me."

My heart was banging so hard against my ribcage. Colette. On trembling legs, I made my way back to the table and stood behind my little sister, holding the back of her chair for support. Her cheeks were shiny with tears.

His voice quieted. "But she was fine." Small smile. "So, then she got cocky."

"So I killed her. I fucked the whole thing up. It came back because of me," said Art. "I liked it better when I thought I was adopted."

"Not because of you. It was because of *her*. It took me a long time to realize that. But she always knew she wouldn't live to be very old. Anything could have triggered it. Minor surgery, a shock to the system. She wanted you children to have each other. She wanted you to be close."

"Well, that worked out," Art said.

"When she got sick again, I couldn't stand it. That was when I withdrew from you all. I tried to drink it away. If anyone precipitated her death," he swallowed, "it was me. She worried. The doctors told us she needed serenity, calm. But I was thinking only of myself. And I blamed myself."

"But you loved her," said Jacqueline.

"I made her last years a misery. And then I went on and did the same thing to all of you. If you hadn't had your grandmother."

We all thought of Mamy. The years we spent living with her in Belgium probably saved us all.

He shook his head. "The main thing is that you did. I hadn't realized it at the time, but the smartest move I could make was to send you to her."

"It felt like you were just trying to get rid of us," said Art.

"Yes," I said. "You were always criticizing us, wanting us to be perfect. We never measured up," I said. "Perfect the way Maman had been. Only she hadn't really since she knew she'd be leaving us motherless and went ahead and had us anyway, leaving us with—" I stopped myself just in time.

"A cold, ungiving, demanding father who spent most of his time drinking." He stood and came around the table to me. "I wanted you to be perfect. And strong. In my misguided mind, I needed you to be worthy of the sacrifice she made, her life for yours."

I stood, knocking my chair over. "Air. I need some."

"Great idea." Jacqueline stood, her hands were trembling. We looked at each other. She headed for the front door. I turned and headed to the kitchen. I needed to do something, anything but there was nothing left to do.

Panicked, I slipped out the back door and ran toward the stables, the skirt of my extraordinary dress flapping in the northern wind. My entire childhood was a lie. The image of my perfect mother shattered. How could she have done this to us? My father who had to live with the guilt of not saving her, with us there to remind him every single day. My story, my feelings of never ever measuring up, never ever being good enough. There was nothing I could have done. The person I'd been trying to become all my life had never existed. The rules of the game were written in concrete. I never stood a chance.

I gasped for breath in the frozen air. The stables had been my refuge when I was a kid. The smell of hay and horse sweat would comfort me. It was also where I spied on my father, wishing at times that I were his horse instead of his daughter. His voice when he spoke to them was soft, his gestures tender. They could even make him smile.

"Hey! Wait up!"

I turned and saw Colette in her white boots and red-and-orange geometric minidress hurrying after me. Her long white coat was open and flapping in the frigid air.

I rubbed my arms. I'd run out of the house without my coat. The sky had turned heather, a sign of snow to come.

"That was . . . insane," said Colette. "You okay?"

"No. It's too much. It's as if I don't make sense anymore. You?"

"Same. To think I was worried about him getting on my case about being an unemployed old maid."

"And I was worried he'd think I looked fat!"

We made a feeble attempt at a laugh.

"Seriously, Gali," she said, grabbing a handful of fabric from around my waist. "You're not fat. I'm going to have to take this in. It's about time you made peace with your body."

"Hi, kettle."

We were doing a lovely job of dancing around our heavy hearts. After a lifetime of experience, we were good at it. Colette pulled a pack of Lucky Strikes from the pocket of her coat.

"Want one?" she asked.

"They still make those?" I glanced toward the house. "Why the hell not?" I took one, lit up, and inhaled. My first cigarette in over nine years, it tasted like what spewed out of my Volvo. A second drag made my head spin.

"It's not really that bad," said Colette.

"What? Smoking?"

"No. Knowing what really happened."

We smoked in silence, watching the clouds of smoke rise and vanish into the air.

"What really sucks is that he's doing this at Christmas." I pulled hard on the cigarette. It would be really easy to fall back into smoking. "He's still just thinking of himself. This is supposed to be such a peaceful, fun day. And look what he's done with it. He's put us on an emotional spin cycle. The part I can't grasp, either with my head or my heart, is that Maman knew she was going to die. That every baby was a risk. And she went ahead and did what she wanted, regardless of the consequences."

"She thought she had it beat. That she was stronger than the disease. So we can't really blame her, can we?" Colette asked.

"I don't know. It's just that we've held the image of the perfect mother and monster father for so long." Tears came to my eyes. "Hubris." I felt as if I were committing a sacrilege. None of us had ever criticized her.

Colette was crying too. "The higher the pedestal, the farther they fall. But Gali, she couldn't have known he'd be so cold and hard with us. And you heard what he said. Anything could have triggered it."

I shrugged and wiped my tears, but they kept falling. I didn't know anything. I didn't even know who I was. The whole driving motivation for my entire life up to this point had vanished. If I wasn't the person who tried to please her father, to make him proud, to try to become the woman my mother had been, then who was I?

Had I done anything because it was what I wanted?

An idea was beginning to jell. "I guess he wants us to move on, get over it. All of us. Start fresh."

"What? The truth will set you free?" She laughed. "Get over it. Just like that?" She snapped her fingers. "A lifetime of . . . you know that voice in your head? The one that criticizes, that tells you you're not good enough, smart enough, pretty enough, successful enough?"

I nodded. "Intimately." I had a crushing desire to brush my teeth.

"Mine was always his voice."

"Mine too. But maybe we could, I don't know . . . take a stab at it," I said.

"At what?"

"At . . . making decisions that are independent of what we think he wants. Not worrying about him sitting in judgment on our lives. Hey, or how about listening to each other instead."

"Oh Gali. You say that as if it were as easy as changing your hair color."

"Maybe this was all just to show us that we should try. Break away and lean on each other." But it was as if it were a play and the curtain had risen on a new act where the actors were the same but the scene was so altered that they no longer knew their lines or motivations. Someone had rewritten it without telling them. Colette was right.

Footsteps sounded behind us. Art was running in our direction, panting, his breath coming out in frosty white puffs in the cold.

"You two have got to come talk Jacqueline down off the ledge. She's totally losing it. I can't calm her down, she won't even look at me." He shook his head. "Like it's my fault, or something."

We each crushed our cigarettes beneath our heels and hurried after Art, dropping the butts in the garbage can as we passed by the garage.

Jacqueline was slumped against my car, a vision in her smashing dress, but when I got closer I saw her hair was tangled and there were dark streaks on her face. She was sobbing.

"Here," said Colette, handing her a tissue from her pocket.

"Thanks," said Jacqueline. "Now, go away."

"No." I put my arms around her. "Go ahead and cry."

"You don't understand. You can't."

"I'm pretty sure I do," I said. "You were a little girl. It wasn't the . . . kindest thing you could do, but—"

"Art is the way he is because of me!" Her voice swerved out of its normal cool speaking range.

"Hey! I'm standing right here and I can hear you. I'm not saying it didn't factor in . . . It's a pretty big paradigm shift. To add to the rest." He put both palms on his temples and closed his eyes. "But"—he opened his eyes and looked straight at Jacqueline—"I think we are who we are regardless."

"Oh, please! I'm not a fool!" She pressed her lips into a thin line. "Why are you even trying to be nice to me?"

"Jacqueline." Art stepped in front of me and put a hand on her arm. "Do you think that adopted or not, if I'd felt loved, I would have stayed away so long? In a way, it's almost worse knowing the truth, because he didn't even love his own son."

"But he did," I said. "It's just that—"

"I know. I remind him of his dead brother. But I was just a little kid. Fuck!" He turned away from us and lit a cigarette. "As if an 'I'm sorry' could wipe the slate."

"Remember he wasn't exactly warm and cuddly with any of us either," I said. "And now we know why."

Art just stared at me. I took a deep breath of the pine-scented air. There was a foul taste in my mouth from the cigarette. "It was worse for you. I know. You were so little. But you had us."

"I had you. And Colette."

"Not an adequate replacement, but we loved you. Love you."

"I used to crawl into bed with you when I got scared, remember?"

I nodded. "Until you started to run."

"It didn't work. The demons were always there. So I started capturing them." He fingered the camera slung around his neck.

On the front porch, Daddy was watching us, smoking, looking like he'd like to come over but didn't dare.

"It's a lot to take in. For all of us. But maybe we could . . ." I nodded toward the house. I was freezing. My teeth began to chatter.

"Jacqueline," said Art. "You didn't ruin me, okay? You were a little kid. We all remember what it was like inside that house."

"Let's go back," said Colette.

"No," said Jacqueline. "It's more than that. That lie has come back to haunt me. You don't know."

"Since you won't tell us, no," I said.

Fresh tears trickled down her cheeks. She shook her head and set her mouth in a grim line. Her lipstick had worn off and it made her look younger. "Forget it. Go back in. I'll join you in a bit."

"Why don't you just say whatever it is and get it over with. We seem to be on a roll here today," I said.

"Leave me alone."

"Oh, come on," said Colette.

"Fine. It has come back to haunt me, okay? The lie. I can't have kids, no matter what I do, how many treatments, nothing works. And now Laurent . . ." She leaned her head back and let her breath escape toward the sky.

"Wants to adopt," I finished for her. "Is that it?"

She nodded.

"Let me get this straight," said Art. "You think this is some kind of cosmic justice or karma or something? You're being punished?"

She looked at Daddy standing on the porch.

"Man, you are even more wacko than I am. It doesn't work that way, Jacqueline," said Art.

"He's right." I folded her into my arms.

"You can't know that," she said.

"But I do know that adopted kids are usually loved as much, if not more, than natural children." Colette put her hand on Jacqueline's arm.

"So I've been told," she said. A ghost of a smile brushed her lips. "It's just . . . forget it."

Colette twisted the end of the scarf she was wearing around her hair like a headband, eyes down. "You'll have to tell Laurent, right?"

"Well. We are here for you. We are here for each other. For better—

"—or fucking worse," finished Art.

"We'll figure it out." I felt drained.

Art took Jacqueline's hand in his. We stood in a huddle, probably looking like some high-fashion escapee sect from Cirque du Soleil.

Thank God for food. We devoured everything except the table-cloth and silverware. I hoped we'd still be hungry enough for Christmas dinner.

I took a deep shaky breath. "Daddy. Why are you telling us all of this now?" Might as well face the truth head-on. Now he would tell us he was dying and it would take us the better part of our lives to get over this Christmas.

"Because . . . because it was time."

"Daddy," said Jacqueline, "are you in some kind of therapy?"

"Don't be ridiculous."

"So, are you . . . sick?" asked Art.

"No. Not yet. My liver isn't in the best shape but I have a clean bill of health. I have been cutting back, though." He looked wistful.

"Wow," said Colette. Then silence.

"Good," I said. I knew I sounded flat. I thought of my gift to him. A very expensive bottle of single malt scotch. If you weren't going to drink as much, it might as well be the good stuff. "And it doesn't smell like cigarettes in here. And that's a first."

"Also cutting back." He nodded toward the back porch. So he was smoking outside.

"So, in conclusion," he said, "I am deeply, deeply sorry. You are all I have. And it's a lot. And I almost threw you away." He rubbed his forehead, as if he had a sudden headache. "It sounds trite. But I felt I . . . owed it to you to apologize in person. And all of you at the same time."

"So you're not sick," I said.

"No. Is that what you thought this was about?"

I nodded.

"I'm sorry you got that impression. I hope it's not too late for us, for me. I understand if you can't forgive or forget so easily." He rubbed his eyes. "I've written you each a letter."

"But why now, Daddy?" asked Colette. "What brought this on?"

He shook his head. "It wasn't one moment, rather a sequence of small events. But it sounds paltry."

"Tell us anyway," I said. He owed us that. After engineering the most wrenching Christmas in human history, we had the right to know which spark set him off.

"So it started following my divorce with Cynthia. I knew this was it. The last time. Because I could not go through the process again. But being married kept me in check. More or less. Alone I would go to bars, eat poorly, drink too much, come home, go to bed. One night, I caught a glimpse of myself in the mirror behind the bar. And there sat an old man with bags under his eyes, a man I no longer recognized. As if the person I had been, the person your mother fell in love with, was buried so deep inside, he was already dead. Years of self-pity had made me pathetic. When I woke up alone the next morning, I realized that every day was going to be the same unless I did something. The train was leaving the station without me."

"You're not old, Daddy," said Colette. She put her hand on his. He stared at it.

"So in conclusion, if you'll let me . . ." He sat up straighter. "I'd love to be a part of your lives. And"—he looked at me—"a part of your children's."

There really wasn't anything to say.

"Now," said my father. "I have a favor to ask you. A big favor. Again, I understand if you refuse. There is one thing I would like us to do today."

Here it was. I knew the other shoe was going to drop at some point. I wasn't sure how much more I could take.

We hadn't been to the cemetery as a family since the funeral.

The drive was much the same as I'd remembered it. Even the weather was similar.

I glanced at Colette, sitting next to me in the backseat. The years almost melted away. But this car was much too luxurious, lacking the wet-dog smell and crushed crayons on the carpet of our childhood Volvo station wagon. And Art was in front next to Daddy. Jacqueline was on my left. Today, no one had fought over who had to sit in the middle. There used to be a huge bump in the middle and we had to take turns sitting on it. Although Jacqueline, being the eldest, always found a way to finagle herself out of her turn, professing a series of mysterious ailments attributed to her status as eldest and her artistic temperament. And Art had been too little.

If truth be told, I hadn't minded the middle space as much as I'd let on. I gladly suffered the discomfort for the privilege of sitting up a little higher than my sisters. I loved the view through the front windshield, framed by Maman's head on the left and Daddy's on the right. She'd loved to drive and Daddy always said he didn't really care for it. For a few years I'd hated that she always drove, as if it emasculated my father, diminished him in my eyes compared to my friends' fathers. I would perch above my family, watching the road unspool beneath the wheels of the old Volvo station wagon we'd had forever. I remembered that car taking us to Brownie meetings, sports meets, and later Jacqueline's recitals, Colette's art shows, my majorettes, the junior prom, even.

Mom always wore a scarf around her head and, usually, sunglasses covered her eyes, even on the many days when the sun was absent. Sun wasn't a requirement, daylight was enough of an excuse. She'd followed fashion, but at a distance, remaining tasteful, European, always a little foreign, looking as if she should be driving a little two-seater convertible in the Tuscan hills, off to a picnic of crusty bread, pecorino, fresh tomatoes, and the local wine, rather than to a Girl Scout meeting.

She'd loved the Jaguar but, with us kids, hardly ever got the opportunity to drive it.

I breathed deeply and the new-car smell filled my head as my father pulled into the entrance of the cemetery. The five of us prepared to get out of the car, and I wondered again how I had let myself get talked into coming here today. I'd had enough. It felt as if I'd been ripped apart and put back together in the space of a few hours. But my father was trying so hard. And it was Christmas.

I switched off my mind, closed the curtain of consciousness, drew the blinds to be blind. I could get through this.

I almost started to cry again, but caught myself, and opened the car door. I regretted not having had a nice, comforting shot of cognac before leaving. Or Grand Marnier. Or rubbing alcohol, for that matter. Even Listerine would have done. The frozen air almost knocked me out after the warmth of the car. I pulled my coat tight around my throat, cursing myself for not having worn a scarf. Where did I think I was, Florida? The doors slammed one after the other, like gunshots in the still, icy air.

"You'd think there would be more people here. It is Christmas," I grumbled to Colette, staring at the empty cemetery.

"Yeah, you'd think. We've certainly been regular visitors all these years."

"It's not the same."

"How do you know? Did all the other people with dead relatives call you up to tell you? *We understand your reluctance to go visit your mother's grave, dear, but for us, well, we're just heartless. Uncaring.*"

"Maybe we could stop bickering. Just this once." Jacqueline's eyes were still red but she looked remarkable considering the state she'd been in a little over an hour ago. She hesitated, then linked her arms through ours. Art joined us and we walked off in the direction of Maman's grave. Daddy was already crossing the crunchy grass.

I scanned the sky. It had turned taupe.

I could go through with this. Once this day was over, I'd go home and have a nice bottle or two of cognac for dinner. With a couple of gallons of that lovely spiked eggnog Colette had made for dessert.

My breath was a white mist of crystals dissipating into the air.

At her grave we stood in a semicircle. The headstone was simple, elegant. Her picture, in black and white, her name *Camille Dubois-Arnaud, 1940–1983.* I unwrapped the bouquet of white lilies and blood-red roses my father had prepared and put them in the urn, crumpling the cellophane and stuffing it into my bag. Jacqueline poured water from the bottle of Evian she'd brought.

"They won't last," I said.

"Nothing *lasts,*" said Daddy.

When Jacqueline started singing the "Ave Maria" under her breath, I welled up. Her voice was crystal and steel, pure and strong. I wiped my eyes.

The song's notes now rested on the grass around us, alighting on gravestones and naked limbs of the chestnut and maple trees. I hadn't ever wanted us all to come here together as a family until everything was perfect. Until I'd proven myself. Now, I no longer knew what that even meant.

As we turned to go back to the car, it began to snow. I raised my face to the soft, fat flakes.

We were around the feast-laden table, Leo and the girls surrounding me. Syd, Art, and Colette were on my left. My grandmother, Tante Sola, Jacqueline, and Laurent were on my right. Daddy sat at his usual place at the head of the table. I guess that put me at the foot. Everyone was chattering, trying to make themselves heard above the Christmas carols and clang of silverware on plates. The fire blazed and the air smelled of burning wood, roasted turkey, and pine. Laurent and Mamy Elise were laughing, Daddy was talking to Art. We were helping ourselves to the food and pouring wine and water and sparkling cider for the girls.

I was sliding a cranberry-stuffed pear onto Charlotte's plate, careful not to let the sweeping sleeve of the dress Colette made me trail in the gravy, when the doorbell rang. We all looked at my father.

"I'm not expecting anyone," he said, and laid down his knife and fork.

A sharp chill went through me. "Stay, Daddy. I'll get it." I jumped up, nearly knocking over my chair. Not Simon? When I opened the door, I gasped. There stood easily the most gorgeous man I had ever seen.

He brushed the snow off his hair and extended his hand, "*Scusi. Buon Natale.* I am—"

"Dante," I said. Colette had described him to me, or had tried, but hadn't come close to doing him justice. He was half-man, half-angel. No wonder she'd been so devastated over losing him. I stood and stared.

"*Posso . . .* may I come inside?"

"Of course, I'm sorry." I took his proffered hand and pulled him inside. "How rude. I'm Gali."

He smiled. "Magali, *si.* Nico tell me all about you."

Talk about a dazzling smile, I thought to myself, then clapped my hand over my mouth. I'd done it again.

"*Grazie.*" He reddened.

"Here, give me your coat. Are you here to see Colette? Have you eaten? Come in, come in." I was babbling. Under his coat, he was wearing an exquisite suit. I noticed the words stitched into the fabric. Colette's work. This could only mean good news for my baby sister. I couldn't wait to see the look on her face. I showed him the way to the dining room, trying hard not to run.

We entered and silence fell like a blanket of snow. Syd, open-mouthed, put her glass down on the table, missed, and it went crashing to the floor, breaking the spell.

"I'm such a klutz," she said, making a face.

My grandmother tsked and began to stand, but Leo stopped her. "I'll do it," he said.

Colette was staring at Dante, biting her lower lip. He cocked his head with a smile. She rose and went to him, looking like a tiny, multicolored bird about to take flight.

He took her hands in his and searched her face with his eyes.

"How did you find me?" She finally found her voice.

"When you want to find someone, it is not difficult. I use the Internet. I decide to not give you up without fighting." His gaze swept over the seated guests.

"Wayne—"

He put his finger on her lips. Then, he kissed her in full view of everyone. I almost swooned, if swooning were something I was prone to do. Syd looked like she was hyperventilating and even my cool older sister looked a bit pink. Daddy was looking down at his plate, scowling a bit, but he didn't utter a word. Thank God.

Colette turned toward us, holding Dante's hand. She glowed. "Daddy, everyone, this is Dante."

"I'll get another plate," I said. Leo followed me to get the dust pail. In the kitchen, he kissed me.

"Are you okay?"

"I'm not sure. But I will be."

We had just cleared the table and had brought in the *bûche* and dessert plates. My father stood. "There's been something I've been meaning to give you. I'll be right back. Elly, Charlotte, would you like to help me?"

When they returned they were carrying a big cardboard box, which they set on the floor.

"This isn't really a Christmas present, it's not wrapped," he said.

"And it's not even from Santa," said Charlotte.

"Correct. Anyway, these are for you, if you want them. Some things that belonged to your mother."

"Oh my God!" I said. I put down my fork and stood up. I wasn't fast enough, though, because my sisters were already opening the carton. We began to rummage through it. I caught a faint whiff of Chanel No. 5.

"Look at these!" Jacqueline had found Maman's jewelry box and held up a pair of sparkling emerald earrings. "I remember watching her put these on. There was a big party and she and Daddy were going out." She looked at our father.

"It was a benefit for the Museum of Art," he said. He had a faraway look in his eyes.

"They're stunning. I don't remember them," said Colette.

"I guess she saved them for special occasions," said Jacqueline. "These you must remember." She pulled out a pair of pearl earrings set in white gold.

Colette bit her lower lip. "She wore those all the time. Remember those white linen pants and the striped boat-necked top she loved? She wore them with that. They're exquisite."

"She had class," I said.

We found photos, letters, two vintage dresses that almost made Colette pass out, a couple of bags, a Halston hat, some scarves. At the bottom, I found a large rectangular object wrapped in white tissue paper. I lifted it out of the box and unwrapped it. The blood running in my veins turned to velvety melted chocolate.

"Oh!" said Colette.

"Maman's Birkin," Jacqueline said with reverence. "You've had it all this time?"

Daddy nodded.

We all looked at the bag released from its nest of tissue paper.

"It's the most beautiful thing I've ever seen." Colette put out one finger and stroked the forest green leather.

"You must find a way to share it. Its purpose is to bring you together," said my father.

"Wow," said Syd, "I've always been like a sister to you, right?"

Art put his arm around Syd. "Guess there's nothing in that box for me, huh?"

"Of course there is. There are letters and photos." But that sounded lame to my own ears.

"I never found her diary though," said my father. "I can't imagine what happened to it."

I swallowed and opened my mouth, then changed my mind. The confession to having filched the diary could wait for another time.

"But, Arthur, I do have something for you." He stood and went to the Louis-Philippe bureau, similar to the one Jacqueline had in her Brussels apartment. He slid open the top drawer and pulled out a key. Casually he threw it on the table in front of Art. "It's in the garage," said my father.

Art held it up. On a tarnished keychain dangled the key to our mother's car. A cream-colored Jaguar convertible.

"Does it still run?" asked Art.

"Like a charm."

My brother grinned, lighting up the whole room. "I don't know what to say."

"You don't have to say anything."

Elly cleared her throat.

"Oh, of course. You know the biggest box by the Christmas tree?" asked my father.

"The one with our names written on it?" asked Elly.

"Wrapped in candy-cane paper?" asked Charlotte.

"That's the one. Why don't you go open it now."

I'd never seen them leave a room so fast. We followed them. They tore into the wrapping paper.

"A dollhouse!"

And not just any dollhouse. Handcrafted, entirely made of wood. It was an exact replica of Madeline's Parisian boarding school, complete with vines made of some sort of fabric and twelve little beds.

They jumped up and down, squealing.

I stroked the bag in my arms. It was like touching my mother. It was her: vintage, classic, beautiful, never outmoded, but, I realized now, not perfect. The bag showed signs of wear that were the essence of its beauty.

It was a true gift. Returning a part of our mother. Not the icon but the genuine, flawed woman she'd been, blemishes and all. And just maybe, we'd get a father. Not the one we'd always dreamed of, but a father nonetheless. Everything was different yet still the same. It felt as if I'd moved to a foreign country, one where I didn't have to keep proving myself. I could stop living on hold until everything was perfect. Because when I looked deep inside my heart, I knew I had two great loves. My family, real and extended. And food. And they were both right here.

Joyeux Noël.

Le vrai chocolat chaud belge
TRADITIONAL BELGIAN HOT CHOCOLATE

Although I've rarely met a cup of hot chocolate I didn't like (barring the dreadful milky-powder-add-water variety), this is the *chocolat chaud* of my childhood. It is for the best and worst times. Maman would make this on Christmas morning. Or for the first snow. For the first day of school and the last. For the first boyfriend, the first heartbreak. Any great success. This was hot chocolate for special occasions. The secret ingredient is a spoonful of brown sugar. It is rich, deep, and velvety and will stop time just for the moment you savor it.

Count 1.2 to 1.5 ounces (35–45 g.) of high quality, very dark Belgian chocolate per cup of milk. Choose Callebaut, Galler, Neuhaus, or our family favorite, Côte d'Or.

Heat the milk, dark chocolate, brown sugar, and a pinch of sea salt per cup in a heavy bottomed saucepan over medium-low heat, stirring with a wooden spoon until the chocolate has melted. When it is hot, but not boiling (tiny bubbles form around the edges of the pan), remove from the heat and whisk briskly until frothy.

If you want to "cheat"—and I do; just don't tell my grandmother—pour the hot chocolate into your blender or Vitamix and mix on high for 10 seconds. Serve immediately with buttered *craquelin, cougnole* or, in a pinch, challah or fresh baguette. Or just on its own.

(This is the basic recipe and can be jazzed up any way you choose. With spices, a bit of cognac, real whipped cream, grated chocolate . . . the possibilities are endless. Of course, it's perfection just the way it is.)

Acknowledgments

I am humbled by the people in my life who have helped make this book what it is today. I would like to thank:

My rock-star agent, Paula Munier, the best of the best. You give breadth and depth to the words hard-working and dedicated. I am so lucky to have you on my team.

My stellar editor, Michaela Hamilton, and her wonderful assistant, Norma Perez-Hernandez. You have both turned my blood to champagne. I am the luckiest of writers to have you guiding and championing my book.

My dedicated copy editors, who saved me countless times. You are my heroes.

Kensington. I am thrilled to be a part of the family.

My early readers: Ginna Getto, keep flying in the right direction for the chocolate; Barbara Zaragoza, who, while living in Italy, took the time to send me her insightful comments; and to my Barb Alpern, baker of bread, who brings love to every relationship, every act.

Robert and Angie for years of coffee-drenched writerly meetings in coffeehouses all over San Diego.

Shilpi for those wonderful writerly lunches. Tammy, for being such an inspiration.

The SMU Writers Program, who set me on this path so many years ago. And my many teachers in countless classes and workshops. I am indebted to you.

Sara Lewis Murre, who predicted this. You are always right.

My own merry band of expats who bear no resemblance to the characters in this book but have saved my sanity, made me laugh, served as inspiration, taken my kids, and have stood in for my family in times both joyous and tough.

My real family in Belgium, so far, yet locked in my heart and ever in my thoughts. For teaching me the meaning of family, as well as how to cook.

My writers group. Words can only skim the surface of the gratitude and love I have for you. Brent Johnson, champion friend and wordsmith hero. Suzanne Frank, my sister in ink and in life, whose answer to "Can you stand to read it one more time?" was always "Yes!" And it would take an entire chapter to properly thank Daniel J. Hale, whose unconditional support, faith, and help have kept me afloat. The three of you make it real. You make me want to be better than I am.

My daughters. None of this would mean a thing without the two of you. You are my joy, the song I sing, the texture to my days.

And finally, I wouldn't be here without my husband, the love of my life, my best friend, problem-solver, and chocolate mousse chef extraordinaire. You are the one. I owe it all to you.